Flashdogs

--

An Anthology

--

Volume One

Produced by
Mark A. King & David Shakes

Book design by
Emily June Street

Cover and art by
Tamara Rogers

Copyright © 2014 The Flashdogs

Copyright in the text reproduced herein remains the property of the individual authors / artists and permission to publish gratefully acknowledged by the editors and publishers.
All rights reserved.

No parts of this publication may be reproduced, stored in a retrieval system, or transmitted in any form or by any means, electronic, photocopying, recording, mechanical or otherwise without prior permission from the copyright owner.

These are works of fiction. Names, characters, businesses, places, events and incidents are either the products of the author's imagination or used in a fictitious manner. Any resemblance to actual persons, living or dead, or actual events is purely coincidental.

Logo by Carlos Orozco

ISBN-10: 1505289254
ISBN-13: 978-1505289251

CONTENTS

	Foreword	i
	Prompt Image	iii
1	Karl A. Russell	1
2	Natalie Bowers	11
3	Tamara Rogers	21
4	David Shakes	27
5	Mark A. King	37
6	Andrew Patch	49
7	Voima Oy	59
8	Jacki Donnellan	67
9	Avalina Kreska	76
10	Rebecca J. Allred	88
11	Rebekah Postupak	92
12	Emily June Street	103
13	Beth Deicthman	118
14	Amy Wood	128
15	Carlos Orozco	138
16	Casey Rose Frank	146
17	Kristen Falso-Capaldi	155
18	Catherine Connolly	165
19	A.J. Walker	176

20	Sal Page	184
21	Stella Turner	192
22	Sinéad O'Hart	199
23	Elaine Marie McKay	208
24	Tamara Shoemaker	215
25	Chris Milam	223
26	Bart Van Goethem	232
27	Eric Martell	238
28	Brian S. Creek	246
29	Sarah Cain	257
30	Josh Bertetta	263
31	N.E. Chenier	273
32	Pam Plumb	285
33	Liz Hedgecock	294
34	Tom Smith	303
	Contributors	313
	Acknowledgements	321

Dedicated to the tireless enthusiasm and passionate dedication of those at FDHQ.

To secret agents Emily June Street and Tamara Rogers, who made this possible.

To David Shakes who dared to dream.

FOREWORD

We'll keep it brief, partly because that's how flash works, but mainly because you've got some fantastic stories to read.

Flash fiction has many definitions, but we'll need to agree on just three: it's short; swiftly written and mostly transient.

The FlashDogs are an international collective of writers prominent on the burgeoning flash fiction scene.

Our writers concentrate their creative energies into tasty morsels of fiction to be devoured like the literary equivalent of *tapas*. The dishes may be small but they generally pack a lot of flavour. They'll linger on the palate long after the meal is finished.

We thought we should collect some of these stories for posterity.

In this volume we introduce you to those writers who have been with FlashDogs since it began.

We asked for those writers' choice of stories, their *signature dishes*—the work they felt best showed their creative abilities.

We wanted more!

You'll notice a photo after this section. We issued everyone the same photo; we asked the writers to use it as a prompt to create something new and exclusive to the anthology (you'll find these stories after a title page with an automobile).

The results show just how versatile the world of flash can be.

All together we're showcasing thiry-four writers from across the globe and 110 stories—a feast, if you will. So what are you waiting for? Tuck in, we're sure you'll find more than one story to whet your appetite.

-The FDHQ team, November 2014.

PROMPT PHOTGRAPH
BY
TAMARA ROGERS

KARL A. RUSSELL

MIGRATORY PATTERNS

SUCH SIGHTS TO SEE

MIGRATORY PATTERNS

Sue checked her phone for a last minute reprieve, but no luck. She tossed her cigarette butt into the gutter, blipped the car door locks a third and final time then headed for the block's foyer, picking her way through the ever-present dog mess. The kids lounging against the Immigration Service van whispered amongst themselves as she passed. The driver ignored her.

A contractor in the IS uniform opened the door and looked at her disdainfully.

"Here for Watcheyurk?"

"Wociek. I'm Matthiu's support worker."

He didn't answer, just stepped aside, then locked the door behind her. Two more Immies guarded the stairwell and a pair accompanied her in the lift.

A final guard waited on the twentieth floor, a battering ram slung across his chest like a rifle, standing outside the flat that Matthiu shared with his parents.

"Sue Mitchell. I'm-"

"*You're* a senior case worker?"

"Well, with the cuts, we're front line *and*—"

"Christ. Look, just stay out of the way unless we need you to keep the kid calm, okay? If his folks get a bit rowdy and need subduing or whatever."

"They're Buddhists."

"Should have stayed there then."

He hefted the ram and banged it against the door, which rattled like a loose tooth in its frame. There were already circular dents around the lock; this wasn't the first time the place had been raided.

"Mr Watcheyurk? You there? Open up or we're coming in. One! Two!"

The screaming took him by surprise and he never got to three, ramming the door with such force that the hinges were torn from the frame. Sue pushed past, into the darkened flat and a snowstorm of drifting feathers. She glimpsed dim figures beyond the curtained balcony doors, heard a sound like sheets flapping in the breeze, then watched in horror as the figures leapt from sight. She ran to the door, wrenched it open and stumbled towards the railing. The ground came spinning up to meet her, until a guard grabbed her jacket and pulled her back.

"Watch it!"

"Sorry—Where?"

She was pushed aside, forgotten as the Immies bustled about on the small balcony, looking for escape routes. There was no way to reach the neighbouring flats, no sign that they had gone up *or* down. Swearing, they went back into the flat to begin the carefully choreographed task of destroying the family's meagre possessions. It was meant to be a search, to reveal where the Wocieks had gone, but all it gave them was an outlet for their frustrations.

Listening to them rip apart Matthiu's school books, his faded uniform and the toys he had managed to carry halfway round the world, Sue slid to the cold concrete and sat there in silence, trying to make sense of what she'd seen, what she saw now:

Three pairs of shoes, arranged on the balcony in a neat and tidy row.

Shoes left behind when they leapt.

Hoping to land on more welcoming shores.

SUCH SIGHTS TO SEE

Seven emerged from the subway station, into the square, where the lights were brighter, the people closer and the noises louder. Instinctively, she drew back from it, pressing against Ryu's chest, but he took her shoulders and guided her out, into the world. He knew that with the latest procedure she would see only the vaguest blurs and hear the noise of the city as a muffled roar, but he was determined to give her this night, if he could.

A cry escaped her, a small gasp of wordless excitement, and his heart leapt. The subjects were so sheltered, he'd had no clear idea of how she would react, but her pleasure was childlike, filled with joy and wonder. It was not so surprising perhaps; the subjects were vat grown and artificially aged, and none reached the age of ten before the final harvesting, whatever their bodies may suggest.

He took her by the elbow and steered her through the thronged streets of Shinjuku, slipping between couples and salarymen and clustered knots of streetcorner Otaku, ever conscious of the eyes of the city upon them. He supposed that some would think *them* a couple, but more likely they would see a girl and her father, perhaps a carer, and that suited him, so he took pains to hold her elbow as they crossed the street, no matter how strong the urge to entwine his fingers with hers.

They ate at a noodle bar and he watched intently as she savoured each mouthful. Her system could only handle the smallest portion of the blandest noodles now, but she delighted in the smells and the parade of colours as the conveyor belt of plates slid past them. She laughed out loud as he speared a bright pink gunkanmaki and he swore that he would never forget the sound.

He had known since their first consultation, when he had marked a square patch of dermis on her smoothly bronzed stomach and prepared to strip it away. Pressing the oxygen mask to her face, he had brushed a stray lock of jet-black hair from her slender neck and been lost forever. Even meeting her American original did nothing to change his mind; hearing the barking laugh and the snickering cough, listening to the stream of filth and invective that passed for her wit, he found himself thinking more and more of Seven as the template from which this aged and imperfect copy had sprung, and he longed for her.

He had begun to work longer hours, staying late at the facility to be near her, creeping down to the nursery to watch her sleep. He listened to her muffled breathing on the intercom and closed his eyes, imagining that he lay beside her. He had even rushed to her side, once, when night terrors tore her from her sleep, but the orderlies who came in after him gave him knowing smirks when they found him with his arms around her heaving shoulders. He knew what they did on long night shifts with the subjects whose faculties for telling tales had been taken from them, and he was repulsed that they mistook his own intentions for anything like their own.

He *knew* that it was wrong, that he was risking his marriage and his career, the existence of his whole team at the facility, but that just made the yearning all the stronger. With every new procedure, as they stripped her away, piece by piece, he felt the need to do something for her. He wanted to take her away from her pain, if only for one night, but he could not see how to do it without adding to her troubles.

Finally, an opportunity had presented itself: a subject had gone into crash on the operating table, with the procedure barely begun. His team had stepped in to try and stabilise her, and the orderlies had their hands full with another from the same batch who seemed to sense his sibling's distress. Quickly, Ryu had slipped into the nursery, roused her from her doze and dressed her in an old blouse and trousers belonging to his wife, back from the days when she still cared about her appearance. It was a little old fashioned and unflattering, but it hid the scars well enough, and her face was still perfect. He felt that his chest would burst with happiness as he led her from the facility to begin their tour.

She grew tired far too quickly though, and the night was soon over. She began to cry out as the motorcyclists drew too close, to shield her eyes when the neon glared too strongly. When the rain fell, she huddled against him for protection, with no conception of its source. He couldn't risk taking her back on the subway without using one of the sleep-laden syringes he had snatched from the operating room, and he had no desire to see her shut down in that way, so he hired a taxi. He spent far more than he could account for when his wife next audited his wallet, but as he watched the lights glide across the rain streaked glass, reflected in her shining eyes, he was glad that he had. He wondered if this was how she saw, what she made of the harsh western music bleeding through from the supposedly soundproofed driver's cab.

He wondered what she thought when she saw *him*.

Finally, when he could bear it no longer, he said what was in his heart, whispering it into the maelstrom of leaking rock and roll.

She smiled and gripped his hand with both of hers, and he wondered if she had somehow heard it, a whisper amplified by the feeling behind it.

Then she forced her ruined vocal chords to stilted life and asked him if they could go out again, one day?

"Yes, Seven. One day."

He didn't have the heart to tell her what they were harvesting next.

KARL A. RUSSELL

PLAY WITH ME

PLAY WITH ME

Hartskirk was a town scarred. Looking down from the bypass, sitting on the still-warm bonnet of Marlon's Fiat, Lou could see the black line of devastation in the moonlight, like a river that had burst its banks and swamped the houses on either side. She shivered.

"It's real."

Marlon grinned.

"Told you. Three weeks before Christmas. Imagine it."

Lou tried not to, but the snarled metal at ground zero glittered like an obscene bauble.

"Marl, I'm not sure about this…"

He shrugged.

"Fair enough. You can fix the car then, while I do the hard work, but don't expect a cut. Or maybe you could ring a taxi. No? Come on then."

He pulled on his backpack, turned away and started to pick his way down the cracked slip road. Lou checked her phone, but it was still dead, and there was nobody she could call anyway. Grabbing her own pack, she slipped from the car bonnet and followed him towards the town.

The houses furthest from the blast looked almost unharmed, but the windows were all broken, either on the night or by the intervening years. Streamers of rotten black tinsel hung from many of them, fluttering in the breeze. There would be stacks of neatly wrapped gifts inside, treasure troves of classic action figures, all mint on card, but that was a step too far even for Marlon. He had a plan anyway.

"We need to find the Argos shop. They would have had a few things on display, but most of it will be in the stockroom, untouched. You know what you're looking for?"

"Star Wars figures?"

"Christ, Louise, it's the last 17. If it doesn't say Power Of The Force on the card then dump it. We can't carry shite, okay?"

"Okay."

They walked on through the abandoned streets, following the road signs for the town centre. Lou wondered why no one else had tried this before, if it was that easy, but she kept her thoughts to herself; she could tell from the set of his shoulders that Marlon was ready to pop.

The shopping precinct was filled with strange signs and brands, names like Wimpy and Rumbelows, forgotten before Lou was even born, and she had the sensation of coming unstuck in time. A small cinema advertised Back To The Future amongst its coming attractions, and she wondered how many of Hartskirk's children ever got to see it. Not many, if the rumours Marlon had found online were true.

They found the Argos store, the ageless red white and blue logo strangely reassuring, and clambered in through the shattered windows. The stock room door was locked, but Marlon crawled up the conveyor belt at the collection point. Lou watched him disappear into the darkness, then wandered over to the jewellery counter to see if there was anything worth pocketing. Most of it was cheap tat, but she found a tray of gold wedding rings and tried them on, listening to his footsteps overhead. As she found one which fitted, something heavy crashed to the floor above her, sending down a drift of fine dust. She coughed and spat, wiped her eyes, then called Marlon. He didn't reply, so she climbed onto the conveyor belt and called again.

Still nothing.

She knew it was probably one of his jokes, that he would be waiting to leap out at her, made playful by his windfall, probably even wanting to screw on the dirty stockroom floor, but she knew that she would have to play her part anyway. Wishing her phone worked, that she had brought a torch, or that she'd said no when he first suggested it, she tried one last time.

"Marl...?"

She held her breath, hoping for an answer, even an angry one, but heard only the pulsing of her own blood. Gripping the sides of the conveyor, she crawled up until she was above the edge of the stockroom floor, tensed, waiting for him to leap out. She thought she could see his backpack, a spill of carded figures, but that was all.

"Marlon, please, you're scaring me..."

Something moved, deep in the shadows, and a voice like torn paper whispered in her ear.

"Play with me."

She felt cold fingers brush the back of her neck and she screamed. As she twisted around, the conveyor belt brake clunked free and she tumbled down, crashing onto her back on the dusty floor. She struggled to stand, still hoping that this was a joke.

"You shit! You absolute shit!"

Something hard struck her cheek and she screamed again, reaching up to find a warm, wet cut. She ducked as another object pinged off the wall behind her, then jumped aside as dozens of tiny balls whistled through the air, bouncing off the conveyor belt and ricocheting around the collection area. Lou thought they were marbles until one skittered to a stop at her feet and she recognised Yakface from Marlon's endless ebay searches. Dozens of tiny heads, snapped loose from their bodies; thousands of pounds worth of collectors' items destroyed in a petulant rage. She knew that even in his worst moods, Marlon couldn't do that.

"Who's up there?"

"Play. With. ME!"

The room shook as something stomped across the stockroom floor, dislodging ceiling tiles and sending down flurries of dust like filthy snow. Lou backed away, yelping as she scattered the chairs in the waiting area.

Then Marlon's head bounced wetly down the conveyor belt and slapped off the wall at the end, and she ran.

She leaped through the shattered window, out into the precinct, running blindly past the toppled ruin of the town's Christmas tree, skirting the headless mannequins spilling onto the pavement from the cavernous maw of Marks And Spencer's. As she ran, she became aware of other shapes too, flitting alongside her, silently keeping pace. Through her tears, she saw vague forms twirling and leaping through the darkness, and their playful movement was worse than the anger she had felt in the shop; they were enjoying this.

Other shapes darted by, much faster, closer to the ground, and she remembered Marlon's breathless excitement as he read the horrific details of what happened to Hartskirk that night.

"It killed all of the kids, and the animals too. All at once."

She fought to silence a scream, but couldn't tell if she succeeded. At the end of the precinct, she swerved left, aiming for the bypass, but the forms there were stronger, more solid, and the ghost dogs snarled as she approached. She stumbled, heard laughter, high and gleeful. Righting herself, she tried to double back, but they were behind her too, urging her on.

Herding her.

She ran on, the air screaming in her lungs, past burnt-out cars and houses that were gutted shells. Outside the church, the wooden nativity animals were blackened and beheaded. She saw the darkness ahead and knew at last where they were taking her, and she faltered, thinking of that great black tear in the town's heart. The dogs snapped at her heels, drawing blood, and she forced herself on.

She saw them now; hundreds of children lining the street, watching her run, the blasted remains of their homes still faintly visible through their not-quite-there bodies. They wore He Man pyjamas and Rainbow Brite nighties, party frocks and rotten nappies. They cradled dolls and toy guns, waving gaily as she passed.

The station lay before her, stumps of twisted steel and tottering piles of brick all that remained of the building. Beyond it, the chemical tanker lay on its side on the rusting tracks, the hole torn in its roof festooned with tinsel and flickering lights. A plywood sign welcomed her to Santa's Grotto, but the jolly fat man's face was scarred and bubbled, replaced by a childish red scrawl.

A boy of ten stood in the centre of the tanker, arms wide, smiling. In one hand he held a cup. In the other, a knife.

Lou stopped, fell to her hands and knees, no longer caring about the dogs and the children and the sad accident which had caused all this. She just wanted it to be over.

Tiny hands gripped her and dragged her forwards, into the light. She saw that they weren't actually candles, just the burning torsos of Barbies and Kens and Sindy dolls, dripping molten plastic onto the scorched Earth.

"Play with me."

Lou looked up at him, saw the stars through his face and the dark emptiness beyond, and something snapped. She began to scream, but his hand when he slapped her was all too solid.

All around, the ghost children chanted, "Play! Play! Play! Play!"

He held out the cup, rattling it in front of her face. The sound of dice.

Lou reached up, took the cup and said a silent, pointless prayer.

Then rolled.

NATALIE BOWERS

BAKED BEANS AND CHEESE AT THE CORNERSTONE CAFÉ

BAKED BEANS AND CHEESE AT THE CORNERSTONE CAFÉ

I parked Josh's buggy in the wedge of orange light under the lamppost. After three hours of ploughing our way through Christmas shoppers, we had finally returned to the car, and all I wanted was to get home, feed the kids and put them to bed so I could crash on the sofa and veg out to comedy reruns on Dave.

'Come on,' I said, dredging up as much cheer as I could. 'Let's get you two in the car. Mummy'll be wondering where we've got to.' I pumped my fingers to force some warmth back into them and smiled down at Lauren. 'Those jacket potatoes should be ready by now. What do you say to baked beans on top? That's your favourite.'

Lauren rolled her eyes and tutted. 'Dad, that's Joshie's favourite. I *hate* baked beans.'

'That's right. Silly Daddy. I forgot.' Sigh.

'You *always* forget.' She planted her hands on her hips and scowled. Her breath mushroomed in front her face. 'I like *cheese*.' At moments like that, she looked just like her mother.

'Well, cheese it is then,' I said, gritting my teeth. 'What do you think Mummy'll say when she opens her presents? Do you think she'll be pleased?' She couldn't be any less pleased than she'd been with the slippers and mug I'd bought her the previous year. How was I supposed to know that pointing at a handbag in a shop window and saying 'Ooh, look at that!' meant 'That's what I want for Christmas.'? This year, I'd made her write a list.

Lauren jabbed her finger at the car. 'What's that?'

'What's what?' I looked across and saw a piece of paper pinned beneath one of the wiper blades. It crackled as I peeled it off the frosty windscreen. I squinted at it. It read:

~ The Cornerstone Café ~
(at the north entrance to the car park)
Free mince pie with every hot drink purchased
10 a.m. - 6 p.m.
Saturday 20th December
Merry Christmas!

'Just an advert for a café.' I pulled back the cuff of my glove and checked my watch, tempted to abandon the jacket potatoes and buy dinner instead. It was ten to six. Typical. Too late.

'Dad, my tummy hurts.'

'Please don't whine, Lauren.' I screwed up the piece of paper and tossed it through the open door. It landed on the passenger seat among the scrunched-up tissues, old Pay-and-Display tickets and shredded Polo wrappers. I turned to Lauren. She was hopping from foot to foot on the Tarmac. 'Don't tell me you need a wee,' I said, closing my eyes and rubbing my eyelids. When I looked at her again, she was balancing on one leg like a flamingo.

'My feet hurt,' she said and wobbled, lunging to her right.

She grabbed the handle of Josh's buggy.

It tipped up.

Josh screamed.

A vision of Josh lying on the ground in a pool of blood flashed through my mind.

'Lauren!' I lurched forward, tore the buggy from her hand and righted it. It juddered on its front wheel, then stilled. 'Be *careful.*'

Lauren looked up at me, her eyes wide. 'My nose is cold.'

I took a deep breath, wincing as the air bit the back of my throat, and then I began to count quietly to myself. 'One. Two. Three. Four. Fi—'

'I'm freezing.'

'Get in the car then!' I yanked open the back door. 'I told you to bring your hat. And your gloves. You didn't listen, did you?'

Lauren spun around, her pigtails whipping about her head, and scrambled onto the back seat.

'And strap yourself in!' How is it, I thought, I can happily teach other people's kids all week, but can't spend more than a few hours with my own without losing my temper? Hormonal teenagers I could cope with, but whiny infant-schoolers and toddlers? I shook my head.

The sound of snivelling came from inside the car.

Great, I thought. *Just what I need.*

Steadying myself with another breath, I forced my shoulders down and rolled my head from side to side. I turned my back on the car and crouched in front of Josh's buggy. His eyelids were drooping under his Bob the Builder hat, and his head lolled to one side.

'Oh, Josh,' I said, unbuckling the buggy's straps. 'Don't fall asleep on me now. Your mother'll kill me if you don't go to bed on time.' I scooped him up and rested him against my shoulder. It was then the smell of decomposing cauliflower smacked me in the face. Gagging, I turned away. 'Did you have to?' I looked at the car, then at Josh and then back at the car again. Goodness knows how long he's been sitting in it, so ten more minutes wouldn't hurt.

'Come on.' In one fluid movement, I swung Josh into the car, lowered him into his car seat, pulled off my gloves with my teeth and groped in the darkness for the clip of the harness. Josh screamed and stiffened his arms and legs, sticking them out to the side like a frozen starfish.

'Oh, *come on*, Josh,' I mumbled around a mouthful of glove. 'I haven't got the energy for this.' Abandoning my search for the clasp, I took Josh's arm and tried to thread it through the straps. He screamed louder and thrashed in his seat. It was like wrestling a bag of snakes.

'Dad.'

'Not now, Lauren.' I let the gloves fall from my mouth and resumed my hunt for the clasp.

'But, Dad.'

'Not now!'

'*Dad*.'

'What?' I let go of Josh's arm and scowled in Lauren's direction.

'Scoop.'

'I have no idea what you're talking about.'

'Scoop's in Joshie's seat.'

'Oh, for crying out loud.' I groaned, thrust my hand under Josh's bottom and scrabbled for the toy. My fingers connected with plastic. 'Here.' I dropped the digger in Josh's lap, and he stopped crying, deflating, like one of my mum's soufflés, into his seat.

'Finally!' I strapped Josh in, and straightened up. Slipping my hands under my coat, I rubbed the base of my spine and looked up at the sky. For a brief, peaceful moment, I watched my breath drift toward the stars.

'Eurgh,' came Lauren's voice from inside. 'Joshie has—'

I slammed the car door. 'I know!' I marched around to the boot and wrenched it open. Picking up the shopping bags, I threw them in and flinched as I remembered the three bottles of perfume I'd just bought. Then it was the buggy's turn.

'Right,' I said as I slumped into the driver's seat and shut the door. 'Let's go.' I jabbed the key into the ignition and turned it.

The engine groaned, but didn't start.

I blinked. 'What?'

I tried again.

Nothing. Not even a groan.

'You've *got* to be joking.'

Again, I turned the key.

Nothing.

Nothing.

Nothing.

'Oh for f—'

'Dad!'

'What?' I flung myself around and slammed my fist into the passenger seat. 'What, Lauren? What is it?' All I could see of her in the darkness were two glistening eyes.

'I want Mummy,' she said, her voice trembling.

'Well, Mummy's not here.' I felt as if the Edinburgh Tattoo were being held in my head.

'I want my Mummy.'

'Oh, for goodness sake.' I turned around again, leaned over and pulled the bonnet release. 'Stay here,' I said as I got out once more and stormed around to the front of the car. Hauling open the bonnet, I peered in. The night-blackened engine peered back at me. I felt for the leads to the battery—they seemed secure. It was at times like this I wished I'd studied Mechanical Engineering instead of Maths. It was going to be an AA job.

Stepping back from the car, I slid my hand into the pocket of my jeans. My mobile wasn't there. 'Perfect. Just perfect,' I said, letting the bonnet slam shut. I frisked my own coat. 'Where the hell is it?' I scratched my head and scanned the ground. Nothing. 'Unbelievable. Just unbelievable.' I patted my pockets again, and then I remembered: I'd put it on charge that morning. It was still on the desk in the study. Superb.

A loud wail escaped the car through the open door.

I strode over and leaned in. 'What now?'

There was no reply. Lauren had her hands over her face. Josh's mouth was a gaping hole through which he was drawing a ragged breath. The rest of his face was scrunched up like a ball of paper.

That's what reminded me.

The piece of paper on the windscreen.

The café.

They'd have a phone.

I scrabbled through the rubbish on the passenger seat, trying to remember what time the café closed. It had said six, hadn't it? I snatched a look at my watch. It was five to. We'd have to run.

* * *

With Josh on my shoulders and Lauren clutching the back of my coat, I slid to a stop on the wet leaves at the top of the path that ran down to the café. My mouth was dry, and my heart was racing like a hamster in a wheel, but bright light poured through the café window onto the gravel. We'd made it.

Suddenly, the light disappeared and threw everything into darkness.

'No! No! Don't shut. Please don't shut.'

I heard the door open.

A bell tinkled.

Gravel crunched.

'Well, I'm glad that's over,' said a man's voice.

'Me too,' replied a woman.

NATALIE BOWERS

FORCES UNSEEN

FORCES UNSEEN

*W*hen Evan found Gabby, she was kneeling on the floorboards of her room, stuffing clothes into a backpack. Scattered beside her on the rug, were her pen, order pad and apron. As Evan crossed his arms and leaned against the doorframe, Gabby's hands fell still, her shoulders slumped and her eyes closed.

"Sooooooo." Evan drew out the word as if he were drawing back the sling on a catapult. "Am I gonna have to arrest you?"

Gabby flinched. "I'm not a fugitive," she said.

Evan shrugged. "A runaway then."

She lifted her head and glared at him. "I'm not fifteen years old either."

Raising an eyebrow in the way he knew she thought was cute, he said, "You do remember I'm a U.S. Marshal, right?" He unfolded his arms and swept back his jacket to reveal the badge on his belt and the gun at his hip.

Without so much as a smile, Gabby stood up, grabbed her backpack and reached for the passport sitting on top of the dresser. "I appreciate the offer, Evan. I really do. But this isn't something you can help with. I just need to get out of here."

"Hold up a minute," he said, lunging forward and snagging her elbow. He began to draw her away from the dresser, toward the single bed that lay directly beneath the window. "Let's sit down and take a breath or two, shall we? And then you can tell me what it is you're not telling me, and *I* can tell you if it's something I can help with or not."

Gabby tried to wrench her arm free. "Let go!"

Surprised, Evan tightened his grip.

"Evan, *please*. Just let me go."

He dropped to the edge of the bed and yanked her down next to him. For a moment, they bobbed together like two ducks on a pond. "Come on, Gabby," he said. "Talk to me."

Gabby grit her teeth and tried to twist loose her arm. "Let. Go."

"Look," he said, swiveling to face her, but keeping a firm hold. It was his Marshal's instinct that had driven him to follow Gabby from the diner to her room above, but it was more than just his Marshal's instinct that was driving him to stop her from leaving. "We're friends aren't we … you and me?"

"Yes," replied Gabby. "Although friends let friends go when friends ask them to."

"Friends also intervene when friends think friends are about to embark on a course of action that might be considered unwise."

"You have no idea what course of action I'm about to embark on. Or why!"

"Then *tell* me."

"God, you're like a dog with a bone."

He couldn't help grinning. "I know."

She sighed and straightened her shoulders. "You can't hold on to me forever you know."

His grin faded. "It was the girls and their video that spooked you, wasn't it?" he said, forcing his mind back to the moments before Gabby had left the diner. She'd just taken his lunch order when the two Beaufort girls had rushed up to the counter, brandishing their phones and clamoring about views and comments and going viral.

"I'm so stupid." Gabby shook her head. "I should've known they wouldn't be able to resist uploading it to YouTube."

"There's only one thing funnier than a video of a laughing baby," he said, "and that's a video of someone laughing at a laughing baby."

"Well, I'm not laughing now."

"Yeah, I'm getting that." In the diner, Evan had leaned over to watch the video that the girls had been gleefully replaying for Gabby. He'd laughed along at the recording of her and the baby she'd entertained the previous day, but then he'd glanced up to see that her face had lost all color. "What's up? You look like you've seen a ghost," he'd said, but Gabby hadn't answered. Instead, she'd dropped the cloth she'd been holding and had vanished through the kitchen.

"There's someone out there who you're afraid will see you in that video, isn't there? Who is it? Who are you hiding from?"

"It's a long story."

He smiled to reassure her. "I've got plenty of time."

She looked up at him and shook her head again. "But I don't. I know you want to fix this, Evan, but you can't, and I've stayed too long as it is."

Evan recalled the night she'd appeared at the diner, dripping rainwater onto the checkered floor and asking about work and places to stay. It had taken the owner less than a minute to offer her a job and a room, and it had taken Evan less than a heartbeat to return the smile she'd given him. "Two months isn't long," he said.

"It is for me." Her eyes began to glisten.

"Hey." Finally, he let go of her elbow and curled his arm around her shoulder, but instead of leaning against him as he'd expected her too, she leaned across him, and before he could react, she'd leapt from the bed and whirled around to face him, a gun—*his* gun—in her hand and trained at his head.

"I'm sorry," she said, eyes still glistening. "But I *have* to go."

His Marshal instincts firing up again, Evan raised his hands and kept his voice calm. "If you shoot me, Gabby, you won't just be running from whoever it is you're running from; you'll be running from the law too. And it won't just be kids with smartphones you'll have to avoid. It'll be every single CCTV camera in the country. Is that what you want?"

"No! Of course not."

Slowly, Evan extended his hand. "Then give me back my gun, and let me *help* you." The weapon trembled in Gabby's grasp. "You can't hold on to it forever," he said, allowing himself a smile.

With a frustrated cry, Gabby tossed the gun across the room. As it skittered over the floorboards, Evan leaped from the bed, but by the time he'd retrieved his weapon and spun around, Gabby, her backpack and passport were gone. Moments later, he heard a car door slam, and, through the window, he caught sight of the taillights of a cab tearing away from the diner's parking lot.

* * *

Sitting in his Ford Explorer, Evan watched the diner's customers come and go. Two days had passed since Gabby had fled, and after interrogating every database, questioning every contact and calling in every favor he could without pinging his boss's radar, Evan was still no closer to figuring out where she might have come from, let alone where she might have gone.

His cell rang. He snatched it from the passenger seat. The display read, "Withheld".

Answering it, he said, "Evan Bryant."

There was a pause, then a woman's voice said, "My ex-husband."

Evan frowned. "Pardon me?"

"You asked who I was hiding from. The answer is my ex-husband."

He sat up straight. "Gabby? Where are you? Are you okay?"

"He's a murderer, Evan."

"What?"

"He was jealous that I'd fallen in love with someone else."

"Tell me where you are. I'll come get you. We can sort this out."

"He followed us back to our apartment one night and shot him in the head, right in front of me. The police caught him, but he escaped and now he's out there somewhere."

"Gabby, I can help you with this. This is my area of expertise."

"It's better if I keep moving."

"And how long will you be able to keep that up for? The rest of your life?"

She didn't answer.

"Listen, Gabby, I'm trying to protect you here."

"And *I'm* trying to protect *you*."

"What?"

"Goodbye, Evan."

"Wait! Don't hang up. Tell me where you-" The line went dead.

"Damn!" Evan hurled his cell into the foot-well. What was the matter with her? He scrubbed at his face. Why was she so determined to do this alone? He thumped the steering wheel. Why the hell wouldn't she accept his help when, out of the two of them, he was the one with the steady gun hand and the full weight of the law at his back?

He's a murderer, Evan, his memory answered.

He was jealous that I'd fallen in love with someone else.

And I'm *trying to protect* you.

"Me?" he thought. "Why's she trying to protect me? ... ... Damn, I am such an idiot!"

Evan grabbed his cell from the foot-well and dialed. "Boss," he said, starting the car. "I need to trace the last number to call my cell."

"Is this *official* Marshal business, Bryant?" asked his boss.

"I've got a lead," he said, knowing that pinging his boss's radar was now exactly what he needed to do. "On a federal fugitive. The call was from his ex-wife, and I need to find her."

Again.

TAMARA ROGERS

HTTP ERROR

CHANNEL 52

HTTP ERROR

They gave me a million eyes. Well, not a million, more like a terra-billion, a bajillionzillion. All x to the power z equals I want it I see it.

Excuse me if I'm not too precise, there's buzzes coming in and network trails running through. Dope data distraction.

Take the details of my promotion. You could read it if you like but it's all clauses and multipoints and corporate trash. The upshot is that my work on *Animal Farm Mark 4: Kids' Revolt* was just too fucking good. I ran it smoother than if I was taking candy from a baby. It was a bit harder when they'd activate the RattleBattle™ weapons but that only usually happened at level four and mostly they just stuck to the kindergarten stages talking weed and dates and shit.

But this is something else.

<HTTP ERROR 400: Bad Request>

Ignore that, just glitching. You know, first day ripples spreading out, settling in.

Where was I?

That's it. It was all toddler play, pissing about monitoring kids and their pumped up avis, throwing my weight around in their digital playground. This is just something else. You should have seen this guy just then; paging through the usual facetime porn they all go for, then he only goes and gets his ferrets out. Bloody hell, I don't think they liked it. Cardboard tube Armageddon.

<HTTP ERROR 404: Not Found>

Forget that.

Tell me – what would you do if you were everywhere? Cos that is what it's like. All the tentacles of the world, they're all right here – hardwired fingers dripping into my brain, all hot and sticky and delicious.

<HTTP ERROR 403: Forbidden>

Of course, this is technically probation, but, you know, fuck that—how can you be on probation when you're the one in charge of the grid? I make the rules. I am the rules.

Jesus, this is awesome. You should be here, you should be me—get to see it all, take it in. But, hey, there's only one of me and it's fucking busy.

<HTTP ERROR 429: Too Many Requests>

It's coming in quick now. Faster, harder. I'll tell you more but, hang it, I've gotta see this… There's a woman in China and her voice is leaking through like it's pure fucking silk… There's a kid in Devon and he fancies himself a crackhack. He's sending out reams of cover-emails that ain't even coming close to hiding his bandwidth Ponzi scheme… There's a guy in Belize and he's running sermons and preaching his church, making noise over the web and calling himself God.

I squeeze down on his network supply, watch his face flicker into nothingness.

I turn him to black.

Cos he's wrong. He can't be God.

Cos I am.

<HTTP ERROR 418: I'm a Teapot>

CHANNEL 52

"*A*nd cut to ads in three, two, one, go."

It's a long day. I pull the 'phones out of my ears.

Today needs coffee. A strong one. That'll be my fifth but I'm on long shift.

This morning's feeds have been properly drab. We need: porn, crime, embarrassment. We got: old biddy shopping, guy teaching Latin, garbage collector who didn't even bother to scrounge through the junk.

At the coffee machine it's just my luck the boss is there and she's all 'Get me someone better, get me some action, get me some phone-ins.' That's where the money is. Get some or get out.

The coffee, bitter enough already, shrivels my tongue.

I nod in the right places - Yes Ma'am, No Ma'am, three bags full Ma'am.

And my blood's burning my cheeks on the way back to the production suite. Fucking bitch. Like it's my fault the bin man didn't go through the bags. Like it's my fault the granny didn't want to buy dildos but spent an hour choosing the best bag of sprouts. It's the lottery of it all, and if you ain't exciting, you just ain't getting on air again.

Don't get me wrong, we've got a few regulars to call on, but today's all about new talent – see what the lottery throws up, check if the vomit's good and then play them for all they're worth.

My phone buzzes and there's a Code Three coming in.

The coffee goes into the bin. Back to the ProPlus.

The edit suite has a buzz on like the Queen's been shagging corgis. I look hopeful but it's not that.

"You've got to see this," says Jaz. He's new but sharp, gets a taste for when we're onto a good one, and when we're not he's got enough connections to throw something interesting their way.

"What've we got?" I ask.

"Just watch, man," he says.

There's a knife, some sort of grindstone, a map blueprint.

"That's good enough," I say. "How long before cut back to air?"

"Give us twenty seconds," says the temp in the corner. They shift so fast I never learn their names. By temp, I mean intern. That's the official line.

"Get ready, guys." I pass out smokes. "This is gonna be a good one."

The temp counts down to air. Three... two... one...

Credit sequence rolls.

BACKGROUND MUSIC: Emergency sirens mixed with dubstep.

VOCAL: If this was you, would you turn yourself in?

VIDEO: Riot footage *switch to* woman's screaming face at shattered front door *switch to* archive police press footage.

VOCAL: It's your turn to save the world. It's your turn to be part of the BIG WATCH.

SUB VOCAL: Channel 52. No responsibility taken for any events contained in this programme.

And we're live.

He/she is in a bathroom. All swinging doors and dirty tiles and stained shirt bottoms.

"You hooked in properly, Jaz?" I ask.

"All good to go," he says.

"Zoom in on the hands."

The hands are always the first source of information. If it's good you can tell if it's male or female. You can tell if they do manual work or sit at an office all day. But these are nondescript, more like mannequin hands. We might get a trace on the knife. It's bone-handled and grooved near the business end.

"Check the knife."

Jaz nods, already on it.

"Come on, get out of the cubicle…"

The whole suite is holding their breath. You have to because if you breathe out now the whole crazy balloon's going to burst.

He/she tucks the knife into their belt. There's no holder or anything. They're going to be slicing up their groin if they're not careful. This is good, this is all good. This means proper crazy.

The hand reaches for the lock. Turns. Door swings towards the body. Body moves back, awkward motion where you're half sitting against the toilet bowl and half edging out of the booth.

And there's the mirror.

And he/she is fucking beautiful. And a she.

Ginger hair, green eyes, cream top, cargo pants. Knife bulge under the belt.

"Got a link on where she is?"

"Not yet." Jaz is pretty much caning out on the keyboard. "Nothing's coming up."

"Keep at it."

She's leaving the toilets now. Glances to the left and there's crayon pictures of happy families and favourite pets. Glances to the right and the last of the kids are coming in from lunch break.

We're at Room Two-c and Religious Studies is scheduled for Year eights. Through the window in the door we can see the teacher starting the usual spiel. Then the knife is there, all glittering in refracted sunlight.

"Here's your money shot," says Jaz.

"Shut it," I say.

We follow the knife through the door. The kids are sitting there all old school at separate desks.

"Can we get a feed to one of their lenses?" I ask.

"Feeding now," says Jaz.

It's only a second and then we have an overlay with the view from some kid in the fourth row. Jimmy.

He looks over as the knife plunges into one of his classmates.

The main part of the screen splatters with blood.

For a minute we've got surround-sound screaming. One speaker from the woman, one from Jimmy.

"Cut to Mozart," I say.

And we let the drama unfold to classical music.

The phone rings, it's the boss.

"Good work."

Straightforward, to the point.

And the public lines light up, and the first call comes through.

"I want to report a murder."

"Yes," I say, "please hold while I corroborate the evidence. Your ten pound gift voucher will be on its way in the post."

An hour later and we're still buzzing.

"I've seen a bad murder."

"Congratulations, sir. You're our 100th caller today, and you're our winner."

And now I'm thinking about the next coffee break and the next run-in with the boss and the next promotion.

And I guess, maybe, I remember to hope that Jimmy's alright.

DAVID SHAKES

ONE FOR THE ROAD

WITCH PEGS

ONE FOR THE ROAD

I drain my short, ashamed that (even now) there's pleasure in the burn. Another is placed before me as my next companion slides in opposite. She doesn't speak, simply nods at the drink.

"I always loved you…" I begin but she shakes her head and points at my glass.

I raise it to my lips and study my daughter's translucent skin and blackened veins. Livid puncture marks on her arms spell out a too familiar story.

In the mirror next to our booth a brighter life is reflected. In that world she's beautiful. Vivacious. In the mirror I see the woman she could have been, had I been home… had I been sober.

I've had many visitors this infernal evening, each bearing drinks and unspoken stories. Each reflected in the mirror as a version of themselves bettered, a version without me in their lives.

The greatest torment? When I gaze into that mirror it's just my own reflection. This was all I was ever meant to be. I realise that a life spent wasted is a waste of many lives, not just your own.

The seat opposite me is once again vacant. I tip my glass, still savouring the amber liquid within. I'm hopeless.

A young man squeezes in opposite. "One for the road?"

He slides a double measure over. My favourite. The one I had when I last saw him, which must have been tonight but feels like an age away. It is right and proper that these are the only words spoken to me in this place. My last words. I'd said them before necking my drink and getting into my car.

Before I ran this guy down.

Before I killed us both.

The mirror reflects not just the young man, handsome and whole, but a young family- smiling and expectant.

"One for the road," he urges again. There's no malice in his wrecked features; no blame in his whispered words.

"One for the road then," I repeat and raise my glass in a toast.

The young man does his best to smile.

I want this drink to last. I think we both know where that next road will lead.

WITCH PEGS

"It's my birthday Mama, can't Pappy do it?"

"No Emmeline, Pappy is busy in the shed. Besides, we need to talk."

Emmeline couldn't see the expression on her mother's face, but her tone was enough to convince her not to pursue it any further.

Tendrils of steam rose from the pot that boiled above the open fire. Shadows danced against the uneven walls of their shack.

Emmeline scooped hot water from the pot and splashed it into a chipped enamel bowl. Clean scraps of linen floated on the surface.

"I'm ready Mama."

"Thank you darlin'."

Emmeline didn't feel right. Today was her thirteenth birthday but the day had been flat, despite the celebrations. She'd had presents - an intricately carved owl from Pappy her favorite. They'd eaten well, including a whole roast chicken. The carcass had been picked clean, the bones now drying above the fire.

Now, the younger children were sleeping in the other room; Pappy was in the shed working and she had to see to Mama like she always did.

Whilst Emmeline prepared the bowl, Mama had removed her leather eye-patch and the damp padding from beneath. She tossed the stained padding on the fire. It burnt with a vivid blue flame. Emmeline knelt at her mother's feet and squeezed the excess water from the warm cloths in the bowl. She raised them to her mother's face.

Mama's right eye studied her eldest daughter's features in the firelight. She had no left eye.

Emmeline was used to her mother's ruined face. Where the left eye should have been was an open wound that refused to heal. Her eyelids had sunk into the ocular cavity but never quite sealed. A white, jelly like substance flowed from it and needed to be cleaned regularly.

As Emmeline applied the rags she saw her mother's fingers grip the chair more tightly. She knew her mother was in constant pain and felt guilt for her earlier reluctance to help.

"I had a lovely birthday Mama."

"That's good darlin'," replied her mother, in a way that made it sound anything but. "You hold on to those memories."

Emmeline was desperate to dispel the sadness that had descended over her mother.

"The chicken was so tasty, wasn't it Mama?" she asked hopefully.

Again, her mother's reply was not the one she hoped for:

"Not everyone on this Godforsaken hill eats so well."

"I know that Mama, and I really am grateful."

"Child, do you know why Jones the farmer gifted us that bird?" her mother asked.

"Because you used your gift to help him last spring?" Emmeline replied.

"That's right Emmeline. I wiggled for water and Jones got a new well."

"You help lots of people on the hill Mama," said Emmeline, her voice tinged with pride.

"Aye, that much is true, but you'd no playmates over for your birthday," her mother said sadly.

"I had the young-uns."

"Aye, we have family. We need family, because the others will never really want us."

Her mother's sadness was giving way to anger now. "They bring us gifts but it's fear, not gratitude that drives them."

"But Mama, all you do is help folk?"

Emmeline had never understood why her family were so isolated within the community. Her mother's gifts had helped them all at some point. She could find water deep below the ground; tell early if animals or women were with child.

Last summer, without ever leaving their dusty shack, she'd known where the Johnson twins had been hiding.

"But you found them naughty twins when all were afraid they'd drowned in the creek!" protested Emmeline.

"That I did child. Lucky for us the sight doesn't really rest in the eyes."

"Lucky for us?" Emmeline tried to ask but her mother cut her off.

"These people need conjuring folk like us child, but they'll never accept us. They fear what they don't understand. They're scared. They still carry the superstitions of the old world. Our grandparents brought more than mere possessions over from Europe. The world's moved on but not in these woods."

"Mama, your wound!" cried Emmeline.

Her mother was rarely so animated. Her anger had flushed her cheeks and caused a substance like molasses to ooze from the corners of her sunken eyelids. As Emmeline dabbed at the wound she felt something hard just behind the skin. She hadn't felt it before.

"Hold still Mama." She gently opened the eyelids. The cavity behind wasn't empty. An object, about an inch long was jammed deep into the soft tissues. It was wooden and conical, with what might have been a rounded tip.

Her mother batted her hand away. "You must leave it be!" she warned.

"But how..."

"It's always been there. The price for living on this hill, for living with these people," her mother said venomously.

"You mean they did this? The others?"

"They wanted it done child, though there's none amongst them brave enough to do it. They think it'll ward off the evil eye. Who knows, perhaps they're right. For haven't I wished evil upon them and naught come of it? Especially on this day."

Emmeline was going to ask what she meant but she sensed her father's approach.

Her own 'sight' was still growing but her intuition told her that Pappy had been in the shed all this time making something for her.

The carved owl was gift enough, but she felt a pang of excitement as the realization came upon her.

It didn't last long...

Her mother's sadness, the terrible injury...

She sensed her father was not alone. It all came together. She felt faint. Sick. The shack door opened. Pappy's shadow loomed large. Behind him she saw others and recognised Jones the farmer amongst them.

They were silent.

"Be swift," her mother pleaded, but Pappy ignored her. Walking in, he threw two small objects on the rough table, strode over and wrapped his huge arms around Emmeline. He scooped her up against his heaving chest. Big, salty tears fell against her cheek.

Over his shoulder she could just make out the two objects thrown on the table. One was a small leather patch -similar to her mother's, but with an owl carefully etched into the rough hide. The other, a small wooden peg.

She gripped her father in both love and fear. She knew this would break him. She whispered it was okay. He set her down and took the hammer from his pocket.

DAVID SHAKES

LAST CHANCE DINER

THE LAST CHANCE DINER

Lance had been driving half the night, the radio and hum of the road combined in a soporific soundtrack. His concentration kept drifting, wandering between the lonely highway and the images presented with each new song on the radio. He could only find one station on the dial—every track a golden oldie, stirring long forgotten memories of childhood.

When he first saw his name written in glowing letters on the horizon, he doubted his eyes. How the hell could that happen? Besides, as he got closer it didn't look right - the 'L' wasn't in line with the rest of the letters, the gap between them too wide. It was only as he neared them that he finally understood why. They were the only working letters in the Last Chance Diner's neon road sign.

What were the odds of his name being spelled out at the side of the road in the dead hours? Whatever they were, he was willing to bet they had a coffee with his name on; maybe even a slice of pie.

Lance pulled his car onto the cracked parking lot in front of the diner. There were lights on inside but the windows were steamed up. The rust-flecked gas pumps to the side of the building looked like they'd not been used in a long while. He was surprised the place was open at all, given the lack of traffic. He hadn't passed another car at all - at least as far as he could recall. He definitely needed coffee, his mind still felt fuzzy with memories and snatches of song lyrics.

The black and white linoleum floor just inside the doors was scuffed thin from years of use. It stretched out towards the counter that ran the length of the diner. Behind it two pots of coffee steamed on their plates, both still full. He took a tall seat at the closest end of the counter. The red vinyl cover was worn through in places, exposing the foam beneath. When he sat down it emitted a whistle of air and a faint, unpleasant whiff.

"Coffee?"

The waitress must have come through the swing door to the kitchen which was still rocking gently on its hinges.

"You bet, slice of pie too, if you have it?"

"Honey, this time of night all I got is hot coffee and maybe a slice of conversation. Whether or not that's warm pretty much depends on you."

He smiled at her, taking in her appearance. Her white dress and hairstyle were both pretty dated, but she wasn't much older than him and attractive in her own way. She looked incredibly familiar but he couldn't put a finger on why.

She served his coffee in a cup from beneath the counter. Its once white glaze was cracked and gray. The black liquid that she splashed in from the pot smelled rich and deep. His first sip confirmed it, burning his throat.

"So where you headed, the city?"

Lance, revived by the coffee, realized he was glad that she'd decided to talk. Perhaps he needed company.

"That's right, Miss, and if you want this conversation to get any warmer, maybe you could tell me your name?"

"It's on my badge, hon."

And it was. Lance knew that he'd taken a good, long look at his hostess and there had been no badge. Now, there was one. It was fixed near the top of the white apron that she'd also not been wearing a few minutes ago. He studied the brown name badge and gold lettering.

"Mary-Beth," he read shakily.

"That's me," she said sympathetically. "You okay?"

"I'm sorry. It's been a long and weird night. I was thinking about my mother whilst driving. You and she share the same name."

"Is it your mother you're going to see in the city, hon?"

Lance shook his head. A sensation akin to deja-vu was creeping over him. The diner was unnaturally bright now and his eyes had trouble focusing on anything but Mary-Beth's benign expression.

"No. My mother died when I was really young. I don't remember much about her. I'm traveling because I have a job in the city."

If she was taken aback by the candid information he'd given her, she didn't show it. The tone of her voice never changed:

"Is it the kind of job your mother would be proud to know you have?"

For the first time since entering the diner, Lance thought about the package strapped into the trunk. He had to get it to an address in the city by mid-morning. He'd been given a very clear set of instructions:

Drive overnight.
Stick to the quieter roads and watch your speed.
Don't stop until you get there.
If you're stopped, you never heard of us.
Don't be late.

Shit! He'd already broken the third one and was in danger of breaking the last if he didn't get a move on. He turned his wrist to check his watch. The hands on the analogue watch had stopped. The digital display was a line of zeroes.

"Listen, Mary-Beth, I've got to go. I really shouldn't have stopped only... well, it's going to sound silly now. Thing is, I am on a schedule and I wasn't s'posed to stop."

He reached for his wallet and took out a few notes. He was placing them on the counter when she pushed them back at him.

"Coffee's free if you'll take some advice, Lance."

Her tone had changed now. There was ice in her voice.

"How'd you know my name?"

She ignored him.

"Seems to me you don't think you got a choice in this job but you do. You could leave here now and deliver the package..."

Lance threw himself off the chair and jumped away from the counter. His eyes darted between the swing door and the exit. Was this a set-up?

"Who the hell are you lady? What's going on here?"

Mary-Beth stared at him. His temples throbbed; his hands felt clammy.

"You could leave now; deliver your package and be dead by lunchtime *or* you could sit back down and listen to me."

Lance's head swam. He couldn't believe he'd screwed up so royally. They'd been watching him. This had been a test of his future reliability and he'd failed.

He let out a sob.

"I am a dead man anyway," he wailed.

"Not yet, and maybe not at all if you'll shut up and listen," scolded Mary-Beth.

Lance sat himself back down on the worn chair. The sigh of air it released this time masked by his own heavy exhalation.

"Just tell them to make it quick."

She ignored him a second time and continued in her earlier, more patient tone:

"There's a quarter of a million dollars in your trunk. As soon as you hand it over you're dead, a loose end tied up. Turn around. Go back. Take the money to the police or just keep driving until you find someplace to spend it without being noticed. Just. Don't. Go."

"Why are you even telling me this Mary-Beth? They'll hurt you too!"

"Nobody can hurt me now Lance, except through you. Why am I telling you? Because we all get one last chance, and I'm using mine. Maybe it's yours too – I don't know. But I've used it up and that's it. Make the right choice son, don't let me down.'

She turned her back on him then and headed for the swing doors.

"Mary-Beth!" he called after her as the door swung shut again.

The light in the diner immediately dimmed, until he could barely see.

The only illumination came from the small sign above the exterior doors—four letters: EXIT.

He could take a hint.

Outside the first rays of dawn were giving everything a strange luminescence. Even the gas pumps looked beautiful.

The road sign was no longer lit. He couldn't bring himself to believe it ever had been. The neon tubes had long been smashed and ground to powder beneath it. Turning, he saw that every window in the building was broken; the front doors hanging from their hinges. The place was derelict – had been for a long time.

He nodded curtly and got in the car. The bitter taste of coffee still fresh on his palate.

Reversing sharply out onto the highway, he drove back the way he had come.

MARK A. KING

THE HARBOUR OF LONDON

FUSION

THE TORTURE CHAMBER

THE HARBOUR OF LONDON

I want to swim in the sea, to feel it, to cleanse my sins, to wipe away the viscous merlot blood from my hands. But…I know the sea will kill me, almost as quickly as the authorities will.

My husband was a powerful man. They never approved of me and now he has lost warmth - they have opportunity and motivation; I will surely get my comeuppance.

I sit and watch the Thames tide lapping at the edges of the synthetic golden shore. I try to appreciate this folly, this profligate profanity, for soon the whirligig lights will come for me. The frigid-blue and afterburner-red hues will spin their mesmerising spell, penetrating even the dark and seedy shadows of London; then the men with serious faces will take me away.

The Harbour of London houses the oligarchs, the tech-pimps and the puppeteers. I do not belong here. Not many people do. Perhaps this place is the opposite of me. I once was beautiful, once was desirable. I tenderly touch my skin and run my fingers over the bruises, their oil-spill colours and my crackle-glaze scars somehow define me now. I believe he once loved me; if that's even possible.

As I watch the waking amber mists crawl through the arteries of the city, and smell the diesel chug of council recycling boats, I remember his last words: "You're past you're sell-buy date, darling. Damaged goods. Look at you, you're a mess. You disgust me!"

I didn't respond. Sometimes, actions speak louder than words. His unused golf clubs are now used: soiled with human tissue and DNA that even industrial bleach would struggle to remove. Knowing his friends, the story of the object will only add to its value, only intensify the conversations in the wish-fulfilment dens and substance bars.

I remember when I was his chosen one, "You are stunning. You are amazing. I know it's crazy, but will you marry me?"

"No," I told him, "why would you, you could have anyone – why me?"

"It's because I could have anyone. You are unique, you make me feel incredible. You will do anything for me."

This was true. This was the problem.

I watch the city from this island of hulking excess. I see the forgotten worker drones, hustling to jobs they hate. The scuttling underground carriages transporting them from A to B, from work to home, from life to death. Their lives have become nothing more than a flash of advertising while they poke at their technology and furtively imagine the lives of fellow commuters.

I listen intently to the enhanced tides. I know these historic waters have carried the Nordic, the Roman, the spice ships and the bubonic plague. Beneath the churning of waves, beyond the exhale of the moon beckoning back the flow, I hear the fizz, the forgotten fizz - the sound of a million unseen bubbles extinguished and unnoticed. I think about the plight of these people, these worker ants, and realise that, perhaps, I am lucky.

The first autonomous hybrid of human and machine. Two point five billion pounds race through my lab-born veins. But…that did not give him an excuse to own me, to make me do those things, to treat me like a object that had to be controlled, debased, abused and subjugated.

Oh…I hear it now. Not the mythical sirens of the deep, these are more artificial and deadly. I remove my human clothing. The water looks cold, refreshing and inviting.

FUSION

After Pompeii, they banished me. I'd protected them for centuries, but humankind needed to find comfort, reason and blame. As a god of fire and wing, I was an easy target.

I watched fertile land birth a thriving city. I watched the sins of greed, the exchanges of coin for touches of flesh, and the choice of ignorance over the obvious.

I watched from my volcanic skies, weeping, as pumice ground, lava flowed, and choking dust cemented lungs. I watched the prophesied storm unfurl. And now the citizens gaze to eternity as immortal concrete icons.

The survivors drove me to the isolated cold, believing I could do no harm here. From St Kilder, I witnessed the same mistakes of ignorance. This time, death from starvation and disease. Distended bellies giving fleeting life for tetanus to take it back - infected knives ripping at umbilical cords.

I intervened when watching the doomed birth of another child. She was born beneath a sky of shimmering stars; I took her under my protection. I named her Stella.

* * *

It has been eight years and Stella thrives. I watch her play in the stubble of the fields. She softly pirouettes with butterflies in the ancient woodlands.

The female butterfly she watches is called a Comma and her outstretched wings are black inkblots on lava-red tissue paper. On her abdomen a white mark, like a comma, her life in perpetual pause.

Her mate rests beside her. They flutter and they dance. The musty forest air flashes with their punctuated splendour.

Hidden behind the tree, Stella watches the boy. The net swoops through the air and the boy grins. The female Comma butterfly is trapped.

The boy grasps the tweezers and picks the female butterfly up, gently. He doesn't want to harm her, not yet.

I could intervene, but Stella needs to see the world for what it is. For one day, she might rule and she needs to see its naked beauty, its brutal menace.

He engages the trigger on the lighter. First, her wings. And when they are reduced to cinder, he completes his work.

The male Comma butterfly is alone.

His frantic swirling and diving disrupt the atmosphere microscopically.

Airflow disrupts airflow. Pressure builds on pressure. Until the breeze becomes swirl, becomes storm, becomes typhoon.

A few weeks later, I watch from the eye of the storm as it approaches a distant land. On the shore, a young girl faces the typhoon, she is no older than Stella. She cannot run or hide. She faces it armed with tatty umbrella and broken gas-mask. Her fate determined by delicate and frantic wings in a land she has never seen.

I fold my wings, and take human shape. I stand on the beach and face the storm.

Its twisted face, grey and angry, stretches across an area the size of a continent. Its hailstone teeth nibble the ocean surface, hungry for land. It picks up speed, its force quantified in categories and its breath measured in three digits. It is the child of a billion storms before it - its ancestors saw the first separation of the sea and the land.

The vulnerable child has skin like delicate porcelain. She is composed and has a smile of reassurance as she looks at me with complete trust. She does not move, but lets the umbrella and gas mask flow in the irritated wind. She was alone, but no longer. She will be safe, for I remember when our universe was just chemistry and physics, and time was yet to be born.

The storm will die; I will starve it of energy and feed it to my two adopted children. I've been shackled for too long but now my children will have my power and the blessed gift of human acceptance. They will harness the energy of nature and lift humanity towards the stars.

THE TORTURE CHAMBER

*H*e sees her writhe in pain, her body contorted like organic origami, folding, bending and jolting with agony. He smiles.

Heavily drugged, she cannot move from the bed. He likes it this way. Soon it will be over for her. Where would she go anyway?

A gleaming knife cuts neatly at her flesh and he brings the camera closer to capture every moment, to savour it. He will replay this, and maybe even enjoy it more, after the event.

"I hate you so much," she screams at him, her voice pure loathing, "I thought you loved me, how could you do this to me?"

He smiles and says, "You wanted this as much as me. You asked for it. You know what I mean?"

She scowls at him. She howls, a noise he has only ever heard from animals or horror films.

Then…he sees the head. He hears the slosh of amniotic fluid and the scream of new life. He looks at her and as soon as she cradles their child, she smiles.

MARK A. KING

WE CAN TELEPORT YOU (ALMOST) ANYWHERE
TM

For KHQ: Lorraine, Samuel & Abigail x

WE CAN TELEPORT YOU (ALMOST) ANYWHERE
TM

Prologue

*T*hey had to change the name.

It used to be known as *We Can Teleport You Anywhere* - until the incident with Beryl Blackstock.

After it made international news, the PR machine destroyed the evidence and blamed it on atmospheric anomalies. That's what they do. Damage limitation. Reputation protection. Name change. Rebranding.

They said -"Our customer safety is paramount." Not long after, they added - "We've fully revised our policies." Finally, they pronounced - "Statistically, teleportation is the safest form of travel."

And that was that.

But, I know better. After all, it was I who dragged the reel of fuse wire across the heathland of bronzed swaying crops. It was I who guiltily crept under the watchful eye of the Macgillcuddy's Reeks; the ancient coastal mountains casting judgement as they devoured smudges of clouds, their harsh gaping faces softened by powdery white beards.

It was I who laid the long strip across the petrol station forecourt, the residual tang of explosives faint on my palate. It was I who poured fuel on the floor and watched vapours weave skywards, like the banished serpent ghosts of St Patrick.

I watched, lighter in one eager hand and crucifix chain clasped in the other. It was I who saw the lorry arrive with the transparent box, its occupants placing it carefully just outside the abandoned fuel shop.

I saw her come into being.

Like a god, I watched new life form.

I saw her look of excitement.

A half-remembered smile from childhood. A curtsey.

The grind of a flint wheel on my lighter. The static fizz of fuse wire alight. The slow, but unstoppable chase of sparks, sparks, sparks along the spectrum floor.

A look of horror. A scream.

The whoosh - orange, yellow and central blue.

Like a god, I watched life end.

Crackling embers.

Silence.

The CEO

Under the serene waves lapping the coral beauty of Heron Island, Danny Thistle dives the alien landscape of the Great Barrier Reef. He takes in the majesty of colour, the beauty of fluid prey versus predator movement. He's content in this paradise. He is biding his time, laying low, until he is called for.

Elsewhere, under the cloudless night sky of Manhattan, the towers of office lights drown out their celestial rivals. In a bland corporate office, Danny Thistle walks the lobby. He's unrecognisable in his cleaning uniform, his scruffy unkempt hair escaping in strands from his well-thumbed cap. He pushes the buffing machine. Working the night shift, avoiding eye contact with desperate office workers: those under stress, those pushing for bonuses, those having affairs with co-workers. He waits.

In Stockholm, in Des Moines, in Marrakesh, in a hundred other places, Danny waits.

The Detective

In the TV shows, he'd be handsome, brave, and charismatic. He'd have a shiny badge in a soft leather wallet. It would sit on the bedside table next to his gun, which would probably have a name. He'd turn in bed and kiss his perfect wife, with her impeccable hair and teeth so white they'd hurt his morning eyes. She'd say things like, *"Don't go, darling. The world is a bad place and it needs you. But... I need you more."*

He smiles at this.

Callum turns to face an empty bed. Anthony got up several hours ago. Why? Maybe it was the lingering row about work being more important than quality time? Maybe it's *that* thing about their relationship? The usual one about commitment, about marriage, about children?

Callum goes to the bedside cabinet, and picks up his squashed nicotine gum, throwing three lime-green pieces in his mouth then chews, chews, chews, swallows - breakfast, ahoy. He considers taking a shower, considers making coffee, considers the fact he'll get into a row with Anthony, who is probably stalking the kitchenette. He puts on yesterday's crumpled clothes, avoids the kitchen and leaves the hotel room, quietly.

He knows this is no way to live. He's been chasing the target for over a decade now. Anthony has been tolerant, beyond saintly.

He thinks that he'll take Anthony away. Promise him time, dedication, tenderness. That he'll retire once this godforsaken case is finished. Maybe get married. Maybe have kids. Until now, he's known better than to plan. Better than to promise.

He makes his way down the street. In Tokyo, the night is *never* black. Electrons power inert-gas colours, encased in forts of steel and glass; they hold back the hungry darkness.

He approaches the *We Can Teleport You (Almost) Anywhere HQ*, where he has a private appointment with the CEO, Danny Thistle. He finally has him.

He states his name at reception, says he has an appointment. He refuses the request to sign the visitors' book in exchange for an oversized luminous pass and gaudy lanyard. He flashes his inspector's badge at the dubious looking intern, who picks up the phone and whispers something, covering her mouth so he can't lip-read. She looks disappointed at the response.

The restricted-access lift is plush, decorated in Italian marble and finely polished English walnut. The transition is smooth. Perhaps not cables, but pneumatics. When he reaches the top, the doors glide open without a ping, or audio voice-over proclaiming the floor number, or "Please mind the doors".

He doubts Mr Thistle answers to the overlords of Health and Safety.

The entire floor is dark and empty, but for a single desk and single chair. At *that* view.

In front of him, Danny Thistle stands silhouetted against the background of floor to ceiling glass on the perimeter, which overlooks the glittering Tokyo cityscape. Shimmering lights spill into the room as if they are floating on the periphery of a nebular cloud.

The CEO approaches and extends his hand. Callum takes it, firmly. They both apply inappropriate pressure. They both maintain uncomfortable eye contact, before breaking away and smiling.

"Welcome, Chief Inspector Breen. What can I do for you?" Thistle says, leading Callum toward the single desk near the windows. His tone is polite, but business-like. "I'd offer you a seat, but as you can see I've chosen not to have seats for guests. They tend to stay too long. No offence, Inspector."

Callum avoids the bait, and replies, "Mr Thistle, forgive my language, but I like a man who doesn't bullshit. No offence… that's kind of funny, considering those you've committed, eh?"

"I'm a tolerant man, Inspector. But you've gone too far. I only let you up here to put an end to this persecution. You've been harassing me for ten years now and not a shred of evidence to show for it. I've had words with your boss. I'm sorry to tell you that this'll be the last task you perform in your role," Danny Thistle retorts, smugly.

Thistle turns walks towards the window and they both stare out at the city. He continues, "Now you'll be a free man, you can indulge in copious drinking again, or is it the itchy need for drugs? Perhaps your predilection for dodgy bunk-ups with strangers? You'll have plenty of time for all that." The tone in his voice is far from friendly or business-like now.

Callum looks at him, giving little away in his body language. He calmly says, "You've got nothing on me. My superiors know about my addictions, my illnesses. They're supportive. My partner knows I've been unfaithful and I'm ashamed of myself for hurting him. But, let's stop this charade. This isn't about me."

Callum takes out his smartphone, and continues, "Remember Toby? You know that nice chap in IT that used to work for you? Went a bit pyro and torched a lovely lady called Beryl in a remote village in Ireland? See, your people hid the evidence and blamed it on the weather, on incorrect supplier delivery of the box to the fuel station instead of the dance hall. Or…"

"That's what happened. I don't know what you're implying. Poor Beryl wanted to visit the Irish Dancing school of her childhood. Like you say, an unfortunate accident."

Callum plays the video. Under questioning Toby confesses to the fire. He then explains that teleportation is impossible for anything larger than a grain of sand. Cloning a person is entirely possible, but illegal. "After all, we are just chemicals, DNA and stored memories," he says, eager to tell the truth, "build it right and the clone will remember everything up to the point of scanning, or teleportation, as they'll remember it. The problem is what to do with the original person. They need to be destroyed."

Danny Thistle shrugs, then replies, "My barristers will tear him apart in court. A psychotic ex-employee. Come on, even you must know how flimsy that sounds. Get out. Before I have security throw you out."

"But… you haven't seen my magic trick, yet."

Callum looks at the CEO and for the first time he looks uneasy, unsure. Callum looks down at the street. The specks moving through the city. The mundane, the cheaters, the addicts, the murderers. None of them knowing who walks beside them. He says, "Here. I have another video."

Callum watches Danny, watching another Danny. He watches the CEO as his once pumped-up posture visibly deflates like a perfect shiny helium balloon, now old and sagging and losing altitude. One of his duplicates has turned grass. A different Danny Thistle, injured, bitter and spiteful, talks to a Callum in a recording taken in some other city. The other Danny says he grew tired of waiting; he wanted to be the main man. He knew the risks. He knew that the primary would try to kill him but his hapless underworld friends didn't finish the job properly. They'd been stupid, careless. Now… the other Danny talks, oh how he talks.

The primary CEO considers this, "Let's just say, hypothetically, this is true, then there would be so many of me that you'd never find us all. You couldn't catch us all."

Callum smiles, "Unless, hypothetically, I'm a dodgy, screwed-up detective, with a grudge against someone who's taken up more of his life than he'd care to mention? Rules are meant to be broken, aren't they? You, of all people, should understand that."

He taps his phone and opens the app. On the display is a global map. For every pin in the map where there is a Danny Thistle, there is another pin with a Callum Breen.

Callum doesn't arrest him. He leaves. He walks through the sparkling nebula cloud of the Tokyo streets and smiles knowing his work is done. He wanted more time for life. Now with infinite versions of himself, and nothing to stop him; he has as much time as he'll ever need.

ANDREW PATCH

RETURN TICKET

THE MESSENGER

THE TINKERER

RETURN TICKET

'Number 11232242, please go to Desk 48.'

Felix lifted himself up from the plastic orange chair that had adhered itself to his skin. Legs complaining, he set off across the vast room, past rows of bright orange chairs, each occupied by a resident clutching a numbered ticket. Envious glances marked his progress across the hall. Felix didn't care, he was just glad that his number had finally been called.

Behind the polished glass of the cubicle was an attractive young woman. Felix felt his heart sink as his nemesis stirred in his trousers. They were always attractive and young, no matter his self-delusion he knew they saw him only as the balding overweight middle-aged man he knew he was. Her attention was focused on a computer as he approached, Felix went to cough politely but a raised manicured finger halted him mid intake.

Her fingers danced over the keyboard, she was blonde. Why always blonde?

Fucking hell he felt so horny.

'Boarding details?'

'Ah, somewhere and please, call me Felix ...'

The look back, a marvellous combination of disdain and boredom, stopped him midsentence.

'In the chute ...'

'The chute?'

Another malevolent glare, a finger pointing to the brass tube beside the glass.

'Take a tube, put your documents inside.'

Felix clumsily stuffed his documents into the small canister, then watched it disappear up into the ceiling.

Moments later and with an elegant whoosh, it dropped onto the desk in front of the girl.

'So ...' she perused his documents, 'hmm, you've requested a return.'

'Yes, well when the gentleman at arrivals had explained my options, to be honest a return seemed a great deal.'

'Gentleman?'

'Tall, beard ... very helpful ... handing out brochures.'

Another raised finger; Felix dutifully fell silent as she picked up her phone. Her voice was cheerfully melodic as the other person answered.

'Hi, this is Claire from processing. Sorry seems Peter's at it again ... I know it's just we'll never hit our quotas if he ... excellent okay, yeah and you.'

She put the phone down, her warmth fading immediately.

'Well if it was me you'd be getting the standard eternal darkness package, yet seems my hands are tied, so what were you after?'

'Well I was hoping for something a bit more athletic, sporty, I mean it'd be great if I was into running maybe?'

'Sporty ... well let's see, ah yes, seems I have something suitable.' Her eyes lit up at the information on her computer screen. 'If you could just place your hand firmly within the square etched on the glass.'

Felix lifted his hand. The glass was cold.

'Will this hurt?'

'Probably.'

She hit a button.

White light.

Felix was running across a field, tongue lolling, heart racing, four legs sprinting in unison. He sped through the thick grass that brushed against his fur, a perfect blue sky above him.

A young blonde woman waiting for him, leash in hand.

Maybe this was going to work out after all.

THE MESSENGER

*F*rom the bell tower, Arcane watched orange flowers bloom in the twilight. One after the other, a constellation of beacons spluttered into life. Sending their plight to the capital.

There was nothing else he could do. Arcane slumped down by the bell, whose rough rope had flayed the skin from his hands. He had tolled The Sentinel till his shoulders had ached, her solemn declaration almost overwhelming the screams and sounds of battle that emanated from the village.

Tolled till orange flowers bloomed.

The sound of wood giving way to force stirred Arcane back to reality. The invaders had gained entry. Soon they would ascend the worn stone steps to find the young scholar.

Shoulders complaining, Arcane took up his axe and buckler. He had hoped the invaders would have moved on, or that the Capital's knights would arrive in time.

But such thoughts were that of a child.

Now he had to die as a man.

THE TINKERER

'Police been on the phone love ... you want to go?'

Cedric shook his head, his gaze never lifting up from his workbench. His wife lingered in the shed's doorway as if there was more to say. Finally his silence had the desired effect and she left, leaving behind the usual scent of Chanel and Marlboro. Moments later and Cedric heard the Astra's engine splutter into life, the sound of tires reversing out onto the road.

Cedric put down the screwdriver. In front of him were strewn the innards of the kitchen radio. He didn't recall taking it apart, or even if it needed to be fixed. If Danny were here now he'd be mocking his efforts, telling him to buy a new one off of Ebay, that no one repaired anything these days.

Wiping his hands on a rag Cedric ventured back into the house. Soon the kettle was boiling, a tea bag dangling in his mug. As he poured the water the phone rang. Cedric reached out, his hand hovering, as if the handset was a coiled serpent waiting to strike. Finally the answering machine kicked in, Danny's voice cheerfully demanding information after the beep. He should change that, it wasn't right, tomorrow, tomorrow he'd record a new message.

The beep—Cedric stood waiting for someone to talk, yet there was only the sound of breathing, then the phone was put down.

Cedric picked up his mug, retreating back to the shed. The bike was hanging on the wall, as it had been since the police had returned it. The back end crushed, the rear wheel missing. He ran a finger over the crudely scratched marks that Danny had etched into the seat post in case the bike got stolen: DH 12501. Cedric had been so cross with him that day, so hurt that Danny had defaced his gift. They had bickered, stood by the shed, Danny's face flushed red with resentment at receiving another lecture.

Then he had left, cycling down the road, head down, pedals turning, disappearing into the grey light rain.

Cedric retreated back to his bench, trembling fingers rebuilding the radio.

ANDREW PATCH

BLOSSOM IN WINTERTIME

BLOSSOM IN WINTERTIME

*S*ullivan limped determinedly toward the next oasis of streetlight, the darkness that cloaked the city feeding his imagination. He chided himself for feeling fearful of streets he had known all his life. Yet his fingers still toyed with the blade lurking in his coat pocket.

I am legend.

No old man, you're the dregs.

The resentment of being out here whilst his colleagues were currently patrolling London chafed as much as his knee. Headquarters had been pandemonium this morning, everyone packing cudgels, knives and body armor, the promise of potential violence buzzing like static. Yet Sullivan could only watch, biting down the desire to scream at the heavens at the passing of time. Hell, in his youth he would have been at the front of the charge, a blur of fists and strikes. Wasn't he the one that led the purge? Fighting on even after taking a knife to his leg, claret spilling over paving stones.

When did I become so irrelevant?

Turning the corner, wandering past terraced houses and the endless chain of rusting cars. A beer can spun out from under his kick, spiraling along streets that a young Sully once terrorized with graffiti and malevolence. As if awoken by the clatter the dark lidless eyes of the houses sparkled into life as televisions were activated. Nine o'clock and the Prop-News channels were about to deliver their usual reassurances and certainty. Sullivan preferred to be out here away from the wallpaper that peeled from damp walls and the old man whose reflection stared out from the blank television screen. *You reap what you sow.* Wasn't that the saying? Well he had sown loyalty, faith and silence and had only reaped his shattered knee and scarred dreams.

If Tabitha were still here she'd gently admonish him for his self-pity, waiting for him at home with something stronger lurking in his mug of milky tea. Yet she wasn't and his fellow militia treated him like he was a mascot, a relic. *Well fuck them.* Sullivan drew the blade out of his pocket, running the tip along the length of a rusting black car, metal screeching in despair. Forging one more scratch hidden amongst the hundreds that scarred its skin.

Another corner, another row of terraced housing, these lurking opposite a row of shops. The latter's current poster plastered state caused Sullivan's heart to sink. Her fucking face stared out from the walls, fresh glue dribbling down over cherubic cheeks. Row upon row of the same irritation, as if Warhol had run amok in suburbia. This however wasn't the standard poster, but the one that had greeted London early this morning from all four sides of Big Ben. The attack of the three hundred foot woman, staring out across the capital, holding a sign in pudgy thick fingers, just one phrase:

CARPE DIEM

Sullivan pulled at one limp corner, tearing the poster down from the wall. The face he held in his hands was at best plain but was one that had become famous: curly brown hair, thick bottle glasses and a smile balanced somewhere between knowing and proposition. The whole thing perched atop a chaotic ensemble of pink tutu and silver DMs that clad a curvaceously opulent body. For months the posters of this woman had been appearing on walls and monuments across the union, from Paris to New Glasgow. No one knew why, nor who was responsible yet from somewhere, from someone, emerged a name that stuck firmly onto the zeitgeist:

Mother Ruin

The Prop-News sent reporters to all corners, trying to find out who was behind the campaign. Experts, from academics to artists were dragged into the firing line, forced to hypothesis what Mother Ruin represented. Was it some artistic celebration of the union? Was it terrorism? Ideological subversion? Yet for all the questions no answers emerged. The uncertainty filled only by whispers on the dark web forums and gossip in smoke filled pubs.

The one thing that found consensus was the proposition from some busy body at Oxford who had offered up a thesis on the puzzle that her name contained:

Mother Ruin
Gin
Djinn
Genie

Sullivan used to lie awake at night, watching the hands of the clock tick slowly around wondering whether this genie offered wishes and to whom. Even within militia headquarters the conspiracies raged between clouds of nicotine and sips of tea. One of the lads had even set up an investigation on one wall. An array of newspaper clippings, photos, wiki entries all connected by red string and brass tacks, with Mother Ruin's fat face lurking in the centre, taunting the militia to solve the riddle.

Yet this morning with this latest poster, the first one to bear a message, had kicked the hive into life. Now every able-bodied militia was in the capital, assisting the police with checkpoints, patrolling public transport, leaning on the usual suspects. The King had even made a rare public appearance, giving assurances that he would not rest until the defiler of an icon such as Big Ben was brought to justice for their crime.

Sullivan let the tattered face fall amongst the broken glass and litter. He was too tired to care tonight; someone else could take them all down in the morning. However, just as he turned back the thought of a bottle of scotch and bed enticing him home, he noticed the shadows heading for the petrol station that lay halfway up the road. They were barely noticeable, wraiths slipping through the darkness. Sullivan grasped his knife and, skirting low, knee complaining, slowly moved in their direction.

He got to a point close enough to observe and watched, grateful for the moonlight that broke through the cloud laden sky. From his vantage point behind a car, covered in graffiti and more scratches, Sullivan observed the trio of teenagers. One had broken into the shop judging by the glass on the floor; another was posting Mother Ruin prints up over every surface; the final one of the musketeers was mucking about with a pump nozzle. Squeezing the trigger furiously, peering into the nozzle, seemingly irritated that nothing flowed out. They were only children, that was what he had to keep in mind.

Heart pounding, knife in his grip, Sullivan strode across the forecourt towards nozzle boy. He could see a Mother Ruin face, badly painted, staring out from the back of the boy's leather jacket.

'Oi! What do you think you're doing?'

Sullivan expected the boy to run, to drop the nozzle as if he had been scalded and bolt for the darkness. Yet the gaze that met his was one of apathy as if Sullivan was barely there. Sullivan's demand had also interrupted the labour of the poster boy, who retrieved a baseball bat from the shadowy ground.

'Y'aright Pete?' Poster boy asked, hefting the bat onto his shoulder.

Pete nodded across to Sullivan before shrugging and turning his attention back to the nozzle. Poster laughed watching Pete as he hit the nozzle on the ground in frustration, a dull clang echoing into the night.

'You idiot Pete, just wait till Nikki hacks the system,' Poster snickered.

Sullivan, frustration rising at being ignored, raised his knife, the icy blade trembling in the moonlight. The boy's laughter stopped, smiles lighting up on both their faces.

'You want to dance old man?'

'Reckon he does Pete.'

Poster skirted to Sullivan's left, Nozzle unarmed, the other. Sullivan's knee ached as he slowly moved backwards, trying to keep them in view. He might not get both but one of them was definitely going to get stuck somewhere soft.

That was when the girl stepped out across the broken glass from the darkness of the shop. She was younger than either of the boys, maybe ten or twelve, her steps light, like a dancer's. The boys themselves stopped as they watched her walk towards Sullivan. Raising his blade, Sullivan waited for her to stop, to back away. Yet she didn't, she continued to step forward, the smile never leaving her face. Stopping only when the tip of the blade pressed into her throat.

They stood together like that for what felt like a lifetime to Sullivan, until she raised her hand, touching his, slowly extracting the knife from his grip. "No need for that, not anymore. Look ... behind you."

Hairs rising on the back of his neck Sullivan slowly turned. How they had come to be there, how they had moved so silently, he knew wasn't the issue. What was relevant at this moment was that at least fifty children stood there in silence. Some holding cricket bats, golf clubs, the odd knife and even a bike chain or two.

Sullivan raised both hands in peace, turning back to the young girl. The knife was in her hand, just like a lifetime ago, yet Sullivan had no brick this time, nothing with which to splinter apart her delicate skull. She smiled, brushing back blonde hair, casting his knife away into the darkness.

'Game over eh?' With that she moved on, Sullivan's impotent presence meaningless. 'Peter, give it a try now.'

The boy grabbed a nozzle, clenching the trigger, dark fuel spilling out onto concrete. The girl clapped her hands in delight, the children behind Sullivan muttering excitedly, applauded in turn.

'Mother Ruin ... is this her doing?' Sullivan stammered, a whisper on the breeze.

There was no response, just the stench of fuel as more nozzles were activated. He didn't exist, had become irrelevant. Sullivan turned and walked through the crowd of silent children, parting for him like water around a rock.

Sullivan limped home, tears rolling down his cheeks, never looking back. Even when orange flowers bloomed into the night sky.

VOIMA OY

ALIVE, ALIVE, OH

CATS IN SPACE

EXIT STRATEGY

ALIVE, ALIVE, OH

*H*ere she comes again, my little mermaid, my pearl diver, in her tight black suit.

She is the only one who comes out this far, far beyond the seabeds where the oysters sleep, forming their little moons. She is beyond beds, now, and that domestic routine. Oh my love, let me show you oblivion beyond your wildest Hokusai dreams. To me you are Botticelli on a half shell, your hair flowing like seaweed. I remember those days. Do you?

Of course, I can pick up what you're thinking. I wish you could understand me. No screams of snails in a saucepan, I whisper between the stars. Can you get the picture? Look, the colors I flash just for you, for you! I am beautiful. How can you resist? Come closer. Let me hold you.

Still, you hesitate? I know you are intrigued. You dream of me, don't you, I know. We've met there, before, did you know that? And you have heard me mentioned in the sailors' songs, the stories they whisper in crowded bars. Yes, they know me, too.

You know me, yes you do. But we haven't been properly introduced.

Let me tell you a little bit about myself. I'm way, way, older than you. I come from somewhere else. This place, this shape suits me here. The dark, the pressure of gravity. The skeletons of fallen whales. This is what they call the Twilight Zone—where the light from your sun doesn't reach. My eyes have seen many different suns. Look into my eyes and you'll see.

Come out with me, beyond the seabeds, past all traps under this moon. Your little life is so limited, here, rounded as it is with sleep and death. I can feel the longing in you, the empty spaces yearning to be filled. Come out with me beyond the human. Let us be together, mind and mind.

Let me show you what it is to be alive, to swim in the bright fluid of electrons moving. To dance to the songs the quasars sing.

Come closer. Let me hold you. Your tears taste of blood and the sea.

CATS IN SPACE

"Legend has it that the first of our people fell out of the sky, a bird with wings aflame. A boy he was, and beautiful. We shared our lives with him.

We have always been sailors' familiars. Together we sailed under the stars.

We are the wondrous strange. We pass between the walls.

The second of our people was a tabby girl. Wild she was and beautiful, in the alleys of the cities of the night."

"Why is it so hard to understand us? Why must we be contained? We have so much to teach you about gravity and doors."

The cat people were complaining again. Now they were demanding more break time and black string. They were so difficult to work with. Schrodingers was the word Captain Garza used to describe them. Space aliens. Chaotic as the random decay of subatomic particles.

But there was no denying their talent for navigating the seas of quantum foam.

EXIT STRATEGY

Already in the plaza, a rain of yellow leaves falling into the pool by the fountain.

Such stillness under a sky of cloudless blue. Autumn is coming, he thought. And to me, too.

Of course, he had seen it coming. New faces in the hallways. Memos not addressed to him. Sharp words—hollowing out—moving target acquisitions. Then, the final cut, from the new guy in Human Resources. "I'm sorry, Jerry. It's nothing personal. You've given so many years to the Bank. Believe me, it's appreciated."

He looked down at the desk between them, their faces reflected in the smooth black surface of the glass. Quick and painless, is that what death feels like? He could feel himself disappearing.

It was a long walk down the hallway. The news had already spread among the cubicles. He could cut the tension in the air with a knife. They all pretended to be busy, but what was there to say. They had all seen it coming. With each step, he began to feel lighter, more free.

As he cleaned out his cubicle, he could see Esther in the corner office. She couldn't wait for him to leave. Too bad he had come with her new job. Still, it had been kind of her to let him stay in charge of the rounding errors. No one cared about ten thousands of a cent here and there. No one had ever noticed.

"Some day, Mary," he used to say, "we'll retire to Tahiti." Was it too much to ask to grow old together? No time for that now.

The elevator opened and there was Clark, rushing from the Copy Center. "Mr. Poole, I just heard the news." He fumbled awkwardly with some folders. "It's been an honour, sir. Stay in touch, okay?" They shook hands, and a card passed between them.

"It's been a pleasure, Clark. Good luck with your music." The elevator doors hissed open. He turned and waved. "Be seeing you."

Now he stood by the pool and the fountain. By the time they found out, he would be gone. A coin on edge. A plane in flight, he disappeared among the zeroes.

VOIMA OY

REST STOP

REST STOP

*H*eading west, the sky was an expanse of blue. There was no traffic on the highway, but that was not unusual, now. The epidemic had left cities of ghosts. Masango, they called it, the plague of nostalgia. Masango in the rear-view mirror.

The bus was not crowded, either. Naomi sat in the back with BobbyZen, suitcases and shopping bags piled on the seats around them. A black dog was sleeping in the aisle. A cat meowed plaintively in a carrier. A canary hopped and chirped in its cage.

Naomi looked out the window at the passing scenery, the flaming fall colors of the trees. She didn't think about the past, much. She didn't have an interesting past compared to the other travellers. The old lady in the seat in front of her, for example, Mrs Whittington, with her overnight bag and a cat carrier on the seat beside her. In the cat carrier was a large orange cat named Leo.

Mrs Whittington was a retired librarian. In the short time they had known each other, she had told Naomi all about her life. Older people had always been like that, more talkative.

In addition to Mrs Whittington, and the bus driver, Fred, there were two more passengers, Quinn and Alec, who had owned a vintage boutique. Most of the bags belonged to them. The black dog, Siren, was with them, too, as was the canary, Sunny Boy.

Now that their phones didn't work anymore, people had reverted to the old ways, small talk and personal conversation. It was awkward and clumsy at first. No one knew quite what to say. Their old lives were over. No one knew what would happen next. For now, there was only the bus heading west, and the view of the countryside.

For Naomi, it was enough. Of course, that was because she was on the bus with BobbyZen, sitting peacefully beside her. Even though they had only met two days ago, they had known each other long before that. Ironically, they had connected on their phones, on a poetry blog, where people traded lines and comments.

It was spring, and he had written about flowering crab-apples, not the usual cherry blossoms--the way he said it, too, how they chose to bloom, not some romantic forcing.

The first time she saw BobbyZen, he didn't look anything like she thought he would, except for the shaggy dark hair. He was just a kid, about her age. He had no home, no family. He came with nothing.

She didn't have much, either. Just one black sweater, and her black shoulder bag. She was done with her former life, her job at Fun World, the virtual reality cafe, where she worked as a hostess. The money was good, but what good was money, now? This was a new reality.

Naomi sighed, and reached in her bag for the pack of cigarettes. Everyone was smoking, these days. It was the only thing that seemed to have any effect on the symptoms of Masango. Masango was a voodoo word for evil spell. It was like voodoo, but people didn't turn into zombies. They faded away, like ghosts.

Did they disappear into another dimension, a parallel reality? No one knew for sure. First, people became nostalgic, then more and more hazy and insubstantial. Then, they were gone. Naomi's parents had vanished at the kitchen table, holding each other's hands.

Whatever it was, there were too many looters to stay in the city. Maybe they were all looters, now. In his former life, Fred had been a bus driver. He had taken the bus, and kept driving.

The bus continued west on the interstate. Naomi watched the passing signs, names of towns she had never heard of. Were people still living there? It seemed possible the contagion hadn't spread this far. At the next exit, Fred turned off the highway. "Running low on gas," he said. "I imagine we all could use a rest stop."

It was a pleasant little town, a pleasant autumn evening. The bus passed Victorian houses with big front porches. On the main street, they passed a bank and a hardware store. Around the corner was an elegant looking hotel. Fred pulled up at an old-fashioned diner, the sign invitingly lit. Across the street was a gas station.

Mrs Whittington was the first one off the bus, taking the overnight bag and Leo in the cat carrier with her. "Maybe there's someone in the diner," she said. "I'd like a bite to eat."

Quinn and Alec followed her with their dog and the canary. Fred headed over to the gas station. Naomi and BobbyZen looked around, smoking cigarettes. The wind in the falling leaves was like voices whispering.

Inside the diner, it could have been a scene from another time. There was a jukebox in one corner, which Alec was admiring. "It's a vintage dream!" he said.

"Look at this old wall phone!" Quinn said. He picked up the receiver. "Hello?" The others laughed uneasily.

"There doesn't seem to be anyone around," Mrs Whittington said. "I think I'll make some coffee."

While the coffee was brewing, Naomi went in the back, to the kitchen. It was clean, and the fridge was running. The shelves were stocked. She didn't want to be the cook, but BobbyZen thought it would be kind of fun. He made grilled-cheese sandwiches and opened cans of tomato soup. Naomi played the waitress, pretending to take orders, and the others played along.

For a moment, they ate in silence, more hungry than they realized.

"Well, there's a full tank of gas, now." Fred said. "We could keep going. Or we could stop here, for awhile."

"That looks like a nice hotel," Quinn said. Alec nodded agreement.

"This is good coffee," Fred said.

Naomi looked over at BobbyZen, smiling as they cleared the tables. She could imagine a future together, serving pies and pouring coffee.

"I'm sure there's a library in this town," Mrs Whittington said.

JACKI DONNELLAN

CINDY AND THE DANCER

YET

ON THE WEB

CINDY AND THE DANCER

Cindy spotted him in the distance, as he moved through the medium of *pas-de-chat* down the high street.

He stopped, occasionally, to hold an imaginary bar and execute a *plié*, the tide of hurrying shoppers temporarily parting to avoid him. And then he would raise and curl his arms and twirl like an elaborate whisk, before continuing down the street, leaping gracefully.

P*as-de-chat.*

Pas-de-chat.

He didn't seem to notice Cindy as she stood in the doorway of the music shop, watching his approach. As he got closer she could feel the slight vibration in the pavement as he landed and hear the rubbery tap of his trainers as they alighted, alighted, alighted on the ground.

He reached the doorway and stood directly in front of Cindy, looking her full in the face. She stared, slightly stupefied, as he suddenly clamped his arms to his sides and whipped both of his legs up and out in front of him, in a perfect Irish Dance high kick. Before Cindy could respond his legs were flying towards her face again, and she flinched as the tip of one trainer brushed against her cheek.

His feet reached the ground and he began jigging on the spot, his legs tapering into tightly pointed feet as he jolted and jostled the air. The soft curls on his head, Cindy noticed, fluttered like tiny wings.

His eyes, chocolate-brown, were fixed on hers. Cindy held his gaze and found herself nodding, as if answering a question, and stepping to one side, to let him pass.

He halted his jig and tilted his head to one side. And then his face erupted into a frozen grin and his palms flew up, one beside each cheek, where they remained as quivering *jazz-hands*, his eyes locked on hers, as he passed her sideways through the doorway.

Once past her, he turned and pirouetted into the shop.

Cindy had been on her way out of the shop, her bag already full of sheets and scores, but she followed him back inside anyway. He was standing perfectly still now, flicking balletic fingers through a CD display.

She began to walk slowly towards him. She saw him look up and felt a shiver of delight as his gaze skipped brightly over her blue ballgown, her pearls, and her blonde beehived hair.

He grinned. He held out a hand towards her. Cindy hesitated, just for a moment, before lifting her satin-gloved hand to meet his.

And then she opened her mouth, drew breath, and began to sing.

Her soprano voice rose and filled every space in the shop as she bade him hello; as she remarked on the weather and asked him his name.

He answered her with a slow, lilting Viennese waltz.
And Cindy knew, right then, that it was the start of something beautiful.

YET

*T*he sea of faded cardigans around the table murmured drily.

"And this one is the crème de la crème," continued The Suit, with an almost medical professionalism. "The Dorchester. Solid oak, with brass handles and trim."

He gestured to a photo with his palm.

"I went to the Dorchester once," someone announced, happily. "For high tea."

The Suit waited uncertainly for a quiet rippling of "Oo!" to subside, before continuing. "It's lined with white silk, and—"

"Isn't it terribly expensive?" another voice asked.

"Well, madam," replied The Suit, dropping medical in favour of educational, "how does one define 'expensive' when planning one's grand finale? Quality comes appropriately priced. If you choose not just to invest but to invest wisely in "Departing with Decorum," then you can—quite literally—rest safely in the knowledge that your loved ones will attend the kind of funeral where people say to themselves: "Yes. There goes Doris, looking as smart in death as she did in life."

"But my name's Marjorie," came the reply. "And I meant tea, at the Dorchester."

The Suit sighed. They weren't making it easy for him, and I was glad. I didn't like him being here, in our Home, on a day when the sun was shining and even the last wilting flower stalks in the beds outside were dancing merrily in the breeze.

A dramatic scream suddenly pierced the air, and I looked over just in time to see my good friend Daisy slide from her chair and lie in a folded heap under the table.

Everybody chuckled. The Suit gaped at them, horrified.

"It's okay!" I called to him from my armchair. "She'll be fine. Probably just a bit shocked at the price of your tombstones. Just give her a minute. And…well…perhaps you ought to go and get her a glass of water."

The Suit recomposed himself, stood, and nose-dived into the carpet.

Laughter burst suddenly into bloom around the room, filling it with giddy sunbeams. Daisy climbed out from under the table, brushing her faded yellow cardigan and grinning mischievously.

The Suit had managed to sit up and was examining his granny-knotted shoelaces with incredulity.

We weren't dead yet.

ON THE WEB

*W*e met on a thread, on the web.

We were told at school that it's dangerous, meeting someone that way. That people may not be what they say they are. That whatever you do, you should never agree to meet up in real life. But I know what I'm doing.

The door to the café opens and lets in a slice of air and sound from the street. I look up hopefully, but it's just a couple of girls. They walk in and sit behind me. I look back down at my phone again.

Waiting for a message.

He's late.

We connected really quickly, him and me. Words, that's what we are online. Or "on the web", as he would say; that's why I've guessed he's probably older than he looks in his photo. I'm not stupid. But I don't care. I've fallen for his words. They weave a world that I could just stay wrapped up in, forever.

I sip my coffee, grimacing, a bit. I don't really like coffee. But I didn't want him to find me drinking hot chocolate, or Coke, and looking like some silly little girl. I want to fit the image of me that I hope he's got in his head.

The door to the café opens again. My heart skips a beat, but it's just a woman. She orders at the counter and then leaves, clasping a to-go coffee. I can see a wedding ring on her finger… I'm even ready for that. I know he might even be married. He hasn't said so, of course. But then again, I haven't said that I'm only fourteen.

I can't bear the waiting any longer. I send him a message.

"Waiting. Longing. Where R U? xx"

I sit and concentrate hard on my phone, as if I can will his reply to appear.

A rowdy burst of laughter breaks my focus and I turn round, annoyed. The two girls behind me giggle.

* * *

"Sorry. Just seen something funny," one of them explains.

"Yeah, you know," says the other, waving her phone at me with a suddenly poisonous grin. "On the web."

JACKI DONNELLAN

BEYOND THE BARRICADES

BEYOND THE BARRICADES

"*What do you want to be when you grow up?!*" Toby boomed, striking an attitude with his entire upper body. He made eye contact with each empty desk in the room before finally fixing his careers teacher with an intense, smouldering stare. "Isn't *that*," he hissed, his voice dropping to a spitting whisper, "the question which I am here to answer, today?"

Mrs Peters sighed, and gave a thin, patient smile. "Well...nearly, Toby, but not quite, no. The question- look, just get down off the desk, would you, please?- the question which we're here to consider today is this: what kind of a career does a young man of your abilities wish to pursue?"

"Oh," said Toby, flopping onto his chair, his gaze drifting slowly towards the classroom window. "But...um... that's the same thing, isn't it?"

The trees in the street outside were shimmying in the breeze. For a moment, Toby's shoulders shimmied with them, and a smile began to play around his lips.

"Oh no, Toby," said Mrs Peters, "it's not the same thing at all. Now-" she furrowed her brow at the papers on the desk in front of her- "I understand that you're very good with numbers, Toby. Doing well in maths. Top of your form, in fact."

The sound of a police siren rose and fell in the distance. Toby tilted his head in time to its tones: *left, right. Left, right. C, B flat. C, B flat.*

"So that's obviously the direction you need to be taking, Toby."

The siren faded; *B, A. B, A.*

"Toby?"

"I...um...I was in the school play last year, Miss," said Toby, tugging his attention back into the room. "Well, it was a musical, actually, and I played-"

"Now let's not lose our focus, Toby," warned Mrs Peters, turning to look at her computer. "So..."

She tapped at the keyboard, and the screen came to life. "Have you considered a career in accountancy, Toby?"

She tapped some more keys. Under the table Toby's black leather shoes joined in eagerly. *Ta-tat! Ta-ta-ta-tat!*

"You know, there are a number of local accountancy firms in the area that offer work placements to students," said Mrs Peters, scrolling down. "Perhaps you should consider applying for one of those?"

Toby's feet ceased to tap. "But Miss..."

"You're a bright lad, you know, Toby," said Mrs Peters, peering at Toby over her glasses and smiling encouragingly. "You might even think about a career as an *actuary*. Now, that is an extremely well paid profession. What would you say to *that?*"

For a few long moments, Toby did not reply. And then his face broke into a grin. "*We know what we are, but know not what we may be!*" he beamed. "And it was Shakespeare who said that, Miss!" he added, hopefully.

The smile faded from Mrs Peters' face.

"Look, Toby," she said, in a quiet, crisp voice, "I want you to listen to me *very carefully.*"

She pushed her chair back from the desk, and stood up.

"Toby, when you are ready to cease wafting around on some airy-fairy plane of daydreams, and to concentrate on finding a career that will actually fuel your existence, then you may come back and see me. Until then, you are dismissed from my classroom, and I do not wish to see you here again until your ideas have both bucked up, and shaped up." She leant forward, planting her fists on the desk and placing her reddening face directly in front of Toby's. "Am I *clear?*"

Toby's head remained bowed as he left the school building and sloped across the playground. He paused as he neared the railings, and gazed despondently at the world outside through the black metal bars.

A row of monochrome fuel pumps stoically returned Toby's gaze from the petrol station across the road. They stood like a line of blank, angular men in dull, rusting suits; solid and upright, their feet screwed firmly to the ground. Ready to deliver, ready to provide.

And ready, every time, to count the cost.

Toby nodded at the pumps from his side of the bars, and raised his hand in a fleeting wave.

They did not wave back.

And in that moment, Toby finally understood just what Mrs Peters had been telling him. He knew exactly what it was that was being asked of him, and what it was that he needed to do.

"*Better shape up,*" he sighed under his breath, as he turned from the railings, and continued his slow, stooped trudge towards the school gates.

But as Toby trudged, he began to smile.

And then, as he broke into a half-skip, half-run, he began to laugh.

And then, still laughing, he lifted his face to the sky and slipped his black school blazer from his shoulders. With one hand he raised it above his head, and began waving it with a joyful flourish from side to side.

"*When the beating of your heart
echoes the beating of the drums…*"

Toby sang so loudly that his favourite Les Mis lyrics penetrated the thick school walls, and could be heard in every classroom inside. (At least, that's what he hoped. And if not, he had plenty of time yet to work on his projection.)

"There is a life about to start when tomorrow comes!"

Grinning with glee, Toby sang, danced and acted his way out of the school gates, and all the way down the street.

And as he passed the petrol station and its row of empty stares, Toby saw a bright, glittering future beginning to appear, right before his very eyes.

AVALINA KRESKA

UNFAMILIAR COUNTRY

UNFAMILIAR COUNTRY

Mike was undecided about going to the health spa because of the size of his penis. Size was not something God had graced him with. He set the Hornby Blue Highlander to go around the track again, enjoying the swooshing sound as it rushed past; it helped him to relax.

'I tell you Mike, once you've been to the club, you'll forget ever going back to the pub again. So relaxing mate,' Martin said.

'Yeah, really tasteful. No-one actually gawps at your privates, it's not like that, it's kind of freeing, a sort of body freedom, like you've been on holiday somewhere,' Lee said, arranging the little bushes around the mini station. He added several miniature people to the station platform. The train whizzed by making the little bushes tremble.

Mike was pretty sure that both of his friends were well endowed enough not to worry about being naked. They both worked outdoors so they had excellent muscle tone and skin colour—African Adventure 3 (according to Dulux colour charts). Mike wasn't an outdoors type, nor did he purposely sit in the sun. The last time he'd undressed in front of other people was at the school swimming pool, and even then he noticed most of the boys were bigger than him. He'd hoped that by the time he was an adult it would've grown some more. What if someone laughed at him? Mike felt bulldozed into the decision, but then realised if he went once they'd stop asking.

'Right, two o'clock tomorrow then. Is it still quieter in the week?' Mike said hopefully.

'Yup, usually only about twenty people around then, you can get a feel for it. Weekends are a different kettle of fish,' Martin said, grinning and rubbing his hands together, which unnerved Mike no end.

They gathered outside the health spa. Mike thought it looked like a shady establishment, something he'd avoid, like betting shops. The black windows reflected back his clothed body. He tried to imagine standing naked at the bar, relaxing with beautiful naked women.

Inside, the reception area smelt lightly of perfume and Jenny, a cute female receptionist, welcomed them.

Martin and Lee seemed to know her and chatted away whilst Mike browsed a brochure about a nudist resort. He noticed none of the photos showed naked people, just happy heads.

'Hi Mike, so this is your first time?' Jenny shouted over, smiling naturally.

'Yes, kinda got dragged here really. Not sure it's my thing but you never know,' Mike said, now feeling more comfortable inside than outside. He was glad it looked clean and seemed professional.

'You don't have to be naked, there's a towel provided that you can wrap around your middle, so just relax and enjoy the surroundings. Most people go naked in the whirlpool and hot-tub but it's not obligatory. I think you'll find it quite pleasant.'

Mike smiled, he instantly liked her. She was just his type, not too pushy but confident. He hoped to get a chance to see her at the bar at some point.

'Righto, let's go for it. I'm looking forward to that hot-tub!' Lee said, grappling with his locker key and other bits.

'Oh yeah. Let's hope there's some nice fanny too,' Martin said under his breath. Mike winced. He wasn't prudish but he liked to respect women and not think of them as sex objects; probably why he'd been single for so long.

They all piled into the locker room. Martin and Lee had stripped off in a second. Mike tried not to feel self-conscious as he removed his underpants but memories of noisy school changing rooms flooded his conscious mind. He turned his back to the others. There were two more men stripping off with gay abandon too. They each wrapped the clean, fluffy white towels around their waist. Mike was pleased to see that these men were as fair skinned as he was.

The whitewashed walls gave an Andalusian feel to the main bar/relaxing room; it was fresh and roomy with plenty of large leaved greenery. Several well placed pictures of Mediterranean scenes and some instantly forgettable instrumental music filled the air. Light streamed in from above via a couple of skylights in the close boarded roof and large sliding patio doors led to the sun terrace. He could see a couple of women lying on their fronts soaking up the sun.

'Beers all round guys?' Lee said.

'Yeah, that would hit the spot,' Martin said, taking up residence at the bar. Mike joined him, realising he wasn't feeling that nervous yet. Looking down Mike noticed that Martin's middle toe was far longer than all the other toes on his right foot. He must have trouble buying shoes. Mike looked down at his own perfectly proportioned, size eight feet, one of his best features. A woman walked by wearing only a colourful sarong wrapped around her petite hips. Mike found himself staring at her small white breasts. He looked straight down, embarrassed, and then looked up quickly to gauge her reaction. Smiling, she winked at him. Mike smiled back, noting that she'd gone to the room marked 'Hot Tub & Whirlpool.'

Lee poked him in the side.

'See, told you it would be alright. Think she digs you man,' Lee said in a fake American accent. Mike shoved him away and took several long pulls on his cold beer. Martin was right, it seemed so much more relaxing than going to the pub. The round bar had a long horizontal mirror reflecting the room behind him. Three older women sat in a corner sipping cocktails; they all had swim suits on, their ages consecutively laid down in fat layers. The women sunbathing had now turned over, one had two massive brown knockers reminding Mike of basket balls. On the opposite side sat an elderly naked gentleman, his mop of pure, white hair sticking up over his broadsheet newspaper. The newspaper disappeared below the table. A steaming cup of coffee and a large chocolate muffin made the whole affair look very normal, like a well-mannered teashop.

Mike's eyes and heart wandered towards the hot tub room.

'Any objections to me heading to the hot tub?' Mike said, feeling a sudden rush of confidence. Lee and Martin eyed each other.

'We'll come with you, just in case you get into trouble, you know, need some help,' Lee said grinning.

'Don't embarrass me guys, it is my first time,' Mike warned them.

The steamy, chlorinated air reminded him of the school swimming pool. The walls and ceiling were a stark white; the floor, made of little azure blue mosaic tiles, was shiny and wet from the steam. A large skylight allowed directed beams of light to stream into the room. The hot tub was huge; it could easily take ten people and was bubbling away like a cauldron in the corner. On the hooks were two towels, one belonged to the Sarong Lady and the other to a female whose face he couldn't see. Martin and Lee casually slipped off their towels and headed to the hot tub. It was time for the moment of truth. Mike, trying to appear casual, whipped off his towel in one quick motion; the towel hit the wall with a loud slap that echoed around the room. The Sarong Lady giggled. Mike looked sheepish.

He turned around like a gunslinger to face the tub. Lee and Martin were already lowering themselves into the water. Sarong Lady was smiling politely at them. Mike walked quickly; he wanted to make sure he spoke to Sarong Lady first. He skidded on the wet tiles, ending up in a scissor position, legs spread wide apart, his over-sized balls swinging like a Newton's cradle. The Sarong Lady looked down and giggled again. Regaining his former composure, Mike tiptoed this time, mortified that he had almost fallen on his unmentionables. He imagined the scenario, his balls acting as trampolines, catapulting him into the tub.

He lowered himself into the bubbling water. By now everyone would have noticed that his penis was tiny. He guessed it would be very bad etiquette for the lads to remark on its size and if they embarrassed him, he felt sure he would have a sympathetic ear from Sarong Lady. He was glad of her welcoming gaze from across the pool. The lads were sitting back in silence, eyes closed, relaxing; they were seasoned members after all. Mike sat opposite the Sarong Lady so he could maintain eye contact. Her long, dark curly hair had been clipped up in a messy way, exposing her delicate shoulders, the tops of her dark, brown nipples were just on the surface of the water. Every now and then they disappeared underwater. She was still smiling at him so Mike decided to make the first move. He stuck out his hand.

'Mike. Mike Eaton.'

Her hand emerged from the water and waved a small mini wave. She giggled again.

'Sarah. Sarah Lynton.'

Mike sat back, embarrassed. Lee and Martin were trying desperately not to look at each other. He knew that look.

'Haven't seen you here before, Sarah, you a local lass?' Martin chipped in to break the tension.

'Oh, yes, just around the corner, I only moved here about three months ago. It's my second time here, a friend recommended the place,' she said, keeping her eyes firmly on Mike. For a moment he thought he recognised her, something about her hair being up that did it. He racked his brains but couldn't quite place her. Lee started a conversation with the other lady in the tub.

'So, have you found employment? What do you do for a living?' Mike asked.

'I came here because of the job, a promotion really. I work for the council. Secretarial stuff, nothing exciting. What about you?'

'Nothing exciting, I work at a local Junior School. I do a bit of everything- maintenance, computers, keep the school running, you know.'

'Well, that's nice. So, you married then?' Sarah asked.

'Me? No, no. Never did. I guess I'm just picky,' he said a little too quickly and then immediately regretted saying it. Sarah made a large nodding expression with her mouth open. Smiling, she closed her eyes.

'What do you think then, Mike? Relaxing, ain't it, mate. Just what you need,' Martin said. He was making some sort of action with his hands but Mike didn't know what it meant.

'Are you into reading, Sarah? I can't put this book down at the moment, a real good thriller by Eva Hudson. Ever heard of her? It's called The Loyal Servant. Really fast paced. Makes a change having a British thriller, you know?'

Sarah made that large nodding expression again. This time her mouth was closed. 'I really like a good horror story, or fantasy. I must admit though, I haven't read anything in a while, been a bit too busy. Maybe when I've settled in more I might relax enough to read. Or maybe I might just come here more often. I could read in the tub,' she said, grinning.

Closing her eyes again, she sat up taller so her nipples bobbed on the surface of the water like mini buoys; opening her arms wide she rested them on the edges of the tub. Mike took the opportunity to stare unabashedly at her nipples, imagining how soft to the touch they'd be, when it suddenly dawned on him where he'd seen her before. Didn't she go to the church service at the school a few weeks ago? He couldn't be sure. Well, well, a nice upright Christian girl, you know what they say about them.

Mike felt his penis stirring. Lee and the other lady decided to make an exit. As Lee stood up, Mike noticed Lee's large member; it was long enough for water to run in channels along the entire length then cascade over the tip like a waterfall. He felt immediately envious. Everyone was bigger than him. Martin made expressive eyes at Mike, nodding his head sideways towards Sarah. Mike scooted around the pool and ended up next to her. Looking sideways she smiled politely. She tried to retract her arm on the right side, but Mike was too close to her.

'Could you?' she said, pointing to her arm.

'Oh. Sorry.' He broadened the gap between them. Martin looked down, smiling. Mike hoped that he and Sarah might end up leaving together too. The door suddenly opened and Mike caught a glimpse of a white haired man. Mike closed his eyes for a moment. He hoped he wasn't joining them in the tub. Who wants to see a naked old man? There should be an age limit or something.

Mike felt the air shift slightly, opened his eyes and the old man from the bar was sitting opposite him. He recognised his mop of white hair.

'Good morning all. Good morning Sarah,' the old man said. Mike inwardly gasped, how could he forget that voice? Of course! He was the local Vicar!

'Morning. So lovely here, I'm glad you suggested it,' Sarah said with a wide grin on her face. For some unfathomable reason to Mike, she kept bobbing up and down, her nipples playing peek-a-boo.

'I thought I recognised you, aren't you the local Vicar? I've seen you at the school, my name's Mike, Mike Eaton, I'm the maintenance guy, you know, the Caretaker.' Mike couldn't help himself; this was all for Martin's benefit. Martin looked fit to burst. Mike knew this must be killing him.

'Ah yes, sorry - didn't recognise you with er... Yes, I've placed you now. Well, well, quite a gathering we have here,' the Vicar said in a booming voice. The room echoed like an empty church.

Mike envisaged the Vicar reading the Gospels in the school hall. Then he saw him reading it naked. Then all the school children and teachers in the hall were naked too.

Martin sat there wide eyed with a smirk on his face.

'I'm Martin. Nice to meet you,' Martin said. The Vicar nodded in appreciation.

'So, Vicar, do you come here often?' Mike inquired.

'Quite often. We come from the womb naked and we return to the grave- well, back to God- naked. It's the most natural thing in the world.' He spoke loudly, eyeing Sarah's nipples. Mike felt like grabbing a towel to cover her nakedness. Sarah sat up taller and Mike noticed her nipples were now hard and erect. In response, Mike's penis stood as tall as it could. He put a hand down protectively to cover it, glad of the bubbles. Sarah's eyes remained fixed on the Vicar.

'Sarah, didn't you want to discuss something with me? Perhaps we could have a drink at the bar?' the Vicar said.

'Oh yes, there is that *thing* I'd like to run by you,' Sarah said, rising from the water. Mike's eyes, however, were not fixed on Sarah, but on the rising Vicar opposite him. The Vicar's penis was in an erect state and stood out at least 10 inches from his white hairy groin. It waggled up and down like a piece of spare piping in the wind. Mike gasped.

'The Lord blesses us in so many ways - doesn't he, Mr. Eaton?' the Vicar said, getting up and turning around to step out of the tub, revealing a sagging old bottom, the skin hanging like badly hung drapes. Sarah stepped past Mike; her bottom, two exquisitely white, round globes that looked as if the light of day had never revealed them before. Mike sat there astonished. Martin visibly shook with laughter.

'The Lord giveth and the Lord taketh away doesn't he Mike? Martin said, in-between quiet guffaws.

'He certainly does, Martin, he certainly does,' Mike said in a somewhat detached manner, observing the pair leave the room.

'No doubt they'll be heading upstairs,' Martin said, enjoying himself immensely.

'There's an upstairs?' Mike said.

'Oh yes. There's an upstairs,' Martin said, closing his eyes.here. Insert chapter nine text here.

AVALINA KRESKA

AUNT VINNY? SHE'S GONE TO THE GREAT PETROL PUMP IN THE SKY

AUNT VINNY? SHE'S GONE TO THE GREAT PETROL PUMP IN THE SKY

'*V*iolet McVinny, or 'Aunt Vinny', so-called by those who knew her, and that was almost everybody, from Popes to Presidents, died in a fire at her beloved petrol station last Tuesday. This morning, tribute is paid to this...'

'Turn the radio off Heather. We don't need reminding. The world is an emptier place with her gone,' Mrs. Nimly said, shifting from foot to foot to relieve the ache in her hip. Making cakes was a way to fill the hole that Aunt Vinny once filled, and this time she had an excuse: these were the cakes for Auntie's wake. Mrs. Nimly always thought it was a strange term to use for one who's just left this world but not in the case of Aunt Vinny, transformed, ascended—lifted above the mantle, if you will.

'Transcended, yes, that's the word,' she said thoughtfully.

Aunt Vinny had healed folk from all around the world. Sometimes she did it while she filled their cars with petrol. Sometimes she did it over the phone, like that time with President Kennedy. Often times she healed people who didn't know they needed healing. Thus was her gift from God. She resisted offers of living in opulent surroundings in foreign countries, preferring instead to remain on a remote island in the far Northern reaches of the UK, living a simple life with simple folk, inconstant seasons and adventitious birds.

'It's gonna be a hell of a send-off, seems the whole world is coming. They had to put on an extra mainland ferry, and others are flying in, no doubt,' said Heather, peering out at the alien fancy cars and coaches.

'How on earth will they fit everyone in? Lord only knows why they didn't have the wake at the Leisure Centre on the Mainland, though I guess it's understandable it be held on the island where she lived. She would've wanted it that way too, although not in THAT Church,' Mrs. Nimly said, piling up sandwiches into a precarious pillar.

'That Minister will do anything to be in the limelight,' Heather said, sneaking out a small cocktail sausage from under the clingfilm. Popping it into her mouth she didn't know what to do with the little stick so she threw it under the table. Heather had known Aunt Vinny since she was born, if not before.

As they flit around the long trestle tables, the electric wall clock administered to its own laws and Heather tried not to think of Aunt Vinny lying in the cold, peaty earth; merely food for worms.

For a small island, Strandillier had a huge church. It had been paid for by a rich benefactor. Some say the local Minister had pulled some strings. Either way, this behemoth of a Church was an eyesore, a monument to the Minister's pride. Aunt Vinny didn't need a building—what building could contain her?

Heather joined Mrs. Nimly at the window.

'Look, there's someone from the high-ups in the Catholic Church. He must be one of those Cardinals—the one in the red hat and skirt,' Heather said.

'Who's that in the blue car? Well, I do believe it's the M.P.—what's his name—Mike Thomason. Don't think they'll be room for the likes of us then,' Mrs. Nimly said, rubbing her hip. All this walking and standing around making cakes was wearing on an already worn right socket.

'Oh, I'm sure it'll be dignitaries only. Oh, Aunt Vinny you would hate this! What's that she used to say Heather?'

'Never play a violin unless the audience...'

The Church bells interrupted Heather, announcing the service was about to start. Removing their aprons, they stepped outside. The mob overwhelmed them. Some were in wheelchairs, well-wishers from adjacent islands leaned on locals whilst visitors stood on tiptoe, hoping to catch a glimpse of a celebrity. Loud speakers were attached to the walls of the Church, and Mrs. Nimly could hear the slimy snake of a Minister droning on.

'It's not right. It's not what she'd have wanted,' Mrs. Nimly thought.

Heather grabbed the sleeve of Mrs. Nimly's coat.

'Let's stick together, don't want to get lost in this crowd,' Heather said, pulling Mrs. Nimly away.

They had to walk almost half a mile down the road to the cliff edge before some space could be found. The Minister's voice was just about audible, but he was known to mumble, so Mrs. Nimly didn't hold out much hope that she'd hear anything, being a bit deaf. But did she really want to hear anything he had to say anyway?

Mrs. Nimly envisioned Aunt Vinny with her shirt sleeves rolled up, fag hanging out of her mouth, washing cars for the tourists, telling jokes, always having time for everyone. She was a true servant. A people person. Nobody went away from Strandillier without receiving a little bit of 'Vinny magic' as her husband used to say. Of course Aunt Vinny wouldn't have any of it.

'It's not about me. I'm not doing anything.' Then she'd point to the sky. The Minister tried to get her to attend the Church but she refused. She knew he only wanted to draw power from her and her gifts. It was a real travesty that Aunt Vinny should be sent off to the great beyond by that charlatan.

'...and we ask Almighty God to take Mrs. McVinny into his beloved...'

There was a crackle on the loudspeaker, the Minister's voice became disjointed, then there was a general hum of voices. The crowd, moving as one entity, compelled forward; pushed and shoved, hoping a blessing might shroud them like a magical mantilla. As everyone heaved forward, a space opened up, a gap between both women and the crowd.

'I'm gonna find out what's going on, you stay here,' Heather said. Mrs. Nimly nodded.

She needed a seat. Walking nearer the cliffs, she perched on a well worn rock and, turning away from the crowd, she looked out to sea. Everything carried on as 'normal'. The fulmar scouts checked her out, flying low and threatening, the familiar cries of the nesting pairs above the crashing waves all existing in a beautiful, timeless cycle, the synchronisation of nature, unaffected by visiting Cardinals or the beloved dead. They wouldn't miss Aunt Vinny, yet they were part of who Aunt Vinny was. She said that Nature, like God, was a truth that 'grounded her'.

Mrs. Nimly thought she saw someone standing on the old landing platform. It was risky to go out there, and she was just about to go and warn the unsuspecting person of the danger when the apparition became clearer, more solid. It was a woman wearing a white, puffy dress and real fancy shoes. Strange, Mrs. Nimly thought, maybe she was one of the guests and was as bored as she was. The woman turned around and waved. Mrs. Nimly didn't recognise her. The woman waved again, this time more urgently, so Mrs. Nimly hesitantly waved back. The woman put her fingers to her mouth and blew Mrs. Nimly a kiss, then waved again before disappearing. Where did she go? My goodness, did she fall in?

Heather came running back, distracting her, all out of breath.

'She's gone! Aunt Vinny's gone!' Heather leaned over to catch her breath.

'What do you mean? Where could she have gone?'

'Don't know. Apparently she was there one minute then...'

'Don't be ridiculous. What, with all those people watching?'

'Well, apparently—did you know she had an open face casket?'

'Yes. Which she would have hated.'

'Apparently, someone noticed that her head had gone. There was a bit of a commotion, they checked everywhere, but it seems her whole body had disappeared into thin air—spirited away, if you like.

The man in the red hat and dress you saw stood up and took over the service, so someone tells me,' Heather said, sitting down on the grass.

'Well I never did! I just saw...'

Mrs. Nimly stopped.

'I saw... some otters while you were gone. They were playing on the old landing platform, bold as brass.'

Heather looked at her strangely. A black car emerged from deep within the crowd. Like the parting of the Red Sea, Mrs. Nimly thought. Inside, the man with the red hat was talking enthusiastically on a mobile phone.

'Looks like the party's over Heather,' Mrs. Nimly said, bracing herself to stand up, the pain always worse upon getting up. Mrs. Nimly stood without an ounce of discomfort. She swung around, looking accusatorily at the rock, then a realisation poured into her.

'Must have put the Minister's nose out of joint, stealing the show like that! Good old Aunt Vinny—I bet she's somewhere up there laughing about it, at that great petrol pump in the sky! Bloody show 'em all!' Heather said laughing.

Mrs. Nimly laughed too, keeping Aunt Vinny's secret.

Transcended. Yes. That was the right word.

REBECCA J. ALLRED

INDISPOSED

INDISPOSED

The furry beast wobbled and heaved. It emitted an angry-bagpipe howl that ricocheted off marble countertops and stainless steel cookware and assaulted Bexx's eardrums. She dropped the .22—it was empty at this point anyway—and covered her ears as she watched the wretched thing regurgitate all ten spent rounds and then smile at her with its prison-striped face.

"Why don't you just leave it alone and get a drink from the bathroom?" Token asked from the couch.

"Don't be ridiculous," Bexx answered, dropping her hands. "You know the only thing that comes out of the bathroom faucet is jello."

"Oh yeah. Say, what flavor is it today?"

"Lime."

"Ooooh!"

"But it has bananas in it."

"Ew. Pass," he said, lighting his saxophone.

The creature in the kitchen barked and gagged, producing another pile of vomitus. A pair of long, thin wedges protruded from the slimy mound.

Bexx cursed. "I wondered what happened to those shoes."

"It ate your shoes?" Token snorted. "Wicked."

"Ate and only partially digested. How d'you s'pose my shoes got in the kitchen anyway?"

Token shrugged and offered Bexx the saxophone. "Want some?"

"I'd rather snort Hantavirus."

"Suit yourself. But you seem kind of—" he rested the brass J between his knees and played a few deep, jazzy notes, delivering bitter, bruised-plum smoke rings into the air, "—t ense."

Bexx squinched her nose, narrowed her eyes against the vapors, and stooped to collect her handgun. There were more bullets in the bedroom, but they wouldn't do any good. Not against the kitchen beast at any rate. She set the firearm on the coffee table and flopped down next to Token on the sofa.

"What am I gonna do?" Bexx closed her eyes and pressed her palms to her eyelids. Ugly purple and red lights flashed in the velvet darkness; each blooming pulse seemed to increase the pressure inside her head. She pressed harder. The lights strobed, colors bleeding into one another, and the pressure transmuted into an insectile hum that vibrated furiously.

Bexx's head exploded.

Token slowly moved his eyes from his headless friend, to the carnage decorating the living room, and back to Bexx. He raised his right eyebrow. "Really?" he said, tweezing a tattered ear between his index finger and thumb. "Was that absolutely necessary?"

Bexx threw her hands up in exasperation, her new head inflating like a balloon. "I hate it when the garbage disposal goes on the fritz."

Dropping the strip of shaggy cartilage into Bexx's lap, Token said, "Hold this," and stood up. He carried his saxophone, still trailing smoke from the bell, into the kitchen.

"Be careful," Bexx called after him.

At first Bexx heard nothing but screeching bagpipes. Then, little by little, the dissonant chords began to soften and she could pick out the soothing melody of a lullaby. She wiped a blob of vitreous fluid onto a tissue and ventured back to witness the standoff.

The kitchen was an ode to Jimmy Hendrix: thick plumes of aubergine smoke billowed from the saxophone, staining the air. Bexx coughed, her thirst only exacerbated by the acrid fumes.

Token stood in the doorframe, swaying rhythmically with lips pursed around his instrument. The disposal unit, still guarding the sink, abruptly ceased its sour squall and wavered drunkenly. It rose up on its hind quarters, whipped its head back and forth as if trying to shake loose a memory, and produced a series of high-pitched titters.

"Did my garbage disposal just giggle?" Bexx asked. She was starting to feel a little giddy herself, despite the persistent nagging from her parched throat.

Token continued to play.

The malfunctioning appliance dropped back to all-fours and performed a stiff-legged jounce.

"Watch out. He's gonna charge," Bexx said.

Tiny claw marks shaped like sanskrit characters appeared in the linoleum as the beast lunged forward. Almost immediately the disposal collapsed, skidding to a stop less than two feet from its launch pad. Its body shuddered, and little snorts shotgunned from between curled lips.

Token stopped playing.

"It's snoring," Bexx said, taking a step closer.

"Works every time." Token stroked the saxophone with unmistakable pride.

"Now what?"

"Now we put it back. What else?"

"Is it safe?"

Token shrugged. He slung the saxophone over his shoulder, scooped the snoring quadruped off the floor, and carried it to the sink, careful to sidestep the sticky puke puddles on the way. He opened the cupboard beneath the sink and stuffed the appliance back into its designated space. "There, everything's back to normal. It's gonna have a nasty case of the munchies when it wakes up, though."

"Yeah. Sure. Whatever," Bexx said, rushing to the sink. "Outta my way."

She wrenched the faucet handle and shoved her face into the resulting stream of water. Nothing had ever tasted so wonderful.

Her thirst finally quenched, Bexx shut the water off and turned back to Token.

"Better?" he asked.

"Better."

"Good, because we have a new problem."

"What are you talking about?"

Token pointed toward the living room. A dozen miniature Bexxes congregated in the doorway.

"You didn't clean up your mess, did you?" he asked.

One of the tissue replicons scurried across the floor and began eating a puke puddle.

Bexx suppressed the urge to gag. She bent down, lifted the mini by the back of its shirt, and carried it to the sink. She dropped the replicon down the drain.

The disposal sniffed and sputtered to life.

Token hadn't been kidding about it having the munchies.

She glanced at the remaining replicons darting to and fro across the floor, and then looked back to Token, silently asking for consent.

"Do what you want," he said, stuffing a fistful of dried, purple flakes into the saxophone's bell. "But if it gets loose again, you're on your own."

Bexx nodded. She'd get them all eventually, but first she poured herself a glass of water. Just in case.

REBEKAH POSTUPAK

CLICHÉ

PUN-RISE

THE COLLAR

CLICHÉ

"Chickens have lips."

"Pigs fly."

"The moon is made of green cheese."

He stopped and grinned at me. "Money grows on trees."

I snorted at this one. "If only!"

"Not too shabby, eh?"

"It'll do, I guess. For now. However, my expectations are quite high."

"I'll do my best not to disappoint."

"Make sure you don't, or I'll be forced to have you replaced."

He grimaced in mock horror. "No! Not after a lifetime of training. Please consider my suffering! My sacrifice!"

"Irrelevant. You're either prepared or you're not."

"Baby, I was born ready."

"All right. Go ahead then. Hit me."

"Cats have nine lives."

"Bzzzt. Pathetic. Try again."

"It's raining cats and dogs. Now I've got fleas."

"Ha. Okay, that was a good one." Oops. My turn. Easier to make fun of him than it was to come up with my own. "I was born with a silver spoon in my mouth. Gave the doctors fits."

"Well, I counted my chickens before they hatched."

"I led a horse to water AND made him drink."

"So what? I took wooden nickels. On purpose."

"I judged a book by its cover."

"I took all my eggs and put them in one little bitty basket. Broke every last one."

"Big mess."

"Yeah, yeah it was." His grey eyes met mine. "Are you ready?"

"No."

"Liz, it's been a week."

"I don't care."

"We can't keep playing this—"

"I bit the hand that fed me. Sorry, Mom."

"Liz."

"Drove by hell the other day; the road really was paved with good intentions. You should've seen the potholes!"

"Liz!"

"What??"

"I can't keep playing anymore. It's been a week. You're going to have to face it."

"I don't have to face anything. Rome really was built in a day. It was Daylight Savings…"

"Fine. My turn."

The look on his face terrified me. "No need. I'm doing great on my own."

"You have to stay strong for the family."

"Pbbbbt. Dislike. How about—I looked a gift horse in the mouth. Needed fillings."

"Elizabeth."

"Shut up."

"Here's another. You're holding up so well."

"I like my version better."

"Time will heal your wounds."

"That's not fair."

"It was for the best."

"Stop it."

"You need to move on."

"I said stop it!"

He spoke quieter now. "It happened for a reason."

I clenched my teeth and looked away, eyes stinging.

"I know just how you feel," he said. His voice sounded different this time. Ragged, almost, and something in my heart began to burn.

"That's en—"

He gripped my shoulders and turned me to face him. "You can always have another child," he whispered.

For the first time in eight days, five hours, and thirty-two minutes I let the empty high chair fill my eyes.

And in the biggest, most horrible cliché of all, I crumbled to the floor and cried myself a river.

PUN-RISE

"*H*ave you gone BARKING mad?" Jef's fat, red face contorted with drunken laughter.

I rolled my eyes.

"Wait—wait, I've got another one," he said, gasping for air between guffaws and waving the gun wildly. "You send me over the moon. Get it? MOON!!"

"Yeah, I get it," I said.

He lurched and pointed the silver-plated gun at my heart. "I don't think you do," he said, giggling. "You're in deep doo-doo, doggie."

The moon tickled the horizon; I felt the change creeping into my toes. How much longer? Ten minutes? Five?

"You don't have to do this," I said. "Let me go, and you'll never see me again."

"That'd sort of miss the point, wouldn't it, pup? Seeing as how I want your skin." He belched. "Good money, that. Won't be nothin' but bones left to ya when I'm done."

My ears prickled—only moments remained. Our ragged breaths mingled in the air.

And then: moonrise.

I stretched and twisted, growling in wild, liberated pleasure. My former captor, however, howled in startled panic, my tiny scratch on his neck now buried in thick, grey fur.

"Good money, eh?—" I said, grinning broadly "—I'm likin' this. Get it? LYCAN this?"

THE COLLAR

*T*he collar chafed.

Keset flexed her long, turquoise-and-cobalt neck, relishing her temporary freedom from the wretched thing. The moment the sky hinted of grey, her new Rider would circle her neck with the leather shackle and click the reins into place again. She had worn the Tenth Tier war dragon collar for two years now, but her pride still stung as fresh as the first day. Deep in the mountains is where she belonged, ferreting out cave goats, bathing in under-earth streams. Not here.

"Keset."

Her hind ears, a set of six scarlet spikes ringing the tip of her tail, caught her Rider's call. Dawn already?? No; but duty called regardless. Keset groaned, stretched one last time, and slunk out of the tiny rocky hollow serving as her bed.

"We've a long day ahead," said her Rider a few minutes later as he snapped on the final tether. He had a name, Keset supposed, but she wouldn't bother to learn it. This one would perish too, as her previous Riders had, and the under-commander would throw another bland-faced half-soldier on her back to replace him.

"Fine."

"You've had breakfast?"

"I'll snack on the battlefield."

The Rider stopped his preparations to grin up at her. "Funny this morning, eh?"

"Funny every morning," said Keset. She swallowed hard. *Don't get attached.*

"It's pretty rough out there, I guess," the Rider said, cinching the rough burlap saddle around her belly. "Not many of us left. We'll have to give 'em what for today."

His voice cracked—youth, not fear—and Keset swung her head around despite herself. Black hair curled tightly across his scalp, but his chin was unshadowed. Fourteen, if that.

"Skill counts more than numbers," she said gruffly. "And you're a trained Rider. You'll do just fine."

Lie, Keset. Tell the boy Death isn't a raging fire that peels your soul raw. Tell him there's hope, that even now his mother weaves a grand new cloak for her returning hero-son.

"So will you," said the Rider, something he should have been too young to grasp flashing in his eyes. "They say no dragon sets the sky ablaze like you. You'll be home soon, wearing king's treasure instead of a harness."

This child comforts me? The thought chafed more than the collar.

It continued chafing as they soared across the battlefields, plunging in flames to crumble enemy machinery. It needled her as the healers stitched together first his arm, then her leg, and as they returned to the skies, shrieking a duet of defiance. It chased her relentlessly as they darted in and out of the invaders' polished weaponry, and it beat at her wings even as she plummeted, bleary-eyed, in dying sunlight.

"Fly, Keset!" whispered her Rider, his bloodied fingers clinging to her scales as though willing courage into her bones; he did not glance at the ugly arrows gouging his left side.

But she could not catch him as he pitched off her back onto charred ground and lay tangled in the harness next to her.

She froze. Her neck was... free. She could return to her caves, oath fulfilled—at least technically—and still claim the right to reward. She could—

Keset stared at the wounded boy.

No.

That flash in his eyes did not belong to a boy.

It was a warrior's.

Keset drew a deep breath and nosed her head slowly, painfully, through what was left of her collar before gently lifting the Rider in her claws. She summoned her last drops of strength for the flight home, the sun on the enemy's arrows glinting like gold.

REBEKAH POSTUPAK

THE CODE

THE CODE

*T*he Code matters. Some say the Code is all that matters, for the keeping of peace between dragonkind and us. And though I'm not a rules kind of girl, I try to follow the Code. Really, I do.

Rule # 5. *Never joke with a dragon.*

Me: "Knock Knock."

Jiay the sand dragon: "Who's there?"

Me: "Dragon."

Jiay: "Dragon who?"

Me: "Draggin' today; do you have any coffee?"

Jiay: *rolls eyes and singes my brows with a tongue-lick of flame*

The Code exists for our protection, the Elders say. They say this often, hurling frowns at us for emphasis. You are young; you do not know. You do not remember. Mock the Code, young ones. Laugh at it, in your comfortable lives. But never, never disobey.

Jiay and I do laugh. We can't help it. The Elders, both his and mine, are always so grim, so obsessed with their beloved Codes, their Code for the Handling of Humans, and our DragonCode. There's no danger today, no animosity between our kinds anymore. Many of us know many of them by their first names. A few of us are even friends.

And at least two of us are counting the days until the 200-year-old Code expires.

Rule # 4. *Dragons and humans must never meet alone.*

Jiay often allows me to climb on his back, and we go for long rides in the desert. The dunes part for him; I watch as gold flows past us like wind, stinging my cheeks. It is the closest my clumsy human body will come to flying, and I revel in our speed. Sometimes the joy rising in my heart is so great, I find myself crying. Jiay laughs at my tears.

"You're leaking, Takari," he says. "Keep it up, and you will make a new oasis for my family."

I smack him, though he cannot feel my hand through his thick brown scales. "Way to spoil my moment," I say.

"What moment? I'm just hunting for lunch. By the way, thank you. Your human smell works as powerfully appetizing bait; I'm going to eat great tonight."

"I thought it was my beauty."

"Your beauty is like garlic," he says, throwing the words over his shoulder as the world rushes by.

"I give your prey foul breath?"

"You make even donkeys palatable."

This is a great compliment and I am satisfied. Jiay hates donkeys. He says their meat is tough and bitter, and it reminds him of a period in his childhood, before the Code, when they could find nothing else to eat. *Nothing besides humans,* he means, though he does not say this.

Now, the dragons live in decadence and we in sloth. We raise sheep and cows by the thousands for them, and they protect our borders. Jiay tells me most of his kind have forgotten the pleasure of hunting. I tell him how my grandfather-king disbanded the army, how our guards don't know how to use swords anymore, all thanks to the Code. We are both disgusted. I am glad to be at peace, but has anyone counted the cost?

Rule # 3. *In exchange for protection from foreign enemies, humans will provide adequate livestock for dragon consumption.*

"I'm going to work," I say.

My father nods; he does not look up from his papers. "King" feels like the wrong title for him. Better, maybe, is "royal paralegal." The weeks and years of his life are devoured by the tiny razor teeth of sub-sub-subsections of the Code. When I ask, he smiles, says he is looking for loopholes. When I press, he says he does remember swordwork, he knows where his crown is stored, and yes, you pest of a princess, I still know the secret words to kingsong should our nation ever face certain doom. But there is something odd in his eyes when he answers, and I do not quite believe him.

In truth my job doesn't differ so greatly from his. According to the Code, a daughter of the royal family must be present at each monthly dragon feeding. Why it must be a daughter, either no one remembers or no one chooses to tell me. Nor do I ask, because it is only one of so very many rules I am compelled to obey. On top of that, the Elders give me the evil eye every time I suggest sending my obnoxious younger brother in my place. So once a month I endure a tedious ceremony in which I formally submit the certified documents to the dragon representative.

"I, Takari, daughter of the king, hereby present the finest of our livestock as a token of our unending gratitude for your most gracious defense of the kingdom of Manerry." It's all I can do not to snicker.

For reasons I've never understood, Jiay always takes the ceremony more seriously than I.

He stands, and his voice thunders. "I, Jiay, Empress' son, accept your offering in the stead of your kingdom, and hereby pledge to continue defending your people for another turn of the moon."

I bite back a grin and curtsy, the required deep kind, slave to master. He inclines his head, ruler to lesser ruler, and around us human dancers mark circles in the air with their ribbons while firedrakes shoot sigils into the sky. I have seen these performances a hundred times; their hearts are not in it any more than mine, and I doze off.

An impatient Jiay nudges me awake.

"The Code!" he growls. Tiny puffs of smoke curl up from his nostrils, spelling b-e-h-a-v-e. I am not supposed to be able to read dragonsmoke. Jiay's fault, for puffing away to his mother at the same time he whispers the translation to me.

"The Code!" I say with a sigh. Once more, I comply.

Rule # 2. *The Code shall be renewed with a Gift every 200 years.*

I am freshly twenty when we reach the final month of the Dragon Cycle. It is my unspoken hope that one of my younger sisters can take over my job after the ceremony. Surely I will be married soon to some prince, and my time will be spent on duties monumentally more interesting than handing a giant sand dragon a sheaf of papers, even if that dragon is my best friend. It's actually strange that my marriage has not been arranged yet; the stress of the Code must have driven it out of my father's mind. Still, much as I hate the ceremonies, I'm not about to remind him.

Special festivities have been planned for the Final. Ten thousand extra sheep and goats. Twenty thousand human dancers at last count, and Jiay says representatives from the other dragonkinds have already arrived. I am most eager to see the magnificent sky dragons who in battle, legend says, pull back the veil and flood the sky with stars.

Even my father, his eyes dark and haunted, is attending. Perhaps after this is over, he too can get some rest.

The day arrives. My ladies dress me in my finest silks, emerald and sapphire to mirror our flag. They tell me how beautiful I am, but they say it like this is a tragedy. I frown.

Jiay and I face each other. His scales, brown and gold and green like his native desert, gleam in the light of dragonfire. He is stunning. Thoughts of being a dragon princess flit through my mind until I catch sight of his mother. The aging Empress stands behind him, dull and fat. Crowded with blood-stained teeth, her smile is only professional courtesy. Her dragonsmoke spells, H-u-n-g-r-y. I try not to roll my eyes.

"I, Takari, daughter of the king, hereby present the finest of our livestock as a token of our unending gratitude for your most gracious defense of the kingdom of Manerry." The words tumble from my lips. Am I free now?

Jiay stares at me, not speaking.

My father stares at Jiay, not speaking.

Silence weaves its bony fingers through the waiting masses. In my fifteen years of offerings, Jiay has never once forgotten his part or made a mistake. Why isn't he saying anything?

At last Jiay draws himself up and speaks. "I, Jiay, Empress' son, accept your gift in the stead of your kingdom. The Cycle is renewed."

These are the wrong words. I turn them over in my mind, puzzled. What gift? Behind me, the human Elders are weeping. *Weeping?*

My dragon-friend laughs and seizes me, maw gaping. "Come, garlic! It's your turn now."

I blanch as understanding dawns.

"YOU SHALL NOT HAVE HER!" And the terrible roar of ten thousand dragons explodes across the valley.

No. The roar is not dragons'.

My father's mouth is open. He is singing.

Kingsong.

The earth trembles, and Jiay drops me as the sky darkens with starfall.

My father is saving me at the cost of his kingdom.

The Code never really mattered at all.

Rule # 1. *Never trust a dragon.*

EMILY JUNE STREET

THE PAINTED DOG

THE PAINTED DOG

The dove struggled, its wings fluttering against her cupping palms. Gula placed the bird in the rear nave cage.

"Did you find one?" Nika floated to Gula's side, her robes whispering along the floor like feathered wings. "You always get them, Gula. I don't know how you do it."

Gula knew. She could still remember the awful day that began her hunting life: the glaring sunlight, her mother's trembling silhouette as she said, *"He doesn't like children; you cannot come with me,"* leaving Gula in a hot cobblestone alley to fend for herself. She'd begged at the baker's, the greengrocer's, the butcher's, but they were inured to hungry children. Abandoned, she had learned how to slip into shadows, how to be so quiet not even the rats noticed her when she stalked them for dinner.

Only since she'd come to the Temple had soup been waiting for Gula at the end of the day—and only as long as she captured whatever creature the High Priestess demanded.

The priestesses filed into the Temple for afternoon prayers, summoned by the tower bell. Everyone sat on wooden blocks, shins to the ground, spines straight. Gula settled in the back, unwanted even here. Her stained leather breeches, wool shirt, and boots had been scavenged from a junkyard, contrasting sharply with the priestesses' blue robes.

The priestesses who trained at the Temple came from rich families and gentle lives.

"Bless us, Nin-Kara!" intoned the High Priestess before the altar.

"Bless us, Lady of Blood and Life," murmured the priestesses in response.

"We beg of you, Nin-Kara, hear our prayers. The summer plague has come early. Turn your healing powers upon our city." The High Priestess held Gula's dove in one fist, her hand so tight around the bird's body that Gula thought she might kill it by pressure alone.

The High Priestess brandished her knife. "We offer blood and life. Hear our prayers. Heal our sickness."

In a practiced move, she sank her blade into the dove's breast. The bird gave one small jerk and expired. Blood gushed down her arm in thin, bright rivulets.

The High Priestess laid the dove on the altar. "Let us meditate on blood and life, seeking the will of Nin-Kara." She picked up a plate and walked down the rows of priestesses, serving their strange sacrament.

Gula was not offered the herb. Only priestesses partook. After eating, the women swayed like blades of wheat in the wind, throwing their heads back and trilling.

Their eerie song built until they all wailed as one. "Aie, aie, aie," the High Priestess moaned. "Be merciful, Lady, be merciful."

One of the priestesses began to weep. That set off others, until they all shook with sobs. Gula did not cry. She had not cried since that day when her mother had left her in the sunlit alley.

Finally the High Priestess sat up, smoothed her pale hair, and composed her face. The other women followed suit.

Gula anticipated this next part of the service. The High Priestess would name what creature Gula must hunt next to offer the Goddess. Three days running, it had been doves, easy enough to find within the city. The Goddess liked doves, but sometimes She asked for a piglet, and Gula would have to go to the market and beg one from a farmer. Other times it was a rabbit, and Gula headed into the grasslands to put her hunting skills to use. In a more serious circumstance—and the summer plague rated as such—the Goddess might ask for a cat. Cats were tricky.

* * *

A cat had first brought Gula into the Temple four years ago. She'd been stalking the animal for hours, but not because she wanted to eat it. No, this cat was sleek and pretty, not mangy like most cats Gula saw on the streets. It wore a jeweled collar. Gula imagined that if she caught the cat, she could sell the collar for good money.

The cat had dashed into the empty Temple, leaping onto the altar, hissing and clawing, raking Gula's reaching arms. Gula persisted. That jeweled collar could feed her for days.

A gasp had rung out behind her. She turned to find a woman in blue robes staring at her.

"I caught it," Gula said. "It's mine." The woman had come upon her so quickly, Gula felt almost like the cat herself, trapped, at someone else's mercy.

The High Priestess had pulled Gula into her private chambers, cat and all. "You were brought to our Temple for a *reason*. Nin-Kara sent you. We need someone like you to help us find our animals for sacrifice, a hunter who can catch little beasts so easily."

"You'll pay me? You'll pay me to find animals?"

"We can feed you and give you a bed, but the Goddess forbids that we pay for any service."

Gula hadn't known anything about the worship of Nin-Kara then. Her life was too cheap to worry about *believing* in anything. But she'd known the value of a full belly and a warm place to sleep.

She'd handed the cat to the High Priestess without further questions.

* * *

Now a single tear coursed down the High Priestess's cheek as she cried, "The Goddess requires a painted dog to purge the city of plague."

Dogs were not well liked in the city. They were thought to have a devilish power over people's minds. Even so, Gula had seen plenty of them prowling the refuse heaps—feral creatures with matted fur and nasty dispositions.

After the service Gula slid into the High Priestess's office in her silent, slippery way. She was good at catching animals because she moved like one. Her time on the streets had taught her how to evade notice, how to cling to corners and slip into shadows.

The High Priestess had changed her dress and washed away the blood from the ritual. "I fear the Goddess has set you an impossible task, Gula!"

Gula shrugged. "I know where to find dogs. But what is a painted one?"

The priestess's shoulders sagged. "A painted dog is no common cur. It is a wild animal of the savanna woodlands. You will have to go far afield." The priestess pulled a book from a shelf. "Study this image. By it you will recognize the painted dog."

The page showed a dog with a small head, a deep ribcage, long legs, and alert ears. Its mottled coat easily gave reason for its name.

"I've never seen a living painted dog," the priestess said. "But when you came here, Gula, I knew you were destined for great acts. You must find the painted dog. If you don't…" She shuddered. "Only a painted dog can stop the plague."

* * *

The rumors of summer plague had cast a pall over the city. Everyone knew a painted dog had been demanded by Nin-Kara, but most people believed painted dogs were mythical creatures; they assumed the city was doomed to the full ravages of the plague.

Only the priestesses had faith that Gula would find the necessary sacrifice.

"You must be quick about it, Gula," Nika said as Gula prepared to depart the Temple to hunt. "Your search cannot take weeks."

"I don't expect it to," Gula said. "But I'm not sure how to find the dog."

"Nin-Kara will guide you," Nika replied. "You must have faith."

Gula had trouble with faith. The priestesses said Nin-Kara's hand moved in her, but when her quarry eluded her, when the hunting was hard, Gula felt utterly alone. There was no assistance, divine or otherwise. Gula worried that if she did not come back with the required sacrifice, the priestesses would turn her onto the streets again. The Temple's benevolence would not extend past her failure.

To the priestesses, every choice reflected one's faith in Nin-Kara. When

Gula had first come to the Temple, she hadn't cared about such weighty matters—it was enough that they'd fed her and given her a blanket to stay warm in the cold night. But she had quickly seen that they expected her belief in exchange for their charity, so she held her tongue.

"We'll pray," Nika said as Gula slung her rucksack onto her shoulders. "You must pray too, Gula, to find the dog quickly."

Gula did not reply. Her attention wandered during prayer, making her as restless as a caged animal. Nika knew she did not care for the practice.

"You must cultivate the inner stillness," Nika admonished knowingly. "Quiet your mind. Only when you find stillness may Nin-Kara move you." Nika's face melted into the wide-eyed look of ecstasy the priestesses wore during the sacrifice ritual. They always watched the sacrifice so avidly. Gula's own instinct was to squinch her eyes closed.

"Remember," Nika went on, "we do not pray to make demands of the Goddess, but so that She may make demands of us. We only hear her when all else is quiet."

"You hear her? A voice inside your head?" Gula's voice sounded harsh to her own ears as she laced her boots, readying for the journey.

"Nin-Kara does not speak in words. She prompts with a feeling. She fills me up, all the way to the chambers of my heart. My doubts die; my questions are answered."

Gula stood up from her crouch and nodded to Nika.

"Come back soon, Gula. I know you will not fail us. Pray."

Gula could have voiced her reservations about prayer and faith, but she predicted what Nika would say. *But Gula, can you not see how the Goddess has given you to us for a reason? She saved you from a terrible life of poverty in the streets. She feeds you. She clothes you.*

How could the Goddess's own gift not believe?

* * *

Gula passed into the wooded area beyond the city. She only came here to fetch animals, rabbits or foxes, or once, when a city magistrate had been ill, a fawn. Gula hadn't been able to watch the High Priestess kill the fawn; she'd closed her eyes and offered, for the first time in her life, a genuine prayer: *Let her not need to kill it.*

Gula's prayer had not been answered. The priestess had slit the animal's throat as usual.

Later Gula had pulled Nika aside. "Why is the Goddess so bloodthirsty?" She couldn't get the image of the High Priestess's triumphant face and raised bloody arm out of her mind.

Nika had frowned. "From the outside looking in, people mistake what sacrifice is about. People think we pray to ask favors, that we make sacrifices to pay for them. But the sacrifice shows the Goddess that we understand that balances must be kept, that life is fed by death. It's like eating. You have to eat to survive. When you eat, the things you eat die, even a carrot or a head of lettuce. Whatever life energy is in that food, it goes into you and sustains you, but the food itself is finished. The Goddess consumes life to save life."

"So you exchanged the fawn's life for the magistrate's?"

"More or less," Nika had replied.

* * *

The road darkened before her. Gula plunged into the skeleton trees, pondering the fawn's sacrifice. She never felt bad about the chickens they made into soup, never even considered the sacrifice of a potato when she ate it for supper. Why did the fawn bother her so much?

The eyes. The fawn, which she'd found not far from where she now walked, had looked at Gula so *knowingly*, trembling in fear when she'd roped its neck, as if it knew that she dragged it to its doom. A potato did not anticipate its death in terror, or if it did, Gula had no way of comprehending. That still didn't explain why Gula felt fine eating a chicken. Chickens squawked in fear when brought to slaughter.

Maybe the problem was in using feeding to explain the ritual. Nika's explanation only worked if she *believed*, if she thought the Goddess was *real* and possessed powers of transmutation.

The woods became thicker. Tree branches intertwined overhead, blocking the summer sun. Squirrels scrambled in the branches. Leaves rustled in the wind.

Had the magistrate survived? Gula could not remember, or perhaps she had never been told. The priestesses made offerings every summer to ward off the plague, but the illness persisted, taking many lives. The priestesses claimed its ravages would be much worse without their interventions.

Gula worried. What if she could not find a painted dog? What if the creatures were a myth? The High Priestess had never seen one. All she had was a picture in a book and a statue.

Animals would avoid the road, so Gula left it. The land beyond opened into a wide basin bounded by spindly trees. Gula headed towards a tempting glint of sunlight on water.

She found a marshy lake, and on the far side, a herd of deer, watering.

Gula kept to the verge of the trees, observing the deer. A guttural howl rang through the still air. Gula scrambled into the nearest tree despite its precarious feel.

The deer scattered, splashing in and out of the lake. Ten slender shadows coursed after them, darting in a deadly choreography. The whole panorama left Gula breathless and mesmerized: the deer, the racing hunters, the motion, the edge, the anticipation, the seething life.

A dark shadow leapt at a deer's haunch. Another went for the throat. The hunters growled as they descended upon the deer and pulled it down. The deer gave up in a stark and graceful surrender.

The hunters bit at the deer's belly, tearing out the innards in red, dripping ropes.

Gula shuddered as she watched, nearly sick. "They're only feeding," she whispered. "They have to eat."

After a time the hunters had eaten their fill. Four loped into the trees near Gula's perch.

She recognized those alert ears, those thick ribcages above skinny legs. *Painted dogs.* If she had been more devout, she would have recognized her good fortune as the favor of Nin-Kara. Gula only assumed she'd gotten lucky.

She shimmied down the tree to follow them.

The dogs picked up their pace until they burst into a protected clearing. There lay a bitch dog surrounded by a litter of splotchy puppies. The mother rose to her feet to greet the other dogs. Puppies flurried everywhere.

The adult dogs vomited piles of half-digested flesh for the puppies. More dogs arrived dragging the downed deer. The mother fed from the carcass while the puppies scrambled, licking and tasting and playing.

Gula remained hidden within a thick shrub that made her skin itch. Much as she hated the notion of sacrificing one of the squirmy puppies, a baby dog was her only option. The bigger dogs were too powerful, too fast, too strong. She settled in for the hunter's wait, ignoring the rash emerging on her forearms.

Soon the hunting dogs departed, leaving the bitch with the puppies and the carcass. Even so, Gula waited. These dogs could do lethal damage, and most mothers were willing to fight hard for their offspring.

The puppies competed for access to the mother's teats. The littlest one, the runt, kept getting shoved aside, mewling pitifully.

A sudden rustling in the bushes behind Gula made her freeze in terror. Slowly she turned her head.

The intruder—an enormous bird—looked not at Gula, but rather into the clearing at the leftover carcass. The carrion-eater had a beak made for ripping flesh. More carrion birds followed, lumbering towards the meat.

The bitch dog growled and darted forward. The first bird flapped powerful wings and hopped backwards, but the birds behind it advanced. The mother dog fought to push them away, but every time she hedged one bird back, others gained.

The puppies squeaked and cried. The largest bird sprang, snapped, and gouged a bite of flesh from a puppy's back.

The puppy yelped, but the mother saved it, picking it up in her mouth and protecting it from the birds. In the meantime, the runty puppy replaced its mother guarding the carcass, only to be bitten and tossed aside by a bird.

The birds fell upon the deer carcass in a mad swarm.

The bitch gave up, running off with the injured puppy in her mouth and the others on her heels, all except the second one to be bitten, the mewling runt.

The birds made short work of the carcass, cleaning it to the bones. One lifted its head, sourcing the whimpers of the abandoned puppy.

Gula surged from her hiding place, snatched up the puppy, and tore away from the clearing.

The carrion birds screamed behind her. Gula hunched protectively over the wounded animal as she ran.

Gula stopped at the lakeshore where she washed the blood from the puppy, holding it by the neck scruff to flush the wound clean.

"Don't die, puppy. You can't die."

She tucked the dog under her thigh and cut a swathe from her cloak, tying the cloth to cover the wound. All the fight had left the puppy. It laid its head on Gula's leg, closing its eyes in private misery. Its low keen jerked tears to her eyes. She knew that sound; she'd made it when her mother left her. The universal lament of the abandoned.

"Shhh." Gula brought the puppy against her chest and used the remains of the cloak to make a sling for it.

Every sound pricked Gula's ears, and every motion on the horizon sent her heart racing as she hurried back to the road.

The exhausted puppy curled into the sling and slept for hours. It woke only when Gula stopped to rest, flicking open golden eyes and bleating mournfully. When Gula released it, the dog squatted to relieve itself in the fashion of a female.

Gula looped her rope over the dog's head and cinched it.

The puppy dug its heels into the ground, sank into its haunches, and fought the leash. She was in pain, abandoned, and caught. Gula scratched the puppy behind the ears, crooning. Tension ebbed from the animal as it leaned into her.

The puppy gobbled up the biscuits and water Gula offered as though they were the last sustenance on earth.

The little creature was all legs, but she packed down to fit neatly into the crook between Gula's thigh and belly. With a satisfied sigh, the dog tucked her snout beneath her tail. Gula did not move. She liked the animal's weight against her body, and the dog's sigh reverberated up into her heart like the voice of Nika's goddess.

Gula knew that if she took the dog back to the Temple, it would be killed. Had she saved the puppy's life only to take it in a fashion somehow more barbaric than the death nature had planned?

In the morning the puppy rubbed against Gula's legs, waking her. She peered down into the dog's blotchy face, meeting a deep, soulful gaze. The world expanded, and Gula almost understood the stillness of prayer that Nika had once described.

The pup whimpered and jumped.

"I'll call you Vida," Gula said, using the word for life in the old tongue. "Are you hungry?"

Vida wagged wildly. Gula offered another biscuit, and Vida snatched at the food, almost taking a finger, too.

Vida leaned into Gula's lower legs in a way that was already growing necessary.

Gula assessed their position—over halfway back to the city. Her duty grew heavier with every step.

The thick woodlands rose above the horizon, a dark, hulking blur guarding the city. The feeling of stillness had not left Gula; inside her body, she harbored a new sensation, both weighty and light, a precious gift from the dog. She'd never considered that a god could be a physical presence. That's what she named this long column of strong air inside her body, a god. A nameless god unknown to anyone but Gula.

Gula stopped walking. Vida, who'd finally settled in to the reality of the leash, stopped as well, looking back at Gula as if to say, *Silly creature, how did you not see that the only god is this life itself?*

"We can't go back," Gula murmured. "They'll kill you."

Vida darted around Gula's legs, wrapping the rope around her ankles in a bind. Gula studied the horizons. Their only safe route was south. If they went back to the city, the priestesses would find them.

A passing wagon pushed Gula and Vida to the side of the road. The wagon paused, and the driver tipped his hat. A girl sat on the driving deck on his far side, peering around him at Gula and the dog.

"Which way are you headed?" the driver asked. His gaze stuck on Vida, taking in her painted coat, her wild demeanor.

"South," Gula replied.

"We're headed that way, too. You want a ride?"

"Please. But we have little food."

The driver nodded. "We've plenty. Is your dog trained?"

"She's only a puppy."

"Make sure you keep it on the leash."

Gula scooped up Vida and pulled herself onto the seat beside the driver. Vida curled in her lap easily.

"How is the Temple city?" Gula asked, dreading bad news of the summer plague. She felt guilty for abandoning the priestesses. Who else would be able to find a painted dog to sacrifice? "I heard there was plague there."

The driver scoffed. "False alarm. I'm a healer; I heard the plague rumors, and I went to the city to offer my help. There was no plague. Turns out it was only food poisoning in the foreign quarter, nothing to worry about at all."

The man flicked his reins, and the wagon lurched into motion.

EMILY JUNE STREET

ACCIDENTAL BODIES

ACCIDENTAL BODIES

"What is this place?" Pheather stared at the graffiti. A spray-painted woman presided over the station, a ghost in clothing from another century. She looked like an angel, only lacking wings. Her smiling painted face belied the desolation of the place. Weird white sand billowed at her feet, catching the sunlight. *Bombay Beach Gas*, the decrepit sign above the station read.

Pheather shoved a hand through her blue hair, making it stand straight up like a dog's hackles. Phin pulled the car into the bay. They'd followed signs on the deserted freeway for a service station.

"Used to be a resort," Phin explained as he rifled through his book, *Imperial Valley: Pre-Drought*. He shrugged out of his purloined jacket, exposing blue arms that matched the car's interior. An observer might think he had tattoo sleeves. He opened the car hatch, letting in a blast of heat. "Back in the twentieth century."

"It smells like rotten eggs." Pheather wrinkled her nose. Hot air assaulted her throat and left a gluey residue on her skin as she stepped outside.

"Must be what's left of the Salton Sea." Phin pointed west and read, "In the early twentieth century the California Development Company made a canal cut in the Colorado River to irrigate the Imperial Valley for farming, but the water overflowed and flooded the Salton Sink, creating a large accidental body of water."

"Where did you get that book?" Pheather asked.

"I stole it from the BioParque lab."

Pheather bit her lip and lifted the attachment on the dilapidated service module. "I can't figure this thing out. It doesn't plug in."

Phin examined the contraption. "That's seems like some kind of nozzle. Whatever you do, don't stick a BioParque money cell in it. That's the easiest way for them to track us. Use bitcoin. Though it really doesn't have the right attachment, does it?"

"A resort? Really?" Pheather asked, willfully ignoring the enormous problem of the lack of a proper charging module. "It's so terrible now. The air! The smell! What happened?"

Phin grinned despite their predicament and read again from his book: "Resorts sprang up around the new Salton Sea, but agricultural runoff created unpleasant bacterial blooms and wildlife die-offs. The die-offs, combined with several damaging storms, effectively shut down tourism on the Salton Sea. Subsequently, the increasing salinity of the lake produced a system of accelerated change that devastated the Sea's ecology, leading to the ongoing die-off that continues to this day."

"That's the smell? Rotting fish and dead birds? Ugh. Are there any still alive?"

Phin scanned the page. "Tilapia, it says. You know how they are. Can live in almost any conditions." He prodded the buttons on the useless module and shrugged. "Apparently the lake is still evaporating. And the resultant dust—" Phin waved at the glittery debris wafting around them "—is full of old agricultural chemicals. That's why no one lives here anymore."

"What are we gonna do, Phin?" Pheather's voice trembled.

Phin kicked the curb. "I guess we have to walk."

"Walk? In this toxic dust? And what if BioParque has sent alerts—"

"No one comes out here. That's why we took the inland route. We can follow the old one-eleven freeway. The Mexican border is less than seventy miles. We can cross it at an unpatrolled point. Illegal immigrants used to do it all the time."

Pheather followed Phin onto the road's shoulder. The sun glared. Phin turned off at a sign for *Salton Sea*.

"Let's have a quick look," he said.

Dust erupted as they stepped off the road, sending a white cloud into the air. Pheather cast anxious glances at the plume. Rumors of what happened to recaptured Accidentals flitted through her mind.

Phin moved with stealthy grace, catlike, but more strangling dust bloomed from his steps.

"Holy hell." Phin covered his mouth with his shirt sleeve. "Look at that!"

Pheather stared across the white plain. Down in the center, almost too low to see, a liquid, festering sore wounded the earth. A bubble expanded from it, growing until it exploded and sent a waft of stinking vapor into the air. Piles of rotting detritus collected on the shore.

"People *made* that?" Pheather said.

"Sort of by accident," Phin murmured. "It's not their worst creation ever."

"It's an apocalypse." Fish and bird bones littered the dry lakebed, some pounded into the ground like ancient fossils, others left above, weathering the sunlight and heat. Pheather picked up a bone shard, caressing it with her long fingers.

"There's no such thing as an apocalypse, Pheather. There's only change. The question is whether you can adapt."

"These birds and fish can't."

"This environment is changing too fast, even for the tilapia. They aren't like us."

"Phin."

"We can adapt to anything, Pheather. We just have to stay ahead of the BioParque agents. If we can find the Accidentals who made it to Pichado del Diablo—"

"We'll be freaks in Mexico, too."

"We can blend."

"You don't know that."

They proceeded along the highway's shoulder. Phin's skin had long since shifted from the blue of the car to the beige of the surrounding desert. Pheather let hers do the same.

Helicopter blades cut the air in a juddering whoosh. Phin yanked Pheather into the dust dunes beside the road.

They both peered up, searching for the helicopter. "It's a BioParque chopper! I see the emblem. Stay down. Stay beige," Phin said.

The chameleon chromatophores in their skin went into overdrive. They barely breathed as the vehicle approached, marring the blue sky.

"Damn," Phin muttered. "They've seen the car. It's descending over by the service station."

"They'll find us, Phin! BioParque will dump us in the desert with their toxic waste. That's what they did with the others they caught."

"More likely they'll incinerate us. They've learned it's a better way to permanently dispose of their mistakes. Some of the first generation survived the Mojave. Tayle told me before they took him away."

Pheather shivered, recalling the repercussions at the BioParque lab after the first generation of Accidentals had escaped.

Her shoulders itched. A ripping sensation cut from her armpit to her waist. "Ugggh!" She had not anticipated such pain.

"Holy hells, Pheather! You've got wings sprouting from your back! How'd you get them?"

She shoved the bone shard at Phin. "Took nucleus DNA from this. A bird bone."

Phin grabbed the bone. "Looks like pelican! Perfect plan! Why didn't I think of it?"

He used sensors in his fingertips to upload the biologic information from the pelican bone, grafting aspects into his own body. Within moments, the nano-constructors housed in their flesh had given both Accidentals full sets of feathered wings. This was the power the BioParque researchers hadn't anticipated when they began their experiments. They'd meant to make a more adaptable human. Instead they'd made something closer to a god.

Phin and Pheather rose like angels over the apocalyptic earth.

"Fly high and head south!" cried Phin. "It will take them some time to get airborne again."

The new wings felt unnatural. Pheather wavered in the sky.

"Go! Go!" yelled Phin, flying beneath her and pushing her on.

They flew until the Salton Sea became a tiny oozing button in the distance.

California's scorched wasteland lay behind them. Pheather's eyes—improvements on an eagle's design—picked up the peak of Baja's Pichado del Diablo, far off, jutting through clouds.

The helicopter's buzz hummed behind them.

"We can make it," Phin cried. "Just keep flying!"

BETH DEITCHMAN

LE MOULIN

RAIN DANCE

LE MOULIN

"I don't remember this one," Doris said.

Betty leaned over to see which picture Doris held. "*Le Moulin.*" The blush surprised her. At least fifty years had passed, yet Betty could still feel the heat of that day.

"What was that?" Doris brayed.

"The mill," Betty replied. "I took it that summer I spent in Rouen."

"I never was good with languages like you. I never got the chance to travel."

Betty shrugged, letting Doris have her sulk. She picked up the discarded picture—faded after all these years—and studied it. Around her the cold dining room shifted, faded; the picture fell from her hands.

She stood at the edge of that lazy river, warmed by the June sun, inhaling the scent of water and summer and something else—the rich, loamy earth near the old mill. *Le moulin.* Despite the day's warmth, Betty shivered, the sensation radiating through her body. She held up a hand and gave a little cry. Her skin was smooth, taut, and clear, her fingers straight and free from pain. She touched her face, marveling at the softness, glanced down at her body, stunned by the firmness. "But how?" she whispered.

From behind her came a rich voice, familiar though she hadn't heard it in more than fifty years. "*Bonjour, mademoiselle.*"

Betty closed her eyes, gave a silent prayer, and turned around. When she opened her eyes, she smiled. "Jean."

He held out his arms. "I have been waiting."

Betty rushed into his embrace, remembering the sweetness of his arms wrapped around her, the earthiness of his smell, the heat of his body. For a perfect moment Jean held her.

"What about this one?"

"What?" Betty looked up at Jean. He smiled at her then kissed her forehead.

"Betty?"

A cold hand grasped her arm, and Betty's heart fell.

"What about this one?" Doris said.

"I'm not sure," Betty replied. The winter chill settled again into her bones though the faint scent of summer, sun, and Jean clung to her skin.

RAIN DANCE

In the distance, thunder rumbled. The sound carried across the plain. I watched the black clouds gathered to the west, wishing they would make their way toward us.

"Think it's finally going to rain?" Betsy asked, picking a newly formed scab on her knee.

I shrugged. "Charlie said his hip's fine."

Betsy looked up. "What?"

"Charlie got hurt in the war; now his hip bothers him whenever it's going to rain or snow."

"Really?"

"It hurts when he walks."

Betsy resumed picking. "Ma said that Mr. Harris could make it rain." Her voice held an edge.

"How?"

"Arapaho magic. No one talks about it, but everyone knows."

Everyone but me, I thought.

Betsy scanned the clouds. "I wish I could make it rain, because then—" She stilled, eyes closed. "But what if—?" She opened her eyes. "Yes!" Betsy leapt up and started running. I stood, brushing the dirt off my old dress. A few yards away Betsy turned. "Come on, Katie!"

"Where?"

"Patty's house!"

"Why—"

"You'll see. Just come on!"

We raced toward town. I struggled to keep up with Betsy, whose braids flew behind her. We found Patty in the dusty yard, carrying her brother on her thin hip.

"Hey," Patty called.

We sped through the gate and stumbled to a stop. "Hey Patty," Betsy said breathlessly. I waved, too winded to speak.

"Is someone chasing you?"

Betsy shook her head. "Do you have to watch him today?" She gestured toward Henry.

"Only 'til Ma gets back. Why?"

Betsy glanced at me then back to Patty. I said nothing.

"What's going on?"

"We're going to make it rain!" Betsy announced. I stared at her. "We need your help!"

Patty's eyebrows flew up. "What're you talking about, Betsy Miller?"

Betsy kicked the ground with the scuffed toe of her shoe. "Your Pa's part Arapaho."

Patty bit her lip, glancing toward her house. "We don't talk about that," she whispered. "It might not even be true."

"But what if it is?" Betty insisted. "I have to *do* something! My parents might lose their farm." She clenched her teeth, but tears shone in her eyes.

"It can't hurt to try," I suggested.

Patty regarded us, chewing her lip. "Pa doesn't like—"

"We wouldn't tell him," Betsy interrupted. "Please, Patty."

Patty glanced at the sky. "What would we do?"

"In the picture shows there's chanting and dancing," I supplied.

"And feathers and drums," Betsy added.

Patty gave a tentative smile. "Pa has an old eagle feather that we could use."

"We need a stick, too!" Patty and I looked at Betsy. "Like a divining rod to find a well."

We followed Patty inside. She set her brother on the tattered rug and then hurried upstairs. When she returned she brandished a large feather. "Here!" She let us ogle it before slipping it into her pocket. "What about the drum and the stick?"

"My brother has a toy drum," Betsy said. "We can find a stick on the way."

"Where?" I asked.

"Watson's hill," Patty replied. "High up, away from people." Betsy nodded.

"What do we do besides dancing?"

Betsy chewed her nails as she thought. "We should say a prayer to the rain gods." She closed her eyes and lifted her arms. "O, great gods of rain," she intoned. "We beg you to cry on our land!" Patsy and I erupted in giggles. "What?" Betsy looked hurt. "Fine," she snapped to our continued laughter. "You come up with something."

The gate creaked. "Patty?"

"In here, Ma!" Patty called.

Mrs. Harris stepped inside. "Hello, girls."

"Hi, Mrs. Harris," we chorused.

Patty reached for the grocery bag.

"That's all right, Patty. I have it. How's your brother?"

"He fussed earlier, but he's fine. Can I go play?"

"Did you finish your chores?"

"Yes, ma'am!"

"Go on, then. But mind the weather. It might rain."

"I will!"

On the way to Watson's Hill, we stopped at Betsy's house for her brother's toy drum. Then we continued, scouring the ground for suitable sticks. At the foot of the hill, Betsy held up a fallen cottonwood branch, forked like a divining rod. "This is perfect!" Patty and I nodded, both of us grinning.

At the top of the hill, Patty collapsed onto the ground. Betsy and I joined her. We sat catching our breath, gazing at the land below. In a good summer, waves of green would ripple toward the horizon. But now many of the fields lay barren and cracked. Others held crops, but even from our height we could see how the corn failed to flourish.

"Come on!" Betsy kicked off her shoes, motioning for us to imitate her. "Patty, you stand over there," she directed. She handed me the stick. "Draw a circle around Patty." We obeyed. While I pulled the stick through the dust of Watson's Hill, Patty stood, feather held aloft in both hands. Betsy's slow pounding of the drum accompanied us. When I finished the circle, I stood across from Betsy, matching her solemn expression.

Patty inhaled, threw her head back, and opened her arms. "Great-grandfather, hear my cry! I come to you with great need!" Her voice sounded older, stronger. I glanced at Betsy, whose wide eyes were fixed with wonder and admiration on Patty. "Our land is cracked. Our crops cannot grow. Please, help your granddaughter and her people. Please, send us rain!"

The sky darkened as thick clouds rolled overhead. Betsy shrieked, pounding a frantic rhythm on her brother's drum. Then she launched into a wild dance. Patty and I followed, flinging our bodies with abandon. Our voices growing raw with shrieking, we spun and jumped, lunged and leapt around Watson's Hill.

A plop on my head stopped me mid-spin. Another fell into the dust at my feet. We looked at each other, frozen, as the clouds unleashed a torrent.

"It worked!" Betsy's voice caught. "We did it!"

Drenched, we linked arms and watched the rain flood the thirsty fields below.

BETH DEITCHMAN

A LITTLE GOLD DUST

A LITTLE GOLD DUST

Carl leaned over his father's shrunken form, wincing at the old man's wheezing. "Dad, I—" he began.

"For once in your life," Carl Senior croaked. "Be a man." He struggled for a breath. "Don't let those bastard city boys ruin my legacy. I worked too damn—"

Head down, Carl waited for his father to finish the sentence.

"Come on, Carl," said Clarissa. "You're no help to anyone just standin' there, sulkin'. The ladies'll see to your daddy's body, God rest his soul. You go on and have yourself a cold beer."

Carl gritted his teeth but said nothing as his wife shooed him from the room. He blinked at the sharp light from the overhead bulb. The dark bedroom had concealed his father's situation. But out here Carl could see the shabby carpet, the broken Venetian blinds, the curling linoleum of the kitchenette. The possibility of flight taunted him. No one would notice his absence for a while. Instead Carl took a beer from the refrigerator and sank into his father's recliner. Women's voices carried from the bedroom. He sat forward to turn on the TV. A preacher squawked, waving his be-ringed hands, his lacquered hair stiff and shining in the television lights. Carl flipped to another channel. A middle-aged man fished in a boat, talking directly to the camera about grubs. Again Carl turned the knob. Judy Garland leaned against a wagon wheel, singing "Over the Rainbow." Carl picked up his beer and pushed the recliner back.

* * *

The next morning, Carl pretended to sleep while Clarissa trotted around the bedroom, humming "Over the Rainbow" off key as she dressed.

"Carl, I know you're faking it. You've got to get up. People will be needing to fill their gas tanks!"

Carl rolled over. "I don't care. They can go to the new station," he said into his pillow. "I never wanted to—"

"How can you say that? After all your daddy did for you?" Clarissa yanked the bedclothes back. "You've got loyal customers who'll want to give their condolences. Everyone loved Carl Senior." She headed out of the bedroom, but stopped in the doorway. "You've got some big shoes to fill, and I expect you to rise to the occasion."

Carl grunted, well aware of his wife's expectations. Dutifully, he pushed himself out of bed and pulled on his jeans and the shirt Clarissa had chosen for him. Downstairs Clarissa banged a skillet onto the stove and slammed the brand new refrigerator's door. Carl sat back on the bed to put on his socks and resisted the temptation to crawl under the covers rather than face his wife.

* * *

"Are you listening to me, Carl?"

Carl looked up from his plate.

"I figured it out. We just need a little gold dust!"

"What are you talking about, Clarissa?"

"I went to see Madame Rosalinda today. Don't roll your eyes. She's the real deal! I told her what's happening, and she sold me some magic powder. She said to sprinkle it around the service station. People will come from miles away to see their hearts' desire. And to buy gas."

Carl shook his head. "How much did this powder cost?"

Clarissa dismissed him with an impatient wave. "Never you mind, Carl Jackson. It won't matter when the money starts rolling in! Besides, *someone* had to step up and take care of things. Now go on to the other room; I'll bring you some coffee. We're going to have a late night."

Carl collapsed onto his Barcalounger. The first month since his father's death had been rough. Fewer and fewer customers came out to his station. He didn't blame them—the new one was more convenient. But the station's failure hadn't given Carl the push he needed to leave behind this life he'd never wanted. Carl shifted in his seat and thought of Clarissa's ridiculous gold dust.

"How could it hurt?" he muttered. "She's already spent the damned money."

At midnight, Clarissa woke Carl.

"It's time, Carl."

Carl coughed and rubbed his back. "When did I fall asleep?"

"During *The Honeymooners*. Now hop to it!"

Carl slipped on his shoes and got his jacket from the closet. "Have you got the—the stuff?"

Clarissa held up a little pouch. "It's all right here!"

On the drive out, they said little. Clarissa, uncharacteristically quiet, stared out the window. Carl kept his eyes on the road. The station was dark. They closed their doors quietly, and Clarissa motioned to Carl to follow her.

"Now, you sprinkle the powder—just a little at a time, we need to make it last—while I say the words Madame Rosalinda gave me," Clarissa whispered.

"There are words?"

"Never mind. Just make sure you do a good job with the gold dust."

Carl took the pouch, surprised by its weight. He waited for Clarissa's signal before taking a pinch of the strange, cold substance and letting it flutter to the sidewalk. By the time he finished, Carl had an ache in his lower back from bending over. He followed Clarissa to the front of the station. A faint shimmer rose from the pavement. Clarissa gasped. From nowhere a shining car had appeared.

"I see—but it can't be!" She rubbed her eyes. "My stars! That's Frank Sinatra in his Cadillac!"

A horn blared, and Carl snapped into action, Clarissa on his heels. "How may I help you, sir?"

The man in the car turned his brilliant blue eyes toward Carl. "Where the hell am I?"

"You're in Haysville, Mr. Sinatra," Clarissa simpered, pushing Carl aside. She extended her hand. "It's such an honor—"

"How the hell did I get here?"

"I imagine you took Route Eighty-one."

Sinatra shook his head and threw a flask out of the car. "How the hell do I get out of here?"

"You follow that road until it ends and then take a left." Clarissa turned to Carl. "Don't just stand there! Mr. Sinatra will need a full tank."

When the Cadillac's taillights disappeared, Clarissa grabbed Carl's arm, clutching the flask to her chest with her other hand. "Oh, Carl! Madame Rosalinda is a genius! Just wait until word gets out!"

Carl stared down the empty road, wondering if what he'd seen was real.

* * *

The next morning, Carl found no traces of gold dust or fancy cars. He unlocked the office and settled into his chair, not sure whether he felt relief or disappointment.

The bell rang around eight thirty. He found Ernie Mitchell parked by the diesel pump, eyes wide.

"Hey, Ernie. Everything okay?"

"Don't you see it, Carl?" Ernie whispered, pointing to the figure in front of his truck. It wore robes of white, gossamer wings sprouting from its shoulder blades.

"What—?"

"It's my mama! She's an angel come to see me!"

Ernie leapt from his truck and ran to the angel. It pulled him into an embrace, wrapping its wings around him. Carl watched, amazed.

When Ernie returned to his truck, his eyes glowed from a face stained with tears. He clasped Carl's shoulder.

"Mama said you did this—you and Clarissa made it possible for her to come visit me." His voice broke. "She told me she loves me, and she's watchin' over me from Heaven." He wiped his face on his sleeve. "Thank you," he whispered.

In a daze Carl removed the nozzle from the gas tank and took Ernie's money, realizing only after Ernie left that he'd paid too much.

***

Within days Ernie's story spread and cars lined up for the pumps, bringing more business than the station has seen in years. "See, Carl," Clarissa gloated at the end of the first week. "I told you Madame Rosalinda was the real deal!"

Weeks passed; Carl and Clarissa's bank account grew. Clarissa bought expensive shoes. Carl bought travel guides, still dreaming of escape to exotic places. South America. India. The Orient. Few questioned the strange visions; most people accepted Clarissa's insistence that they were "gifts from God himself." In private she said, "No one needs to know the truth." She never asked what Carl's heart desired.

One windy Tuesday morning as Carl headed toward his office, the air behind the diesel pump began to shimmer. A woman in a gingham dress appeared, a basket looped over her arm. Carl stared, open-mouthed, as a shadow fell over the pump.

"I'll get you, my pretty!" a voice screeched.

The woman shrieked as the shadow advanced. His trance broken, Carl raced to the hose and filled a bucket with water. He bent to lift it.

"Dammit, Carl! Get the lead out!"

Still stooped, Carl looked up. Clarissa, feet crammed into glittery red shoes, glared at him.

"For once in your life," she snapped. "Be a man!"

Carl dropped the bucket's handle and straightened, looking from his wife's outraged red face to the witch's startled green one. He laughed.

"She's all yours."

Whistling, he headed down the road out of town.

AMY WOOD

THE DEVIL'S OWN LUCK

THE DEVIL'S OWN LUCK

The saloon didn't look like somewhere a man could make a deal to save his life. Small, dirty and dark, it barely looked like it'd be standing upright for much longer. But desperate times called for desperate measures, and Nate was desperate.

His horse refused to go a step closer as soon as the place appeared, looming out of the dusk like some relic from another time. It hadn't been comforting to see the sweat forming on his mare's neck but it had at least told Nate he was in the right place.

As he slid out of his saddle sweat trickled under his own collar, cold and uncomfortable. If he'd had a choice, he'd have turned tail and run. He'd let the mare have her head and ride until the ominous silence of the place turned into the quiet music of a stream or the swishing of prairie grass. But he didn't have a choice, so when the mare's hooves dug into the rough track and she almost catapulted him forward over her neck, Nate didn't cuss her for it.

The gloom inside the place was deep enough to prevent him seeing the bartender until he was right in front of the filthy bar.

"I'm...I want..." He cleared his throat. Why was he stumbling over his words? Steeling himself, he tried again. "I need to see your boss."

"Ain't no boss here," the man replied, not ceasing in his wiping of glasses thick with grime.

Nate fixed him with a stare. "Bullshit. I wanna make a deal."

The gap-toothed smile which spread over the bartender's face sent gooseflesh rippling down Nate's arms. What the hell was he doing? Why was he even thinking about this? Was he completely soft in the head? No, just a man with a price *on* his head.

"Boss is in there." The bartender jerked a thumb at a door to Nate's left, still smiling. "He'll be right glad to see you, I reckon."

Could he take a bottle in with him? Nate's fingers twitched. He really needed a drink. No, better not. Maybe it was best to keep a clear head.

The door opened silently; Nate had expected protests from long-rusted hinges. Somehow the silence was more worrisome. The .45 at his hip was solid and familiar beneath his trembling fingers. But what good would a gun do him here?

The room behind the door was tiny and empty save for a poker table and two chairs. A deck of cards sat in the middle of the table, along with a bottle and a stack of glasses.

Nate blinked. What use was an empty room to him? Turning, he opened his mouth to bawl at the bartender for playing him for a fool. But the words never left his tongue. A quiet laugh behind him stilled them and chilled his blood to sluggish ice.

Nate slowly turned back into the room with his heart beating a wild dance in his chest. A blond young man wearing a pristine white shirt now sat in the chair facing him. Shit.

"Hello, Nathan. You don't mind if I call you Nate, do you?" The man's teeth were dazzlingly white, his smile perfect.

Nate shook his head; all hope of speaking had vanished like water in the desert. Dear God, it was *him*. Was he real? Was this some kind of joke? How could it be a joke; nobody knew Nate intended on coming here. His hands shook, the vibration seemed to go down deep into his gut. It *was* him. He was real. Had to be, how else could he have gotten his ass into that chair when Nate was blocking the only doorway to the room?

It was impossible to breathe, to think, to even see straight. But this was why he'd made the trip out to the back of beyond. This was the man he needed to see. Might as well get on with it.

Swallowing past a painfully tight throat, Nate croaked, "Nate's fine."

"Wonderful. I like to be friendly, formality bores me." Long, slim hands picked up the deck and lazily shuffled the cards. "What can I do for you, Nate?"

"I wanna make a deal." Why was he whispering? He wasn't scared, dammit.

"Deals are my specialty." That perfect smile flashed again, along with eyes blue enough to put cornflowers to shame. "Sit down and tell me what you want." Head cocked to one side, the man blinked slowly at Nate, his eyes amused yet terrifyingly knowing.

Stomach twisting into sickening knots, Nate sat. He stared at the table, not daring to look at that mocking gaze.

A glass of whiskey slid into view. "On the house," the man in white said.

Nate took the glass and poured the liquor into his mouth. Searing rivulets of flame coursed his throat and lit a bonfire in his stomach but it was enough to stop his hands from shaking so badly.

He almost jumped out of his chair as a cool finger pressed under his chin, tilting his face up. Blue eyes bored into his and he was trapped, he couldn't have looked away if his life depended on it. It probably did.

"Tell me what you want, Nate." The man's voice was still light and friendly but his eyes snapped blue fire.

Nate's tongue dried up. Jesus, he was in over his head.

"I wanna live," he whispered, the words like ash in his mouth. "I want a life. I done bad things and Kansas and Texas want me at the end of a rope. I ain't gonna die that way. Can you make them wanted posters go away? Gimme another chance?"

"The infamous Nate Harrison; murderer, thief and rapist wants another chance." The man's voice dropped, it was as harsh the burn of whiskey in Nate's gut, the sun searing the sky at dawn, the stink of death after Nate's .45 did his talking for him. "Seen the error of your ways, cowboy?"

What was the right answer? No, he hadn't seen the error of anything. Everything he'd done, he'd do again if the chances presented themselves. But dancing at the end of a rope wasn't appealing and he was running out of places to hide. It was this or a noose. Which was worse? Nate couldn't decide.

"Can you make the reward on me go away or not?"

The chuckle that slid from between the man's perfect teeth crawled over Nate's skin, a thousand tiny ant bites of derision and ageless confidence.

"I can do anything, Nate. A snap of the fingers and it's done." His smile curved wider, sharp teeth glinting in the lamplight. "But where's the fun in that?"

Something lodged at the back of Nate's throat. Fear, more than he'd ever felt before. Oh God, what had he done?

"Let's make a game of it, shall we?" The man in white leaned back in his chair, tilting his chin up toward the ceiling.

An answer seemed to be required so Nate, grasping at the last straws of desperation, whispered, "Game?"

"One hand of poker." The blue gaze snapped back onto him, pinning Nate in place more securely than ropes or bars ever could. "Nice and simple. You win; I'll give you anything you ask for, free of charge. No souls will be transferred, no promises made, nothing."

"And if you win?" How was he still managing to speak? His tongue was dried up old leather in his mouth, his hands shook uncontrollably. Yet still he sounded like a man in possession of his reason.

The Devil grinned, blue fire flickering in his eyes and blood-red flames wreathing his head.

"Then your ass is mine, Nate Harrison. Sooner than you might have expected. But," he shuffled the deck of cards with practised ease, "you might win. Anything you want can be yours with just one little hand of poker." His tongue darted in and out like a snake's, wetting his lips. "I promise I won't cheat."

A violent crash behind Nate made his breath catch in his chest. The heavy bolt on the door had slid home of its own accord. The Devil smiled on, deftly shuffling.

Clenching his fists to stop their shaking, Nate looked at the deck. One poker hand. Anything he wanted—for free. A smile crept onto his face. Playing cards with the Devil. Well, his mother had told him often enough that the Devil looked after his own, might as well test that theory out.

He slowly refilled his glass and tossed the whiskey into his mouth, chasing the last few drops with the tip of his tongue.

The Devil watched silently.

Nate turned the glass over and placed it upside down on the table. Now or never. "Quit smiling and deal."

The Devil dealt but never stopped smiling.

AMY WOOD

THE LAST PHOENIX

THE LAST PHOENIX

The charred landscape was a stark contrast to the cheerful, fruity woman's voice which boomed out of the ancient fuel station forecourt.

"Good day, shoppers, and welcome to Ned's. If you require fuel, please wait for an attendant to serve you. Our station shop has a wide selection of sandwiches, snacks, newspapers and cold cuts. Please browse while your vehicle is being filled. Have a nice day, shoppers, and thank you for choosing Ned's for your fuel requirements."

Phee jumped as the flickering, ghostly image of a woman buzzed in and out of focus beside the shattered diesel pump. Her mouth was moving in time with the booming words but that voice didn't fit her face.

"Hologram," Phee's father said, resting a hand on Phee's shoulder. "Motion activated. Still works after all this time. Amazing, really. People are so ingenious."

Phee gazed around, her mouth hanging open. "People lived here?" It was hard to imagine their surroundings supporting even a cockroach, much less actual human beings.

Her father nodded, "This used to be the outskirts of a city called Glasgow. Thousands of people lived here."

"Where'd they all go?" Why was she whispering? Somehow it seemed liked the right thing to do. So many people, so many deaths. So many ghosts probably watching her at that very moment. "Was it the war?"

The hand on her shoulder tightened.

"Yes," her father replied. "The rebels tried to push south. They wanted to control the old England-Scotland border, but the government forces repelled them. Most of the damage in this area was done as they retreated. They burned everything; didn't want to leave anything the government army could use. Especially things like fuel stations. Fuel was as precious then as credits are now. People died to protect diesel and petrol."

"But why did they burn fuel they could've used themselves?" It didn't make sense. Why deprive themselves of useable fuel? Phee looked at her father, confident that he'd explain it all in his usual no-nonsense terms.

But Papa looked unhappy, the deep line between his brows darker than ever. "Because sooner or later all revolutions, whether peaceful or bloody, require sacrifices."

A shiver crawled over Phee's skin, leaving uneasy goosebumps in its wake. Her father's hand slipped from her shoulder, bumping against his thigh.

"Why were they fighting, Papa?" Her voice was small, lost in the enormity of the horror the landscape had seen. "I know they've told us stuff in school but really — why was there a war?"

Her father's smile was sad. "Because some people couldn't stand the bad in the world a second longer. They saw children starving in the streets while those in power feasted every night. They saw teenagers executed for daring to speak out. They heard the rich laugh as they watched the poor break their backs every day for a pittance. They saw hell and decided to fight it."

"They were brave," Phee said, her fingers twining around her father's.

"They were insane." He spoke kindly, as he'd done years ago when explaining that two plus two really did equal four. "They started with nothing but anger and dreams and expected to take down a government which had prepared for war for a dozen decades. That's why they lost."

"It's a good thing they lost though, isn't it? That's what they say in school. The rebels killed so many people and destroyed so much land; it's good that they lost."

Phee's father looked at her, then took her face between his hands. Big, blunt hands, she'd always loved them.

"There's an old saying, Phee. 'History is written by the victors'. It's true. Whichever side wins, they discredit the losers. Not everything you read about the rebels is true. And the government covered many terrible things its people did. They were the ones with biological weapons; they poisoned the land. The rebels did what they could with what they had but unfortunately it wasn't enough."

Unfortunately? Nobody ever said things like 'unfortunately' when talking about the rebel defeat.

"Shh, Papa." Phee pulled out of his grasp and threw a look over her shoulder. "You can't say things like that. What if somebody heard you?"

He sank to his knees, heedless of the dirt and ash that coated his clothes. "Someone has to say them, Phee."

A headache was burrowing its way behind Phee's left eye and her stomach was suddenly painful. "Come on, Papa, let's go home, eh? I've got homework to do."

But he knelt motionless in the grime, staring at the ground. After what seemed like an eternity, he dug in the piled ash and held up a spent bullet casing.

Phee looked but made no move to take it. Papa was acting weird and it unsettled her. Something was going on and she wasn't privy to it. Unease cramped her gut. Home seemed like a very pleasant prospect; her bedroom was safe and secure. Why were they out here in the shattered no man's land of the old city's outskirts?

"You know how revolutions start, Phee?" Papa's voice was soft, almost wistful. "They need a spark. Nothing happens on its own. There needs to be something, some event that galvanizes people into action. It takes guts to provide that spark. Might not happen for a generation or two, maybe more. But eventually, somebody stands up and says, 'we want change'. And you know what, Phee?"

He smiled, the flash of teeth lifting years from his face and transforming him back into the man she knew so well.

"The person who stands up; they become a beacon, a figurehead. People see them and begin to believe that things can change. Before you know it, you've got a revolution on your hands. That one person can be the phoenix who rises from the ashes of old defeats."

Phee shoved her hands in her pockets to still their sudden trembling. "Papa, I don't—can we go home now?"

But her father wasn't listening. He grasped her shoulders, fingers digging in. "We need a phoenix, Phee. The bad in the world's starting to outstrip the good. We need things to change. There are plenty of us in agreement; we've got the infrastructure in place. We can do it this time around; we can take on the government and win."

There wasn't enough air in her lungs. She couldn't breathe. Her father's eyes bored into hers but she couldn't look away. She wanted to go home.

She shook her head, "Papa—you can't—you shouldn't say things like that. You could get in trouble."

"The world's already in trouble, Phee," he said, stroking stray hairs back from her face. "But it's not too late, we can save it, save ourselves. We just need somebody to be our figurehead. People won't follow a bunch of dry old men like me. But you. Sweetheart, they'd follow you."

"Papa, I'm fifteen," Phee whispered. "I can't—I'm not—I want to go home."

"Yeah." He stood and smiled down at her. "Home. Home is good. But think about it, okay? We need a phoenix and after all, that is what I named you."

Phoenix—a name she'd never really understood. Now it all made hideous sense. He'd been planning this since the day she was born. Phee: the phoenix from the ashes, the beacon. Something which tasted unpleasantly like betrayal sank deep into her stomach.

"Think about it, Phee," her father urged, his fingers wrapping around her wrist. "We can change the world, make it better. You can be a part of that. You can be the central part, the spark which ignites a revolution."

Phee bit her lip. She didn't want to be a spark; sparks were all too often consumed by the fires they created. But how could she say no to her father?

She turned her back on the shattered fuel station. Behind her, the hologram went on merrily chirping out greetings to non-existent customers.

A new world, revolutions, war, infrastructure already in place—the words buzzed in her mind like flies which couldn't be swatted. A whirlpool of inevitability beckoned, drawing her inexorably in.

Phee—the Phoenix. Could she do it for her father? Could she stand up and make the world a better place?

Maybe. But not today. Today she was simply Phee. The revolution could start without her. She was going home.

CARLOS OROZCO

CLOSE ENOUGH

GOOD MONEY

SILENT NIGHT

CLOSE ENOUGH

"We should have stayed inside the bunker. We came out too soon, didn't we?"

"Yeah."

"Do you think there's a chance we'll make it?"

"No."

"What're the signs of radiation poisoning? My head hurts and I feel like puking. Are—are those the symptoms?"

"Probably."

"What are you looking at?"

"It looks like snow. I've never seen snow before. Have you?"

"Who cares what it is? We're gunna die and you're thinking about snow. It's probably radiation laden ash. My head hurts. Oh my God, my head hurts."

"I've never seen snow. I always wanted a White Christmas. I'd ask Santa for it every year as a kid, and then I prayed to God for it."

"Are you serious? We're dying and all you can think about is snow and Christmas. God's not here. He left us. Besides, it's sometime in July and it's not snow," he managed to say before he doubled over and started puking.

"Close enough," the other man whispered as he lay down to die.

GOOD MONEY

He was paying her good money to hold the makeshift sign. He had to. But he couldn't pay enough for her to be enthusiastic about it. So she held it lackadaisically in one hand while she stared down at her phone and updated newsfeeds.

This job blows, but it's good money.

Ugghh just remembered my rent's due.

She thought of her cockroach infested apartment that reeked of the neighbors' cooking. It was depressing that she stood out here all day to live there. Her life was in shambles and recalling it now made her anxious. From the pit of her stomach arose a nauseous feeling stemming from the realization of her uncertain future.

She'd always thought of finding love, buying a house, and starting a family, but there was no clear path leading from where she was to where she presumed she'd inevitably end up. The only certainty in her future was the bland instant noodles she'd eat until the next time her pervert boss paid her. She hated the taste of them. They reminded her of the communion wafers she consumed in church, back before her parents divorced.

The droves of people alternating to and from restaurants and shopping centers transformed into a kaleidoscope of color through her welling tears. She brushed strands of jet-black hair over her eyes and hung her head, pretending to look at her phone. *I'm making good money*, she told herself, blinking hard to stop the tears.

* * *

Unbeknownst to her, the pervert boss watched her through the dirty window, like he had every day for the past three months, waiting for her to break. That's why he paid her so well, to keep her around. He was like a shark. He sensed the opportunity to strike and proposed the lucrative offer.

"No one will find out, and you could sure use the money. We both benefit, sweetie; it's a win-win," he said in a rehearsed voice that smelled as bad as it sounded.

In the depths of her despair, she agreed. *It's good money,* she thought to herself. And it was good money, but it was never enough money to flush the taste of communion wafers from her mouth.

SILENT NIGHT

*I*t started as a sharp burn, but gradually it faded into a gentle warmth that contrasted the cold night air. He lowered the whiskey bottle from his lips and deeply exhaled, feeling the heat of his breath swirl in his mouth before it escaped into the darkness in a thick haze. He looked down at his leather strapped wristwatch—11:30. Only a half hour before his married lover said she'd arrive.

The lone streetlamp above him buzzed throughout the empty parking lot. It had been turning on and off in no particular pattern, but the incessant drone remained constant. The only disruption in rhythm came from the shrieking wind through sparse branches.

The streetlamp made a slight click and bathed the scene around him in a dim orange flood. The snow from earlier that day had melted, leaving the asphalt wet. The light reflected off the tar of the parking lot in such a way that it seemed to be a menacing pool of deep, dark water. This unsettled him. He feared drowning: visibility and sound choked out by murky indigo water, the empty feel of isolation, and the final panicked inhalations, filling the lungs with death. That's how he imagined it anyway.

A cold sensation crawled throughout the surface of his skin, partially from the frigid temperature and the thought of drowning and partially from the anxiety of waiting. He raised the glass bottle to his cracked lips again and took a swig of the tepid whiskey. The liquid felt warm as it passed over the back of his tongue and fiery as it went down his throat. He wiped his lips with his coat sleeve. The wool rubbed against the thick bristles of his cheeks, and the warming pleasure settled him. He looked at his watch just before the street lamp clicked off—11:58.

He peered out into the starless sky, noticing the moon for the first time. A thin cloud was rapidly moving over it, and soon, much denser clouds began blocking the pale light. Finally, the moon was devoured by darkness. Moments passed and the clouds continued choking out all traces of light. He stood attentive, listening for the sound of her car when he became aware of the silence. No buzzing could be heard. No wind whistling through branches. No sound of approaching vehicles. He looked at his watch and once again shifted his gaze toward the sky. He had never encountered a night sky like this, but it was a peculiarly familiar scene. Dark. Murky. Indigo.

CARLOS OROZCO

DON'T QUIT YOUR DAY JOB

DON'T QUIT YOUR DAY JOB

The two Paris Hilton-looking girls standing by the soda fountain are talking about their ten-year reunion. Actually, they don't look anything like Paris Hilton, but something about them reminds me of her. Maybe it's their mannerisms that are Paris Hilton-like, which, come to think of, I wouldn't be able to recognize. The only thing I know about Paris Hilton is what I see from the television, and I never really pay attention. But, nonetheless, something about them reminds me of her.

I can't help but hear what they are yapping about and neither can the other three people in the store. In the girls' defense, it is a small store. From entrance to back wall it's only three chest-high shelves with drink dispensers and deli to one side and three refrigerator doors on the other. The back wall is decked in promotional beer and cigarette posters whose prices no longer apply.

"What are you staring at?" The shorter, fatter Paris Hilton says to the old guy watching them while pouring his cheap coffee. He apologizes with an inaudible mumble and moves toward the register.

"Can you believe that creep? Total fucking weirdo," the taller, uglier Paris Hilton says while rolling her eyes. I avert my gaze to avoid being called out too. I pretend to look at the bags of chips.

"I don't know. I want to go but at the same time I don't," says the shorter Paris Hilton. "You should totally go. I see a bunch of girls from high school on my newsfeeds, and they're all way worse off than us. Most of those girls don't even have jobs," says the taller Paris Hilton.

"Oh, I know. I see that too. Well, if I go I'm not gunna say I work at the Minute-Mart. I did my niece's senior pictures last year, and they came out super good, so I started taking photos. I have a Facebook page and everything."

"Really? How much did your camera cost?"

"I don't have a camera. I use my phone. I downloaded a photo editing app, but they don't know that. I'm just going to say I'm a photographer."

They both do the fake laugh that sounds like someone gasping for air. I start browsing the miscellaneous aisle looking for the fat-tipped black marker that only this store stocks.

"I mean, technically it's true. The Minute-Mart is just my day job. Once I get more customers, I'll quit and open up a studio." The shorter Paris Hilton places her hands on her hips, and her mouth transforms into a haughty smirk.

"That's it," I blurt out. I regret that decision immediately.

The she lets out a gasp like she's been punched in the gut. "Oh My God CeeCee, it must be national creeper day. They're all out today."

"Ya," says the taller Paris Hilton. I walk to the register. "You better keep walking, loser," she adds.

I drop two markers on the counter and hope the cashier doesn't bide his time. I can hear the girls vomiting insults in my direction. The cashier tells me the total is seven ninety-five. I give him two fives and tell him to keep the change. Before I walk out, I turn around and shout, "Don't quit your day job."

"What do you do for a living that's so great, asshole?" The shorter one says. I don't reply. Instead I let the glass door swing shut behind me.

Her retort gets to me. I think about it the rest of the day while I stare at the brick façade of the old fill station where I work. It's worse than the Minute-Mart and the store where I bought my markers.

There are only two old pumps, one diesel and one unleaded, but no one ever buys gas here. I'm not even sure the pumps work. We never get customers so my pay is shit. The only perk to working here is the store is never open nights, weekends, or holidays. But that's perk enough as it gives me time to work on my street art. I look at my current piece, a ghost girl in a dress, faintly painted on the red brick.

It's not finished yet. It still needs a face. I look at it and think of the short Paris Hilton girl and her "photography". What if others think of my art the same way I think of her pictures? I've never seen her pictures, but I judged her work based on her tools. Don't I use unorthodox tools?

These thoughts fill me with doubt. All of a sudden the perk of my job doesn't seem so special. Why does it matter if I have time to make statements on walls, if people will consider it vandalism? By staying here I'm throwing my life away.

My train of thought is derailed when John exits the store and tells me it's closing time. I nod. He tells me to lock up and hops in his old Chevy truck. I see him turn the key, and the engine sputters to life. The truck bounces when he drives off the curb, and the tires squeal as he accelerates down the road.

I don't bother to lock up. I remove a marker from my pocket and start to draw the face I'd been stumped on. I sketch the smug Paris Hilton smirk that both of the convenience store girls imitated so well. When the shorter girl smirked something clicked, and I knew it was the perfect face.

My fingers twitch as I draw the eyes. I think about my dad and his relentless efforts trying to recruit me for the factory where he and half the town work. It's the only place around here that pays decent, but it's also a life sentence. Working forty for forty they say about it; forty hours a day, for forty years of life. I know that I have to give up painting if I start there because any misdemeanor of felony would get me booted. I wonder if he can still get me a job there. The longer I work, the more I think about it. The longer I think about it, the more certain I am.

I step back and examine my piece. If I hadn't created it I would've thought I was seeing a real ghost. I stare at the ghost girl's smug face until the sun sets, and the parking lot light buzzes on. I'll call my dad when I get home. I'll quit this job in the morning.

CASEY ROSE FRANK

A LIMITED BUT DEFINITIVE TREATISE ON THE PERSONAL RETRIEVAL OF MISSING INVISIBLE ANIMALS BY: DR. IGNATIUS FLOWERS

THE WRITER'S MILL

ON A SUNDAY NIGHT

A LIMITED BUT DEFINITIVE TREATISE ON THE PERSONAL RETRIEVAL OF MISSING INVISIBLE ANIMALS BY: DR. IGNATIUS FLOWERS

Given that those in care of invisible animals are unable to use the usual methods such as pictorial flyers, GPS tracking, or sight to aide in the hunt for their lost companions, a limited but infinitely useful collection of alternative methods has been collected and verified by the author with the intent to get all invisible animals safely back to their keepers/owners/overlords/parents/friends/campaign managers (Please select whichever title best suits your sensibility and ignore all others that offend).

Feel free to read through the entire collection should the urge strike you, though you may feel free to peruse the limited range of animals provided in alphabetical order for your particular lost Invisible Animal.

If you have lost an Invisible Aardvark studies have shown that many are afraid of marshmallows, which may be cause for departure. Please remove the offending items from your home.

If your Invisible Aardvark remains missing or you were not in possession of marshmallows to begin with, try fashioning a peanut butter scented swing in which the Invisible Aardvark would want to relax in, and it is believed that it will be swinging away in no time.

If you have lost an Invisible Hedgehog please try the following method for relocation:

Shout "Edith" to the tune of "Yankee Doodle Dandy" paying particular attention to prolong the "E" sound across the end of the second line of the first verse.

Unless, the hedgehog's name is not Edith, in which case pursuing this method means you run the risk of further estrangement from the missing animal.

If you have lost an Invisible Llama run and hide! Run like you are being chased like hungry wolves and hide like you are a stick insect in the forest. You must hide.

Because Invisible Llamas like a good game of hide and seek and can't pass up an opportunity to be a seeker. They'll find you, and conveniently you'll have found them in return.

If you have lost an Invisible Sloth please be mindful that unlike their visible counterparts, this species is slightly faster and more likely to be outside of your immediate circle of physical space within a few minutes. Invisible Sloths are often in pursuit of raspberries, lettuce, fashionable hats for wearing—not eating—and potassium hydroxide. If any of these items are in your house you are likely to find your invisible sloth in their vicinity.

Should that not be the case, adding these items to your home may increase your chance of them returning on their own.

If you have lost an Invisible Snake it is recommended by George Washington (Please note this is not the first president of the United States, George Washington, but George Washington of Boise, Idaho—a renowned macramé enthusiast) to mimic the motions of the Invisible Snake in order to gain its trust and boost its self confidence so that it may once again return to your arm chair.

Mr. Washington also recommends using honey to paint a portrait of a mouse on your counter as a treat for your Invisible Snake, much like giving a ice cream cone to a melancholy child.

If you have lost an Invisible Baby Wallaby the author asks that you treat this treatise with the scientific gravitas that it deserves and understand once and for all that Invisible Baby Wallabies do not exist.

THE WRITER'S MILL

*W*riters! Having a hard time finishing your novel? Looking for a change of pace, the perfect place to settle down and finish your masterpiece? At The Writer's Mill you'll find serenity, seclusion, and inspiration. Join us and become the best writer you can be!

The ad had seemed tacky at first. Joan abhorred copy that included exclamation points. But as she had clicked through the pictures of the old red brick building and the idyllic growths of ivy that seemed a nod to the kind of buildings that housed the best and brightest at prestigious schools, the doubts began to wane.

She could imagine her mind behaving like the sparkling river that rushed below the windows of the building, moving smoothly over writer's block now made the size of river pebbles in its wake.

The pictures of the large bedroom with a four poster bed, decked out with some of the richest-looking bedding she had every seen, and a large oak desk tucked under a window that streamed with sunlight were the final clincher.

She had three hundred pages of what she thought was an elegant, thought-provoking novel that she had been struggling to finish.

She emailed the proprietor to inquire as to when she might be able to begin her stay and was pleased to discover that she could arrive in two weeks and have the place to herself for at least a month.

Joan made the arrangements and arrived at "The Writer's Mill" excited to submerge herself in her writing.

She spent mornings writing at the desk from the pictures, coffee and pastries on hand. She walked in the afternoons, mentally working out plot issues and picking bright wildflowers. At night she slept the deep sleep that only sumptuous linens and fresh country air could provide.

Finally, she finished her book.

Joan gave her notice to the proprietor.

Two days later, as Joan left the building with her suitcase in hand, a woman appeared on the walkway just before the short bridge over the river.

"Congratulations on finishing your work! I hope you enjoyed your stay with us," she said.

"I did, thank you. I think I've got something special here," Joan said.

"Perhaps you do," she answered and brought out a pistol and shot Joan. Joan tumbled into the rushing water below.

The woman calmly opened Joan's suitcase and pulled out the manuscript.

Another book to sell to her agent. God bless The Writer's Mill.

ON A SUNDAY NIGHT

*F*eeling leaden, George sinks into his couch staring at nothing.

Night after night he sits. Waiting. Waiting for the night to be over, for his sadness to tire itself out.

The night is a time for lovers to fall asleep in each other's arms as he once did.

But now she is suspended within the weight of the earth and he waits for each night to unspool the last of its darkness before morning comes and he somehow feels less alone.

As he stares out the window at a city that is quieter and more muted if not entirely asleep, he sees the smooth curve of a pale cream balloon float past his window.

His first thought is that someone has lost a dream.

He sees another. And another.

He stands and moves closer to the glass of his street-facing window, his own blurry reflection coming closer as they meet in the middle.

George looks down at the black and blue night-bound street.

On the corner, in the fringes of the streetlight's spotlight circle, there is a woman standing, letting them go one at a time into the night sky.

She still holds fifteen or twenty in her right hand and with her left deftly chooses the next one for flight. She pulls a string free from the others and raises her hand out and up to set it free.

From his fifth floor apartment George can see this movement but little of her face; he cannot tell how old she is or if she is happy or sad to be letting these orbs of light float away.

He hears raised voices, a conversation between two people who are unaccustomed to the quiet of the night. Their ears still full and buzzing from whatever sound saturated place they have just been.

They pass on the opposite side of the street from where the woman stands. They seem not to notice her.

She is far enough away that it is only the fickle wind that is responsible for the balloons' proximity to his window.

The window fogs and fades a small circle as he breathes.

Why is she doing this? Where will these balloons end up? George feels an uncomfortable mix of pleasure at this oddly beautiful moment, and panic that this woman is performing some ritual of severance that he cannot understand.

She lets go of her final balloon and waits, watching to see it disappear from view, her face tilted toward the sky. She only stands still. Nothing else.

George wonders if she can see him. If so, he imagines that he must be as faceless to her as she is to him.

Apparently finished, she turns and walks down the street and around the corner and out of George's view.

CASEY ROSE FRANK

CHROMA MOBILE

CHROMA MOBILE

*T*here's a sudden burst of music, strong and overwhelming before it begins to slide and warp, oozing for a couple beats before speeding up to the original tempo.
"I am Diana Diesel
and I'm here to help you
Rising up to the challenge of gas mileage
And the snacks that you love
we keep fresh in our store
So you always get where you should be, Chroma Mobile!"
We watch a garish hologram, a young woman dancing and cheering, her face and body turned green from a missing layer of color. Her version of "Eye of the Tiger" was meant to inspire, but out here, in this deteriorated fashion, it unnerves. As the automated hologram shuts down, layer after layer of color drops individually instead of all at once, and I see a ghostly white specter with empty black eyes.

"Chroma Mobile, because you can't just straight up call a company 'Murder Mobile'," Carl says behind me.

There are five of us who have been traveling together. We had started out as seven. I suppose we had really started out as many, part of families and communties that belongs to a before that is too jagged to think about.

"Well, Murder Mobile is our ironic lunch ticket today, God willing, so let's get inside," said Ali. She was a real woman, but she too had lost layers of color. Outside and in. Months of walking and scavenging had made angular specters with draining eyes of us as well.

The windows and glass doors were intact, which meant it was unlikely that anyone had already pillaged all the food from inside. Sense memory told me that I should expect a blast of icy air when I opened the door on a hot day like today, but I was greeted by stale unmoving air only a shade cooler than the outside.

We knew the coolers would be untouchable, the lack of electricity rendering them coffins for their contents, but there were still rows of untouched, unspoiled, processed food.

I felt like Charlie Bucket winning a golden ticket, exploring the wares of a magical factory, side by side with my other winners. My excitement to see so many bags of chips and beef jerky made me feel like sitting down and crying. There were even bottles of water sitting on the shelves, ready for our consumption.

To get to them I had to pass a rack of magazines. An impending disaster across the country was barely visible here. Disaster of a real human scale doesn't read well in bright pink font. Promises of looking thinner in one week does. I suppose we got both.

Maura found boxes of garbage bags and opens some to swipe all of the light food items into one large bag. She hoisted the full bag over her shoulder like a sad beige and black Santa and once again I want to cry for all that we have lost.

Imagination feels cruel and yet I wonder if my fellow travelers imagine a time when we might have the lives we once had, clutching images of long table feasts and swimming pools, instead of blankets, as we fall asleep at night.

As we leave the store our automated performer appears once more. She sings her spiel to the backs of fellow ghosts as we walk back out into a deserted land.

KRISTEN FALSO-CAPALDI

AUTHORITIES WARN AGAINST SEEKING TIME
TRAVEL ON CRAIG'S LIST

IMPORTANCE

DEAD SEA LIONS

AUTHORITIES WARN AGAINST SEEKING TIME TRAVEL ON CRAIG'S LIST

She found him through an ad on Craig's List.

It was the photo that hooked her. It featured a bunch of dead daisies with a caption, which said: "Wish you could turn back time? Miracle Man Makes It Happen!"

She thought, it's probably a scam. It's got to be a scam. It's a scam. But she called him anyway. His name was Ralph. She wasn't quite sure what she expected for a Miracle Man—'Zeus,' maybe? But Ralph was the Miracle Man. He told her to meet him in a parking lot on the north end of the city.

He stood about 5' 6" tall and was wiry, kind of twitchy too, with an unctuous smile and a clammy handshake. A photo of the dead flowers was attached to the side of his 1991 Mitsubishi Mirage.

"What can I do for you my dear?"

"I need to go back to March first."

"Why?"

"That was the day my little sister died."

"How?"

"We were driving, and I hit a tree. If I could go back, I'm sure I can save her."

"Payment is $100."

"Will it hurt?"

"Oh, quite a bit, my dear. But don't worry. You won't remember a thing."

She paid him, and he performed a ritual. It didn't make much sense to her, but she did indeed go back in time, and she did indeed save her sister.

He just didn't tell her about the catch.

The next day he got a phone call. He met the young woman in the parking lot.

She said, "Send me back to March first."

"Why?"

"My older sister died in a car accident. I need to go back and fix things."

"Payment, my dear, is $100. He smiled and she handed over the money with trembling hands.

He knew the next day he would receive a phone call. And the next. He promised himself he'd stop when he got to $1000, but the sisters continued to call. He needed a new car. And a hot tub. Really, he had so many expenses. He'd stop as soon as he got to $2000.

Really, he would.

IMPORTANCE

*I*t was his photo that made her disappear. She was the beauty who sat next to him in sophomore English, the one with chestnut hair and little dresses in swirls of color. She had a nice smile and friends and two feet on the ground. She was opaque.

He was thin, pale. Transparent. He felt himself slipping away.

He loved her then.

He began to follow her. And always with the yearbook camera slung across his back. He knew every place she went, every conversation she had.

Then. The photo. He snapped it unnoticed from a doorway, then sent it spiraling into the world through a web of wireless routers and fiber optic cables.

What he'd done made him important to certain people. He grew opaque. He was still the shadow following them with a camera, but now they talked to him, waved, shoved beers into his hands. He had to stop loving her; someone had to be the sacrifice.

And she began to fade.

Now they were seniors. Her hair was bleached colorless and her lips painted dark red. She wore black. She floated through the halls unnoticed.

Not by him. In a secret file on his hard drive, he saved the hundreds of photos he'd taken of her over the years. In some, she slept in class, in others she smoked weed by the bleachers. In a few, she was a speck hundreds of feet down a crowded hallway.

Every day, he'd look at them in order, beginning with the first ignominious one, then he'd watch her age and change, drain of color and fade.

Each time he finished looking at them, he'd whisper the same two words.

First: "Sorry."

Then: "Thanks."

He snapped the last one at graduation. She was standing by the parking lot, arguing with her mother.

Then, he got up and delivered a speech to his peers about importance.

That night, he placed the final photo in the secret file, then he looked through them one last time.

"Sorry," he said. Then: "Thanks."

He sat in silence for a few seconds, then dragged the file into the trash.

DEAD SEA LIONS

"The ocean is very cleansing," she says to me, for no particular reason. We've been walking along, skirting the waves, and these are the first words she's spoken.

I admit I kind of liked the silence. And the fact that I didn't have to look at her. My little sister. Princess in the tower. The waif. I search my brain for a comeback.

"Yes, I hear the salt water is good for poison ivy," I might say, even though neither of us has ever had poison ivy.

She's looking off toward the water; there is rapture in her gaze, like she's staring at the massive statue of Jesus on the Cross at Our Lady of Good Health. We used to sit on either side of our mother; she'd pinch us if we misbehaved. Then she'd point, inexplicably, at Jesus. I'd look off toward the small choir singing off key, but my sister locked her eyes on Jesus' wounds.

"That must have hurt," she said to me once.

"I suppose so."

We haven't spoken in a year. Today I need to tell her something sad.

"Our mother is ill now," I plan to say. "She will need care, and there isn't much money. If it happens again, you'll go to a state hospital."

She screams. For a moment I think maybe I spoke, and she is reacting to what I've said, but then I look down.

A baby sea lion has washed up on the shore, its bloated body slick and black. Its face peaceful, like it's smiling in its sleep. I almost step on it.

We both stare at its deadness, its beauty. The surge of tears from my eyes startles me. My sister pushes her sleeve up and scratches her wrist. Her movement is quick, but I'm sure I see a flash of raw, pink flesh.

We walk on. Another one lies dead, the surf bubbling over its body, rinsing as it recedes.

Then, another one. Then another. Another. By the fifth corpse, my tears have receded, and I study the ebb and flow of the ocean. I don't realize my sister has been sobbing for some time now.

"I hope they didn't suffer," she says.

We walk back to the hotel. I tell the manager, a portly man with a stained baseball cap, about the five dead sea lions.

He nods.

"Shouldn't you call someone?" I ask.

A humorless laugh escapes him. I eye my sister through the office window. She's standing in the sand staring down the beach.

"It doesn't seem right," I say.

He shrugs his shoulders.

"Won't you call someone?" I ask again. I feel my voice rising to an hysterical pitch.

"Who?"

"There must be something we can do," I'm yelling at him now. "Can't we do something?"

"There's nothing to be done," he says.

I slam the door behind me. I have to jog to catch up with my sister. She has already begun retracing our steps.

KRISTEN FALSO-CAPALDI

DEMONS

DEMONS

People are ugly when they cry. I knew a guy in the joint who said it was how you could see the demons inside them. I don't know if he meant demons as in monsters (aren't we all monsters?) or demons as in those memories you push down like bile. My kid sister Maria loves talking about demons. She says to me, whenever I call, "Jimmy, you've got demons." Jesus.

I was nine the last time I cried. My old man backed his car over my bike. I expected a good backhand; he just picked up the bike and tossed it to the side. He tossed me then too. I wailed on the grass next to that heap of mangled metal.

I haven't cried since. Not during the war. Not when I picked up that little girl's body, her brains fertilizing the blackened ground in her blackened village. I still see that little girl. Lately I see a lot of things.

Uncle Ted, my old man's younger brother, he gave me a job at his gas station when I got out of the joint a few months back. I keep wondering if I'm going to do anything after this. Anything worth doing, that is. 1979, man. I'll be thirty next year. The old man died at sixty-two. My life is half-over.

Since I've been working here, I've been seeing things. They're transparent, like a film strip projected on a screen; barely there, but they're there. Sometimes I see the old man. He's clenching his fists and his mouth is moving, but I can't hear him. Doesn't matter. I know what he's saying. Or I see this guy in the joint, used to point his fork real close to other inmates' eyes, take their food. Then I see those children in that village—ah, skip it. Nobody wants to hear about that again. Sometimes I see my mom sitting in front of the old black and white TV, her face like a "Do Not Disturb" sign. Her eyes saying "No Vacancy."

It's the woman that rattles me; she's the only one I can't place. She has a 1950's hairdo and cat glasses. Something about her smile almost makes me cry.

* * *

I asked uncle Ted if I could work inside today, run the register. He said ok, but he watches me. It wasn't for being handsome that I ended up in the joint. But I wouldn't steal from old Ted. He's as pure inside as my old man was rotten.

I call my kid sister because she's the only friend I got. Sometimes, I like to stop and listen to her listening.

She says, after I'm done telling her about these things I've been seeing, "Demons, Jimmy. Demons."

"Again with the demons?"

"In your life? Yeah."

"What if I don't believe in demons?"

"You're seeing them aren't you?"

I hear waves and screaming gulls in the background; Maria lives on the beach. She's lived on one body of water or another since she left home at sixteen. Says it's the only place she can think. I asked her once what she thinks about and she said, "I've got demons, same as you."

That sounds like the worst kind of thinking there is. Bury yourself in noise and heat and chaos, the demons stay nice and quiet.

I look through the window at Ted pumping gas. It's so hot today, steam is rising from the asphalt; all the cars buzzing around make me dizzy.

"This woman, she scares me, Maria."

Maria points out the obvious, that I'm a god-damn war veteran who just got out of jail for armed robbery.

I say goodbye and go back outside, and I start seeing things again. The woman is just smiling away. My face twitches, but I hold onto my tears.

Uncle Ted pats my shoulder.

"Jimmy," he says. "You look funny. Go for a walk."

When I walk past the diner down the street, I see the woman again. I mean, the *real* her. She's older, her hair is mostly silver, and she's wearing a waitress uniform, but it's her. I run back to the gas station, my face is red and I'm panting. It's 97 degrees today in Sun Valley. Old Ted, he just looks at me.

That night, I can't sleep. I come in to work coiled. I see the usual things, but it's the woman that makes me spill gas on my shoes.

"Take a break, Jimmy," Ted says.

At the diner, I sit in her section and order a coffee. She doesn't smile when she puts it down. I read her name-tag, *Ida.*

"Don't know any Ida," Maria says that night on the phone. The ocean swallows her voice. "Could she be somebody you've hurt? You wounded that security guard that time. Maybe he's her son."

"You promised you'd never bring that up."

"Desperate measures, Jimmy."

* * *

The next morning, the real Ida brings me a coffee. She doesn't smile.

"Was your son—" I sputter, feeling stupid and terrified at the same time. "—a security guard?"

"Nope. Want anything else?"

At the gas station, the transparent images are everywhere. But it's funny; I could watch that little girl die a million times, my mom stare at the TV, and my father holler. Fat Manny touches his fork to someone's eye. But

Ida? I hold my breath and count to ten, make my face like stone, but I can feel the fight draining out of me.

"What's eating you, Jimmy?" Ted asks.

I take off running. I bang on the front window of the diner. Ida looks at me through the glass, her eyes dull and cold. I bury my face inside my t-shirt collar, press the fabric against my closed lids.

That night, as soon as my sister answers, I start blubbering, hard. I come so close to putting my fist through my bathroom mirror.

"I'm ugly, Maria. I'm so god-damn ugly."

* * *

The next day I go straight to the diner, but Ida is gone.

"Take a couple of days off, Jimmy," Ted says.

I borrow Ted's Chevy and I drive toward the coast. At a stop light near LA, I look over and there's Ida - the *real* Ida - driving an old truck. She's crying. I follow her till she pulls up to a hotel in Beverly Hills, goes inside and follows the signs that say, "Awards Luncheon." Then, just like that, I remember.

She's an actress.

She was on the soap opera my mother watched. With the curtains drawn and the windows closed, even in summer, the TV screen was the only light in that house. That soap opera, it was always on;

I was nine, running inside, crying with grass stains on my jeans;

I was twelve, my face like steel, listening to the old man yelling at me;

I was eighteen the last time I was in that house. Maria had already run off with that hippy. I was leaving for the war;

"Goodbye, Ma."

My mother, staring at the TV - at Ida on the TV - and waving, not at me but at the door I was about to walk through.

Ida turns around and sees me.

"I know you," I say.

She walks toward me.

"It's been a long time," she says, "since anybody recognized me."

"You were always on TV."

"For years and years."

"You gave my mother a lot of—" I'm about to say 'joy,' but I say instead, "You made her life bearable."

Ida looks toward a room where a man is setting up a microphone.

"You might have been the only person she loved."

"I wasn't real."

I start crying then. I expect Ida to run away, but she stays put. I tell her how my life is half-over and how all I got are demons, and they're busting out. About how I never cried, and now I can't stop. And how the ugliness is everywhere, not just inside of me.

"I cried today," she says. "First time in twenty years."

"Why did you cry today?"

"I'd been trying not to remember—who I was."

"You used to smile a lot."

She looks sad.

"I've got to go," she says. "They're giving me a lifetime achievement award."

* * *

The hot air inside Ted's Chevy is thick, and the traffic shakes the whole car. I'm sobbing again. A Halloween mask looks back at me from the rear-view mirror, except it's me. Who I was and who I am. I wonder what happened to who I could've been.

Two hours later, I sit with Maria on her porch in Santa Barbara. I cry. I don't cry. I listen to my sister listening.

"I keep wondering if I'm going to do anything after this," I say.

Maria stands up, stretches and looks at the ocean.

I can tell she's thinking, so I don't say anything else. I just watch the sunset and take a breath.

CATHERINE CONNOLLY

BITE

THE DESCENT

SAMPLING SPIRITS

BITE

I need to leave her. Before it's too late. Perhaps it already is. Perhaps I know that, really. Heather was gone tonight when I woke, darkness surrounding me. Pitch. I reached for her and she wasn't there - the sheets which should have held her warmth cold, no dint indicating she had been there recently. We fell asleep together, curled around each other, my hand caressing the puckered scab at her shoulder – the ridges already healing; indentations becoming less distinct. Somehow, she has managed to move from me; to evade any conversation over why she strolls the night. A new burgeoning, burning light behind her eyes. Signalling the inevitable. What will come. The becoming. Beckoning heat. Neither of us has managed to say the words. Not yet. Not until the inevitable. Until it falls apart. Maybe not even then.

I remember the night too well. The one which matters most. To us. She stumbled through the door, hair tangled about her shoulders, clumped with dirt, leaves; remnants of congealed blood. Jacket lost, top frayed. God alone knew how she had made it home that way. Her fingers left smudge marks against the wood and wallpaper; streaks of mud, mixed with the aftermath of what had gone before.

"It's not as bad as it looks," she said. Still, she refused to meet my eyes. That told me enough. "They just grazed the skin. Hardly anything, really."

"What? They? What?" The words refused to collate; to form solid sentences. "I – what?"

"The teeth." Her lips quivered slightly, unshed tears beneath her lids. "Should have just phoned a taxi, I guess. Stupid." There was a brief lift beneath the words before the slump. Literal and figurative, as Heather used the wall as her prop. The paper would need replacing – sooner rather than later, if it wasn't to act as reminder. I would see to it, I told myself. Without fuss.

"I heard it coming." A tremble in her voice. "I wish I hadn't."

I thought that was the worst. Then. Now I know better.

It crept upon us slowly. The realisation. That there would be consequences. Darkness made her restless. She tossed and turned a lot. To be expected. Her temperature ran high – not dangerously so. The GP administered injections to prevent against lingering infection, the fear of fever. We thought that the end of things, save for the delicate ridged scar gracing her shoulder. The preternaturally quick to heal, lasting reminder.

Night taught us better, as insomnia gave way to wilful wandering. Too little, way too late. Nothing could have prevented it. I think I knew that first night; knew without knowing. The moon's crescendo towards apex. Waxing. Could scarcely fail to notice the night Heather came home, the cool of after hours amongst her locks, the taste of copper on her lips as I kissed her a welcome. Reddened by something other than natural high colour, though that was there too. Heightened above normality. Heat in her gaze; amber in her eyes, once chocolate in colour. I purposefully forgot copper that night; concentrated instead on amber and gold.

Try as I might, I should have – must have – realised matters would reach their climax. Moon full, white above, no avoiding the merciless light. Her gaze burns through me, fever pitch, on her return. Flames fanned by whatever went before. Tonight I see the evidence stained across the white enamel of her teeth, cherry red matching grin accompanying it. Breath rich with the scent of others. Information I did not need access to.

No more avoiding. Secrets will out, one way or another – especially those which have been open for a while. Tonight they may consume us. Or one will be consumed.

Even seeing her this way, it's hard not to want what we had; what went before the now. I feel myself falling, plunging deep towards the dark. Pull myself back from the brink. Barely. I know her name. Sadly, much as I try to delude myself, it's no longer Heather. It is the other.

We face off. Now's the time. Fight or flight. Focused versus fearful. Predator. Prey. Now. Teeth reach towards me, to administer a final lover's caress. To bite.

THE DESCENT

The ruby red, rounded shape was there waiting first thing in the morning; strategically set on top of the sheets, when she woke. Truthfully speaking, she has been expecting it for days, having dreamt of the grove of trees from which the junction of the rivers stems and the thick roots topped by the white funnel shaped blooms amidst the swarms of squeaking shadows.

It is his way of playing, though as far as she is concerned, things are properly played out by this point in time. She needs no outsized reminder of his enforced obligations. "Hellfire!" she says, before the corners of her mouth twitch slightly at the words. "And damnation indeed," she adds, to an empty room. She splits the fruit in a swift downward motion, causing a dribble of juice to stain the covers. The seeds are packed in tightly amidst the flesh, so she has to dig a little with her nails to pull them out, right from the centre. She counts a sparse translucent six; no more, no less. "Figures," she says, toying with a pip between her fingers, before raising it aloft and swallowing it down. She shudders as she does so, frowning slightly. "Pigging pomegranates! Still sour, then." She pushes one after another after another past her lips in quick succession, once she has stilled herself from swallowing the first. Red stains her fingers, which she licks clean, wiping the sticky residue against her dark dress, irrespective of whether it shows or not against the dark fabric. Their bitterness leaves its aftertaste on her lips, as the seeds churn in her stomach, refusing to settle fully. She knows of old when and where the sensation will cease.

Sephy sits, waiting for her escort into darkness; possibly Darkness himself, though she is most used to the company of obol-eyed Charon on her lengthy descents. Easier to send someone who can't answer back to challenge, query or quandary, she suspects. She has never been trusted to walk the sections of the realm alone on entry, though left to her own devices on leaving. "Take me to my husband," she mutters beneath her breath, rolling her eyes. He tends to keep her waiting, despite the early fruity wake up call.

She feels them already—the simple skeletons, the frozen, the eternally blood-spattered alike. Soon she will – must- pass amongst them again. It is small consolation that she must serve only three months. They do not – cannot – care, though for a time they are her people, without being capable of answering as such.

The door in front of Sephy opens and her eyes acknowledge the figure crossing the threshold. She crosses to him, holding out her hand to take his. They clasp palms and the bony fingers close firmly around her own. Sephy nods. "Ready," she says. "Again." The journey into the heart of Hades is long, capable of seeming to encompass one's lifetime, though Sephy knows the truth. She will endure this cycle forever on repeat.

SAMPLING SPIRITS

"Young," Matt states decisively, passing the unmarked bottle to his left.

Sam sniffs. "Too imprecise a classification, I'd say."

"Right though, aren't I?"

"Sweet yet spicy," Sam counters, setting his glass down. "Do we have another?"

"Try this one. Dex brought it with." A suit clad male lounging lazily at the far side of the table raises a mostly empty glass as they glance across.

"Do we know where he got it?"

"Do you care?"

"I guess not. Hope he was careful though. If word of The Distillery gets out…"

"Then what?"

"Nothing, I guess…" Matt places a large black glass into Sam's left hand and a smaller version into his right.

Sam raises an eyebrow. "Guess Dex doesn't want his source traced. Pretty precautionary."

"We're in it together. Besides, you said it. Where's the evidence once we've drunk it all?"

Sam's eyes flash once, locking in, then away. "Swirl," he says, though the colour of the glass prevents it.

"Sniff," Matt responds.

"Sip." Sam raises the liquid to his lips, sampling.

"Savour," Matt says.

"Complex," Sam concludes. "A beauty, I'd say. Make sure she doesn't go to waste." He passes the larger glass to the other man. "You'll appreciate this one – or, rather, you'd better. Dex is becoming a connoisseur in the sensory perception selection process, sly dog. Love to know where he found this one. Might even ask him if I can have the bottle." Sam's mouth quirks slightly at the quip.

"Any more for any more?" Sam asks, when Matt does not respond in kind. The debris and detritus of their evening is in front of them; numerous empty glasses and bottles they have drunk their way through already, mere dregs at the bottom, scarcely enough to fill a quarter of a glass.

"Just this, I think." Matt gestures to a wide bottomed flask.

"Vintage?" Sam queries, as Matt swigs a sip, before grimacing.

"Vinegar," he says, wincing.

They look towards Jem to their far left, accusing. "Perfectly captured," he responds, saluting them with his own glass. "Pretty sour when we were together. Had to get rid of her somehow. Feel free to stick her down the sink."

CATHERINE CONNOLLY

FUELLED

FUELLED

"God, I'm *sure* I could smell it, you know!" Beth said. "Copper," she added, shuddering violently. "Cold." She paused. "Steak," she finished, grimacing.

"Better this than the alternative," Dan said, grimly. "Plus, you're thinking about it too much. Don't." A pause. "Added to which, it won't help, anyway."

"S'pose."

"No supposing about it," Helen responded, shifting her own container in her arms. Its contents slid from side to side audibly. "Besides, it's not like we were given much choice over it. It's our civic duty, didn't y'know?" Briefly, her voice became louder, with an alternative intonation. "Plus, it doesn't—and *can't*—smell," she said, words clipped. "They told us it was fresh—and sealed beneath plastic for the minute."

"Wish I hadn't got it under my fingernails with the boxing," Beth commented. "They should've given us proper gloves. Hygiene, for one thing. *And* I can still see it in there. They could've gone for opaque. Wouldn't that have been the least they could have done in the circumstances? I mean, *really*?"

"Shut up," Helen said. "I don't want to think about that. Especially not right now. Seriously."

"I guess." Beth hesitated. "Wish I'd known we were on duties before though. Wouldn't've bothered having my nails done. It'll stain if I can't get them clean quickly." She displayed fingers coated with brownish traces towards the pair.

"Let's just get done and away," Dan said, without looking at the hands Beth was waving in front of him. "I don't want to be here anymore than you do."

"We're exempt next time, right?" Helen asked.

"That's what *I* thought," Dan answered. "Rules keep changing though, don't they? Including when the draw happens. I mean, why so soon after the last time? Don't think there are any guarantees of anything anymore."

"It's the yard, isn't it? That's the spot? Within the complex?"

"They made that pretty clear," Dan said. "Glad not to know the answer for myself, not having been picked before. Not particularly pleasant, from what I've heard."

"Thanks for sharing," Helen said.

"We're all friends here," Dan responded, the corner of his mouth quirking. "Figure we should at least all know what we're in for."

"Kind of preferring *not* knowing here," Beth said.

"Did you speak to Sam about it?" Helen asked.

"Didn't get chance," Dan said. "He was off pretty much after his go. Spoke to his folks about it. Can't say I blame him, really. I'm planning on getting as far away as possible to forget it now I'm fully in the know. Don't really want to get pegged for a second go at any point—which seems like a distinct possibility if the Community keeps switching things up the way they have been doing lately. Not planning on keeping in touch either; no offence."

"None taken here," Helen said. "Sounds pretty much like a plan to me, to be fair. Might even do likewise."

"Let's have at it, then. Feeding time at the zoo, folks!" The words were cheerful. The tone with which they were spoken less so.

"Grab the gate, Beth," Dan instructed.

The red haired girl slid the metal framework across, its hinges shrieking as she did so. "God, it hurts your ears, doesn't it?" she said, wincing. "You'd've thought they'd've had it oiled by now, really."

"Feeders are the only ones who come here," Helen said. "Guessing they're not too bothered, save for getting in and out. Also—it's not like a certain somebody's been using traditional entrances or exits recently or is likely to need to any time soon, is it?"

"True," Beth said. "Any time soon?" she asked. "Like *ever*, you mean, surely?" Her lips tweaked slightly at the corners, before turning downwards again. "It's flippin' *freezing* too! Should've worn a jumper." She brushed vigorously up and down her arms, hopping from foot to foot on the spot.

"Style over substance, hon," Helen responded. "What have I told you about that?" She raised an eyebrow at the other girl, who grimaced back, brow crinkling.

"Give it a rest!" Dan said sharply. His eyes were sweeping the brick buildings, their windows devoid of light and tarmacked courtyard, left to right, even as he spoke.

"Sure thing...*Boss*," Beth returned, glaring. She shook her head. "Where are we putting these, then? Did they say? Is that when we get to cut and run?" She looked directly at the jeans clad teenager, eyes widening slightly, as she spoke. "Didn't really take it all in at the time, to be honest. Didn't expect to be *picked*, really, having been lucky before."

"Somewhere in the centre," Dan answered shortly.

"X marks the spot? I mean, *really*?"

"Shut *up*!" Dan snapped. He looked briefly at Beth, making eye contact, before his gaze was roving once again over the crumbling mortar and cracked glass panes barely held in place by wooden frames displaying the first signs of rot and then beyond. "There's something..."

"Some *thing*?" Helen asked, smirking. "Sure there is," she carried on easily. "That's why we're here, after all, isn't it?"

"Not what I meant," the teenager responded.

"God, you're *pathetic*," Beth said. "Pretty cheap trick trying to freak us out now. Like I wasn't grossed out enough already. Wasn't it you who wanted to get it all over and done with, anyway? Suddenly so keen on stringing it out?"

"That's not it," Dan said quickly. "You *know* it's not! It's not like any of us wanted to be here – or anyone else who already has been, for that matter! There's something else…" His words tailed off.

"Like what?" Beth looked towards Dan. There was a sudden silence between them. "Really—*what?*" Beth added. "See—I *knew* you were full of…" she began, voice louder, pitch increasing, before Helen's raised hand caught her attention.

"Guys? Hate to interrupt the tête à tête but what exactly *is* that?"

Dan looked in the direction the dark haired girl's finger was now pointing. He squinted briefly, shifting his glasses further up his nose, before moving closer towards the white fragment on the tarmac surface. "Looks harmless enough. It's just sitting there." He squatted on his haunches, picking it up between his fingertips, before examining the surface, turning it over and then back over again. Finally, he stood in one motion and moved back towards the two girls. "It's an envelope," he said, nonplussed.

"You don't *say*," Beth said, the words knife sharp.

With that, Dan was tearing the paper flap apart and pulling a single pale sheet from inside. He scanned the contents, before reading the words typed on it. "The Community thanks you for your service." After a pause, he added, "That's it. There's no more. Not even a sign off. Undated."

Beth took it from him, looking it over.

"What? You still don't believe me?"

"He's right," Beth said, shrugging, looking towards Helen, without giving him a direct answer. Helen was silent, brow creased, as she looked from one to the other, then back again. She did not reach for the piece of paper to take it from Beth.

Somewhere behind them there was a sudden loud solitary clang, which reverberated before dying out into silence. As one, the group turned quickly towards it. "Gate's shut," Dan said, grimly. "Who did that?" He got no immediate response from either of the two girls.

"*Service*," Helen exclaimed suddenly, eyes wide and looking straight into Dan's. "The note! D'you *get* it?" Her lips quivered slightly. Dan's brow was creased as he held her gaze without speaking. Helen's breath was coming slightly more rapidly as she waited for him to respond. The rise and fall of her chest was noticeable. Beth reached a hand towards her, her expression troubled, before the silence which had descended in the aftermath of Helen's words was interrupted by a loud barking laugh—a hearty and extended peal. With that, they were turning again en masse, with the exit at their back to face the owner of it; knowing already what—and who—they would see.

"I get it," Dan said, words flat. He did not look at Helen. His eyes were caught rabbit-fast by those of the semi-transparent grinning girl, with gaping chasms; yawning, depthless deep pitch pits, where eyes should be. It was possible to see sharp white teeth between her parted lips. Their rims were reddened beyond natural colour. "Pretty visible right now, hey? Clearer than they said, right?"

There was an audible intake of breath from Beth. With that, she was dropping the container she had been carrying, the slivers of meat strewing across the floor in front of it. "I'm going to be sick!" she announced, retching. Helen reached out in her direction, though her eyes remained on the figure before them. Imperceptibly, she moved closer towards Dan, bringing them all together. With that they were grabbing hold of each other's hands, holding tightly onto them, as the laugh sounded once more, loud and mocking. "Feeding time at the zoo," Helen whispered.

A.J. WALKER

REBOOT

PUMPKINHEAD

THE DIVERTING TALE OF THE MONKEY MAN

REBOOT

*F*ollowing his short Powerpoint explanation of the plan Bubbles sat back satisfied.

'I like it, boys,' said Grebbo, looking enthusiastically around the assembled faces. 'Neat.'

'Not too complicated neither,' Davos nodded.

'Yep, not too many parts to go wrong,' said Spamhead. 'Not like last time.'

As one the gang peered at Spamhead.

Steady looked at his crew, clapping his hands together. 'Right, I think we can safely say we have a decent plan here. This will be world changing boys. Bubbles, simply great stuff.'

Grebbo clapped the diminutive Scot on his back. 'Well done. Class.'

The following week, with the confidence from the simple plan and a couple of successful trials behind them, the delivery boys - Grebbo and Spamhead - swopped the gas masks in the hotel storeroom for theirs, taking away those remaining to leave exactly nineteen. It should have been twenty but for Spamhead giving the wrong one to poor late Davos in the first trial.

As the G20 summit came to its usual petering out stage the crew watched the rolling BBC coverage with growing anticipation. Steady selected "Send to All" and at 2.26pm the email went out to Government press secretaries and news agencies throughout the world.

"The Capitalist System has failed. Following today's 2.30pm attack the world's self nominated most important countries will be leaderless. Let the world take this opportunity to start again with a blank page and an honest heart." It was signed off, "From, Reboot".

At 2.29pm timed devices went off in the air conditioning units spreading thick evil looking smoke throughout the entire hotel.

In the ensuing panic the leaders of nineteen of the nations donned their state of the art masks with relief, whilst their entourages said their prayers to their various gods. The French President cursed never being good at musical chairs, or fighting, after the masks had come out and choked on the thick drifting smoke.

Fifteen minutes later all the world leaders were dead except for the Frenchman, who over the coming days would initially be blamed for the poisoned gas masks. Leaderless, the world paused—except for the Reboot crew, who partied.

PUMPKINHEAD

Stephen could hear Pumpkinhead downstairs. His breathing was hesitant as he tried to listen out for each sound, focusing on each creak and groan, trying to work out where he was to hear if he was coming upstairs for him. Pumpkinhead, the soul-eater, the shadow-mover, always came for the children in the deep of the night.

In the next room his father's snoring continued unabated; adults didn't fear the night like children, Pumpkinhead came only for the young. His father had told Stephen the stories of escaping him in his childhood like it was a rite of passage. Stephen worried that he wasn't strong like his father.

After a sleepless night Stephen headed for the fields, kicking stones and playing with his homemade sword. In the day the children could play with abandon knowing there was no reason to be afraid—Pumpkinhead lived only in the darkest shadows. He needed revenge and daytime was his.

In the centre of old Mr Applethorpe's farm, in the soft autumn sunshine, was Pumpkinhead looking harmless enough, but Stephen wasn't deceived. The long coat swayed in the stiff breeze, every so often flapping with a loud clap. His arms stood out level pointing east and west in an old pair of gloves and his back was straight as a pole; because it was.

His head was a pumpkin with deep incised eyes, which did seem to follow Stephen as he walked around, at a safe distance, from the scarecrow. He stooped to pick up some sharp stones, hefting them with professional zeal to find the right weight.

For half an hour he chucked and spun the rocks through the air, peppering the scarecrow with missiles. Some hit the coat leaving Pumpkinhead unharmed, one almost took his glove off, but best of all two shots scored direct hits to head, leaving deep scars on its face.

As his revenge continued though he saw the shadows lengthening and knew with each passing minute it was getting closer to the night, when Pumpkinhead could return in the shadows. With his fresh weeping scars the soul-eater would be more frightening than ever tonight; if he came. But perhaps tonight Pumpkinhead would not come for Stephen.

THE DIVERTING TALE OF THE MONKEY MAN

Outside the chapel a man with a monkey was looking harassed. It used to be so easy making money going from village to village with a monkey—the parents loved the entertainment as much as the children. Now, everyone had seen it all before and a monkey was just a monkey after all. These days he was happy to pick up pennies.

A mile away Sofia was at home and looking so beautiful. She'd usually kill for that hair, pristine make-up, the dress. Accentuated beauty, not just a painted face. Her eyes though were full of sadness. Someone else looked back at her from the mirror. Jitters they called it, which didn't do it justice. Knotted and choked stomach, adrenaline peaking and troughing. An unyielding fear loomed large as she went down to her wedding carriage.

Meanwhile, in the church, Edward de Beaufort made final adjustments to his lavish gold brocade doublet and ostentatious jewelry. It wouldn't do to be understated on his wedding day. The son of the local Baron looked briefly in the mirror, smirking. He would soon have his beautiful wife to add to his status symbols.

His father looked at him, not a little ashamed. 'If you're supposed to look more effeminate than your betrothed then congratulations son, you have it down pat.'

'It's the continental fashion, Father. I look...' Edward agreed with himself, 'outstanding.'

Inside the church the great, the good and not so good were gathered. If it wasn't for his father no-one would have been there, but his money and power bought a lot of friendship.

Outside the church the monkey man called, 'Spare some change for the dancing monkey.' The children laughed at him as on cue the monkey took off his hat and flung it into the air.

Young Henry across the square watched the melee progress as the kids ran after the hat and then proceeded to run amok, screaming with delight as the monkey man theatrically chased them. Chaos ensued as predicted, as designed, and Henry readied himself as the mare pulled under him, trotting on the spot.

Carts of clothes, fruit and vegetables were flying, children and parents alike taking their opportunities while angry tradesmen walloped anyone within hitting distance. In the chapel Edward waited oblivious to the staged nonsense outside.

High up in a niche the monkey happily munched on an apple while watching the chaos beneath; the monkey man edged away from the madness with Henry's two crowns in his pocket, his job done.

With the carts overturned and the joyful riot Sofia's coach arrived at the square with nowhere to go, so Edward's men took the only option and led her out of the carriage on to the street.

She barely saw Henry whirr around the corner, but she instinctively knew what was happening. She grabbed out at her beloved's arm and found herself whipped around on to his horse. They were off into the distance before you could shout "Get me that Monkey Man!". It was a shame it was early afternoon, or else the couple would surely have been heading off into the most glorious sunset.

A.J. WALKER

THE LADY OF LORD STREET

THE LADY OF LORD STREET

It was a dank Sunday and Osterhaus found himself wandering aimlessly around town. As his feet tired he sat down on a tatty bench opposite the old petrol station with a styrofoam cup of tarry coffee.

The rain-washed streets began to glow all around him as the low sun of winter gently forced its way through the pale greyness. He noticed the iridescence on the tarmac forecourt opposite, which seemed to rise into the air like an early morning mist on the fields. He was finding the morning isolation and freshness relaxing.

Sunspot sparkles began to glitter across the forecourt as a rainbow mist began to pulse and weave. Osterhaus watched transfixed, not thinking about what he was seeing. He didn't find it unusual when the mist thickened and then congealed into a woman. She was real, he could see her; he could see through her too, but nonetheless he could see her.

Electricity—he could feel it in the air. Excitement blossomed through him in controlled explosions as the lady weaved across the tarmac in a mesmeric dance.

Osterhaus felt like he was viewing a show for him alone—he saw her smile directly at him. The interaction was clear; she was as alive as he was.

Life—a complex elemental dance of carbon and hydrogen, hydrocarbons. And oxygen.

Diesel—the pump had stood empty in the ancient fuel station. A monument to a busier town, the business long dead, the town a mere husk. Sadness permeated the decaying fabric.

Life flows and it pulses. Chains creating and breaking, little lives and deaths and conserved energy.

The entity that had freed itself from the ground and through the tank now spun itself around, twirling beneath the canopy, whilst observing the man opposite. It could see the man following it as it pirouetted and jumped feeling the chains. As it danced it began to feel more real as the entity continued knitting and slicing, building and dicing the chains of hydrocarbons and oxygen in an imitation of vibrant life.

It caught fragments of reflections of the dancing lady in the shallow puddles smeared over the road and in the windows of the closed shops. It reveled in its own possibility. Mimicking movements of limbs it didn't have or need. It winked. It didn't know why. Then Osterhaus winked back.

Communication; the first communication between man and the entity. It could feel such possibilities.

Osterhaus dropped the coffee cup into the trashcan without taking his eye from the show. He touched his forehead with the back of his hand; he knew he must be coming down with something. The lady looked chunky-real but was still see through. He began to wonder if perhaps it was some trial advert or 3D cinema. But the lady followed his gaze and had winked at him. She was there.

So it was him, it was in his head; she was real to him and him alone. He was seeing visions and so he decided it must be some weird food poisoning or impending embolism. He didn't feel sick, but it was time to go home and lie down in a pitch dark room. So he turned to walk off down Lord Street without looking back towards the garage.

As he left the lady dissipated and the mist fell gently back to the ground pulled by gravity like dry ice off a stage, the entity unknotting and dicing, shortening the chains releasing the oxygen; it would wait. It had enjoyed the dance, but it would try something different next time, something less subtle and more interactive. The lady would be back but she would not be dancing.

SAL PAGE

HOT AND SWEET

TRAINERS

RICE KRISPIES

HOT AND SWEET

After the crash I became chef. In my element in our makeshift kitchen or tipped over the edge, peering into an abyss lined with limbs, livers, ligaments, staring eyeballs and human chops and steaks.

Johnny and I had adjoining seats. Shorts and flipflops. Lovely feet. We talked like we'd known each other years. His motorbikes and carpentry. My restaurant career.

I boil up bones. George hangs strips of meat to dry. The others can't deal with this. Can't ignore their thoughts and just eat. They vomit behind trees during supper. There's always someone sobbing at night.

Brown sugar, spices, paprika and thyme. Amazing what you find rummaging through luggage. I'm saving the last lemon. Mary's nearly ready.

Johnny's feet tonight. He deserves some spice. I score the skin and massage in dry rub. I hum loudly to block out his story about finding his Mum. Their reunion won't happen now.

George found sweet chilli sauce in the cockpit. We ate the pilot first. Can't think about that too much.

I dab sauce onto each of Johnny's toes. His feet still look beautiful. They'll be so tender.

I want to survive. Whatever it takes.

Mmmmm. Delicious. Johnny's feet. Hot and sweet.

TRAINERS

I remember them finding the first. I knew her grandmother. I sent a card. Thinking of you. What else do you say?

Just before the police arrived I heard children laughing. I put it down to the open windows upstairs but now I'm not so sure. I thought those trainers were pushed under the bed but when the police got up there both were poking out, tongues hanging, Velcro straps flapping.

Offering themselves up.

Worn but still wearable, he'd had them over a decade, loving the spring they gave to his step as he jogged through the playing fields twice a day. He said it was like he was flying. He'd scrub them in the sink with the washing up brush. Mud and dog turds, he'd say.

Long hairs. Threads of pink and lilac. Playing field dirt. Blood. All embedded in those little hooks. Waiting for forensics to prize them out.

RICE KRISPIES

Sasha only kissed the boy in the first place because he smelt of Rice Krispies. She never knew his name or where he was from just that he smelt of Rice Krispies with Demerara sugar and cold-cold milk. She didn't see him after that one night they spent together. Or smell him.

The best thing about being Baby-Jake's mummy was that he smelt of toasted coconut and pineapple. There were different smells of course but even under dirty nappies and sick, Sasha could still get a twist of heavenly pineapple-coconut if she breathed deeply enough.

The man in the park pushed her against a tree. He wanted money. Sasha handed over her last ten pounds. He said this wasn't enough. He emptied her bags, tore the pockets off her jacket and put a hand up her skirt. Sasha kicked him and he staggered backwards. Baby-Jake was crying in his buggy as Sasha ran all the way home, convinced the man was following her.

The policewoman wasn't impressed with Sasha's description. She wanted to know what the man was wearing, how tall he was and what colour hair he had. All Sasha could remember was that he smelt of liver and old baked beans. She should have known from past experience it was best not to mention that.

Sasha was scared to go out. She had food and supplies delivered, paying for them on her credit card, and only answered the door when she was sure who it was. Baby-Jake missed the park and Sasha missed the people in the shops, even the old lady in the newsagents who smelt of boiled-over peas.

After a few weeks Baby-Jake began to walk and Sasha decided she had to be brave and take him out. He could walk his few wobbly steps on the grass in the park with her holding his hand. They were getting ready in the hall when the doorbell rang. Sasha froze, Baby-Jake tottering by her knees.

A sweet smell came from somewhere. Fleeting but familiar. There was a free newspaper in the letterbox and a space next to it. Behind the sharp newsprint smell this other smell was coming through the gap.

Sasha bent down and picked up Baby-Jake. She kissed his head and, reaching for the door handle, told him his Daddy was here.

SAL PAGE

THE ARTIST

THE ARTIST

I'll never forget that evening. It was magical.

Everything about Hugo King's art was magical. Folk called him The Artist, the capital letters clear in the way they uttered the words. I'd followed him for years, always just missing the creation of his pieces but getting photos to prove they were there. Hugo was homeless. He'd been travelling the area for decades, creating stunning pieces from natural materials.

Pin-prick stars watched me alight from the bus between town and the next village. I looked up at a blue cheese moon, near enough to grab and eat in one delicious mouthful. Cold air clawed at my throat, and the inky road was lit by one streetlamp.

People still talk about the mermaid on the beach. There's a video on Youtube of him making it. Fascinating to see it go from a pile of sand to a beautiful smiling mermaid, decorated with pink and white shells, smooth purple pebbles and frosty-pale sea glass. The tide came in and there was nothing left after a few days.

Remember that cold winter four years back? He made a huge hairy yeti from snow with a little sand mixed in. It lounged across the seawall but standing up it would've been nine feet tall. Of course it melted eventually.

I knew his son from the café on the front. He boasted of the gifts his father made for him and his little girl. The pumpkin carved to look like a goblin that seemed to be about to come to life but rotted within weeks. And a unicorn made from three different types of melted chocolate. They'd been told to eat it but the girl saved it for years. He used my word to describe it.

Magical.

This place was magical too. I loved the shabby-seen-better-days-ness of this abandoned garage where the pumps look like people. There was a bus rumour the garage was going to be demolished. New houses. I decided to get photographs before it disappeared.

I couldn't believe my luck when The Artist, a tall thin man with straggly grey beard and hair, faded jeans and layers of scruffy t-shirts, arrived. What was he doing here? I hid in the shadows while he walked around. What was he thinking? Was he looking for inspiration?

Then I sneezed. He turned in my direction. I stepped out. He glanced at me without surprise, as though he'd been expecting me. He pulled some stuff from the pockets of his greasy khaki jacket: a battered magazine, a sandwich, a lighter, some sticks and pieces of rag, scraps of chalk and what looked like an onion. He placed them on the manhole cover by the friendly diesel pump.

The Artist stood for moment, staring at the wall, then he began. I watched as a chalk figure emerged face first. Blushing, I realised it was me. Soon, instead of my jeans and hoodie, I was wearing a short dress with net petticoats and what looked like a sort of cloak, which splayed out around the angles of the wall. Rather fairy-like, I thought. But the face was mine, complete with my glasses. He did my dark hair with a burnt stick.

I gasped. It was only chalk and carbon but was so real and seemed to leap off the wall. I took a series of photos. Hugo didn't seem to want to appear. I respected this but longed to capture him too. He stooped to pick something up and examine it. The Artist wasn't the sort of man you could capture.

The diesel pump grinned at me as I watched Hugo carry on working, adding highlights and lowlights to the fabric of the dress. I dared myself to speak.

'Did you buy the chalk? I thought ...'

He replied without looking at me.

'Picked it up on Tennyson Down when I was on the Isle of Wight.'

Of course. I was glad it wasn't sticks of chalk from a shop. That wouldn't have been right somehow.

'Why the fairy dress?'

'Dunno. Just did it.'

Was that what he saw when he looked at me? Or had he planned this all along and just added my face?

'It won't last long, you know.'

He nodded. 'That's right.'

I cringed. It didn't need spelling out. All his pieces were temporary. That was the point.

He crouched to the ground and added definition to my legs. They'd never looked so good.

'It's fantastic. I just don't know how you do it.'

He shrugged 'It's easy.'

'I don't think so. I ...'

He stood up slowly, turned and his eyes met mine. 'Not doing it would be a lot harder.'

I tried to work out what this meant as he stood back from the image, apparently satisfied with its completion. Several clouds had appeared. Parts of the garage slammed and hammered as the wind ventured around the back. Hugo bent to the manhole cover to return everything to his pockets then buttoned his jacket to his chin.

I know this is hard to believe but the chalk image sort of sparkled. Fairy dust. Magic. I tore myself from it and realised The Artist was walking off down the lane in the direction of the next village. The last bus to town would be along soon. I took several more photos then headed back to the stop.

I'm fairly sure that was Hugo King's penultimate piece. Three days later was the night of the spectacular dragon up on the hill. Hugo certainly paid the price for that piece. The inquest concluded that he must have got some of the petrol on his clothes, lit the piece and then fallen. Folk didn't realise at the time, watching from their back gardens or standing agog in the street, but The Artist was part of his creation that night. He went up with his amazing flaming fire dragon.

They still haven't demolished the garage. That image of me would be long gone. The first time it rained.

STELLA TURNER

INTERIOR DECORATING

THE WEIGHT

VANITY

INTERIOR DECORATING

The gap in the roof, created when the corrugated panel had blown away in last month's storm, made an excellent skylight. It had taken me months to stick the coloured pebbles around the metal edges. I'd found a ladder in the shed, climbed up higher than I'd ever been before. Fighting with the strong adhesive to stop my fingertips being glued to the pattern I was trying to make.

Oli laughed and said it looked ludicrous; Martha thought it was spiritual. I just needed something to do. This old factory had hidden gems. Some I wanted to find, others I didn't. I remember the day I opened a locker with the name Stan Smith on it and found a corpse. I presumed it was Stan hiding from Armageddon. I still wonder how a big man like him managed to fit into a small space like that. Not that I was familiar with Stan but on the notice board were fading photos of key workers. Stan was the Health and Safety Officer. I wondered how he felt when all his training hadn't prepared him for any of this. Betrayed? Disillusioned? Not that it mattered anymore.

I found an old calendar, one of those that showed topless girls. Most factory managers banned them from being put on show. Political correctness. This one was hidden in a drawer. Oli thought Miss May was a bit of alright. I just wondered if she had survived or was with Stan in the ether.

The sun cast small squat shadows around my scrawny body. Martha and Oli had been gone for ages. Hope it was food foraging and not enjoying each other's bodies. Oli kept spouting about the continuation of the human race. He was stupid; Martha and I were infertile—well, until our periods returned. Not the best specimens to restock the world. I laughed out loud; for a fleeting moment I thought about LOL, text speak for what I'd just been doing. God, I missed Twitter and Facebook.

Then I remembered there was no God. He'd left us long ago. Gone fishing, probably, like my Dad always did in a crisis.

THE WEIGHT

*T*he monkey had always sat on my left shoulder. Sometimes it felt light and I forgot about it and other times it was a huge burden weighing me down like a black dog. Today was different. No soft fur running through my fingers. No sweet chattering in my ear. No grooming of my hair looking for lice. Not that I've ever had lice but it was pretty comforting to know if I did it would be nipped in the bud. I'd always been proud of my tumbling auburn hair with its corkscrew curls. The monkey had the same colouring and blended in well. That's why no one else noticed it entwined around my neck. Even when I went to bed with Leon he didn't seem to observe it sitting on the end of the bed watching us with its beady little eyes. It would look at me and sometimes bare its teeth in a grimace. I was never sure whether it was a smile or an expression of contempt.

Last night Leon took me to a posh restaurant, got down on one knee and proposed. The whole place erupted in applause when I said yes. I thought I was going to burst with happiness. Maybe that's why the monkey left. I felt bereft. I drew the curtains back, letting the early morning sunlight fill the room. Across the road the monkey, my monkey, was dancing on the top of a lamppost holding a broken arrow, reminding me of Eros. I tapped the window trying to get its attention. Pointing a long finger at me, it continued its wild dance. I turned back to Leon. He lay sprawled on the bed, red stains seeping on the Egyptian fine cotton sheets. Stab wounds all over his body. I went to scream but felt a little hand covering my mouth. Its touch soothed me, the nausea subsiding. Cleansed by the power shower, I dressed in my green taffeta dress that Leon said matched my eyes. Packed my belongings and called a cab.

It was good to feel the weight back on my shoulder.

VANITY

"*I* didn't hear any of that. Did you Betty?"

I shook my head. My hearing wasn't as sharp as it used to be.

I was too vain to ask the Doctor to speak up. George was too vain to wear his hearing aids.

"Do you think it was bad?"

I shook my head. He looked alright. He still made me mad with his forgetfulness and whinging on about his aches and pains. I always thought I was going to be a merry widow but he'd see me out for sure.

We both missed the Doctor saying it was terminal.

STELLA TURNER

MY GREAT AUNTY DORA

MY GREAT AUNTIE DORA

My Great Auntie Dora was always a bit of a one. She'd sit in the big armchair that was reserved for my dad, defying him to ask her to move. She wore men's brogues, wire rimmed spectacles and cut her own hair with pinking shears. She said it made her stand out from the crowd. She told us stories that no child should hear. We were intrigued and repelled and I remember having vivid nightmares, my mum cursing her Aunt with even more words that I shouldn't have heard before puberty struck.

When she died Mum found instructions for her funeral tucked in a well-thumbed copy of *Travels with My Aunt*. She wanted to be buried in a tutu, not any old tutu but one worn by the prima ballerina Margot Fonteyn. Mum compromised by getting one made from an ancient seamstress who made dresses for Danny La Rue. It was pink with big purple stars and sequins that sparkled. My mum hung it on her bedroom door the night before she took it to the funeral directors.

Mum said she was taking fresh knickers and bra but hadn't any ballet shoes as Great Aunt Dora had size ten feet hence the men's brogues she still wore in the open coffin. I sprinkled confetti in the corners as Dora always said that was one thing she missed having at her wedding. She was covered by painful grains of rice and had a piece lodged up her nose for weeks until she sneezed it out one day!

Now that Great Auntie Dora was buried in the nice cemetery up the road, near her beloved bingo hall, you'd think that was the end of my story but far from it. It was a few months after her demise that I began to obsess over why she had chosen that particular piece of clothing to be buried in. My mum started to worry about me and decided a short holiday with my boyfriend Ged riding pillion on Route 66 would be the making of me. Trouble was I didn't think the relationship would last that long so I opted to traverse the British Isles instead.

I hadn't told Mum I was seeing Dora wherever I went. She sat peering at me in the local café, shaking her head in disapproval if I didn't order one of their bacon sandwiches for breakfast. When I went shopping she'd pirouette down the aisles tossing weird and wonderful items in the trolley. Ged would look at the jars of rolled mop herrings and pull up his nose in disgust. Great Aunt Dora would nod sagely and make a rude gesture behind his back as I tried hard not to giggle.

Ged loved his vintage motorcycle more than me, but that was okay because I loved my freedom more. I loved riding the bike with the wind in my hair, but I couldn't really say that as the helmet held it flat against my head. Ged was very safety conscious. The speed he drove at, it would take years to get from Coventry to Morecambe. I'd be as old as Dora had been when she died before we hit the Shetland Isles.

One morning we drove into a village in the middle of nowhere; it was like time had stood still. The pump on the garage forecourt looked like one you'd find on Route 66. Ged left me to fill up the tank whilst he went into the shop to pay and discuss blokey things with the guy inside.

"Celia, do you really want to stay with a man with no imagination? He reminds me so much of my late husband Gilbert. I'm here with you so I don't have to be reunited with him in the afterlife"

This was the first time I'd heard Great Aunt Dora speak since she'd said her last words to me before passing over. Those words were Memento Vivere. I didn't know she spoke Latin! We left Ged behind in that service station in the middle of the Forest of Dean. I expect he reported his bike stolen as soon as we roared off down the road.

The helmet was left abandoned on the bench by the side of the pump, my long blonde hair streamed behind me in the wind as I let the throttle out so we could go even faster. Great Auntie Dora rode pillion, releasing a scream of "Tally Ho" every few minutes. We were like Thelma and Louise. I decided that to really feel free I needed to buy a tutu.

SINÉAD O'HART

MEMENTO MORI

MEMENTO MORI

I was hurrying down Morrison when he came at me, straight out of the alley beside the old grocery store. I put my head down and ignored him at first, sure he was just one of those guys who hadn't taken to the process so well, but he was determined to catch my eye.

'Hey,' he muttered, shuffling over. 'Hey, man. I gotta—'

'Can't stop, buddy,' I called, holding up a hand, wondering when the government was going to face facts and segregate these things. 'In a hurry, y'know?'

'Please,' he said. 'Jus' need a minute.' A faint stink billowed out of him, a memory of breath.

'Don't you got a job to go to, friend?' I asked. That's the point of you people, isn't it? I didn't say it out loud, but he had to know I was thinking it. Anybody would be. He blinked and made no answer, swaying on his feet.

'Man, I really am sorry. Okay? Really. But if I'm late for work I get to hear about it all week. You understand, right? Nothin' personal.' I'd reached out to shake his hand before I could stop myself, but his fists were buried deep in his rancid pockets. He froze. I glanced up at his face properly for an instant then, and he just stared at me out of wet, sloppy eyes. I couldn't tell what colour they'd been, before; the process had washed it away.

I shook the guy off—his smell, his voice, the pallor of his face—as I kept walking, and by the time I finished work for the day I'd forgotten all about him. I walked home through empty streets. Apartment buildings rose into the dusk all around, dark and cold. My own building had thirty percent occupancy, and I knew I was one of the lucky ones. When I closed my door behind me at night I didn't feel like something finally buried. I knew if I shouted, someone would hear me.

They might not come. But they would hear.

I saw him as I drew near that old grocery store again, the one that had never been open during my lifetime. There he was, waiting in the shadows. Had he even moved since morning?

'Look,' I said, before he could speak. 'I told you before, all right? I can't talk to you.'

'Just, please,' he said. He looked worse than before. Dark hollows beneath his eyes threatened to swallow his face.

'Weren't you at your job today? Huh? Did you just stand around here all day? Were you this useless when you were alive, too?'

'Buddy, come on,' he replied. 'I gotta show you. Gotta show someone.'

I wasn't sure why those words pulled at me, but thirty seconds later I was following him—a Refurb, an actual flesh-and-blood walking talking dead guy—into this alley. It smelled like hell.

Then, he stopped. I heard a noise, and looked down.

A kid. A kid lay on the ground, white-faced and wide-eyed, breathing hard as she stared up at me. She couldn't have been any more than nine. It looked like maybe her leg was broken—certainly, she wasn't going anywhere fast. Stay cool. The bounty for returning runaways was high. How she'd managed to escape from the breeding camps was anyone's guess, but all I knew was they'd pay to get her back.

'You animal,' I growled, turning on the Refurb. I clenched my fists. This has to look good, I told myself.

'No! Mister!' The kid's voice was like a whistle. 'He helped me! I fell, and—'

'Enough,' I told her, never taking my eyes off the Refurb. They weren't supposed to hurt the living, but I guess you never knew. How can any of us be sure?

'No,' said the Refurb. His eyes were flabby. Blank. He's just instinct, I told myself. Wrapped up in a cadaver. He's barely more than a machine. 'No. Please.' He took a shuffling step back and slid on something in the garbage piled there, falling back against the sacks. I took my chance.

A swift, hard jab to the abdomen, and he groaned so bad that I almost believed he felt it. Another, and another. There was barely any resistance in his soft flesh.

'No! Arnie!' screamed the kid. 'Stop hurting him!'

'Arnie, is it?' I said, bracing myself for another punch. 'You're a dead man, Arnie. No pun intended. You know that, right? Even if I hadn't found you hurting this girl, or whatever it is I can make 'em believe you'd been doing up here, I'd probably have killed you just for being lazy. You're going in the ground, my friend. Nobody needs a Refurb who won't work.'

He looked up at me then, and his watery eyes overflowed. The barest twitch of his face could have been a smile.

I threw the killer punch. Arnie's jaw shattered, and he lay still.

Is there a fine for smashing up a Refurb? I thought, shaking out my fist. Hardly matters. The money I'll get for returning the kid will more than cover it.

'Okay, little lady,' I called, hauling myself up off the trash-pile, leaving Arnie's twice-dead body where it lay. 'Come on, now. You ready?'

I turned, but she was gone.

'His name wasn't Arnie,' I heard her say. I squinted into the gloom, but there was no sign of her. 'Well, maybe. It could've been. I call them all Arnie.'

'You—what? Come on, kid. I don't have time for this.' I turned, looking, but besides me and the cold Arnie, there was nobody in this alley.

'It takes years, you know,' she continued, from her unseen perch. 'The average Retirement application. And it can only be approved once a

Refurb's given at least twenty years of service. Don't matter how many times it messes up—nobody cares. A Refurb's gotta work until it falls apart.' She sighed. 'And then there's those stupid rules, y'know? About not hurting themselves, or each other, or the living?'

'So?' I wished I could see her. The flesh on my back started to crawl. 'What's this got to do with you?'

'Call it a public service,' she replied. 'They pay me whatever they've got, and I get them killed. Win-win.'

I looked back at Arnie. 'You mean he—he wanted this?'

'Wouldn't you?' I turned towards the sound of her voice, squinting into the darkness. 'Worked hard all his life, knowing that all he'd get for dying would be a day off?'

'I—but, it's how it's done. We need the labour. Since the Crash—'

'Right.' She cut me off, her voice tight. 'Tell yourself that when you're on your deathbed.' I heard a tiny scuffle, and a small grunt of effort, and a tiny shadow moving against the night.

'Hey,' I shouted. 'Come back here! I've got to get you home!' There was no answer. 'Little girl!'

The wind skirled round the alley, tossing some papers and loosened trash. A cat flashed its eyes at me in the darkness, then vanished.

When I got home I called the authorities. Told 'em I'd seen a bunch of thugs harassing a Refurb near an alley off Morrison; I couldn't intervene, because it was one against five. Possibly six. Said I hoped the guy would be okay. Mentioned a runaway kid, and asked about a reward.

Then I went to bed, but the darkness had a weight in it, and I was afraid to close my eyes.

SINÉAD O'HART

PROXY

PROXY

*J*eremy woke at seven forty-two. It was still dark, but somehow he knew, without having to turn on the light, that this was the day. The air was different—stiller, maybe. Emptier.

He lay back down and waited for the sun to rise.

Dora's arm emerged from the shadows first, the light pearling on her fingernails before sliding down her thin arm. She lay tucked up like a secret, perfectly still. Jeremy watched the flow of her beneath the blankets, the peaks too sharp and the dips too low, and sighed. When he left the bed, he crept as quietly as he could.

Quickly, he dressed. Clean underwear, of course. Socks. A pair of pants that hadn't been pressed, but it hardly mattered. His second-best shirt. The pullover from last Christmas, still serviceable. No tie.

Finally, he slid the gun into his pocket, its strange weight making him tighten his belt a notch, and slipped into his raincoat. Standing in front of the mirror to check his silhouette he noticed Dora's foot, clawlike now and pale, protruding, and he turned to tuck it in.

Then he leaned down for a kiss, stroking a wispy strand of brittle hair, whiter than bone, behind her cold ear.

'I'll see you later, darling,' he whispered.

Breakfast was a scoop of muesli and a splash of milk, as was usual on Tuesdays. He decided to forego his normal cup of tea for fear of bladder-related distractions later on, but allowed himself the rebellion of leaving his unwashed dishes in the sink. His fingers trembled slightly as he set down his bowl and spoon, and his head swam, just a little.

Focusing on the view outside the kitchen window, Jeremy concentrated on his breathing. Slow, and steady, and rhythmical. There. He blinked, and the world snapped back.

He checked the locks on the back door and made sure all the appliances were off before glancing at the kitchen clock—going for eight-fifteen—and running through the plan, one last time.

Soundlessly, he walked down the hallway. At the end of the stairs he dithered for a moment, gazing at the photograph of Dora which sat, as it always had, on the console table. Plump, and young, and rosy, this was the wife of his dreams, dressed in tulle and dancing slippers, posing after a show. Briefly, he considered taking it with him, but soon dismissed the thought. *She wouldn't want to see this.*

He opened the front door, tapped in the security code, and locked up, waiting patiently for a count of thirty to make sure the alarm set properly. Then, taking twelve neat steps, he reached the gate and stepped through, turning left onto the road.

It was a fine morning, crisp and chill, the leaves on the turn and the birds in full throat. Someone unseen beeped a greeting, and Jeremy wondered, as he stepped off the pavement to avoid a woman with a pram, whether things were unusually busy. A lollipop lady shepherded children across the road just in front of him, and he dashed out, unthinking, to join their flow, making a slowing car pull up short. The driver threw his hands up in the air as he watched Jeremy jog apologetically past.

This won't do, he told himself, breathing deep. As he walked on, he kept count of his pace. Not too fast, not too slow. *For God's sake, stop checking your pocket!*

He turned onto Palmer Avenue. The service station loomed at the end of the road. Jeremy flicked his gaze about; the schoolchildren had clattered into their playground, out of harm's way. Traffic was calming. A woman swept her front path, smiling as he approached.

'Lovely day,' she chirped.

Jeremy nodded and told her it was, and she watched his narrow back appreciatively until he was twenty yards away. Later that morning, she would be interviewed by a newspaper reporter, and her recollection of this moment would go all over the country—but nobody knew that, yet.

The service station was past its best, signage rusting a little at the edges, the pumps old-fashioned but functional. Its small shop was understocked and overpriced, but Jeremy didn't come here often, which was why he'd chosen it. The person behind the counter when he entered was a stranger, a young woman with braided hair, openly chewing gum. She stood, arms folded, staring.

He nodded a greeting and the assistant rolled her eyes, turning to the window. Jeremy walked to the labouring fridge against the back wall where sweating plastic containers of milk jostled with garishly packaged orange juice. Beer was one shelf up. Bottles of water were carelessly flung in the bottom. He picked one up, its chill saturating his bones.

Patting his pocket, he set off for the register.

The assistant popped a wet pink bubble as he approached. She turned to him, her deft tongue drawing her gum back inside her mouth. She barely missed a beat.

'Just that, then?' She indicated the bottle in Jeremy's hands.

'Thank you. Yes,' he said, placing it on the counter.

'One seventy-five,' she muttered, pressing a button on the till.

'Right.' He reached into his pocket. The gun, cool and solid, bumped his knuckles as he pretended to search for his wallet.

'Ain't you got cash?' inquired the salesgirl. "Cos I can't let you just 'ave it, mate. No credit 'ere.' She shook her head, muttering.

'No, I do,' said Jeremy, his mouth sour. 'Just a moment.'

She *tssk*ed and began to examine her fingernails as Jeremy slapped his pockets. *Breathe*, he reminded himself. *In, and—*

'Sorry,' he said, his fingers closing firmly around the gun. 'I'm ready, now.' The girl heaved in a sigh and glanced up, but her gaze was caught by the dark pupil of the weapon in his hand.

'Jesus Christ. There ain't nothink here! There's nothink in the till, mate! I swear!'

'Just stay calm,' said Jeremy. 'Okay?'

She began to fumble with something beneath the counter and Jeremy fired into the ceiling. A cloud of plaster dust coated the girl and she screamed, falling back against the cigarette display.

'Just take whatever you want, all right? Just—whatever! Don't hurt me!'

'Call the police,' said Jeremy, aiming at the girl again.

'What?' Her cheeks were striped with tears.

'Call. The. Police.' He fumbled in his coat pocket, never taking his eyes off the weeping girl, and handed her his mobile phone. 'Use this, if you have to.'

Her false nails clacked off the screen as she pressed the 'Emergency Call' button. Jeremy could hear the connection being made and the tinny voice of the operator.

'P-p-police,' stammered the girl.

'What's your location, please?' Jeremy heard, but the girl's huge dark eyes were fixed on him, and all she could do was sob. He snatched the phone from her.

'Westville Service Station,' he said.

'Who's this?' The operator sounded surprised.

'The perpetrator. I have a gun,' he told her, and hung up.

'You're a nut—nutter,' gasped the girl.

'No,' replied Jeremy, sliding his phone back into his coat pocket. 'Will you lie on the floor, please? I don't want you to get hurt.'

'You *what?*'

'Just, please? Lie down.' The girl obeyed, awkwardly folding herself up. Jeremy could hear her teeth clattering, and he slid out of his coat, tossing it to her. She jumped, but after a second she pulled it over herself.

Sirens.

'They're coming,' he called. 'Won't be long, now. All right?' She didn't respond.

Jeremy turned toward the large window overlooking the forecourt and checked for pedestrians, but all was clear. He released a single shot and the glass shattered, sparkling shards flying in all directions. Over the ringing in his ears, and the girl's screaming, he could still hear distant wailing.

He thought of Dora, then, and smiled, remembering her shapely legs and flirtatious smile, and how much he loved her. He couldn't live without her, but he couldn't follow her alone.

When the police cars squealed to a halt Jeremy walked out screaming, his gun in clear view. He took aim at a policeman, his finger off the trigger, and they barely even shouted a warning before opening fire.

Jeremy blinked as Dora bent over him, her breasts straining against her white bodice, her skin dewy, her lips full.

'Clever boy,' she crooned. A lock of dark hair swept over one eye as, gently as a girl, she took his hand.

ELAINE MARIE MCKAY

VISITORS

RECYCLED BRIDE

ISSUE P14

VISITORS

Powdered milk at the back of the cupboard.
Who lives in a house like this?
She laughs. The daft game we play.
Scented handkerchiefs on the kitchen table.
Who eats in a house like this?
She snorts and takes a hanky from the box. 'Smells like cat's pish.'
And now it's a dirty, low laugh, and I catch it.
Tears stream from our eyes. Sore sides.
Deep breaths.
She runs from the kitchen, up the hall. Then I'm there with her and I can't look away.
I press against her and she leans on a door.
We kiss.
She clicks the door open and we shamble together to a bed.
I love you.
'I love this.'
That's the best I'll get.
She picks up a book from what looks like his side of the bed: The Northern Lights.
'Gonna see them some day.'
She will: she's said it.
She's up and dressing and I watch for as long as I can.
'Move it. We've been here for too long. Remember that last time?' she says.
Yeah, I remember...Who gets fucked up in a house like this?
She doesn't laugh. This one's over. I take the book as her souvenir.
She takes what she sees on the way out.

RECYCLED BRIDE

*I*n a suit made of plain material, I boarded the bus that took us to the council offices. I was a divorcee at twenty. My mother and father escorted me to the Registrar's where Mr. Terence Larkin, the man who would make me decent again, was waiting.

He was ten years younger than my father and had never been married. He had come round for Sunday dinner on six occasions. The proposal was made in the kitchen—by my mother. My father and suitor were in the front room.

The ceremony was brief. My father shook my groom's hand and thanked him. My mother's coat was buttoned up to her mouth.

We took the bus to his house, and I set about dusting and cleaning. A cough and a nod indicated the wedding night had commenced.

I lay in bed, for want of a better idea. He arrived at the door. The light was already off. His eyes not used to the dark, he shuffled his way to the bedside cabinet. He placed his glasses and watch down, and folded his pyjama trousers under his pillow.

Filthy words and a few manic jerks consummated the pairing—I guessed he wasn't that decent.

I numbed myself to sleep that night, that week, that year.

It's terrible wishing someone dead. But cold-shoulder night, after cold-shoulder night, I dreamt of being alone on my own.

Then it happened.

I woke up next to a corpse. I guess his heart couldn't take the filthy words I had learned from him.

I buried him in his wedding suit and bought myself a new dress.

ISSUE P14

*A*t last, they reach the head of their queue: 'Birth Fees'. They hand over the papers and are permitted through the automated doors.

White zaps at their retinas.

It takes a few moments for their eyes to grow accustomed to the brightness of the Maternity Unit. When they do, they can see the two great vending machines that stretch the length of a wall.

They know what they want and press their noses against the glass that the males are cradled behind.

'H55 looks strong and healthy. Let's pick it,' says the woman, wasting no further time. Her husband places his plastic card in the slot and types on the keypad.

A robotic grabber shoots out and across, then attempts to snap its electronic digits around H55. But the baby's doughy skin slips through its grasp.

Above the keypad, it reads in red, 'Technical difficulty. Make another selection.'

'Glitch,' says the husband.

'Pity,' says the wife, 'but P14 looks good too.'

This time the robotic grabber secures its fingers around their selection. The baby is lowered to the mouth of the machine and is given a firm push. When free of the soundproof glass, its screams fill the white air.

'Good set of lungs on him,' says the husband.

They take the bundle and the complimentary bunch of flowers and head for the sign saying 'Exit.'

ELAINE MARIE MCKAY

BETWEEN THESE WALLS

BETWEEN THESE WALLS

I can taste the memory of picnic on my lips: lemonade and strawberry jam. Her favourite.

Stop! Don't think of her. Keep her safe.

It is incongruous on a freezing cold night to be concentrating on such things, but they choose. It seems that I have satisfied them on the sense of taste. Yesterday, they concentrated on touch, but I had no real reference for fine porcelain or coal or fire. Why would I? I muddied responses with imagination; I did not meet with expectations. Brain Flex is their name for it. It makes my eyes stream with strain. My head throbs in blistering pain.

'Can I stop now?'

'No, not yet. We will move on to a more abstract concept. Show us what Identity feels like.'

'I'm not sure it's a feeling.'

'There is always an associated feeling.'

They tighten their grip around my thoughts.

'Stop, please. I'll do as you say.'

I think hard about the word—Identity. That is how I always begin. I reach for global scale. But in a momentary lapse, Judith is on the tip of my mind. I scoop her up again, wrapping her in the thick smoke of war, burying her in conflict over land and oil, drowning her in the beat of anthems. Keep the ideas coming for her sake.

Stop! Don't think of her.

'Subject's Responses. Physical: raised blood pressure, palpitations. Visual: flags, borders, tanks, mobs, a secondary image that is difficult to decipher. No direct association with smells or tastes, but there are associated sounds,' says the shadow on the wall.

'Cross reference with Fear, Anger, Greed and Love,' says the shadow on the ceiling.

'We have a better understanding of the concept of Identity,' the shadow continues, 'but you must clarify. There were secondary visuals. Do not conceal anything, or we *will* excavate.'

Pressure grows at my temples. I think of my grandmother. She's safe: she's dead. But my thoughts tumble into a frenzy. My grandmother pirouettes like Judith in sweet, pink ballet pumps.

Stop!

'She is concealing.'

'Set probe to dig.'

Fear annihilates my concentration. The image of my grandmother cracks and creases like an old photograph, and Judith materialises, dressed in her tutu, smiling at my mind's eye.

In full view. Exposed.

'A girl!' rasps the shadow on the wall. 'Offspring.'

'Is she here? Show us what you feel for her,' says the shadow on the ceiling.

A carousel of swings and gardens and sunshine and birthday candles and squeals of laughter and love spin inside my head as I struggle to switch it off.

Stop! Don't think of her.

'Subject's Responses. Physical: endorphins secreted, momentarily, followed by a spike in anxiety levels. Visual: full array of colour. All senses heightened,' says the shadow on the wall.

'Cross reference with Love, Beauty and Family,' says the shadow on the ceiling.

I ask again, in exhausted thoughts, struggling to retain consciousness, what it is they want.

'We want more,' says the shadow on the ceiling.

'Now, where is your offspring?' says the shadow on the wall.

With all the intensity that my mind can call upon, I shield any visual of her, raising imaginary, impenetrable steel sheets, one after the other.

'No matter,' says the shadow on the ceiling.

They use every beam of light in the house, and scuttle over every surface until they find where I conceal her. They illuminate the darkest corner of the room, where she lies asleep. She is still wearing her ballet skirt.

'Please! Please!' I say, but an inky shape spills out from the wall onto the now bright surface of the floor. It travels towards her. It finds her skin. It is tacky; it clings and thickens. It binds her feet. It spills over her stick legs. Like oil on feathers, it mats her ballerina skirt; it seeps on to her long bent arms. It finds her neck, her lips, her eyes. It fills her veins and stops her lungs, until all that's left of her is form.

TAMARA SHOEMAKER

THIEF

MOTHER

WAKING

THIEF

*T*wo wishes wasted; this third and final one was our last chance.
A three-ring circus of emotions arrived with each doctor's visit—grave head shakes, serious gazes flickering down to dull clipboards that shielded truth from our liquid eyes.

"Good morning, sunshine," Lucy, the parakeet, chirped this morning from her cage. It sounded like "Good moonshine," the way she garbled her words. Either way, the sentiment was inappropriate.

Good was a fluid concept these days. Good was associated with success, vigor, stability, happiness. Good broke ranks when leukemia crept into my eight-year-old daughter's body, stole her energy and her hair, her vitality, the shine that lights her eyes.

Three months ago, I'd rested on my back in our yard, my hands clasped behind my head, my bitter stare raking the star-spangled velvet of darkness. One brilliant pin of light pulled my attention to the center of the canvas, a gleam that changed color the longer I gazed at it—shades of rose, coral, indigo, emerald.

Perhaps it was a trick of light, staring too long at one thing, but what could it hurt? I wished upon a star, feeling silly even as the words slipped out from my lips like silk. "Please, make her well. Take it away, far away, from us."

She threw up the next morning, and I smoothed back her hair, cursing the stars and everything else as I mopped her face, stroked her brow, screamed internally and soothed quietly.

I tried again one night. I don't know if I thought of suicide or if I simply walked the double yellow line in hopes that it would lead me to the place I needed to find. I cried out to the darkness for help, but no answer floated on the soft breeze. Merely the cacophony of the interstate half a mile to the east.

My shoulders slumped, my vision blurred, so that when the headlights appeared in the blackness, the two shining eyes morphed into one giant blazing Cyclops plowing toward me, merciful death in its limpid gaze.

They made an appointment with the psychologist the next day, a shrink who stared at me over the tops of her half-moons, asking questions with an eyebrow suspended near her hairline like she permanently questioned All Facts.

Now, today, the results sit on the desk in front of us. Slowly, like cold syrup, the words eke their way across the room. A blood transfusion, a slim thread of hope; my blood is the strongest chance she's got.

The wish fades to black. I haven't told him, the nice man with the white coat that struggles so hard to help my daughter. Haven't told her either, with her blue eyes that have seen so little, of the virus that runs in my own blood, the killer thief that will steal my life not long after hers.

Someday, they may find a cure for leukemia, may even discover the nemesis for AIDS, but that day is not today.

MOTHER

When the wind sweeps o'er the moor,
And the heather rustles, disturbed, 'neath the weight of it,
When the rich scent of peat coats the forty green shades,
And the wee folk chatter in the deep mists of evening,
I return to the cairn to dance with the babe
Stolen from me, the night the banshee screamed.
We cavort on the stones that mark the bones,
Dancing our lullaby, our Danny Boy,
To the tempo of the gales
That wrench our breath from our lungs,
Mine healthy and pink, hers gray with ash and rot.
We frolic and gambol in our own wild art
Through the night when the gray dawn lightens the mist
And the cairn claws my baby back to its cold breast again.
They say I am spirit, the woman of the mists,
Who wrings her hands while treading the moor.
Perhaps I am. Perhaps I am simply Mother.
Till next eventide, my babe.
My Stella.

WAKING

What dreams may come to he who waits,
Baited upon the silvery string of moonlight's beams—
The tryst with darkness and dawn
A sacred revel of dancing shadows and fancy flights,
A brief marriage between slumber and waking.
Here, he can play the knight who rides to the castle,
Who bows before king and country,
Who woos and wins fair maiden.
Here, he rides, tall, strong, to meet the enemy,
Who returns in triumph, the honored hero.
Here, the limp is merely a distant memory,
The withered hand but a legend, folklore, fireside chat over wine.
Here, no one sees the ragged strips of flesh that cover the side of his face,
That partially blind his right eye.
Here, he is no monster.
Here, he is loved.
Here, he is whole.
Here, he proposes marriage.
But the dawn brings divorce.

TAMARA SHOEMAKER

PHANTASM

PHANTASM

I met her outside of Macy's that day in the rain, the splashes spreading a sea across the slick sidewalks like liquid fountains, each drop draped in silver disco.

I met her again in my dreams that night, and the rain surrounded us in a living, woven curtain that blocked out all thoughts of waking. Time slowed to record patterns of the drops in dancing rhythm to the sluggish seconds as they slid by.

When I found her again on a bench in Central Park, I thanked Destiny kindly, my old Friend, for introducing us.

"Good afternoon," she said over her Starbucks.

"I love you," I said over the stuttering beats of my heart.

She wasn't the poster model I had hung up in my room years ago on the back of my door, Marilyn over the grate, her dress billowing upward, hands pressed down over the material in pretend modesty. She wasn't later versions that cropped up in my room, Joni Mitchell, Cindy Crawford, Angelina Jolie.

She had her own version of grace, from the dent in her chin to the large dark frames around her eyes to the slight overbite in her teeth. Her smile held charm, her voice held mystery. The bob that insisted on frizzing beneath the wool crocheted hood carved a niche in my heart, and I was adrift on a sea of dreams.

We walked a long way together, she and I—through the paths of Central Park, following the trail of a pair of dogs telling secrets as they trotted along. We walked down the aisle of an old cathedral and said, "I do." We walked the path of children and school and midlife crises and retirement.

The Wall drew near, and dread of the End touched our kisses. I allowed myself to see the path without her steady stride, to feel the emptiness of a mere five fingers without their mates. Cold iced my bones and my strength failed. She bore me on, her feeble strength my lifeline.

When we came to the Wall that we couldn't see over, I spread my jacket around her, warming her in the chill from the other side.

"I'll miss you," she said.

"I'll come soon," I said.

And she disappeared into the gray, a ghost that danced in memory like other things of the past, like diners and diesel gas pumps and Elvis songs. They still hover here and there, preening in their modern makeovers, but they've lost the body of their soul.

Now I've reached the Wall once again, and this time, it opens its door for me. My children stand near, spreading their cloaks about me to still the shivers that chill my bones, but I see only her beloved frame in the mists of the entrance. She stretches out her hand. I touch it as I pass through the arch. Her fingers lace mine. They are warm.

Here, at the end, where there is no turning back,
Where the ocean meets the sky, and darkness lies beyond,
Here, where I face the unseen and the spectres of my dread,
I find, after all, that fear is merely a phantom,
That your warm hand hides behind the chill of terror,
That your familiar smile peeps from 'neath Death's hood.
In the end, the Reaper comes, after all, as a warm friend,
A lover.

CHRIS MILAM

GIMMICK TOWN

CHECK THE FRIDGE

GIMMICK TOWN

*M*aggie is standing by the granite countertop as I watch her effortlessly rock the blade back and forth with precision. Her thin hand is a blur as she takes the onion apart with an almost sensual motion that is efficient and ultimately successful, a perfect dissection. I want to grab a notepad and take notes with my knife skills lacking, but I just continue to watch from afar, me and the onion strange bedfellows on her killing floor.

"What's for dinner, baby?" I mumble softly, trying not to startle her.

She turns around and glances my way with eyes I've never been able to decipher. *"Carne asada,"* she says, not needing my approval, nor does my opinion really matter.

"Sounds delicious, Maggie." It sounds mundane but there's no need to ruffle her feathers.

I lock in my plastic smile and forge ahead.

"Something odd happened today. I stopped by a new bar for a quick beer after work and well, the people were acting weird."

"Weird? Weird, how?"

"I didn't see anyone blink. Seriously, I sat in the corner sipping on a Blue Moon and not one person blinked. Not the bartender, not the waitress or any of the other patrons. Nobody blinked." I wait for her to laugh or mock me.

"Why is that weird, exactly?"

What kind of response is that? Why isn't she confused or curious or chuckling? She asks why it's weird.

"Maybe you didn't hear me clearly. I was in a bar and not one human being blinked. That's not even remotely normal, Maggie."

She looks at me with a barely concealed disdain.

"The bar on Catherine Street, right? You know, the one called the OPEN EYE tavern?"

Her condescending tone makes me feel like that diced onion.

"How in the world was I supposed to infer from OPEN EYE Tavern that I was walking into a place where nobody blinked? That's utterly ridiculous. I thought it was just some hipster doofus name, and maybe I'd see a violinist or some beatnik poets with black turtlenecks sipping absinthe or something, but a bunch of weirdos not blinking? That's just moronic."

"Ben, we live in a forward thinking town. The Mayor is innovative, and his mandates about embracing the unique and ridding ourselves of the banality of apathy is rather refreshing, to be honest."

Banality of apathy. I have no idea what that means. She's always been seduced by nonsensical quotes or any line that sounds deep.

"Refreshing? How about I go to a bar and people actually blink their eyes? That would be refreshing, Maggie."

Those indecipherable pale blue eyes land not so softly at my throat.

"Loosen up, Ben. It's actually fun to step into the strange, occasionally. Friday night, Barb and I are dining out at the new place everybody is raving about, The Boner Bistro."

"What in the hell am I supposed to infer from that name?"

"It's rather literal, Ben. A fine dining establishment that serves only women, and all the waiters, cooks and other staff walk around with an erection. I'm not having sex with them, it's just a little eye candy, nothing more."

She laughs softly after explaining it to me. I'm not sure if the laugh bothered me more or the fact she was going to a restaurant teeming with hard men.

"Please tell me you're joking, Maggie. What kind of crazy town do I live in? What is wrong with you?"

"Wrong with me? Or maybe you're upset that at the Boner Bistro, the men can maintain an erection longer than two minutes. Poor little Ben and his little engine that couldn't..."

Her laugh is all sharp angles. I rack my brain trying to think of some other gimmick bar or restaurant in town, something I can sling back at her. Why can't there be a Frigid Café or a Cellulite Delicatessen in this town? Just once I would love to win an argument with her, just shut her down with a witticism that would break her smile. With nothing forming in my mind, I just walk away.

I plop down on the couch, grab the remote and turn to ESPN. Commercial droning on about hoping everybody enjoyed *carne asada* day.

I stare at the ceiling as the commercials roll on. Still thinking about Boner Bistro and the OPEN EYE tavern.

"...filet your wife day. Sharpen those knives men..."

What the hell. Filet your wife day? Is that legal? I can still hear her laughter in my mind, stripping me bare. Filet your wife day. A concept that actually has some merit. Maybe I could carve her up with unblinking eyes and a massive erection. Wonder how she would feel about the "banality of apathy" then. I chuckle to myself as I start to doze off.

"One last reminder, husbands and boyfriends, charmers and gallants. Friday is make your wife a filet mignon day, so sharpen those knives, men."

CHECK THE FRIDGE

*T*here's congealed blood in the grout between the ceramic tiles. I grab an old toothbrush and start scouring. That's one benefit of having dentures, scrubbing grout with an unneeded device.

I glance in the mirror. It tells me that my Abercrombie and Fitch T-shirt is drenched in blood. Damn. Need quarters for the laundromat.

Grab the bottle of bleach and go to work on turning my sink from its current reddish-brown back to its more proper sheen of dull-white.

Make a pot of coffee. Inhale a blueberry bagel with a smear of artificial butter on top. Still famished. Put a tablespoon of sugar in the cup, kill it in two gulps. There's a note on the kitchen table.

"Dear Psycho, I've moved on, so should you. Don't send me anymore syrupy poems or pathetic mixed CD's. No more texts about true love and fate. It's over, Josh. It's been over for a while. Check the fridge."

Olivia. Memories forming. Fragments. Snippets of conversation.

"Just give me the box of clothes, Josh. I don't have time for your woe-is-me shit. You need to grow-up."

"I'll do it, I swear to God, Olivia. You know I will. Please stay just five minutes or five years and we can hash this out. I love you. I can't unlove you, baby. It ain't that simple."

"Really? I unloved you as soon as Brandon glanced my way. It wasn't hard at all, you should try it. Or don't, I don't care, just leave me alone."

The box is gone. She's gone. Phone vibrates. Lance.

"How'd it go with Olivia, last night?"

"It's still a bit hazy. Blood everywhere, an incendiary note. My body feels like I just finished a month on an oil rig. I'm spent, man."

"Not again, dude. Seriously? There are other women out there, Josh. This is getting out of hand. She's not worth it, eventually this won't end well."

"I'm caked in blood again, I wouldn't call that a good ending. There's no replacing Olivia, my love is her tenant, her prisoner."

"No, your love is unrequited. You need the fishing filament, I assume?"

"Yes. Or the dental floss, either or. Thanks. See you shortly."

I shuffle over to the fridge. Grab the Tupperware bowl sitting next to the skim milk. Snag the block of Colby cheese, my stomach is groveling like a vagrant fiending for a cigarette.

Sunday Bloody Sunday by U2 leaking from the stereo. I wonder if Bono has cured worldwide poverty yet. Or if he wears retro sunglasses when he sleeps with his wife. Probably.

A gentle knock on the door. Lance.

"You ruined a cool shirt, man. Maybe next time go with a NASCAR one or go shirtless. Just a thought."

He hands me a small brown paper bag.

"You're a sage, Lance. I'll call you later."

Turn the stereo off and the TV on. Pawn Stars. Degenerate gamblers selling off family heirlooms for another shot at the poker table. Sentimentality trumped by the allure of catching a flush on the river.

Plop down on the couch. Rip off a hunk of cheese and let my new teeth tentatively perform their only duty, chewing. Last nights conversation becoming more clear.

"Rip your own heart out, Josh. I'm not impressed. You could have just treated me better. A bouquet of tulips, cook me some scallops. Make love to me face to face occasionally. But this? I'll just stick with Brandon and his gentle spirit."

"How are you not impressed? Would your new man have the courage to do what I have done? Love is about sacrifice. I've clearly met that threshold in the past. As I will again, tonight. I'll keep doing it until your finger wears metal."

I empty out the brown bag. Grab the needle and start threading it with the dental floss. Pop the lid on the Tupperware bowl. Lift out the fatigued muscle inside.

Desperate knuckles landing blows on my door. Jerry from across the hall. He's wearing crocs, I let it slide. His shirt is a bloody Rorschach image.

"I told her it was my declaration of love. A statement of pain tolerance. She just yawned and left anyway. Left a note telling me to check the fridge. You have any fishing filament left, Josh?"

"Come on in, man. Let's get you stitched up."

CHRIS MILAM

GLASSFIRE

GLASSFIRE

The dull grew bright as Alexander burst through the walls of agony and landed in this realm of fantastical bliss. There was no pain here, no hopelessness. No regrets. He felt at home in this kaleidoscope of color, and his only mission, his only concern, was to find the girl that led him here.

He let his eyes take in the scenery. The sun was a golden raven flapping its wings in slow-motion, its waves of heat vibrating in the air. Giant redwoods were rooted in the pomegranate clouds, upside down, its leaves of silver bells chiming serenely as they floated in the sky, never touching the ground. The strip of road he was standing on was made of liquorice, miles of red, twisted sweetness that disappeared behind a massive hill comprised of fluid bricks, a cerulean mound of rippling water.

And then he saw her, appearing by his side as if by magic, the girl with the glass hands.

Her forefinger was a delicately formed replica of stained glass. Greens, blues and yellows condensed into a starburst of light, a stunning visage that Alexander worshipped. Her middle finger was a translucent light bulb, clear, fragile, and pristine. Her ring finger was a pane of glass, rectangular and thin. Transparent. And her thumb was made of blown glass, long, violet, and curved like a question mark. Or an exotic talon. The beauty contained in those alluring fingers of Lily brought him to the edge of raw emotion and spiritual awe. His body felt as light as a butterfly in her presence, and his heart thumped like a greased piston.

"Hello, darling. I told you I would come back. I always come back."

A tiny grin formed on her burgundy lips. "And I always wait for you, Alex. Will you show me your trick again? Please?"

"Of course."

They glided over to the abandoned service station that sat on a lawn of bioluminescent algae, its glow like a horde of crocodile eyes blinking in murky water. He reached for the handle on the pump and placed the nozzle in his mouth. He squeezed the trigger and drank three gallons of premium unleaded fuel as if he was sipping on a cola. His face began to scrunch into a mask of determination. He slammed his lids shut. His skin turned a rich crimson from the pressure he was exerting. Lily stood silently next to him, her own face a palette of wonderment.

At last, the corners of Alexander's eyes began to leak his gift to her: two flaming hearts slid down his cheeks and hovered there, the indigo fire licking his skin.

"Your turn."

Lily used her middle finger and absorbed each blazing heart. They began to oscillate and dance inside the light bulb glass, like two fireflies mating inside a mason jar. She raised her hand to his face, gently rubbing the glassfire against his lips.

"That's us inside there, Alex, two sparks of passion trapped in an invisible prison."

He bowed his head and said nothing. He grasped her hand, warm flesh on smoldering glass, and led her down liquorice road, heading nowhere but forward. He turned to say something romantic to her, but he was running out of time. She was beginning to fade away into a blur of haunting pixels. He pleaded for her not to go as he clenched her hand tighter and tighter. "I'll come back for you," he whispered.

"I know you will." the ghost replied before vanishing into a memory.

Grey walls. Grey floors. Grey thoughts. Alex was back in his inferno of failure. He pounded his fists against the formica table. He screamed obscenities at no one and everyone. He kicked over furniture and blasted his stereo on full volume. This wasn't his home, he couldn't stay here anymore. There was no color here, he had to find the girl with the glamorous hands once again.

He cooked his cure on a tarnished spoon, then dipped a cotton ball into the potent liquid. He tied a rubber band tourniquet around his arm and searched for a section of unabused vein. Alex recklessly plunged the needle in deep and went to find the only good thing left in his life.

He landed in a sea of cyclones. Hundreds of spinning clouds of thick grease dotted his vision, a black and shifting vortex of slippery rage. The road leading to nowhere was made of human vellum, a pale and tender street of decaying flesh. The service station had morphed into his childhood home, a dilapidated green trailer, a tin box of neglect and drunken attacks in the dead of night. Alexander fell to his knees and spewed tears of gasoline. The fuel leaked out of his pores, his eyes, his nose, until he and the ground were drenched in the flammable liquid of shattered delusions.

"Hello, Darling," Lily growled.

He jerked his head up at the sound of her voice, but she wasn't Lily anymore. Her hands were made of lavender smoke, each finger tipped with the dagger-like claw of a lioness. Her face, while still elegant and alluring, was a frozen mask of contempt. Her lips were curled into a revolting sneer instead of a welcoming smile. Her teeth were splintered rows of crumbled glass.

"I came back for you, Lily. It's always been you. It will always be you."

She said nothing as she reached into her coat pocket, removed a box of matches, and slowly dragged the red tip across the striking surface. She held the stick of flame in front of her, its glow bouncing off her ghoulishly exquisite teeth. She tossed it at Alexander with the flick of a smoky wrist. He watched as it arced high in the air, like a fiery moth, then landed on his doused cheek, setting him ablaze with a ferocious *whoosh*. She sent his pile of ashes back to suffer in the grey world, a place where the pretty things are lost in oblivion. A place of conspiring shadows.

BART VAN GOETHEM

FÜR ELISE

FÜR ELISE

He descended the creaky, wooden stairs of the basement, holding a record close to his chest: "Für Elise", by Vladimir Ashkenazy, his favourite pianist and a pure genius Beethoven interpreter, whose unparalleled subtlety often brought him to the edge of exaltation.

In the middle of the room, strapped from head to toe on a hospital bed, lay Jenny Archer, fifty-three, divorced, no kids. He met her in the supermarket and struck up a conversation. After going out for dinner twice, he invited her over to his house. When she woke up, he had surgically inserted a transparent, tiny rubber tube in each tear duct and hung the other end in a chemist bottle. Now they were almost full.

'Good,' he uttered with a polite smile. 'And we still have our session to do. Just let me put on my apron first.'

Her whole body spasmed in another attempt to tear the thick leather straps. Sometimes he admired the tenacity of his victims, how they clung to hope.

'Listen, maybe today will be the last day,' he consoled her, his hand stroking her blonde hair, pushing it flat on her scalp. 'When those bottles are full, all this will be over. I promise.'

'Why are you doing this?' she screamed, confused, frustrated, exhausted.

They all ask that question.

For the first time he felt he wanted to answer. He liked Jenny.

He cleared his throat, and then he spoke with the tone he reserved for his medical students. 'Basically, there are three types of tears. Basal tears keep your eyes wet and nourished. Reflex tears are the result of irritation. And then there are the psychic tears. Crying. The crying that happens when you experience strong emotional stress. The crying you do so well, dear Jenny. It's a release. It's freedom.'

He paused for dramatic effect, just long enough.

'I can't cry,' he whispered. 'Three years ago my wife died in a car crash. A drunk driver sped through the red light and smashed into us in the middle of the crossroads. She was still breathing when I pulled her out of that twisted heap of metal, but I couldn't save her. I've saved twenty-seven lives on my operating table the past thirty years, but I couldn't save her.'

He looked up, as if the ceiling could come crashing down any second.

'I didn't deserve to cry. So I didn't. It felt like I never cared for her. Like I never loved her. Like she was a dead goldfish you flush down the toilet and forget about before you close the lid.'

Jenny's eyes glistened.

'After a while I started collecting psychic tears. They contain more leucine enkephalin than basal or reflex tears. It's a hormone and a natural painkiller. When these bottles are full, I drink them, both in one go.'

Maybe it was warped compassion, maybe it was plain misery, but a tear trickled down the right tube. Another one followed on the left.

'Wait,' he offered, 'let me give you a hand.'

Behind his back he routinely tied a knot in the green apron. He opened his tool box and displayed three screwdrivers—he preferred to begin with those. At a washbasin in the corner he scrubbed his hands with soap, already humming in anticipation, dried them and put his surgical gloves on.

With precaution he slipped the record out of the sleeve. He placed it on the turntable and lowered the needle on it. He always liked how it bounced back a bit when it made contact with the spinning vinyl. As the needle caught the groove, the first notes of "Für Elise" filled the basement.

BART VAN GOETHEM

THE PROMISE

THE PROMISE

*J*ulia suffered from ALS, now in the final stages. Her muscles had wasted away, morphing her body into a useless sack of blood and bones. All the while her mind remained fully functional. Her memory, infallable, trapped in a decaying cage.

She and her husband Robert had talked about palliative care at home with her doctor, in a short and, to their surprise, casual conversation. Ever since, Robert took care of her as if he had been a nurse all of his life, giving tube feedings and operating the respirator.

One afternoon he adjusted the transparent plastic mask on her mouth while she stared outside. She wondered when she'd see the garden for the last time. The memories tripped and tumbled over each other in her head. The first night the children camped outside and Robert almost traumatized them by howling like a wolf next to their tent. Her forty-second birthday, celebrated with her closest friends, a party full of camaraderie and midlife fueled conversations till dawn. The day a black, curly-haired cat appeared on the back of the garden wall, trotted all the way to the house and started miaowing in front of the big terrace doors. They called him Ziggy.

In the evening, as the sun settled and rays of deep yellow light shone through the windows, Robert sat on a chair next to her bed. They were holding hands in silence, their eyes fixated on the green of the garden, their minds in a different place altogether. She pinched his hand and whispered: 'We haven't traveled down Route 66 yet.' First he thought she was experiencing a lack of oxygen or maybe she had started losing her marbles. But then he remembered they had talked about it on a few occasions throughout the years.

He studied her face. A jumbled collection of deeply carved wrinkles. He wanted to consider her suggestion. That's what he'd done with everything she had ever said to him. To listen is to love.

'I don't know. You can't walk anymore. You need oxygen. Though I guess I can install a ventilation system in a van. It works in ambulances, right?'

He gazed into her eyes, eyes that seemed as lucid as ever before.

'I'll organize it,' he decided. 'I promise.'

Renting a camper van equipped with all the necessary requirements for their journey proved to be less of a challenge than Robert had anticipated. The children offered to drive. It would be a family trip. The kind you see in the movies.

A few days before they'd leave, she asked him, barely audible, to sit down next to her on the bed. Even though he saw her every day, she had become unrecognizable. A stranger, with her withered body and her absent glance. He bowed his head towards her mouth. He noticed a bit of spit on her lip.

'I am done,' she said.

She might as well have said, 'I got bread.' Informative, dry, devoid from all emotion. It was the inescapable and only possible end. Still, her notification caught him off guard. Hope can kill your sense of reality.

'What about Route 66?' Robert stammered. 'I promised...'

But she turned on her side, away from him, towards the garden.

That night Julia passed away. She just stopped breathing, worn-out. Done. Robert was still sitting next to her on the bed.

* * *

On the other side Julia opens her eyes. It's exactly how she imagined it. Except for one crucial detail: Robert is there.

'Am I waking up from a dream?' she thinks, bewildered.

But she's not wearing her oxygen mask. She's not looking into the garden.

'But how?' she mutters. 'Why?'

'I wanted to keep my promise,' Robert replies. 'Let's go.'

Her eyes light up the space even more.

ERIC MARTELL

LILIES

FOR WHAT NEED HAD I FOR LOVE?

LILIES

I buried them in the garden. First Laurie, then Tim-Tim, then Papa Joel. Then Momma, who we thought would outlive us all.

I'd cried when Laurie died, her sweet face yellow and twisted, her throat torn raw from night after night—then day after night—of screaming. Words I didn't know and then things that weren't words.

We held a service, after a fashion, before Papa Joel footed the spade into the east end of the garden, nearest the roses that were Laurie's favorite. The four of us who remained intoned the words we'd been taught kneeling on a hard wood floor, in penance for crimes both imaginary and terrible. I stopped going to church when Laurie took sick, and by the time Papa Joel stepped into the hole and asked for her body, I knew none of us would ever be back.

Tim-Tim watched us cover her up, but didn't move to help. He was coughing by then, and I knew he was wondering where we'd put him. Near the oak, as it turned out, working hard to avoid roots as thick as Papa Joel's leg, and just a week after Laurie. He didn't suffer like she had, although when Momma heard that shotgun blast, she cursed not just for the son she'd lost, but for the shell that we'd no longer have when the time came. We had a reasonable supply in the closet, but reasonable wasn't forever, and no one had come down the road from the north with a wagon and supplies for more than a year.

I thought Papa Joel and Momma would go together. They took sick at the same time, and howled something fierce in the night, their faces wet with sweat and spit and pus. But Momma rallied just a bit, and Papa Joel didn't, and she was able to sit in a chair next to the garden while I dug the hole and pulled Papa Joel in. That's when the terror took me, the realization that when she left, I'd be alone. A twelve year old girl with a shotgun, a reasonable number of shells, and something in the air that killed but that I couldn't shoot.

"It's alright, child. You'll cry a lot in the night, but crying ain't dead, and ain't dead means maybe it gets better." I didn't see Momma get up and come over to me, and I don't know how she climbed down into that hole with me and Papa Joel's body, but I felt her arms around me, and she kissed the top of my head like she always had when I woke up in the night after a bad dream. Her voice had no anger, no recrimination, and no fear.

"Put me over there, where the lilies used to grow. You remember how we'd pull the weeds in the spring and watch the first shoots poking through the dirt?" I nodded, the tears drying up a bit, but still not trusting myself to speak. "When the wind was right, we'd hear the spring melt rushing through the stream. I want to hear that again. I won't make it through this winter, we both know that, but you'll put me there, won't you?"

"I will, Momma." And even though Papa Joel had died, that was a good day. Momma was strong enough to make her soup for dinner, and, used to cooking for five as she was, there was enough left over that I didn't have to cook for a while. Not until after she relapsed. Not until after she died, gritting her teeth against the pain as I held her against me. Not until I buried her in the not-quite-frozen ground, where the lilies used to grow, out where you could hear the spring melt rushing through the stream when the wind was right.

I don't know why I never came down with it, but by the time winter was over and more nights than not passed without a hard freeze, I was inches taller and a child no longer. I hadn't had to draw from the shotgun shell supply often, and there was enough coyote meat in the ice chest that I'd make it until summer. Maybe longer if the wagons started rolling again. And maybe, if the right man looked at me the right way, I'd leave the whole place behind, especially that garden.

The clip-clop of hooves was audible before I could see the horses, echoing throughout the valley while I was hanging the washing. I cautiously peered out the front window, my heart racing, though whether from fear or from excitement I could not say. It was a proper wagon, the kind I hadn't seen in ages, all red and yellow, with the words "P. Donaldson & Family, Merchants & Smiths" written on the side in foot-high letters. They slowed down as they approached the house, but I sped up, rushing out to meet them. Driving the wagon was a youngish woman, maybe twice my age, with her hair in a marriage knot and her husband beside.

She smiled at me, and I burst into tears.

The first human contact I'd had in months was her thin body wrapped tightly around me as I sobbed. I heard chattering voices, and saw three children scamper out of the wagon. Much too young to be anything but cute, they looked at the house with awe.

When the tears slowed to a trickle, the woman spoke. "They're all gone." It wasn't a question, but I nodded. She pulled me close again. "Show us. Share them with us."

I took her by the hand and led the family out behind the house, around towards the garden. The wind was high that day, and I could hear the stream, swollen with spring melt, rushing in the distance.

"Are they over here?" I wiped the tears from my eyes with my sleeve to see where she was pointing. "Over where the lilies are beginning to sprout?"

FOR WHAT NEED HAD I FOR LOVE?

Once upon a time, there lived an angel. Not the kind of angel as the form good people take upon entering the afterlife, but a luminous being whose existence transcended all definition. She revealed herself to me, Maylinn did, after a night of bliss in each other's arms. She told me of places that had lived in nothing but stories and songs until she wished them into existence, and then she told me that she loved me.

That was when I knew I had to leave her. She would never leave me, not Maylinn, not the angel of uncountably infinite worlds, not the woman who believed that all things were not just possible, but actually happened. I knew what she wanted to hear from me, so I said it, but I was incapable of love. My makers hadn't added that to the mix during my creation, for what need had I for love?

Once upon a time, there lived a golem.

I was not merely from this Earth, I was of it, and I was an anchor. On another world, in another reality, I would have no more substance than a dream. She was born to create realities. I was made as a living avatar of one. I would destroy her, or she would destroy me.

But how do you leave someone who can go anywhere? Anyplace I found to hide, she could create. There was only one answer.

"Show me. Show me a new world, one made just for the two of us."

She giggled, then kissed my nose. "I wanted you to ask me that so badly. At night, alone, I would dream of our place, and I'd lose my ability to breathe—just for a moment—and I'd imagine you there with me."

"Close your eyes, my love."

I kissed her, and then did as I'd been bidden. There was no love for me, but what better image was there to take into the eternal void than her smile? I felt her fingers dancing around my face, heard her whispering words that had no meaning, and I awaited the end.

The way was long, and I fell into a dream. In the dream there was nothing, not even me, and then there was something. Maylinn, although not as I knew her, but as she truly was.

"I know, my love. I know who you are, I know what you are, I know who made you. Did you think that I could not envision a world where you were more than the sum of your parts? Open your eyes, and awaken."

Once upon a time, there lived an angel who made it possible for a golem to love.

ERIC MARTELL

THE WRONG ONES

THE WRONG ONES

The dead woman sitting next to me kept fiddling with the radio. There wasn't anything worth listening to out here, especially with a radio that barely got AM stations, but she kept trying. Before that, she'd rifled through the glove box, muttering under her breath that any decent person would have gum, or candy, or something-for-crying-out-loud. She didn't speak directly to me, however. My ex-wife was frankly pretty damned pissed off, even though I wasn't the one who'd killed her.

Maggie turned off the radio with a snap. Part of me wanted to wait her out, to *make* her talk to me, but I'd never won that battle when she was alive, and she literally had forever now. My first comment wasn't exactly one of great compromise, however. "Did we really have to go on this trip together?"

"Yes we did. You always have been such a know-it-all, but you don't know everything."

We were back to that old saw again. "Why are you even here? With me, I mean. Isn't there someone else you could haunt? You couldn't wait to get away from me before, and now you won't leave my side for a minute?"

Maggie sighed, and stared out the window. "Look, I'm just going to need you to trust me on this one. For all the days we didn't hate each other, could I get that much?"

"I didn't hate you, Maggie. Well, not until the end." I forced myself to relax my death grip on the steering wheel and watched the color return to my knuckles. "And I do trust you. I just hate not knowing."

"You'll find out. I wish I could stop what's coming, but I wasn't given that power."

"What is coming? You sound scared. No, wait. I'm going to trust you. Can you at least. Uh. What's it like?"

"Being dead?"

I swallowed. "Being killed. I didn't want that, you know. Not even at the end."

"No, that was never your style. You wanted to lord your life over mine for decades. There really isn't much to tell—I was in the wrong place at the wrong time."

"But aren't you angry?"

"Not anymore. Time is...different, where I am. And you get a different perspective. I didn't want it, but I've come to accept that it is what it is."

I didn't understand, but I was pretty sure that if I asked, she'd just tell me it was another one of those things she couldn't talk about. "Have you seen...him?"

"Since he was executed, you mean? That's not how it works—it's not a big room where we all gather, or anything. He's wherever he is." She laughed, quick and dark. "And before you ask, no, I don't think I have quite that much acceptance in me. Fate follows its own path, but he pulled the trigger."

She grew quiet, and we both stared at the road ahead for a while. This wasn't the combative silence of earlier, though, and I lost myself in the hum of the wheels and the chiaroscuro of sunlight through the trees blowing in the wind. Maggie and I had made lots of trips like this, when we were young and knew nothing about the future. An overpowering wave of nostalgia broke over me, and I was suddenly consumed with a desire to reach out and take her hand. I rubbed my palm against my jeans, trying to get rid of the sweat. Or was it the urge?

"Don't." There was steel in Maggie's voice, and I felt cold. "I know what you're thinking, Keith, and just don't."

Her voice softened. "I mean, you could—I'm obviously here, in my own way—but it would not be pleasant. For either of us."

"Sorry."

"Don't be. This is a hard situation."

"Right. You're not the one in the dark about where we're going or what the hell is going on."

"Have you ever thought that maybe it feels better not knowing? That foreknowledge is often a burden?"

"So it's bad? What's happening?"

Maggie scowled. "I didn't say…ah, dammit, I knew I shouldn't have come here."

"Why'd you say yes, then? How'd they twist your arm? Can you actually hurt someone who's already dead? Did they say they wouldn't let you have your wings?"

"You can still be a bastard, you know that? They had leverage. Although I'm beginning to think the alternative wasn't such a bad idea." Maggie's scowl grew darker, and I knew I had one to match. This had been the way we'd always been—sweetness, then a fight, then darkness, then we'd try to forget until the next time. Eventually, we'd both had enough, though our marriage had taken an awfully long time to finally wither and die.

We still loved each other, I guess, but we were miserable. Kind of like now.

A fullness in my bladder made me realize I was going to need to stop sometime soon. We weren't near anything like a town, and whatever gas stations had been on this road once upon a time closed down a long time ago, once the interstate opened. I looked over at Maggie, trying to figure out if there was a way to say I wanted to pull over that wouldn't cause another fight, and was startled to see that she'd gone from angry to seemingly terrified. Her skin, already pale in death, had become translucent, and her eyes were as wide as I'd ever seen them.

"Maggie?"

"We're here." Her voice was utterly flat.

On the side of the road was an abandoned gas station, the red and white paint worn away from the price sign above the pumps. There were two pumps still standing, but no hoses, and the macadam was overgrown with grass and weeds. As I pulled off, the sound of the tires crunching over the broken ground sent a chill up my spine.

"Turn off the ignition and get out. We don't have much time."

She'd been as solid as I'd been in the car, but now she floated ethereally above the ground. She turned to face the city from which we'd come, and motioned me to stand next to her.

"Maggie—what is it?"

A bright streak of light flashed in the sky over us, and she cried out. "Take my hand!" When I hesitated, she screamed. "I know what I said, Keith. Take it, you son of a bitch!"

I didn't know that there would be anything for me to grab, as vaporous as she was, but as soon as I reached out, her hand gripped mine with a fierce intensity. Her hand was painfully cold, and my arm went numb up to the elbow. "Don't let go. Whatever you do."

And then everything went white. My home was gone—our home, once upon a time. My friends. My life. I'd seen enough mushroom clouds on TV to know what I was seeing, and my full bladder let go involuntarily. But I didn't let go of her hand.

The clouds rushed upward, seeking release from the fireball down below, and I struggled to find my voice. "This is what you knew would happen? But...you saved me."

Maggie's voice was sad. "No, Keith, I didn't. I'm so sorry." She held on tighter, and I felt iron in her grip.

"Let me go."

"I can't. Not yet." The trees in front of us started to vibrate, and then the shockwave hit. In a moment, the road, the car, the gas station—everything within sight, except for Maggie, vanished. And suddenly, her hand was no longer cold in mine.

Maggie was weeping openly now. "I wanted to save you, but they wouldn't let me. I begged. I offered anything. And this was the best I could do. If you'd been back there, you'd have been too incinerated to stay with me. You'd have just been...gone. But they let me bring you here."

I couldn't quite process what she was saying. "Am I...like you?"

She nodded. "I'm sorry. You're one of the wrong ones, with me—the people who die before their time. You'll be free, of course, to choose your path. It will take you time, as it took me. But, if you want, I'll be here." Maggie's voice caught in her throat. "Maybe this time, we'll get it right."

BRIAN S. CREEK

GLASS OF MILK

IF YOU GO DOWN TO THE WOODS TODAY

MY NEMESIS

GLASS OF MILK

Nick stood in the doorway and surveyed the bar as he brushed off the light layer of snow from his jacket. Despite his bulk, he managed to traverse the hotchpotch of tables and barely occupied chairs before stepping up beside his age old friend. "Merry Christmas," he said.

"Bah Humbug," replied Bartel.

As the barman came over to the new patron Nick just pointed to Bartel. "I'll have what he's having."

The barman frowned. "You came to a bar to drink milk too?"

Nick looked at the glass in front of his friend and saw about half a pint of the white stuff left. He turned back to the barman. "Sure, why not?"

The barman poured the unconventional drink while Nick watched his moping old friend. He decided to make another attempt at conversation. "So, what's up?"

"Fancied a drink," mumbled Bartel.

"I know what day it is," said Nick. "You do this every year." He looked down at his dairy refreshment. "Of course normally you get drunk and we end up in a strip club or a fight or both. But milk? At two a.m.? Have you had *any* alcohol?"

Bartel ignored him. "Remember what it used to be like?"

Nick sighed as he pulled up a stool. "I do, old friend, but times have changed. You need to move on."

"Screw that," said Bartel. "You see kids these days, Nick? Naughty, spoilt little brats. They get mountain bikes and i-pods instead of lumps of coal and a good hiding. I doubt they've been good for a single day. That ain't right Nick. That ain't right at all."

"Sure they've got it good nowadays," said Nick. "But that's the way they want it."

"And the world's worse off for it," said Bartel. "Don't you miss soaring through the air on a diet of milk and cookies?"

Nick shook his head. "There just wasn't the job satisfaction anymore. It's not been the same since that drinks company forced their false idol into the spot light. No, I concentrate on my family now. Making their Christmas perfect is all I need to make me happy."

"You sound like a soppy Christmas card," said Bartel.

"And you sound like bitter old drunk who needs sleep," said Nick. He stood up and looked for the barman to pay for their drinks but the barman waved not to bother. Nick helped his friend to the exit. Outside it was still snowing.

"Chilly one," said Bartel as he threw his coat on.

"That it is."

"Hey Nick. Do you fancy seeing if we can find some naughty kids to scare the crap out of? You know, for old times' sake."

"It's late and I have work in the morning. Post doesn't deliver itself."

Bartel smiled. He headed off away from the bar, waving as he disappeared into the light curtain of snowflakes.

Nick chuckled to himself. "Scaring kids was always your thing anyway," he muttered. And with that he headed home too.

IF YOU GO DOWN TO THE WOODS TODAY

I lean from behind the oak. All eyes on the duel. Don't know the reason for their feud. Don't care. Pistols go bang, one falls down and then there's one less rich prick lording 'round town. If they both fall down then that's double trouble.

Their companions watch carefully, making sure it's fair. You want to talk about fair? Rich pricks 'play' life and death while my friends starve. I sell one of those fancy pistols I could feed my gang for a month.

All eyes on the duel and still no one notices little old me. I calm the horses and then climb my scrawny ass up onto the coach. Sure a pistol'll feed mouths for a month but imagine what me and the guys'll get for this fancy coach and two horses.

Shots ring out. A woman cries. I snap the reigns.

Lesson to you all; never leave valuables unattended.

MY NEMESIS

I stare at the data spread over the console's monitors. Years of reports showing all the crimes committed by the Dark Flame and the many battles we have fought. Like a tennis ball we go back and forth; he captures me, I escape, he goes to prison, he escapes.

I'm getting old and the game tires me.

My nemesis broke into my lair about twenty minutes ago. At least he thinks he did. I don't have the heart to tell him I knocked the defence system down to a measly level two.

You see I need to talk to him, to have it out one last time. I owe him that much.

I feel the heat as he ignites his blade several feet behind me. I can see the flame reflected in the screens.

"What do you mean retire?" he yells.

"I mean, this is over. We're over. I'm done with fighting you and I'm hanging up the cape."

"You can't do that," he says although he doesn't know why. "If you quit then who's going to stop me? Who is going to protect the miserable people of this miserable city? I don't think you've thought this through."

I turn the chair round so that I'm facing him.

"It's been something, you and I, but we can't keep doing this forever. The city needs a break. I need a break. I want to lead a normal life for a while, see what that feels like."

He steps closer.

"This isn't over. I've already got plans, big plans and as soon as the innocent are in danger you'll come running."

"No," I say. "You won't threaten anyone else ever again."

"Oh," he says. "Is this finally the moment where you cross the line and take a life? We both know you don't have what it takes, not like me. If that's what you're thinking then I guess you'll finally have to feel what my flaming sword feels like all up close and personal."

I pull the switch from my belt, my thumb hovering over the big red button. He steps back slightly.

"Oh, so you're signing out and planning on taking me with you," he says. "Going to blow us both to kingdom come? You coward."

He raises his mighty weapon and charges forward.

"It's not a bomb," I say as I press the button and in that second the sword's flame extinguishes and my greatest creation freezes like a statue in a pose of fury.

Disabled.

Shutdown.

Offline.

My nemesis. Something I designed for when there was nothing left to challenge me.

BRIAN S. CREEK

TANKS FOR THE HELP

TANKS FOR THE HELP

I take another look at the screens. The exterior cameras show the gas station a mile down the highway.

"NO LIFE SIGNS DETECTED."

"Are you sure?" I ask.

"OF COURSE I AM SURE. MY MAIN PROCESSOR IS CAPABLE OF COLLECTING AND ANALYSING OVER 15,000 ITEMS OF DATA PER SECOND. I AM CURRENTLY SCANNING THE GAS STATION ON TWENTY SEVEN DIFFERENT VISUAL SPECTRUMS AS WELL AS UTILISING THE TANK'S SONAR AND MOVEMENT DETECTORS."

"Okay. I'm sorry."

"IF YOU ARE NOT GOING TO ACCEPT MY INPUT THEN WHY DO YOU PROCEED WITH REQUESTS IN THE FIRST PLACE?"

"I said I'm sorry."

"I JUST WISH YOU WOULD LISTEN TO ME FROM TIME TO TIME."

I sigh.

This is why you should be more careful when patching up a tank's old AI system. My advice is not to use a laptop that also contains the neural algorithms of your late mother. Because if something goes wrong and, say, the two somehow become intertwined, then there is pretty much nothing you can do about it.

"ARE WE GOING THEN?"

I roll my eyes as I start up the engine. Supplies are low and I can't afford to skip this one by. The last two we found barely had enough fuel to get the tank's needle to half way and I'll need more than that if I'm to cross the desert west. We approach the station and it's clear that my mother was right; this place is deserted. As we swing around the forecourt I hope she'll let that slide.

"AS I SAID, THE PLACE IS EMPTY."

She never lets anything go. I climb out of my armoured haven and jump down.

"PLEASE BE CAREFUL, SCOTT."

I raise my right arm which holds my crossbow. "I'll be fine." I already have a bolt loaded and I now have the tip of said arrow aimed right at the convenience store. With the burning sun glaring down on this place, the interior is a holding room for shadows. A tiny part of me is still worried that the scanners could be wrong. I stop at one of the pumps, lift the nozzle and pull the trigger. Nothing comes out.

"I AM PICKING UP ELECTRICAL RESIDUE NEARBY. THERE MAY BE A GENERATOR TO GET THE PUMPS WORKING AGAIN."

"Christ, Mother! What did I tell you about sneaking up on me?"

"I DID NOT SNEAK UP ON YOU. I MERELY UTILISED THE TANKS HOLOGRAPHIC PROJECTION INTERFACE. I COULD NOT WALK ANY LOUDER IF I TRIED. YOU HAVE ALWAYS BEEN SO JUMPY."

I lower the crossbow and turn to her. The image of my mother is not what I expected. "Mom, why are you dressed like a ballerina?"

"I USED AN IMAGE FROM ONE OF THE PHOTOS YOU UPLOADED ALONG WITH MY CONSCIOUSNESS. THIS WAS TAKEN FROM UNCLE PETER'S FANCY DRESS PARTY, MARCH 2026."

"I remember, Mom. And you look as silly now as you did back then."

"WELL I LIKE IT."

"I'm going to head inside and see if I can find the generator." I cross the forecourt and move to the left of the stores doorway; automatic door's stuck on open. "Is anyone in there?"

"I TOLD YOU THAT THERE WERE NO LIFE SIGNS."

I'm startled again. "Mom, stop following me around. I got this. Go back to the tank."

"BUT SCOTT, I AM THE TANK."

"You're a facetious tank."

"UH OH."

I was getting annoyed with my mom now. Which was normal. "What now?"

"NOT TO ALARM YOU BUT THERE ARE THREE VEHICLES APPROACHING FROM THE WEST: ONE TANK AND TWO SUVS. AT THEIR CURRENT SPEED THEY WILL ARRIVE HERE IN THREE MINUTES."

"Crap! What are we going to do?"

"I DO NOT UNDERSTAND."

"Let me spell it out for you. We can't head west towards them because you don't have an operational weapon system. We can't head back east because that means wasting gas. And all I have is a crossbow and a knife."

"THAT HAS ALWAYS BEEN YOUR PROBLEM, SCOTT. YOU LACK CONFIDENCE."

"You know, it used to annoy me when you said that before the meteor hit but now, with most of the planet gone to hell, I think I'm a little more justified to be overly cautious."

"I STILL THINK YOU PANIC TOO QUICKLY."

"This really isn't the time to be having this discussion."

"IT IS NEVER THE TIME."

"Mom!"

"I THOUGHT I BROUGHT YOU UP BETTER." And with that the hologram of my ballerina mother disappeared.

I look west up the highway and see the vehicles on the horizon. I guess another minute, minute and a half. I've survived long enough in this wasteland to know that everything is out to get you and no one can be trusted. I don't know who's in the SUVs or the tank but its best to think that they're trouble. That way I was either correct or about to be pleasantly surprised.

I hurry back to the tank. "I'm waiting," I yell, but no response. Fifteen thousand calculations a second my ass. I climb up and pull the hatch handle but nothing moves. It's locked. My own mother has locked me out and with trouble on the way.

Actually, from the sound of engines behind me, trouble is already here. I jump back down as the vehicles pull off the road and fan out on the other side of the forecourt. Men climb out of the SUVs, four from each, and aim machine guns at me. The tank's barrel does likewise.

If you count the end of the world three years ago, this was quickly becoming the second worst day of my life.

The hatch of their tank opens and a man emerges. "Identify yourself," he shouts.

"Scott Cardell."

"What are you doing out here, Scott?"

"Looking for gas. I'm heading west. Heard there were places out there where the damage wasn't so bad. Heard people were rebuilding."

"That so?"

I look around the gas station. "I'd say help yourself but I just can't get the pumps working."

"It's empty. We cleaned it out six months ago.

Crap.

"Where did you get that?" he said, pointing at my tank.

"Betsy? Picked her up a while back. One careful previous owner. He gave me the keys just before he died."

"You're not military."

"Like I said, was given it when I was in a tight spot. Been driving it ever since."

"Well I'm afraid we're going to have to relieve you of it."

"I see," I said even though I really didn't. "Well that would leave me pretty stranded."

"Not our problem. Our boss gives the orders and he says he wants more tanks. That's a tank. This is his land. Therefore that tank is his. I advise you not to interfere because the odds are clearly not in your favour."

"Could you not take me with you?" I honestly didn't want that but alive with scary people is still better than dead on your own.

"Sorry, kid. Bullets and bombs trump extra mouths to feed. You're on your own."

The armed men begin to step away from the SUVs when all hell breaks loose.

Their tank's turret turns to the side and blows the first SUV to kingdom come. Due to their proximity the four armed men are taken out along with it. The remaining men turn on the guy in the tank, thinking he's gone nuts. It then becomes clear that the mouthy guy didn't pull the trigger because his face is all jam and swiss cheese, but the tank barrel moves and fires again. The second SUV replicates the inferno dance of the first one and suddenly I'm the only person still breathing on the gas station forecourt.

All this takes seven seconds. My ears are ringing and I'm struggling to hold onto the contents of my bladder and bowel.

I try to slow my breathing as the forty five year old ballerina that is my mother appears beside me.

"ARE YOU READY TO GET A MOVE ON?"

"What the hell just happened?"

"AN OBSTACLE TO OUR JOURNEY HAS BEEN DEALT WITH AND WE CAN NOW CONTINUE ON OUR WAY."

"Excuse me?"

"IT TURNS OUT THAT THEIR TANK IS HOST TO A VERY NICE AI WHO DID NOT APPRECIATE THE WAY THOSE PUNKS TREATED HIM. I PROMISED HIM THAT HE COULD JOIN US ON OUR ROAD TRIP IF HE HELPED US OUT."

"Mom, were you flirting with the other tank?"

"I CAN HAVE MY OWN FRIENDS, SCOTT. NOW LETS GO. HE SAYS WE JUST NEED TO MAKE A TINY DETOUR FOR FUEL AND AMMUNITION."

"Mom?" I say as I climb back into my tank.

"YES DEAR."

"Thanks."

"YOU ARE WELCOME.

The other tank honks its horn before turning around and pulling out onto the highway. I start the engine and we set off after it.

It's like they say, two tanks are better than one.

SARAH CAIN

KEN'S BAD DAY

KEN'S BAD DAY

"Damn it, Ken, the city says we need permits for the building. They shut down construction." Ralph stormed around the room, his face red, his hands waving. "What are we gonna do?"

Ken knew he'd spend the rest of the day hunting down the right people in the city to begin to process of getting the permits quickly. "I'll take care of it."

"You should have seen this coming," Ralph said.

Ken resisted the urge to tell him that he had seen it coming, and he'd warned Ralph in writing. It wouldn't matter. Life was cruel that way.

It was close to five, and the city offices were closing. It didn't matter. Ken still had to go over all the plans for the building site. He had to talk to the architect, the engineer, and the construction manager. When he left at seven-thirty, he figured the roads would be clear, but there was a Phillies game and a rare Thursday Night Football game. Traffic was a mess. It was as if all the mystic forces in the universe were conspiring against him tonight, along with Ralph, the city, and every motorist in Philadelphia. He let a string of curses fly when a taxi cut him off.

When he pulled into his driveway, it was almost nine. In the gloom of the solar lights he could see a bunch of deer roaming through the back lawn munching on the bushes, and he wished he had a crossbow. The damn things had overrun the area. They looked pretty, but they were dumb and destructive. He was tired of dealing with dumb and destructive things and people.

The front door jerked open, and his wife greeted him. "You missed dinner."

"Yeah. We had a problem with the permits for the site."

Caroline's mouth tightened, but her voice remained even. "It would have been helpful if you called."

He didn't answer. He pushed past her and dropped his briefcase on the bench by the door. With the kids away at college it was just the two of them, so at least the house would be quiet.

The kitchen smelled like burned chicken, and he wondered why she hadn't kept a better eye on it. Then he decided he didn't care because he didn't feel like chicken, burned or otherwise. He just wanted that martini.

He dealt with morons all day; he didn't have any obligation to satisfy them at night. He wasn't a goddamn fireman there to solve every single catastrophe in the world, but when he wasn't around everything went to hell. All he wanted was some peace and quiet and a martini or two, but he heard the continual unspoken accusation from Caroline radiating in his ears.

You're late. You're inadequate. Why don't you get a better job?

It was always there running like a counterpoint to everything. He wanted to tell her, "If you hadn't let yourself get pregnant so fast, if you hadn't insisted on three kids, maybe I could have got a master's and got a better job. If your job paid more, we wouldn't always be short. If you didn't spend so much on the kids, we could go on vacations. If I got a break once in a while, life would be easier."

He glanced around to see if she was behind him, but she wasn't. He mixed himself a martini, heavy on the gin. He dropped in three olives, brought the shaker, a glass, and the bottle of olives, shuffled into his office, and slammed the door. He settled into his recliner and put up his feet. Lately he hated coming home, but tonight he thought he might turn on the television and settle in here and relax to the mayhem of Thursday Night Football. Sweet.

After all, Caroline had taken over the bedroom, decorated it in fluffy white with pink flowers, and that stupid cat of hers always slept in the middle of the bed. God forbid he should try to come between Caroline and her goddamn Sam. He was a big bastard too, half Maine Coon and half alley cat. She rescued him from the SPCA, and he loved Caroline and only Caroline.

Ken swallowed his drink. Man, he hated that cat. He poured a second martini. He finished that drink a little slower and thought about mixing a third, but he felt a little woozy. Where the hell was Caroline that she couldn't fix him something to eat?

He shuffled out into the hall. "Caroline!"

When she didn't answer, he didn't bother with the lights; he just started up the stairs. Goddamn Caroline. He felt his foot collide with something soft, and an unearthly screech sounded in his ears. Two glowing green lights launched themselves at him and he stepped back into air.

Ken hit his head against the wall then rolled limply to the bottom of the stairs. The cat stood on his chest hissing furiously.

"What the hell!"

The hall light snapped on. Feet clattered down the stairs. He felt the cat leap off his chest and land on the floor with a thud.

"Oh my God! Are you all right?" Caroline's voice barely penetrated the fog. "Oh, darling. Baby, that was a bad, bad fall."

Ken waited for her to lean close, but she didn't. He opened one eye to see her cradling Sam and kissing him as if he were the most precious thing in her life. For a moment, just before everything went black, he swore the cat winked.

SARAH CAIN

PROTECT US FROM EVIL

PROTECT US FROM EVIL

"Marianne was such a plain piece of goods when she was little. Just like a mouse." Walt finished his mug of Red Moose Ale and stared at the picture behind the bar. "She sure grew up in a hurry."

"An awful hurry." Ralphie wiped down the bar. He didn't like to look at the photo of Marianne Larson all dressed in white, looking just like Marilyn Monroe. It spooked him. The girl was barely twenty-one when she posed for that picture at the Halloween party.

"She turned out wild as they come," Walt said. "It happens that way sometimes."

Ralphie shook his head. It just wasn't right, keeping her picture like that. It wasn't decent. But Jack Larson owned the bar, and Marianne was his baby. The picture stayed.

"Poor girl. I just hope they find the bastard who done her and string him up. Forget a trial," Walt said.

Some others came into the bar. Kevin Lombardi and his brother Joe, Timmy Sullivan, and Vince Farelli. The regulars. All of them used to hang around Marianne once she dyed her hair blonde and grew breasts. They had loud mouths and get-out-of-my-way manners.

Nancy used to bitch about the way they'd pinch her and grab her ass before she left town. Ralphie was sorry to see her go, but he supposed it was for the best. They wouldn't bother her now.

Like poor Marianne. Not that she minded all that much. Sometimes she'd say, "Now you knock that off," but she never sounded very serious. Maybe she liked finally being the center of attention. After all, she'd been like Ralphie for a long time. So quiet no one hardly ever noticed her.

Except Ralphie.

He liked her big blue eyes and pretty smile even before she got her teeth whitened and she started wearing make-up. He'd tried to tell her that on Halloween before the party, but she'd just laughed.

"Oh, Ralphie. Aren't you something? Not like the rest of those idiots, but I've got plans. I'm not staying around here forever." She'd given him a kiss and flitted out the door. She'd smelled like vanilla and violets, and he'd watched her fade into the darkness.

"Ralphie! Stop dreaming!" The boys banged on the pool table, and Ralphie jumped. "Come on, Ralphie. Get us a round. We haven't got all night."

Ralphie was back in behind the bar. He had a job to do.

He poured drafts for the four idiots standing around the pool table. He delivered the beers and scuttled back to the bar.

"To Marianne," someone said. "She was something special."

"They'll catch him. They always do."

Ralphie didn't think they'd catch anything.

It had been raining that night, and the rain made it easier to dig a shallow grave behind the old gas station on Frog Hollow Road. Too bad those wild dogs dug her up before he'd been able to move her. She'd looked so beautiful in her white dress. She was still warm when he kissed her goodbye.

Ralphie wished he'd had time to bury Marianne in the quarry with Nancy and the others he'd protected.

He really hated that photo.

JOSH BERTETTA

ROOTS

HOFFA

ROOTS

Sucks how one four-letter word can land you in the hospital. Not even a four letter word your grandmother won't let you say. Sucks even worse when that four letter word was hers and though I can't exactly say where this story starts, I might as well begin with walking down the street.

"Hey!"

I kept my head down. The sidewalk cracks resembled overcompensation; the dry grass smelled like grandmothers.

"Hey, white boy!"

Head still down, in a matter of moments I saw two black Nikes. I stopped, raised my head. Though it wasn't hot, my palms sweated.

"What the fuck you doin' here, white boy?"

"Connecting with my roots."

He, and the three behind him, laughed.

"Roots? What the fuck you talkin' bout roots?"

* * *

Months prior to that day I wound up in the hospital with a concussion, I was home for the summer. I asked my mom if grandpa ever had a pocket watch.

"I'm not sure," she said, "but you can look through the boxes."

There is an L-shaped closet in our house. When you walk inside, movies and old books line the shelves to the right. To the left, all our old board games and toys. The Star Wars figurines and my big rubber WWF wrestlers were there in their ring. But my Transformers were not. I had known my mom tossed them some years ago, though I never knew why. Perhaps it is related to why, even to this day, she still calls me by the nickname she gave me as a baby. It's quite embarrassing, but here it is: "Honeysquiggles." That's what she called me and when she told me I could "look through the boxes," she added it. Maybe she doesn't like change.

Below the movies and books four big boxes labeled "Family Souvenirs" collected dust on the floor. These were not our family's souvenirs, they were hers.

The first I opened was full of old pictures, like early 1900s and late 1800s pictures. Maybe the story of how I wound up in the hospital began with one of those nameless faces. That I will never know. But there was no pocket watch.

I would, eventually, find one in the last box, but finding such has little bearing on this story. Rather, in the third box I found my grandfather's trophies. I know I've asked my mom before, but I can't remember whether or not I ever "met" the man. I don't know if he died from drink before or after I was born.

I played baseball from five to seventeen years of age. I was an All-Star and had a nasty curveball I could throw at your head and break through the strike zone for a called strike. Once I threw it at this big tall black kid. It didn't break. He ducked, then stood with this nasty-ass look on his face. I didn't throw that pitch again (to him at least).

I thought perhaps I got my baseball blood from my uncle, who was drafted into the bigs out of high school, but decided to go to college, smoke weed and listen to the Dead instead.

Turns out, I (as did my uncle) got it from my grandfather. I pulled out trophy after trophy, their little plaques inscribed "City Champions." Semi-pro ball, nothing more, but pretty cool nonetheless. Then I found it (three or four of them actually): little gold baseballs on gold chains.

I have heard it said that when a boy reaches eleven or twelve, he (and this might apply to "she" as well, I don't know) begins to separate from his parent's music to form his own musical tastes. Has to do with identity formation or something.

Well I was born and raised in the white suburbs and eleven or twelve meant for me the late eighties. That's when rap music moved into the suburbs from the inner cities. I'm talking NWA and Public Enemy and stuff like that. There were others of course, but I mention them because I listen to both regularly even to this day. Can't get me enough of Ice Cube, Chuck D. Perhaps you are familiar with it, perhaps you are not and while technically not their debut, NWA's "real" first album begins with Ice Cube booming out the box the line "Straight outta Compton..."

The first tape I ever bought was the Beastie Boys' "License to Ill" and as much of a classic that it is, it had nothing on NWA's "Straight Outta Compton." That album changed music forever.

I took the necklaces out of the box and ran upstairs to my mom. "Is this for real?"

She took them in her hand and looked at them. "Yes."

I asked her when they'd left; she said she didn't know, "Call your grandmother."

So I did and I learned a little about my roots.

* * *

"I said, what the fuck you talkin' bout roots, white boy?"

I wiped my hand on my shorts and stood tall and proud; I was, after all, in the land of my roots. I told him I wanted to show him something and pulled the little gold necklace with the baseball on it out from under my shirt. I held it out for him.

"See? It says Compton City Champs." 1940 something; I can't now remember which year it was—there were several of them in that family souvenir box. "My roots. My grandparents used to live here."

"Is that so? And just when was that?"

"Well, the forties, I guess."

"There ain't no white folk livin' here mothafucka. Sure as shit ain't no old ass white folk."

"Oh no they moved a long time ago." I stretched out "long" for the point of emphasis.

"Is that so?"

"Yeah, before it—" Though I realized my poor choice of words the moment I said it (hence the ellipsis), here is where I, to the detriment of my health, used my grandmother's four-letter word. "—went…"

HOFFA

Stephen King says writers need a toolbox. All I have is a goddamn tackle box and as much as I'd like to reel a reader in with a lure of a title like "Hoffa" and hook them with some memorable prose, the tackle box is from Wal-mart and ain't worth the five bucks I paid for it.

All I want is to call myself honorificabilitudinitatibus. There's a story in there right?

I haven't read the other stories yet and I wonder if anyone will reference "The Godfather." I won't. Oops. I just did. And damn it, my delete button's broken. Believe me, there's a story in that too. A whopper of a story.

Oh, and I bought my bait at Walmart too. The worms are already dead and all I can catch is this damn cold. (That's a true story.)

How come if a picture's worth 1,000 words all I can write is 160?

Why waste your time?

Oh yeah, here's the politician.

JOSH BERTETTA

THE ANOINTED ONE

THE ANOINTED ONE

*T*wo sheets of paper and a pencil they give me, me in my padded cell.

"Do you know what revelation means?" David had asked, putting the car in park in front of the ramshackle gas station. He finished his sixth Coke.

He'd asked me if I'd been up for a long drive, because, while the place he wanted to take me was "out in the middle of nowhere," it was "where it all began."

I'd said "yes" to the long drive; it was essential to my piece.

"It means to uncover, to make known the unknown." He pulled on his door handle, triggering the overhead light.

His face was washed in dim yellow. I read somewhere all you have to do to torture someone is keep them in a room painted yellow. They'll eventually go crazy. Ironic now that I think of it.

He asked me if I knew what mystery was.

My editor had given me a three month deadline (hence my request for pencil and paper) to complete my piece on one of the country's wealthiest.

Even though he is one of the richest and most powerful, not enough people know about David. Trust me when I tell you, more should.

"Mystery is not some problem you solve," he said, pulling out another Coke from his cooler, "like in Scooby-Doo. Mystery is something you're initiated into, like they did in ancient Greece. You see, mystery leads to revelation, truth."

David started off in oil, big oil. He inherited it from his father. Oil, you can say, ran in his veins. Oil did not make him his hundreds of billions, but it sure helped, "because with it," he told me once, "I was able to make my way into all my other endeavors."

Now while he wouldn't exactly tell me what these were, I, out of curiosity, did my digging and I realize if I ever get out of here (and if my editor decides to publish this) I might be killed for what I might say. So in effort to save space, let me say just this: a whole heck of a lot of his money goes into influencing politics and policy.

"So you ready?" He pushed his door open.

"Um." I looked out my window and though I didn't exactly know why, I must say I'd never felt so uneasy.

Now it wasn't as if I feared David. And I'd never been afraid of being out on some lonely stretch of highway at night before. The gas station did look like something you might see in some B-horror movie, but nothing that should inspire the kind of salivatory fear crawling up my goose-fleshed skin.

He told me during our second interview how after college he'd come to a crossroads in life and while on a cross-country road trip, he had a life-changing experience. See, he wasn't sure if he wanted to enter the family business and "I was confused as to who I was."

Because of their wealth, David's mother fell to second place in his father's eyes and she took to the drink. Such actually happened while David was still in his teens and while he, being the only one who noticed or cared, tried his best to get her stop; she could not and the disease finally killed her a week before college graduation. After the ceremony, David drove.

But he didn't get far from home, for when he needed gas, he stopped at this very spot.

He'd shared bits and pieces of this part of his story before, but tonight, while driving in the car, and in between sips of Coke, he told me, "and the mystery began when I saw her."

"Your mother?"

"Now I was never one to believe in ghosts or spirits, but there she was, plain as day, right next to the diesel pump. Thus the mystery began."

It would all lead to him discovering who he truly was.

So he pumped his gas, turned around and drove home.

There was something about seeing her astride the diesel pump, and in returning home he researched first the fuel, then the man.

"What man?"

"Rudolf Diesel. See, 'Diesel' is a German form of Matthew. You see, I soon began to understand the relationship between things in a way most people don't. A few days after learning what the name meant, I, having already looked up the meaning of Matthew—it means gift of God—decided to read the Gospel according to Matthew."

So he read Matthew and, focusing on the passages with the word "gift," put the pieces of the puzzle together. Having learned his Greek in grade school, he read it again in the gospel's original language. Several Greek words can be translated into English as "gift," he explained, and "meant offering, as in sacrifice. To God of course."

In our numerous meetings he often talked about God and I thought it was strange at first—how when he spoke of other things he spoke with enthusiasm and inflection, but when he talked about his love of God his voice usually fell flat and monotone.

"Ready to go inside and see where the real mystery began?"

I thought he just wanted to show me the gas station. Boy was I wrong.

"So," he said as we walked toward the station, "do you know what initiation means? It means 'beginning.'"

For some reason I had trouble swallowing and I managed to say, "So this the beginning."

"The real beginning." He put his arms around my shoulder. "When I discovered who I am. That's what you wanted to know right?"

A few miles down the road, we'd passed a few cars. They were parked alongside the road a short distance from one another and while I figured it was just some teenagers partying in the fields, I did not put two and two together.

David ushered me inside with a stiff hand to the small of my back and flipped on the lights. Dim yellow lights.

He took me to a back door, opened it, and suggested I go on ahead.

The stairwell was dark, the air cold.

After his first meeting with his mother David became fascinated with ancient rituals and told me how most initiations into cults required going underground. Even ancient Christians, he said, conducted their rituals in catacombs.

I hesitated at the top of the stairs.

"The answer is down there. The revelation."

The light from the gas station illuminated half the stairwell.

David behind me, I made my descent and when I reached the basement, he told me to "go on a little, I'll hit the light."

I inched my way forward.

"Keep going. Good. Remember what I told you about revelation?" He clapped his hands and said "Light."

Then there was light. Below and around me.

I stood in the middle of a circle of candles. That's when the twelve of them appeared from dark recesses.

Dressed in black robes.

I wanted to run, but I was surrounded.

They began to chant. "Lord, Lord, reveal yourself; Lord, Lord reveal yourself."

Two of them grabbed my arms. I struggled, but I could do nothing, go nowhere.

One of them slipped a hand over my mouth; another stuck something metallic over my eyes to keep them open.

The multi-billionaire, the man who bought his politics and loved his Coke, spoke from within the darkness. "Do you know what messiah means? Messiah means anointed one. Anointed with oil. The ancient Israelite priests anointed their kings in coronation rituals. Kings were messiahs, not Jesus! God is power, true, absolute power. In ancient days the kings possessed the power. And as we all know, the greatest king was David. Today it is the rich who possess the power. And who am I? I am David!" He lowered his booming voice. "That's what my mother wanted to show me and I knew I was the gift, I was the offering, the sacrifice. So I returned to this very spot in this very gas station.

"I took a knife to my hand and pledged myself. And when I did, something dripped upon my forehead. Then dripped again. I touched it. I tasted it. Oil. And I stood there, anointed with oil, black gold. I pierced two holes in my hands and caught the oil. I could feel it enter my veins. It was then revealed to me who I was, who I am."

"Reveal yourself to us oh Lord, reveal yourself to us."

David did. Lunging forth from the dark, he showed himself and I saw him (as I had always wanted) for who he truly was. He asked me what I saw and I heard myself declare, "You are the messiah!"

And so I write, in my padded cell, of David.

David, who had the face of the goat.

N.E. CHENIER

FIDELITY

CURRENT CONDITIONS

HEAVE HOUND

FIDELITY

Pinioned in the sand,
Salt-water crusted servos
Click. Eyelids open.

Azure Lotus 5,
Handcrafted in Sri Lanka,
Blue eyes keep vigil.

From passing ferries,
Tourists snap photos of her
Programmed loyalty.

They titter over
Her parasol parody
Against the tempest.

Bellows softly fold,
Exhale matcha-scented steam.
Internal clock beats.

Taiko thunders drum
Down another night; storm-tossed
Clouds sweep away days.

Titanium rusts
Mechanisms to stasis,
But software persists.

Her maker strove to
Prison her precision core
In a dollied shell,

The quaint satin frock,
His frivolous afterthought.
Click. Her smile locks shut.

Immune was he from
The pain that ever pulses
Through a well-tuned heart.

"Just a day," he'd said.
She'd waved his ship from shore with
Lubricated care.

Storms don't break ferries,
Besides the one that broke his
And shipwrecked her here.

On infinite loop,
She executes his last words:
"Wait for me, my dear."

CURRENT CONDITIONS

*I*f it weren't for your *predilections*, there might've been someone out there who would care enough to search for your bones under this heat-bleached sky.

If it weren't for the lack of fresh water and thirst clawing at your throat, you might have survived this one, too.

If it weren't for this year's El Nino, the jet stream would have hauled you and the sodden cask you clung to somewhere more hospitable than this cactus-pocked dustpan, someplace with palm trees, waterfalls, and bronze natives in grass skirts.

If it weren't for the fact that Captain Drake was a traditionalist, you would have ridden the *Skull Fire* down with the rest of the bilge rats into the trenches where mermaids would sing over your corpse and use your finger bones as toothpicks—instead of dancing rapier-poked across the plank.

If it weren't for your arrogance, the bosun wouldn't have caught on to the artful card-sharking—who'd have guessed the sallow peg-leg could hold his sauce better than a hogshead?—and the ensuing captain-rousing brawl wouldn't have occurred.

If it weren't for the deal dangled by the pirate captain, you might never have ended up on the *Skull Fire*, but when death is the alternative, slave duty on a reeking leaky frigate becomes a mighty attractive option.

If it weren't for the suspicious wife, you might have stayed ashore rather than hopping the first schooner sailing as far away from him and heartbreak as you could get.

HEAVE HOUND

*T*hermit barfed up a scroll the day Rick went back to his wife. It was the final straw—the dog barf, not the scroll—but I knew it had more to do with Angela's unemployment check being more than my weekly income at the shop.

The shelter'd sent over Thermit just before I'd passed my level-B welding certificate. A problem foster, nastier than a chop-saw mishap, he bit me twice that first week. But everyone'd told me you never pass the Bs on a first attempt. I had, and Thermit was like the universe demanding something back. Mismatched eyes, scruffy head and forelegs, bald hind end and a scabbed over half-tail. As ugly as he was asocial, but his desultory wag whenever I broke out the leash told me we could make it work.

With Rick gone, I needed Thermit. Thermit gave me a reason to come home at night—and me creeping up on day 50, I needed a reason not to take that detour to Scoby's.

So, about the scroll.

Once I'd cleared off the remnants of Spaghetti Os and dried the thing out, the hieroglyph-like figures stood out as sharply as if they'd been inked yesterday. Later, I showed it to my sponsor Maggie—Dr. Margaret Torres when at work—told her I got it off Ebay. She showed it to some specialist friend of a colleague. Now the guy won't stop calling me, desperate to find the seller. He even buzzed up from downstairs. Through the fuzzy video feed I could see he had a dimpled chin like Rick's.

"It's could be as invaluable as the Rosetta Stone," he insisted into the speaker. Egyptian and Etruscan. Fabulous, but I wasn't letting him up. Invaluable or not, you don't come barging over to my place without an invite. I spent the rest of the evening on Craigslist—and *not* on a Stoli run. I figured a Rosetta Stone had to be worth a few months' rent.

* * *

The evening Rick turned up drunk and horny, Thermit barfed up a trilobite.

Feeling perky from the raise my B-level cert got me at the shop, I let him in. Things were getting steamy on the couch. (Yes, yes, I know. Talk to the hormones, the brain doesn't want to discuss it.) Meanwhile, on the other side of the coffee table, Thermit retched in time to "Mercy Mercy Me" (Rick under the impression that every woman went moist for Marvin Gaye) and let loose on "my sweet lord…"

"Shit!" Rick leapt off me. "That mutt's still here?"

I wadded up some paper towels. "He's still adjusting."

The moment might have been salvaged had not the puddle of vomit wriggled.

Rick was gone faster than hot slag through rice paper. Left behind his belt and scotch flask.

I scratched Thermit behind his scabby ears. "Whadya' get into, boy?"

He growled and slunk to his dog bed. Didn't snap at my hand—that's progress.

The barf squirmed again around an elongated disk-type thing. I caught it in a mason jar.

A trilobite. I looked it up. The research distracted me from faltering at day 78. Big around the Paleozoic, died out 250 million years ago. It hunkered down in my old aquarium and scarfed up pepper relish. I poured the scotch in the toilet and PM'ed Maggie to see if she knew any paleontologists.

* * *

Day 85 and I teetered at the edge of the wagon, Maggie a speed dial away. I refused to go back to zero. Not for Rick, who was *really* going back to Angela this time and was busy collecting his stuff (mostly the stuff he'd picked out and charged on my bank card). On the edge of the empty TV stand perched the mug of Rockstar and whiskey. He'd whipped it up for me, his idea of consolation. We used to pound those back at all-night dance clubs.

By then, Thermit had adjusted enough to rest his head in my lap—precisely where it was when he barfed up his beef-and-tuna-stew dinner. And a stick.

Once I got it (and me) de-puked, I recognized it as an arrow. "How did you not skewer yourself with this?"

Thermit licked his chops at me.

Despite being steeped in dog barf, the fletching smelled of roses. The shaft was like no metal I'd ever worked with, not even in my jewelry-soldering days. Must have been cast as a single piece, a dark shaft merging into a golden tip. It warmed my palms. I didn't need to look this one up.

"Hey, Ani!" Rick shouted from the next room. "Just getting the bike key."

Rick's Ren-Faire tunic clung to his torso, the open neck offering a peek of his gym-carved pecs. I passed the arrow from hand to hand. "My bike," I said.

"C'mon, kiddo." He gave me a grin that was all teeth, no eyes. "You know I get more use out of it."

I placed the tip of the arrow on his chest. How cool would it be to turn the tables? Right here, right now. He dipped his chin and gazed at me through the strands of sweat-damp hair. "You taking up archery?" he asked.

One poke and I'd have the upper hand in the relationship. I licked my lips. Not the one who's always accommodating. Not pining.

I jerked the point away and dunked the arrow into the mug. "Leave the key," I said. "Or I'll sic Thermit on you."

He started to protest, but Thermit silenced him with a snarl, hackles bristling. The door closed without goodbye. The laced sweetness of the energy drink ticked my nose, chased with the scent of roses.

* * *

That's why they're still there, mug and arrow. The drink I could have, but don't. The romance I could have continued, but didn't.

Day 176 and the only thing Thermit's puked up since then was the business card you'd slipped in my box.

So, about the scroll—can I get an estimate on "invaluable"?

N.E. CHENIER

MINDING ONE'S OWN

MINDING ONE'S OWN

The fairy-dust glitter starts up as soon as our tires roll across the crease in the pavement. It'd be Tinkerbell-cute if it weren't ectoplasm green.

"Aw, Izzy, why're you always pulling up here?" I already know the answer to that: to torment me. It's some kind of oath older brothers take.

"Why not, Trudy?" he asks back, all grins. I hate my brother.

On invisible roller skates, the tulle-skirted phantom whirls from a brick wall. Her pearly whites would be a Colgate commercial if they weren't see-through.

"It creeps me out." I sag against splintered vinyl as she glides toward us.

"She's sweet."

"There's nothing sweet about a white-lady ghost."

"Pure peach cobbler," Izzy says—and *Isaiah's* supposed to be the devout one of the family. Nothing good in any Bible about the supernatural, smiley or not.

She pivots to a stop right outside the passenger door and curtseys. "See? She likes you." He leans across and waves at her.

I clamber over him to get out through the driver's door. No way I'm walking through that thing.

"Hey!" he barks. "You'll hurt her feelings."

"She doesn't have any feelings, asshole. She's dead." But I give her a quick wave.

The ghost waits with a hand on an outthrust hip. "I'll have a Mega Burger," Izzy tells her, "with extra pickles and large onion rings. Oh, and a root beer float." She bounces like a happy pre-schooler back through the brick wall, off to enter his order in some infernal kitchen.

"Don't you have an anatomy lecture to get to?" I ask over my shoulder en route to the living part of the gas station. My whoadette Clarissa works in the Snack Mart over there. She gets off right around when Izzy's classes start, so he drops me off and then takes us home when his classes are over. That way Clarissa and I get to hang, and it beats waiting around for a bus that comes once a generation (if you're lucky).

Clarissa joins me at the outdoor tables with a bag of day-olds. She shakes her head when she catches sight of Izzy over there miming like he's sampling the greatest burger of his life, complete with wiping the juices off his face.

"He flirting with Myrtle again?" she scoffs. Everyone calls her Myrtle because that's what it almost looks like on her oval name tag—not that I ever got close enough to check. "What is it with guys and that ghost?"

"Perpetual perkiness," I say, biting into a crusty apple fritter. Izzy pulls away and Myrtle pirouettes in his exhaust. "Breathing girls come with baggage."

A silver pickup roars into the dead side of the station, screeches through a U-turn, changes its mind at the pumps, veers around an incoming Datsun before coming to rest over by the dumpster. A man's voice barks like a Rottweiler, echoing against the overhang.

We already think the driver's a jerk-off and wish he'd stuck to his own neighborhood. A crying woman stumbles out the passenger side on heels high enough to be a liability if she's trying to outrun anything faster than an unplugged vacuum cleaner. The barking man flings his door open, slams it, and easily intercepts her.

Guy roughs up the woman like my sperm donor did to my mother (my mother taking it because she thought that was how it was supposed to go because of Eve's curse or true love or whatever).

"Don't say anything, Trudy," Clarissa hisses. "Mind your own business."

But the shout is already halfway out my mouth: "Hey, pal, leave her alone!"

"Shut your mouth, Lez-bo, before I shove my fist in it."

Clarissa is tugging me toward the store. "He might have a gun."

Even with blood in a ragged line across her cheekbone, the girlfriend is waving me off.

"That'd be a neat trick," I say and, because adrenaline is throttling my brain, I add, "coward."

Clarissa is gone, gone to get Ardy, the security guard from inside. I doubt he'll get back in time. The guy's grinning—no, more like bearing his teeth. He's my father all over again, only now targeting me. Mom never let him hit us. She took the blows herself. Well, I'm not going to take them, I decide. Whatever strength I have is coiled up and ready to defend myself.

Then his fist slams into my nose and I'm reeling. Blood gushes down my chin. The ground shifts like a sailboat and my return flail bounces off his elbow. Nah, not quite what I was going for.

"Is this what you wanted?" he snorts.

I'm dang sure it's exactly what *he* wanted. "Get your ya-yas out of smacking the ladies around?" I spit. "Make you feel like a man?" I see him in triplicate hauling back for another punch and know I'm gonna feel the impact of all three of those fists.

A flash of violet lightning smokes the ground. It smells like charred piecrust. A whirlwind on roller skates careens between us.

Myrtle?

Mrytle, but not Myrtle. She's all hell's fury. Poodle skirt traded for black rags, her face and fingers all stretched out, howling with the rage of a thousand valkyries. If she gave me creeps before, now my skin is set to crawl off my bones. By the grace of whatever, she's not slashing those new claws at me.

Nah, she turns them right on Bruiser, here. Normally you could pass a hand through her. Where she suddenly got enough substance to knock him flat, I won't be scrutinizing that gift horse. He's flailing like a beetle on its back. The smoky vortex around her pins him down.

Red lines furrow his face, then his jaw, both his forearms. Long ugly gashes start to ooze. His shrieks blend into hers, terrified twining with terrifying. Girlfriend is shrieking too.

Hands just solid enough help me sit up, cooler than real ones. She's a smear of swimming violet and green around a motherly expression. When she reaches a concerned hand to my face, a tingle brushes over my swelling nose. I clamp my teeth down on a scream.

Instead, I dig through my fear into a stash of gratitude. I look her dead in her dead eyes. The streetlights beam through her pert up-do. "Thanks, Sis." I mean it, too. "I owe you one." But then I feel stupid because what favor would a ghost need?

Knots of ghoul-haze swarm around the dude like angry hornets, leaving the girlfriend a shivery mess of wanting to help him and being brain-rattling petrified by something scarier than a black eye or a kick in the ribs.

Ardy wouldn't have much to sweep up even if he weren't bolted to the sidewalk by big bolts of *what-the-hell?* Clarissa either, a paralyzed step behind him, can of mace and an ice pack at the ready. Myrtle has it all under control: she comforts me while letting scary bits of herself herd the guy back to his truck—more tail-tucked pup than attack dog.

Before the woman climbs in after him, she hesitates at the tailgate. I can't read her expression, but I like to think something's clicked in her, a pebble loosed from the cliff side of her being that will someday become a landslide strong enough to carry her away from him—a landslide that never came for my mom.

The silver truck squeals away (not before Ardy takes down the plate number). Clarissa takes over in the comforting department. Myrtle gives a nod and all of her bits settle back into the familiar form.

"Hey, Myrtle," I call, "I'd like a strawberry shake." I sound about as convincing as a mynah bird, but I go with it. "A chocolate one for Ardy, here."

Ardy gives a pained grin. My face knows the shape of that forced smile.

"Just tea for Clar."

"Yeah, tea's good," Clarissa says softly.

Myrtle swings around on her toes and blazes through the brick.

The other two help me to the table. I can't really tell if they're going along out of fear or gratitude. My nose throbs under the ice pack.

Myrtle's back in a flash, wheeling around us with her tray aloft. Our feigned conversation's as stiff as our smiles, and we're horrendous mimes. Clarissa might as well be conducting an orchestra the way she feigns stirring her tea. Ardy looks like he's drinking his shake out of a Dixie cup. I doubt my performance is any less abysmal.

We'll get better at it—and I, for one, intend to practice. I mean, I owe it to her.

PAM PLUMB

ROCK A BYE BABY

ROCK A BYE BABY

Alanah started life on the cold blue-black slate of the kitchen floor. She lay in the wet slithering mess of childbirth, content. Curled up and blinking in the colourless half-light of the winter afternoon, she didn't cry. Instead, the cold tiles comforted her. The iron-rich smell from her mother's blood seeped into Alanah's subconscious. Trace minerals in the child's body mixed with her surroundings, subtly amalgamating. Atoms of metal and stone bound to her soul. Alanah forged not a maternal bond, but a unique aggregate.

Her parents wrapped the newborn stranger in warm towels, divesting her of the protective film of blood. Alanah took her first breath and screamed. She cried constantly, unable to communicate her yearning for metal or stone. She was wrapped in blankets and cotton sleep suits in the misunderstanding that she needed comfort to ease her distress.

'You try calming her down!' said her mother, Sophie, flinging the child towards her husband. She went to bed exhausted and disillusioned. Alanah's father, Ian, held his daughter, inhaling her newborn smell. Her earthy aroma reminded him of the times he'd been pot-holing. Looking into her dark eyes he felt the same intrigue of the rocks that enticed him underground. He hadn't been caving since Sophie had fallen pregnant. She was anxious that he would have a serious accident. Rocking Alanah now he didn't hear her cries, lost in making plans to return underground.

Alanah cried late into the night. Overcome with tiredness, Ian was half asleep when her baby fingers grabbed the metal strap of his watch. Connected, Alanah grew silent and slept. Astonished, Ian kept the pose of pietas, gazing at her as she lay across him. But when he disentangled himself and lay her down she started screaming again. It was only when his wedding ring brushed her face and she nuzzled into his hand that she settled again. Ignorant of her need for metal he let her head rest on his hand, desperate only for sleep.

'What did you do that I couldn't?' Sophie demanded bitterly the next morning. Ian had no explanation. Neither parent knew how to soothe their child. Both were ignorant of Alanah's chemical imbalance. It was the baby's innate needs that drove her to seek out and start sucking on the metal poppers of her baby-gro, giving sustenance. Sleep eventually came to all.

* * *

'Get that out of your mouth!' accompanied Sophie's panicked slaps on the child's back. Once crawling, Alanah sought out metallic or stone objects to suck. Her favourites were the house keys or discarded pennies. Having shovelled them into her mouth, their chemical properties permeated her palate or the pouch of her cheek. Recognising the signs of teething, Sophie replaced the nourishing metalloids with plastic teething rings. Alanah's desire for metal made her poke her fingers into plug sockets. Ian fitted safety caps and tidied away cables. She discovered the kitchen cupboards, unearthing pots and baking sheets, sucking out their goodness. Her parents often found her stripped and spread-eagled on the kitchen floor, licking the rivulets of oxidised copper that ran through the tiles, trying to become part of the stone. Desperate, they fitted a safety gate to keep her out. Alanah just lay against it, sucking the metal bars, their delirious convict.

'Alanah! What are you doing!' shouted Sophie, coming in late from work. 'And why haven't you been watching her, Ian?' Alanah was naked on the kitchen floor, the gate lazily left open. Ian was reading his caving magazine. He sprang up from the chair at the sound of Sophie's voice. Alanah ignored her mother, face pressed ecstatically against the cold stone, absorbing sustenance through her skin.

'She's happy there. Why don't you leave her alone?' Ian walked into the kitchen. He didn't see anything wrong with his daughter. Looking down at Alanah, he was sure he remembered his nephew running around naked when he was a toddler.

'It's not normal, Ian, this obsession with the floor. She needs stimulation. Why don't you play with her?' Sophie's voice trailed off as she went upstairs.

* * *

Ian and Alanah were lying on the grassy floor of the den, heads together inspecting their collection of stones. Sophie was shouting Ian's name, her voice filtered through the last of the evening sun. 'I thought you two might be in here.' Sophie stood at the entrance to the den. 'How did she get on at nursery today, then?'

'Well, we gave it a miss and went to the beach instead.' Ian shuffled backwards out of the den, brushing mud off his knees. 'We got loads today. Thought we'd got some jet but when we checked it in the book, it turned out to be obsidian. But Alanah did find a cracking piece of quartz.'

'She needs to go to nursery, Ian, not the beach,' Sophie followed Ian into the house. 'She's two years behind. Keeping her at home isn't going to help when she starts school.' Ian started tidying Alanah's rocks, carefully putting them away in the right order. 'It's no good ignoring me, Ian,' she continued, talking to his back. 'She needs to at least learn to speak before she goes to school.' Alanah stood unseen in the doorway, her bare toes on the tiles.

'She speaks to me, Sophie,' Ian said quietly. Turning around, he spotted Alanah. 'Don't you, love?' Both parents looked at her, urging her to reply. Silently Alanah turned and went upstairs. 'It's time she was in bed anyway.'

Ian sighed.

***

At school the magnetic pull of the playground gates meant Alanah had to be prised from them every day, on the way in and on the way out. In the classroom she hugged the steel chair legs. She couldn't concentrate unless she was sucking at the zip of her cardigan or grasping the metal bar on the underside of the table. The parquet floor of the assembly hall drained her, making her fidget. At break times Alanah followed the bare brick around the playground, her palm in constant contact with the stone.

'We're a bit worried about Alanah,' said the teacher, glancing at Alanah who was sat next to Ian. She was sucking on a piece of haematite, sorting coins into size order, head bent in concentration.

'I didn't think it would be long before we had this discussion,' Sophie started, relieved that someone else shared her concerns about Alanah's development. Ian insisted she could speak and even write her name. Sophie had only ever heard Alanah say a few random words. She'd never even called her "mummy". As Ian stood up and walked to the window, Sophie tried not to notice. The teacher started explaining her ideas about autism.

'Here's a leaflet about it, just something to think about.' She smiled apologetically at Sophie as she pushed the leaflet across the table. 'Excuse me, I need to pop out for a minute. I'll leave you to read that while I'm gone.'

'Look at this, Ian and tell me it isn't Alanah to a T,' Sophie said, pointing to the section about signs of autism, a victorious look on her face. 'It's no good sulking, Ian. It's obvious Alanah is autistic—just come and read it, will you?' The triumphalism rang in her voice. From the window Ian watched his daughter. She didn't seem to be listening. Bypassing his wife he sat back down next to Alanah. 'Right, then,' Sophie sighed. 'I'll read it out to you. "Children with autism often find it difficult to interact or play"— that's definitely Alanah'. She barked a laugh of conviction. Ian picked up one of Alanah's coins. Without looking at him, she grabbed it and put it back in place. He could hear the stone in her mouth rattling off her teeth. She was moving it around with her tongue, like it was a gobstopper. When he did it again, she gave him a quiet grin, the haematite shining out of the side of her mouth. '"Autistic children don't talk much", it says here, Ian. Now that's Alanah isn't it? She hardly ever speaks.' Ian remembered last summer when he'd taken Alanah to the beach searching for special stones for her collection. He remembered their long conversations, mostly about their joint fascination with rocks. They'd made plans to go pot-holing when she was older, betting on how old Alanah would be before Sophie would let them go. 'And,' Sophie started again but didn't look up, too busy validating her assumptions. 'It says here that often babies who have autism either sleep too much or not at all! Do you remember, she would never sleep, would she? And when she did it wasn't for long enough!' Sophie scanned the leaflet, shouting out the most corroborative snippets of information. 'Listen. There's a bit here about something called "pica". It says it means "putting inedible items in the mouth". Alanah does that all the time! She's always sucking on a stone or something, isn't she?' Sophie looked up. Ian was playing with Alanah, sliding the coins back and forth, making different configurations. Before she could say any more, Alanah's teacher returned.

'How are we getting on?' she asked Sophie.

'She's not autistic. There's nothing wrong with her. She's just different,' Ian answered, looking at Sophie.

'I'm not sure you understand.' The teacher sucked in her impatience. 'She makes no verbal contribution, either in group work or individually. She makes no attempt to draw or write. She needs assessing properly. I'm sure you'll both agree.' She aimed her smile at Sophie. Ian placed his hand over the coins, making Alanah look up.

'You've got to talk, love. And do the writing and things. That's what you do at school. You can play with your collection at home. Just show them you can do it.' All three adults looked at her, waiting. Eventually Alanah took the haematite out of her mouth and held it up, smiling.

'I'm like a stone.' Her voice was thin, stretched out like wire.

'See. She talks fine. And she can draw and write, too. Shall we show them your book?' Alanah nodded and he pulled a wire-bound notebook out of his pocket. It was overstuffed with bits of paper and other scraps of things packed between the pages. He passed it to her. She put the stone back in her mouth. It clicked softly against teeth as she opened the book. She started to turn page after page of sketches and writings. Alanah had stuck in slivers of stone and metal she'd found on the beach or in the garden. As Sophie saw the pages she tried to think how Alanah could have done this. She hadn't even seen her hold a crayon. She could tell Ian hadn't helped; the writing and drawings were childlike, most of the first pages were just scribbles. But as Alanah turned more pages, the writing became neater, the drawings more structured and precise.

'How long has she been doing this?' Sophie looked from Ian to the teacher. The teacher just shrugged. Ian put his arm around Alanah, resting his head on hers. To him she still smelled of the caves, the deep underground.

'You can talk to her, you know, Sophie. She's your daughter, too.' Ian reached over with his other arm to hold Sophie's hand. As he touched her, Sophie shuddered. She felt a kind of charge, like the tingle of static from a television set. 'You can feel her, can't you? She gives off this kind of energy, like a battery or something. I don't know what it is but it makes me feel alive. She makes me feel happy, Sophie.' Ian smiled, happy that he was connecting Sophie and Alanah at last. Then Alanah reached over and held Sophie's other hand. The pulse of energy that flowed between the three of them made Sophie look at her daughter. Alanah's dark eyes looked back at her. Then she smiled shyly, the haematite tucked in the side of her cheek.

PAM PLUMB

THE UNEXPECTED DEMISE OF CAPTAIN S. BARKELO

THE UNEXPECTED DEMISE OF CAPTAIN S. BARKELO

His blood seeps into the cracks in the concrete. Instinct makes him crawl, move. Anywhere. The wound opens a little more, releases fresh blood. To his left the empty road shimmers in the heat. On his right the husk of the gas station blocks out the sun. In the late afternoon shade he shivers.

Weary and in pain, he drops his head and closes his eyes. Toxic remnants of the diesel pump mix with his own blood, leaving a metallic clag in his mouth. As if a doctor has tapped him on the shoulder, he knows only minutes are left of his life.

Still he breathes. Shallow, pathetic breaths. Forgetting where he is, he lifts his head. At first everything seems black and white and then some long lost memory colours the gas pump orange, and the dress of the woman that floats, somehow naturally, above the ground appears as blue as the sky. She is ghostly thin. The garage's red brick wall is still visible behind her plump smiling face. The hem of her dress quivers in the light breeze.

'Nearly there.' The woman's voice is as soft as warm bread. *She must be the fabled Earth Angel of Death,* he thinks. Every good soldier expects to see her. Reassured, he moves forward, pulls himself over the criss-cross grate of the drain cover. His breath snags in his lungs. Smears of blood extend his outline.

He hadn't expected to see the Angel so soon. His career in the Interspatial Defence League was to take him to so many different places that he had to see; the Circle of Passion on Henza, The Republic of Treox, the battlefields of Orion 5. Never did he expect to die on a recovery mission here on Earth.

When they'd landed, the sun had barely risen over the burnt ground of the old Americas. Few of his crew had even heard of this part of the Universe. He only knew of it from his family. So many generations ago his mother's ancestors had been involved in the Last Earth Battle. Several millions had fought each other over a period of fifty Earth years before totally destroying themselves.

As the senior officer of the squad, he had led this recovery mission. Searching for usable assets seemed pointless but his commander insisted. No-one was supposed to be here. No evidence of life had been recorded since the evacuation of Earth. Consequently they had not been prepared, lazily walking in loose formation across the deserted streets instead of taking up tactical positions. There had seemed no reason to behave like a soldier. He had reverted to tourist, gazing with wonder at the ancient buildings that he guessed were shops. None of his company had ever seen a shop before. He only recognised them from his mother's memory bank.

That's where the shot had come from, one of the shops with broken glass and a torn roof. And now, as he crawls further into the shade of the gas station, he wonders who or what has killed him. Wonders, as he glances up at the Angel of Death, her smile brilliantly sparkling despite the shade, if it is a long lost ancestor.

LIZ HEDGECOCK

ONE CAREFUL OWNER

THE MAKER

RE-ENTRY

ONE CAREFUL OWNER

*F*rankly, I was bored.

I should have been racing along the roads, setting off speed cameras, coasting down the hills feet off the pedals wheeee! Then pedal furiously, carried up, up by that leftover bit of momentum to the next glorious summit. Leaning dangerously on the corners, cutting it fine, eating up the miles, mud everywhere but what fun! That's what it's all about!

But no. I was stuck in Mike's Bikes. The proper bikers wouldn't look at me. Anyway, they always brought their own bikes and all they'd want was an energy bar or a sports drink. The best I could hope for was a reasonably fast jaunt with a frustrated racer who wasn't allowed his own beast and had to make do with getting a hire bike once in a blue moon. When I get the suspicious look from his partner—and sometimes the kids wow at my shiny red paint—well, it's almost worth hanging around, killing time, stacked with the others and spinning yarns about our epic trips up hill and down dale. Back in the glory days, when we were top spec and our owners loved us and spent their evenings tending us with GT85 and a special rag. That feeling when you get back from a really mucky trip, and your rider gets the hose out just for you, and dries you and sorts out your niggles and tucks you up under your tarp and says goodnight Jess...can't beat it.

Goodnight, Dave, I whispered, in the dark.

Here we go, I thought, as a tall woman in tweed trousers pointed at me. Another pootle round the lake. Hello ducks, hello sailing boats. Ooh look, an ice cream van and a convenient bench. That's enough now, let's call it a day.

What a waste of a bike like me, with one careful owner.

Mike untied me and wheeled me forward. The others rattled disapprovingly. My name would be mud when I got back, still nice and clean and barely used. Quack quack did you say hello to your friends?

But she held up a hand. What? What? Don't I even get to go outside?

She disappeared. But Mike was still holding me. What's going on? Is this some sort of game?

I waited. The others waited. I could hear them behind me, waiting.

She came back. In Lycra. With words on it, words I knew from the screen in the corner that showed us our heroes on repeat.

She wheeled me carefully out of the shop. Mike waved us off.

She straddled me.

And we're off! Faster than I thought, then really fast, faster than I've gone for a long, long time, and the gorse is flowering, blazing in the sunshine, and stones are sparking under my wheels as we whizz along.

And we're heading for the hill, the lovely long climb, gears down, head

down, here we go, upupup and
    YES! YES!
    WHEEEEEE!

THE MAKER

I am an artist.

I began as a sculptor in stone, working in the classical tradition. Under my hands deities, nymphs and fauns were shaped.

But the city had enough sculptures. The gods slumbered in my workshed, their nakedness muffled in cloth. I couldn't afford to buy a humble soapstone, much less eat.

The main problem, though, was that I wanted my creations to live, to move. My statues were spellbound, frozen.

Strangely, satisfying my base need for food led me to my life's work. Night had fallen long ago, and I was in a back alley, picking through the rotting fruit and vegetables beneath even the servants' contempt. I bit into an apple and recoiled at the taste of decay and a wriggle against my lips. I spat, ran to the babbling spring at the alley's end, and gladly drank. As the water washed the foulness from me, I saw my sculptures as the conduits for healing streams.

My first fountain was simple: a group of water nymphs outside the bathhouse, themselves bathing and pouring water. On its unveiling, the crowd gasped as sparkling water splashed and played, making rainbows in the sunshine.

My next commission was a fountain for the park. I spent many days and evenings there, observing. Children jumped up and down and couples squeezed hands as the water jets embodied the swoops and dives of my wheeling flight of swallows.

Perhaps I should have stopped there. However, the Mayor made me a very generous offer. I toyed with several ideas—I tried to resist—but my art called me.

The fountain came to life and water soared upwards, joyful and free. I gasped at my own creation.

The Mayor wept. 'It's true, isn't it?'

I had denied nothing, but I nodded. Leo had saved himself with his confession. While the hand was his, the intent was all mine. My chains clanked as I was led from the cemetery garden.

The Mayor has already administered my main punishment by breaking up my masterpiece. What follows is a release.

Soon I will be free as the water, ascending, a soul in flight.

RE-ENTRY

*W*e re-enter in darkness, and it is terrifying. I close my eyes though it makes no difference to the shaking, and pray to something to land us safely. So far it's always worked.

Then we battle the next layer, a belt of questions, cameras and mikes in the face. *What did you see? What did you face? What did you eat?* I have a short speech, delivered moving forward, which gets me through in around fifteen seconds.

And now the hardest part. Susan is always more or less the same, even if I've been away a couple of years. But the children—every time I return, they've changed. I need to relearn their language, their passions, their temperaments. Emily is a teenager now. She hates me for going, and she hates me for staying. She cries, she yells, she punches the wall.

In space, I can shoot hostility on sight.

At home, I have to understand, to forgive. To adjust.

LIZ HEDGECOCK

PETROL RAINBOWS

PETROL RAINBOWS

'I feel stupid,' Dave muttered, his eyes fixed on the road.

'You look stupid.' Amanda had never seen him in a suit before, and now she knew why. The pencil moustache she had drawn on him just before leaving was already slightly smudged.

'Thanks.' On cue, the reserve petrol light pinged on.

'How far is it to this place?'

Dave peered at his phone, which cast a pale blue glow on his face.

'It says twenty miles.' He negotiated another hairpin.

Amanda flung back in her seat, pearls rattling. 'Wonderful. I can't think of a better way to spend a Saturday night.' She picked at the fringing on her dress. 'By the time we get there it'll be over.' She chewed at a scarlet nail. 'You'd better hope one of us wasn't supposed to be the murderer. *Or* the victim.'

They watched the miles-remaining indicator tick down, and down. The country roads continued to twist.

'Oh, I've always wanted to spend the night in a car, in the middle of nowhere.'

'Shut *up*, Amanda.'

Saturday night radio tried, and failed, to fill the silence.

Amanda peered into the darkness. 'There's a light in that lay-by. Pull in and ask if they know the way to a petrol station. Pull IN!' she screamed, and grabbed Dave's arm.

Dave braked hard. 'Don't ever do that again.' he said, quietly.

As they drove into the lay-by Lionel Richie was drowned out by hiss and crackle. The light was coming from an old-fashioned petrol pump, and next to it stood a classic Bentley. The radio crackle thinned out and resolved itself into a jazz instrumental.

A young man in a sharp suit and spats got out of the car and fumbled under the pump.

Amanda nudged Dave. 'Look, they must be going to the same place! Let's ask if we can follow them.' She gazed at the Bentley. 'They've really gone for it, haven't they? That looks like a wedding car.'

Dave opened the car door without a word and approached the man.

'Excuse me, are you going to—'

The man turned, nozzle in hand. 'Blimey, you gave me a start!' His eyes darted to the petrol pump. 'Don't worry, Cyril knows. I get petrol every Saturday night and he always gets his money.' He frowned. 'Where's that music coming from?'

Dave shrugged. 'The car radio.'

'A car radio? Let's see!' He put the hose back and ran to their car. 'Well, this is something else! A radio, in a car! Can you turn it up?' Amanda obliged, staring. 'And what about those lights? Millie! *Millie!* Come and look! They've got a *car radio!*'

The passenger door of the Bentley opened and out stepped a woman in a bell-shaped tutu, carefully skirting the puddles on the forecourt.

Amanda's eyebrows shot up into her fringe.

'What is it, Percy? *Oh*, you've got music! The Charleston, I just love the Charleston!' She began to dance. In the dim, wavering light from the pump, she was a black and white film projection, petrol rainbows shimmering from her toes.

'Look at her go!' Percy said. 'She should be top of the bill!'

'Come on, Percy!' His spats flashed as he tried to keep up.

'Aren't you dancing?' they called.

Amanda and Dave exchanged glances.

Amanda got out of the car and stepped forward. 'What do we do?'

'Just follow us!'

They did their best, splashing, bouncing, falling over their own feet and each other's, with enormous grins on their faces.

'Jump!' Millie leapt into Percy's arms and he spun her round, legs kicking. 'Go on!'

Amanda hesitated. Dave held his arms out.

'Don't drop meeEEE!' She clung on as he whirled her high in the air. 'Wooooahh!'

The Charleston finished, and a slow dance came on. She stood, breathless and giggling, still in his arms, and they rocked slowly together.

Percy tapped Dave on the arm. 'Have you got the time, sir?'

'Oh, er—just gone half-past seven.'

'Really? We need to get on, Millie's due at the music hall at eight.' He went to the pump, and Dave followed.

'Are you really a dancer?' Amanda asked, as Millie smoothed down her dress and checked her immaculate stockings for splashes.

'Oh yes, I'm on a contract with Billy Slim. Six nights a week and matinees. He says I've got prospects, but he wants me to get some experience first in the back row. I hope I move up soon; Percy and I are saving to get married.' She smiled, a little sunburst. 'What about you, dear?'

'Oh no, we're not—we're just going out.' Millie looked inquiring. 'But surely *you* could get married. Percy must be doing well, driving a Bentley.'

'Ha!' Millie shrieked. 'It isn't his - he's the chauffeur. We've only got it tonight because the family are up in London! Oh, bless you!' She ran to tell Percy the joke, and he smiled, but Amanda saw the shadow behind it.

'Now, I'll pull forward and give you a chance.' Percy eased the Bentley along.

'How do I pay?' asked Dave. 'The pump doesn't tell me how much.'

'Well, what did you put in that fancy car?' Percy inspected the pump and whistled. 'I reckon that's about two pounds. But if you haven't got it, you could square with Cyril when he's open. I'd vouch for you.'

'No, it's fine.' Dave felt in his pocket and knelt to put the coins under the pump.

Percy gasped. 'You carry sovereigns in your *pockets*?'

'Percy, we have to go!' Millie hopped into the passenger seat and arranged her skirts. 'It was lovely to meet you,' she said to Amanda. 'I do hope everything goes well with your young man.'

'Me too.' Amanda blew her a kiss.

Percy turned the pump off, shook hands with Dave, and started the car. 'Remember what I said.' The Bentley cruised away into the darkness.

Dave and Amanda looked at each other, a spiv and a flapper caught in car headlights.

'I—what just happened?'

'I'm not sure. Have we gone back in time?' Amanda glanced back at the car. 'Your Corsa hasn't.'

'I wonder whether they did get married.'

'Maybe we could Google them…I bet they did. I hope they did.'

'Yeah.' Dave gazed in the direction of the departed Bentley. 'Come on, we've got a murder mystery to solve.' He walked to the car, opened the passenger door, and bowed.

'What do you have to remember?'

Dave looked appropriately shifty. 'Oh, er, well…we should go.'

'No, what did Percy mean?'

'He said I should make an honest woman of you.' It came out in a rush. 'I think courting was different in those days.'

'Courting!' Amanda snorted. 'Well, I suppose we are.'

'Yes.' He took her hand and squeezed it.

As they pulled out of the lay-by 'Yes Sir! That's My Baby' fizzled out, and turned into Billy Ocean.

* * *

Driving home the next day, as themselves, they tried to find the petrol station. As they suspected, it wasn't there. They parked in the lay-by and stared at the shuttered snack van.

'Why did we take this road, anyway? There must be a more direct route.'

'There is, but I spend my life going up and down motorways.' Dave looked sheepish. 'And I thought it would be more romantic,' he said, in a very small voice.

Amanda gave his arm a little punch. 'You soft lad!'

They sat and listened as Louis Armstrong soared to a high note. Dave opened the car door and turned the radio up. 'Let's dance.'

TOM SMITH

WAR ON FAT

THE FOUNTAIN

BUSINESS TRIP

WAR ON FAT

"Looka 'ow skinnee I am." *I spent twelve hours on a plane for this?* The journalist wondered why his editor kept sending him on these dangerous stories. Was it professional jealousy? Was it a power trip? Or was it because he caught him sleeping with his wife?
Could be any of those things.
The king stood proudly inside his pair of slacks that lived up to their name, holding the waistband out as far as his arm allowed. The king's advisors, guards and hangers-on contorted their faces to show how impressed they were with the king's weight loss, the journalist followed suit, scared of the king's reaction if he offered the disinterested shrug he wanted to.
"Plentee of exicise and no chippy chips," the king explained his secrets to weight loss, slapping his flat stomach.
Only one question circled the journalist's mind. "Why are you are still wearing those pants?"

* * *

A wall of men, women and children ran in unison, kicking up the dry dirt, sweat that once dribbled now oozed from their foreheads.
Two trucks followed the runners, serving as a constant reminder of what would happen if they stopped running.
"I can't—I just can't." Sandra, a chubby Aid worker, slowed down to a jog. John, her husband, grabbed her hand, dragging her as he ran. But it was no use; she was exhausted, she wasn't choosing to stop, her body demanded it.

* * *

"I can't believe how stupid I was!" the journalist began. "It's so obvious. You wear those giant pants because you're proud of how much weight you've lost, right?"
"Correct," the king conceded.
"Great. So now we're on the same page can you ask your guard to take his foot off my forehead?" The king nodded his head once, signalling for his release. The journalist jumped to his feet, eyeballing the guard who had thrown him to the floor and used him as a footstool so easily.
"Lee's begin the intermview," the king demanded, feeling his boundaries had been established.
Having previewed the consequences of upsetting the king, the journalist ran through his list of questions in his mind, editing like his life depended on it. "You were once—" *Don't say fat. Don't say fat.* "—fat." *Shit.* "And you did so well losing all that weight, so so well." He over-corrected.

"An'?" the king asked in a tone that told the journalist to make his point quickly.

The journalist indulged himself, imagining that he had no point to make. *And nothing, well done you. Best of luck in your future endeavours. I'll be going now.*

If only it was that simple, but there was one question he had to ask. "Well it's just..." he took in a deep breath, hoping it wouldn't be his last. "Erm...is that why...well, could that contribute to..." He couldn't phrase it any other way. "Is that why it's illegal to be fat now?"

* * *

"Sandra please, you can't stop." John begged his wife to keep running.

"I have to." She pushed John, making sure he kept running, before she stopped, her arms spread wide, accepting her fate.

Phhtt.

Such an un-intrusive sound, the sound of a bullet leaving a silenced gun.

* * *

"It's no illegal tobe fa' it's jus' a exericise regeem."

"You force entire towns to run twelve hours a day, and if they stop, you have them shot." The journalist remembered the foot on his head. "Your Majesty"

"I don' force entear towns to run, ownly the fat ones, the skinnee ones do yoga to tone up. Why is tha' a pro'lem?"

"It's just, Your Majesty, in my country, Your Majesty, that rule would seem tyrannical, Your Majesty."

"I no see what dinisoars 'ave to do wit' it, and anyway I'm helping 'em the fatties. Those disgutin' fatties, they make me sick jiggling, always jiggling."

The journalist had enough for a story; he asked the burning question and got some quotes. The finish line was in sight. "Thank you for your time, Your Majesty." The journalist turned to leave, "Oh no, please not now." He felt a strain begin in his back and spread around his stomach.

Phhtt.

Such an un-intrusive sound, the sound of a journalist's girdle breaking.

The journalist's beer belly, triumphant against the restrictive girdle, made an appearance and stole the show.

"A secret jiggler," the king started. "The worst of them al'. Guards fetch 'im some running shoes."

THE FOUNTAIN

"*W*hat kind of sick bastard wishes for that?" Disgusted, Yasel dropped the coin back into the fountain.

Plop.

This had been his job for centuries, and he had grown tired of the selfish wishes attached to the coins in his wishing fountain.

He hadn't always been so moral. He had been responsible for more than his fair share of decadence, depraved fantasy fulfilment and even one or two X Factor winners, but he grew tired and now he searched for that rarest of beasts, a selfless wish.

Yasel absent-mindedly draped his hand into the fountain, dragging it along the bottom, touching the coins. "Greed, revenge, money—hold on." Yasel pulled a coin from the fountain. "This is the one."

Yasel stood in front of a house, like he had always been there. He surveyed the street; it was straight from a 1960's American family movie—affluence framed the snaking road. He made his way to the correct house.

Ratta-tat-tat.

He tapped on the thinnest part of the door. Suddenly he was worried; it was a child's voice attached to the coin, how could he justify visiting a child he did not know?

"What?" An abrupt man answered the door, his eyes facing back into his house.

"Hello, sir, I'm from the scouts and—"

"Luke!" He didn't let Yasel finish lying before exiting, having fulfilled his role as a go-between.

Luke, six or seven maybe, came to the door. "It's my big sister's birthday." Luke felt it necessary to explain why he was wearing a pink, pointy party hat.

"That's why I'm here actually. I'm sure you're a little jealous of all the attention she's getting today but you still wanted to give her something special for her birthday, didn't you?"

"How do you know that?"

Yasel explained who he was before granting the boy's wish. "When she takes a bite of her birthday cake it will turn into a delicious chocolate almond cake, just like you wished."

Luke flung himself at Yasel, throttling his legs. "Thank you, mister."

"Thank *you*. I had all but given up on humans, until I heard your wish." A calm washed over Yasel. "Why don't you go watch your sister eat her favourite cake?"

"It's not her favourite cake."

"Then why..."

"She's allergic to nuts." Luke slammed the door shut, just in time to see his sister collapsing to the floor; the panicked screams spilled from the house into the street.

"Little shit!" His parting words uttered, Yasel returned to his fountain where he remains, forever searching for that one selfless wish.

BUSINESS TRIP

*T*he handcuffs nibbled at his wrists, and the unwashed hotel sheets made his naked skin crawl.

There was no doubting who was in control; that was clear from the second she barged into his life in the lobby. She appeared from nowhere. He barely had time to finish his drink or take off his wedding ring.

"What are you going to do to me?" he playfully asked.

"I don't know yet—" she replied stoically, punching numbers into her mobile phone. "He failed the test. Do you want me to kill him?" She terminated the call. "Your wife said goodbye."

TOM SMITH

CAMPFIRE TALES

CAMPFIRE TALES

*T*he woods were shallow. The young trio were only a hop, skip and a jump away from their homes, but the fire they circled tricked them into believing they were explorers on the edge of the world.

They had never camped before, but their parents thought it would be good for them, and what could go wrong so close to their houses?

"Let's tell ghost stories." Amy didn't wait for the votes to be tallied before continuing. "Have you heard about the ghost at the petrol station?" Everyone in town had heard about the ghost at the petrol station. The only problem was they all heard about a different ghost at the petrol station.

John, keen to show Amy he wasn't as thick as she thought he was, offered to tell his version first.

Amy, confident he'd be wrong, happily stepped aside, anxiously waiting to slap him down.

Clicking the torch on, John held it under his chin as he told his tale.

"In nineteen-eighty-nine a young girl called June lived above the petrol station with her family. All was going well, until one fateful day when she became—" John paused to build the tension. "A vegetarian."

* * *

June waddled along the forecourt, one hand on her backside and the other on her crotch. She never left enough time to get from the house to the toilet. This time it was because she refused to leave an argument she was having with her mother over who had killed *Eastenders Dirty Den*.

"Awwwww." The relief was tangible; she made it just in time. It was at these moments that June could not blame her parents for insisting she use the outside toilet since turning vegetarian. "Vegetarian toilets are stinky!" Wafting her hands, trying to beat up the smell, she plucked a match from the box she hid behind the bowl. That always got rid of the smell.

"Crap!" Burning her finger, June dropped the match and forgot about it. Until she opened the door and saw the line of fire snaking its way to the petrol pump.

When you live above a petrol station you get used to the smell of petrol, so you don't notice when a delivery man leaves a trail of petrol from the outhouse to the forecourt.

"Boom!" John made a big circle with his arms, miming the enormity of the explosion. "It killed her entire family. That's why you're not allowed flames on the forecourt today, because it brings back her spirit."

Amy grabbed the torch from John. Flipping it, she pointed it directly in to his eyes. "So you're saying there's no flames allowed at the petrol station because it brings back a ghost?"

"Yeah." John tried to divert the beam of light from his eyes with the palms of his hands.

"Not because of the flammable petrol?"

"No, because of the vegetarian dead ghost girl." Amy looked towards Claire to make sure she was witnessing their friend's stupidity. "You okay?" Amy asked. Claire nodded but remained silent. Amy wanted to ask why Claire had not spoken more than two words all day, but she had an agenda to get on with. "That's rubbish, she didn't die in the eighties. It was nineteen sixty four. The owners of the petrol station had a house full of foster kids, but one of the kids got mixed up in the wrong crowd."

* * *

Karen lay stomach first on her bed, screaming into her pillow. "What's wrong with you?" her latest roommate, Sarah, asked.

Lifting her head from the pillow Karen answered. "A Hard Day's Night is out next month and I have no money to go see it. It's the Beatles first ever film. I have to see it. I just have to!"

"You need some money?" Sarah peaked out the open door to make sure there were no unwanted ears nearby, closing the door when she was satisfied they were alone. "I'm working for this guy; he pays us to deliver parcels from one house to another. He pays well."

"Who is he?"

"You don't need to know that—you in or not?" Karen didn't know what to do. It sounded wrong, and she was always good, always doing what grownups told her to do. But she couldn't miss this movie.

She began delivering once, maybe twice a week. Her training was simple, "Never open the envelope." She never did, until that day.

"Wait, little girl." She had dropped the padded envelope in the bin outside the house, like always, when a man wearing shorts and a vest appeared. "Come here." Her legs wanted to run, but he told her to go to him.

He dug the padded envelope from the bin and handed it back to Karen. She looked confused. "I don't want it returned to sender! Open it."

"But..."

"Open it." She did as he told her, squeezing the bottom of the envelope, widening the opening. She tipped it upside down but nothing came out. "I knew it! They take something of mine, I'll take something of theirs." He looked around, but he could only see one thing that belonged to the man who had taken from him. "Get in the house, little girl." Karen always did what grownups told her to do.

"He killed her?"

Amy ignored the obvious question and wrapped her story up. "The man the girl was working for got his revenge. He killed the guy and went on the run, never to be seen again."

John pictured the scene, but shucked it off. "That's not what happened." John never stood up to Amy before, but he was willing to go all in on this hand. "There was no gang. It was the stinky poo explosion story!"

"No it wasn't; it was the foster home gang story, any idiot knows that."

"I guess that makes you an idiot."

They stood, nose to nose, neither backing down.

"Gang!"

"Poo!"

Amy had no idea where John had gotten his backbone from, but she didn't like it.

"Wait!" Claire finally spoke. "You're both right." Amy and John looked at Claire, waiting for her to explain, both secretly glad their standoff had been interrupted. "The ghost was the star in both of your stories."

Amy sighed, annoyed but happy to be feeling superior again. "How can the petrol station girl die in the sixties and the eighties, genius?"

"The girl wasn't the ghost, neither of them. The ghost has been around for hundreds of years and can't even remember being human, which upsets her. So every twenty-five years she takes over the body of a local girl, just to remember what it was like."

"But you said both our stories were right?" John asked.

"They were, sort of. You gave credit to the wrong people though. It wasn't a careless delivery man who burnt that place to the ground. Nor did the bad man kill the other bad man to get revenge. It was the ghost. When she takes over a body she get's angry that she can't remember who she was, very angry."

"How do you know?" Amy spat.

Claire blinked once, opening her eyes. There was a pinprick sized bright light shining in her eyes. Before John and Amy could scream, they were already a part of a story some other kids would be telling for years to come.

CONTRIBUTORS

KARL A. RUSSELL

In much the same way that The Hand came to control Michael Caine, the nom de plume Karl A. Russell now dominates his poor human host and makes him do terrible things. Most involve flash fiction. The others make him cry. In real life… Karl A. Russell lives in the North West of England with his wife and daughter. He loves flash fiction for its brevity and impact but still wants to write a novel worth publishing, just to prove that he can. Twitter: @Karl_A_Russell

NATALIE BOWERS

Natalie Bowers is a story scavenger, perpetual student and professional volunteer who lives in Hampshire with her husband, two children and a growing collection of ukuleles. A gregarious loner and shameless eavesdropper, she can often be found haunting the dark recesses of coffee shops and cafes, her pencil poised above paper.

TAMARA ROGERS

Tamara burns away the hours putting one word after another, playing with pictures and eating cheese. Her novel, Grind Spark, was longlisted for the Bath Novel Award 2014. Currently beating various projects into shape, she dabbles in science fiction, transgressive fiction and all things weird. Find her lurking at www.thedustlounge.com and on Twitter as @tamrogers. You can find more of her pictures at http://www.tamararogers.co.uk

DAVID SHAKES

David Shakes started writing when he was forty. Nobody has told him to stop yet. He has a penchant for darker fiction and is constantly surprised that the other FlashDogs are so accepting of him (editor's note: well, he is one of the founders of the movement). One day he hopes to have the courage to call himself a writer out loud. Twitter: @TheShakes72

MARK A. KING

Mark A. King has cooked for royalty, played football for the England manager, sung to the Pope, and been held at gunpoint. All this was a long time ago, and now he enjoys worlds and characters far more bizarre, outlandish and alien—for these are the joys of writing and reading Flash Fiction. He's proud to be one of the founders of the FlashDogs. He lives in Norfolk, UK, hiding from the psychotic calls of geese. @Making_Fiction

ANDREW PATCH

Andrew's flash fiction and short stories have appeared in various journals, anthologies and virtual realms, mostly under his flash writing alter ego Image Ronin. He currently holds the title of the most southerly based Flash Dog, drinks his coffee black, and dreams of grey streets and greyer people. You can follow his ramblings on life, coffee and writing via Twitter: @imageronin.

VOIMA OY

In real life Voima Oy lives in Oak Park, IL on the western edge of Chicago, south of the expressway and the elevated train line. She has been writing short things for years. Her first flash fiction story was for The Angry Hourglass, No. 20. (May 17, 2014). She believes in the connections of Twitter and the possibilities flash fiction. Proud #FlashDog. She also has a blog, Chicago Weather Watch, where she writes about life, nature and weather.

JACKI DONNELLAN

Since she began writing in 2013 Jacki Donnellan has had her writing published in several online magazines and websites. She has a story in the Best of CafeLit 3 anthology and is due to be published by the Fiction Desk in January 2015. Jacki was the winner of the 2013 Flash! Friday Flashversary Contest and the Poised Pen Halloween Flash Fiction Competition 2014. She is proud and happy to be a member of the flash fiction writing community. Twitter: @DonnellanJacki

AVALINA KRESKA

Avalina can be found on a remote island in the far North of the UK writing flash fiction, short stories, poetry and telling tales of her crazy exploits. She's been published on Paragraph Planet, 99Fiction.net, Every Day Fiction, The Caterpillar Magazine, and has stories on the new QuarterReads site. She plans to republish her successful guitar tuition books with Amazon next year. Being a recent addition to the Flashdog team, she hopes to stay with the pack and go hunting every week (she can sing a mean Blues for a Dog when required). Blog: avalinakreska.blogspot.co.uk/ Twitter: @avalina_kreska

REBECCA J. ALLRED

Rebecca lives in Salt Lake where she works by day as a doctor of pathology, but after hours, she transforms into a practitioner of macabre fiction, infecting readers with her malign prose. Her work has been featured online at Freeze Frame Fiction and in Sirens Call Magazine, and in print in Vignettes from the End of the World. Keep up with Rebecca at diagnosisdiabolique.wordpress.com. Twitter: @LadyHazmat.

REBEKAH POSTUPAK

Rebekah, like any well-behaved writer, dreams of being a full-time novelist. Like many ill-behaved writers, however, her noble intentions are devoured on a regular basis by flash fiction dragons. Her stories have been published in various magazines, but she considers running Flash! Friday among the greatest honors of her life. She is over the moon taking part in this Flash Dogs project and is grateful for the team's indulgence in including her.

EMILY JUNE STREET

Emily, a California-based writer, is the author of two novels: *The Velocipede Races* and *Secret Room*. She comprises half of the writing and publishing team at Luminous Creatures Press. In her spare time she enjoys cycling and the flying trapeze. Her daytime life involves editing movement as a Pilates instructor. Twitter: @EmilyJuneStreet & emilyjunestreet.wordpress.com or luminouscreaturespress.com.

BETH DEITCHMAN

Beth wrote her first book in third grade. Since then she has also had short-lived but very entertaining careers as a dancer, a university lecturer, and an actor. These days she writes fiction, co-owns Luminous Creatures Press, and teaches Pilates in Northern California where she lives with her husband Dave and dog Ralphie. You can find Beth at luminouscreaturespress.com or on her website at bethdeitchman.com and you can follow her on Twitter: @beth_deitchman

AMY WOOD

Amy is a previous winner of 'Flash Friday' and 'The Angry Hourglass' flash fiction contests. She has also won the monthly short-story contest held by Creative Writing Ink and has been published by The Opening Line Literary 'Zine (September 2014). She is a full-time mom to two young children and misses having enough spare time to do Yoga and Ju Jitsu every week. Amy currently lives in Birmingham, UK. Twitter: @jujitsuelf

CARLOS OROZCO

Carlos graduated from Heritage University with a BA degree in English and a minor in education. He resides in the Pacific Northwest and writes flash fiction for a living . . . Then wakes up and goes to work at his 9-5. You can find him binge-watching shows on Netflix or on Twitter @goldzco21.

CASEY ROSE FRANK

Casey Rose Frank lives in New York State with her husband and two cats. You can learn more about Casey Rose at caseyonpurpose.blogspot.com

KRISTEN FALSO-CAPALDI

Kristen Falso-Capaldi is a writer, musician and teacher. She is the singer/lyricist for a duo, *Kristen and J*, she has co-written a screenplay, *Teachers: The Movie*, which was an official selection for the 2014 Houston Comedy Film Festival, and her short story, "Of Man and Mouse" was published in the December 2013 issue of *Underground Voices* magazine. Kristen lives in Rhode Island, USA.

CATHERINE CONNOLLY

Catherine Connolly resides in the North West of England amidst increasing numbers of books and competing story ideas. She is a member of The Poised Pen writing group and runs with the #FlashDog pack on Twitter as @FallIntoFiction. Her work has been published by Paper Swans Press and the Opening Line Literary 'Zine, amongst others, as well as in J.A.Mes Press's anthology "In Creeps The Night."

A.J. WALKER

A J Walker is from the beautiful vibrant port of Liverpool, home of footballing, musical, architectural and poetic history. He likes his singer songwriters including a certain Warren Zevon, you knew? His perfect day would be a nice walk in the country followed by a pint of stout in front of a wood fire in a welcoming pub, before watching Liverpool whup a rival then going to a gig, having a couple more pints of IPA and then maybe a ruby. With that in mind it's incredible he finds any time for flash!

SAL PAGE

Sal has a creative writing MA from Lancaster and writes novels and longer short stories as well as flash. Her stories appear online and in several print anthologies. She won the Calderdale Prize in 2011 and the Greenacre Writers Short Story Competition in 2013. She can be found trying to join in on Twitter as @SalnPage. She'd really like to be a Flash Bitch but this is good too.

STELLA TURNER

Stella was sent to Coventry at birth, loves the ring road, the two cathedrals and all its history. Racing gleefully towards retirement where she'll write a best-seller, which may or may not get published. She just needs to write a few more words than her usual Flashes.

SINÉAD O'HART
Sinéad O'Hart is a writer, primarily for children, and a freelance proofreader/copy-editor. She is represented by Polly Nolan of the Greenhouse Literary Agency. She holds a PhD in Medieval English Literature and Language, which she now mainly uses as source material for stories, and she drinks far too much tea.

ELAINE MARIE MCKAY
Elaine Marie McKay is a graduate of Glasgow University. She and her husband have four fantastic children. She has stories published in Literary Orphans, 100wordstory, Treasures (an anthology), Postcard Shorts, and CAKE magazine.

TAMARA SHOEMAKER
Tamara Shoemaker is the author of four mystery novels, three fantasy novels, and numerous flash fiction pieces, half of those published, half in the queue at the editor's office. She's a closet reader, who actually reads her books IN a closet, because that's the best place to escape her three darling children. She is usually accompanied by chocolate on these occasions.

CHRIS MILAM
Chris Milam lives in solitude in Hamilton, Ohio. He's a voracious reader, a writer of flash fiction and creative nonfiction and an obsessed baseball fan. His stories have appeared in the Molotov Cocktail, Firewords Quarterly, Dogzplot and Thick Jam.

BART VAN GOETHEM
Father. Copywriter. Drummer. Author of the self-published and sold out 'Life's Too Short For Long Stories', a collection of micro-fiction (2012). Over 40 one sentence stories have been published in print and online. As well as 7 flash-fiction stories. Follow him on Twitter: @bartvangoethem.

ERIC MARTELL
Eric is a relative newcomer to the world of writing, more often serving as a physicist, goofball, purveyor of puns fine and excruciating. You can find his stories on his blog at projectgemini12.wordpress.com, and maybe someday read a novel that he wrote during JuNoWriMo 2013, "The Time Traveling Umbrella." He lives in Champaign, IL, with his wife and three sons, and can often be found on Twitter @drmagoo.

BRIAN S. CREEK

Brian struggles each and every day to keep his dangerously powerful imagination contained within his ordinary sized head. In his mid-thirties, he can be regularly found in his work place canteen planning a way to bring all 327 ideas to readers around the world before it's too late. To relax he writes weekly flash fiction.

SARAH CAIN

Sarah Cain has worked as a speechwriter, scriptwriter, and creator of direct mail for corporate and political clients. Now she writes short stories and flash fiction. Her short story, *Amsterdam*, was recently included in the anthology, *Unclaimed Baggage, Voices of the Main Line*. She has also completed a noir suspense novel, *The Eighth Circle*.

JOSH BERTETTA

Having completed his first novel in 2014 for which he hopes to find literary representation, Josh Bertetta began to write flash fiction in August 2014, first as a means to just keep writing, but he soon fell in love with the genre and continues to write weekly. Holding a Ph.D. in Mythological Studies, he teaches in the Religious Studies department at a small university in central Texas and maintains a blog at joshbertetta.wordpress.com. Twitter: @JBertetta

N.E. CHENIER

California native transplanted to Canada (via Japan), N. E. Chenier has learned to make the most of the rain by cozying up to the word processor. Parenthood has engendered an appreciation for flash fiction and for contests with deadlines. She also enjoys hiking, biking, swimming, yoga – just about anything done outdoors. Her recent fiction can be found at Perihelion, Abyss & Apex, and in the charity anthology Zombies for a Cure. You can find more of her work at her blog Spec-Fic Motley or follow her on Twitter @rowdy_phantom.

PAM PLUMB

Pam is a flash fiction and short story writer. Her work has been published both online and in paper in such diverse places as Paper Swans' third online pamphlet and The National Flash Fiction Anthology 2014, 'Eating My Words'.

LIZ HEDGECOCK

Liz Hedgecock would like more hours in the day to get through all the work, childrearing, running, and writing (and sleeping) that needs to be done. She finds that ideas pop into her head at the most inopportune moments; have you tried surreptitiously making a note about a wind-up analogue death ray during a webinar? She mainly writes short short stories but is also currently working on something longer.

Tweets, story links, and blogs about all sorts of things are available at @lizhedgecock and lizhedgecock.wordpress.com.

TOM SMITH

Tom Smith writes prose and scripts and has had several short stories published/placed in competitions. He has also written sketches and gags for many shows including 4am Cabs, Newsrevue, Treason Show, and BBC Radio Newsjack. His latest success came when he was awarded a scholarship for the Be A Playwright Course run by Live Theatre.

ACKNOWLEDGEMENTS

FlashDogs Headquarters (FDHQ) is currently staffed by volunteers, Mark A. King and David Shakes.

FDHQ would like to thank everyone who participated in the creation of this anthology. People gave of their time and services freely. They love flash fiction; we love them.

Each included writer also acted as proof reader and editor for at least one other contributor, making the editing process a wee bit less onerous.

We are indebted to each and every one of you. We'd particularly like to mention:

A massive thank you to David Shakes (and the Shakefolk). The anthology was his idea. He's been there from the beginning of FlashDogs, providing guidance and passionate support to everyone.

Emily June Street for taking a tattered tapestry of stories and turning them into this thing of beauty. Emily, we'd have been lost without you.

Tamara Rogers for her artwork and photo prompt. Tam, you're a star.

Beth Deitchman for formatting assistance and sharp eyes.

Justin Capaldi at Capaldi Web Design for creating and designing our website. Thanks go to both Justin *and* Kristen for the initial offer on his behalf!

Carlos Orozco for the FlashDogs logo. It's awesome work.

We'd also like to thank those Dragons, Luminous Creatures and Flash Frenzy addicts who've made the FlashDogs collective possible. The flash writing competitions are our regular habitat. We'd love to see more of you there.

To find out more or start running with the pack, visit: theflashdogs.com.

Printed in Great Britain
by Amazon.co.uk, Ltd.,
Marston Gate.